DEATH CACHE

Tiffinie Helmer

ISBN-13: 978-0615897103
ISBN-10: 061589710X

Cover Designs by Kelli Ann Morgan with Inspire Creative Services
Interior book design by Bob Houston eBook Formatting

Publishing History: First Edition
Published by The Story Vault

ACKNOWLEDGEMENTS

To Kristin Morgan for sparking this idea of geocaching when I needed a new fresh survival premise for my Alaskan books. I have enjoyed the time we worked together and hope many great things come your way. When you read Death Cache, I hope it doesn't put you off geocaching. Just maybe don't enter any competitions where you are flown into the middle of nowhere and dropped off.

To Cindy Stark and Kerrigan Bryne for the last minute plot sewing and character weaving. I'm so lucky to have you both on this journey with me.

To Writers of Imminent Death: Mikki Kells, Kerrigan Bryne, Cyndi Olsen, Ariadne Kane, and Heidi Turner. Our weekly B&N Thursday night writers group have helped keep me focused, inspired, and on schedule.

To Anselm Audley for becoming a fan of my work even though romance isn't your genre. Thank you for helping clean up my mess. I have really enjoyed our collaborations and will never forget that Wild Men don't moan.

And to my agent Christine Witthohn for the continued support and whip-cracking motivation.

Thank you!

DEDICATION

For my youngest daughter, Tess. You started out as a surprise and have continued to surprise me since the day you were born. Your sweetness is laced with just enough sour to make you interesting and unpredictable. I am truly blessed to have you in my life. Love you, babe.

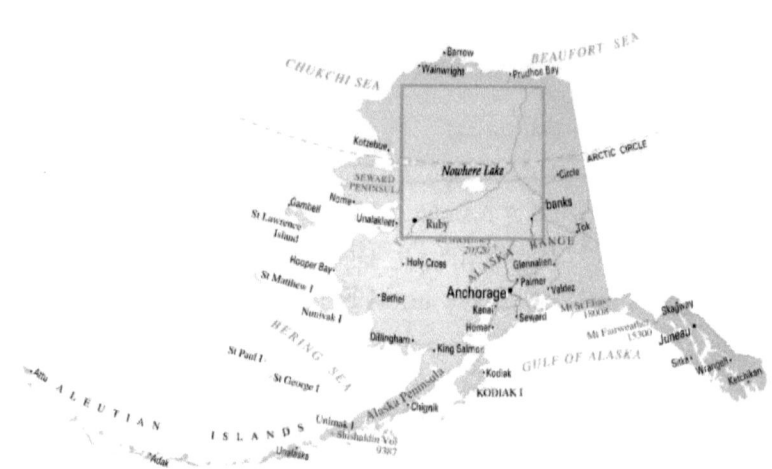

By Special Invitation Only

1st Annual Extreme Geocaching Competition

June 7th – 14th

Time & Place: 8:00 a.m. N64° 49.098', W147° 55.0349'

Lodging: Rustic cabins on a pristine glacial-fed lake.

What to bring: Pack for survival in Alaska's Extreme Backcountry.

Do you dare to be the best?

CHAPTER ONE

"Oh my God, I've slept with everyone here." Tern Maiski's gaze swept the airplane hangar with mounting dread. Good heavens, she sounded like a slut. All four of her exes stood next to the Cessna outfitted like they were headed on the same geocaching trek competition she was.

"Except you refused to put out for me when I wanted to experiment in college." Nadia Hanson, best friend extraordinaire, came to a stop next to her.

See, she wasn't *that* sexually promiscuous. Four men in twenty-eight years didn't make her easy. Besides she'd bet 'easy' would be the last word these men would use to describe her.

Nadia gave a slow whistle at the impressive line-up of testosterone. "Damn, girl. Remind me again why you let these guys go."

All eyes turned their direction. The men stood in a row like a reception line from hell.

Tern tightened her hold on the strap of her backpack. She'd only let two of them go. One had moved her to the friend pile and the other had broken her heart. She had no problem meeting each of the men's stares. Except Gage Fallon's. The bastard had walked out on her without a word six months ago. Just up and disappeared. Not an email or lousy text message to explain the hard dumping he'd given her. This was the first time she'd seen him since their last night together when they'd loved each other into a coma. She wanted to devour him with her eyes, and rail at him for making her worry so much. If she hadn't called and pestered his boss, who'd reassured her that no foul play had befallen him, she would still be worrying and wondering what had happened to him. Obviously he was fine. "I should tuck tail and run right now," Tern murmured.

"You back out now, what do you think that's going to say?"

Right. She'd introduced them to the high-tech sport of geocaching, a treasure hunt where the participants used GPS to find hidden caches. Damned if they'd prove they were now better at the game than she was, not with how wide her competitive streak ran. Nadia's comment had Tern straightening her shoulders and moving forward with a walk that was part take-no-prisoners and part promise-to-rock-your-world.

Addison "Mac" MacFearson greeted her with a crushing bear hug and a kiss on her cheek. A rugged Alaskan Bush guide with a 'No Crybabies Allowed' attitude, he'd been her first love, and still held a special part of her heart. He'd called a halt to their relationship as he was two decades older than her twenty-eight years. He hadn't wanted another family, and she really wanted children, but they had remained good friends through it all. She hadn't seen him in a few months and cheerfully returned his hug. He released her, held her at arm's reach, and cocked a knowing smile. "You're in for a trial here, sweetcakes."

Yeah, she'd gotten that idea the moment she'd seen the stud reunion.

Standing next to Mac, Lucky Leroy Morgan winked at her. His come-hither smile and surfer good looks, tempted Tern to sidle a little closer.

Man, he'd been fun.

"I thought you were in Peru climbing the Andes," she said, staying just out of reach. A lot of good that did her, as he took a step forward and swung her around in a tight clench.

"I was until this little adventure presented itself. Damn, but it's good to see you." He followed the swing with a dip and planted a searing kiss on her lips. When he'd righted her, she was dizzy, flushed, and half tempted to follow up on that kiss. But she knew better. Lucky was a gambler, not only with his money but his life.

"I stopped by the shop last night, but they said you were in Chatanika visiting your family," Lucky said. "Seems lately every time I try to look you up, you're busy."

"Thought I was waiting around pining for you?" Their relationship had ended amicably. Both of them wanted different things—she a home and family, Lucky the next adventure—but he still looked her up whenever he was in the hemisphere.

He covered his heart and his bedroom eyes warmed. "A guy can hope."

Tern introduced him to Nadia, and those eyes heated further in appreciation for her best friend. Another reason she'd cut Lucky loose. The man had a weakness for the ladies, and she didn't share.

Nadia held out her hand. "I've heard a lot about you."

"'Bout time I met Tern's sidekick. I've heard a few things about you myself." Lucky took Nadia's hand in his, his approving gaze roving up and down her body. "We should compare notes."

Oh, heavens. Tern moved on.

Robert Coate was next. He solemnly nodded his head. "Tern," he greeted. His steady gaze had the power to nick her heart. She'd broken his and the guilt of it still weighed heavily on her.

A business owner of a sporting goods store just down the street from her own shop, The Arctic Tern, Robert had made the most sense in her husband search. He was involved in the community, regularly attended church, loved dogs, and was a single parent in need of a mother for his beautiful six-year-old daughter, Chloe, who Tern adored. He was about as close to Mr. Good Enough as she'd found, but an inner voice kept whispering she wouldn't be happy settling. And to be honest, she didn't want to be known as Mrs. Tern Coate.

"Hi, Robert. How are you doing?"

"Fine." He straightened his shoulders, his eyes hooded with scowling brows. It was like this every time they ran into each other since their breakup. Though Tern had tried to let him down easy, easy hadn't worked. She'd been forced to be brutal in order to make it clear she was no longer interested in anything more than friendship from Robert. Since then they had stuck to 'fine' and 'okay' as they felt around for a more comfortable footing.

And then there was Gage.

Tern's heart hurt just knowing he breathed the same air. It had the added benefit of pissing her off too. She had no business caring about a guy who wasn't man enough to pick up a phone.

While she refused to look at Gage as she'd greeted the other men, she'd felt his eyes burn through her. An answering heat rippled under her skin. She'd done her best to ignore it, but failed.

As she finally turned to face him, hunger consumed her, and it was all she could do not to lick him like an ice cream cone, all six feet and three inches of him. He'd changed in the long months since she'd seen him, exuding an edgy danger that unfortunately made him even more attractive. Her blood raced and her heart thumped harder in her chest. She wondered if he could hear it.

His jade eyes were colder, his dark hair longer, and it looked as though he hadn't laughed in a long time. The biting remark hanging on her tongue died.

"Tern," he said, in that same husky, deep baritone that had her insides clenching. "Seems you know all the players. Are you the one who set this up?"

Like she was a masochist. "No. I'm just as surprised to see you as you are to see me." She met his gaze and tried not to baulk. He didn't look happy to see her at all. She'd bet he wouldn't be here if he'd known she'd been invited on this excursion. It hurt knowing he hadn't missed her the tiniest bit.

Deadbeat. He wasn't worth her heartache.

Nadia bumped into her, and she grabbed a deep breath hoping it would settle her down. Nadia greeted Gage with a welcoming smile and a hug. They were both employed by the University, Nadia as a math professor and Gage as a scientist for the Geophysical Institute where he studied the aurora borealis and Earth's magnetosphere. Nadia had been the one to suggest Gage check out her shop when he needed to do his Christmas shopping.

Tern didn't like seeing Nadia in Gage's arms. He returned Nadia's smile, his eyes crinkling at the corners as they caught up with each other. Why couldn't he have greeted her like that? She turned away before she gave in and kicked Gage in the shins or fell into a blubbering puddle at his feet begging to know why he'd left her.

Through the door of the hangar her white Jeep beckoned, promising escape. She even took a few steps toward it, before realizing what she was doing and stopped. She couldn't back out now. Not with Gage's eyes boring into her back. If she walked off, he would know how much he'd hurt her. But then, how could she spend a whole week with him in the wilderness and refrain from killing him? Or worse, sleep with him again?

A sandy-haired man wearing aviator glasses and flyboy jacket entered the hangar. "Folks, my name is Hugh, and I'll be ready to take off in about ten minutes. We'll be taking the DeHavilland Beaver tied up next to the dock. If you'll carry your bags down there, I'll get them loaded, while you take your seats."

"Do we know where we're going yet?" Robert asked, grabbing his pack and following the pilot.

"Everything will be made clear to you once we've landed. Those are the instructions I've been given. Can't have one of you with an advantage."

How about disadvantage?

Tern sure as hell felt like she carried a handicap starting out. It didn't seem like anyone else was burdened with the amount of emotional baggage on this trip that she was.

She caught Gage watching her and felt like a rabbit being hunted by a wolf. Her nipples tightened and excitement swept over her. *Damn her thrill-seeker gene.*

14

"Ready?" Nadia broke through Tern's connection to Gage.

"Nope."

"Ah, come on, Tern." Nadia flashed a smile and gave her newly darkened hair a toss. She'd recently exchanged her natural cinnamon for Tern's raven coloring. Tern was still getting used to the change. "It'll be fun. Once we get there and the games begin, you'll forget all about Gage Fallon."

"Uh-huh, and we'll see stars in the sky tonight too." It would take a miracle as the midnight sun ruled the skies this time of year.

Nadia laughed and hooked her arm through Tern's and pulled her toward the floatplane. "You'll kick yourself if you stay."

They climbed aboard and took their seats. Nadia sat in back with Gage, sandwiching Tern with Lucky on one side and Robert on the other. Mac sat up front with Hugh.

Fortunately, once they took off on the man-made Chena Marina and were soaring northwest into the brilliant blue sky, the noise in the plane was too loud to carry on a conversation without headphones and mics. Mac and Hugh were the only ones outfitted, which suited Tern just fine. There was too much back and forth going on inside her head to pay attention to anyone else.

Why had she let Nadia talk her into getting on this plane? There was no way this trip would end well, other than winning and being named the best geocacher in the state. Regardless if she'd seemed a coward for backing out, she should have run from the hangar and left this crew on their own. The plane bumped along in a pocket of turbulence as though nodding in agreement.

The floatplane dipped, beginning its descent. She caught a view out the windows and anticipation replaced the foreboding that brewed in her thoughts. A glacier-fed lake glistened like an expensive jewel below them. Iced mountain tops, perfectly frosted by Mother Nature, crowded around the lake as though hoping to pick up any secrets it might whisper of time and space. Spruce trees in the darkest blues to greens to blacks competed for room among the birch trees. A clearing revealed a nest of small cabins along the south bank of the lake, directly opposite the glacier that receded above the valley.

The DeHavilland skimmed the placid waters of the lake on a perfect landing, drifting right up to the sandy beach near the cabins. Hugh powered down the Beaver and silence pressed in.

"Welcome to Nowhere Lake." Hugh rolled up his hip waders and stepped out onto the plane's float. He hopped onto the bank and secured the plane to a birch tree before wading into the water. One by one, they climbed out onto the floats and jumped to shore. Hugh unloaded their packs, tossing them the short distance. Tern seized hers just as it would have smacked her in the face. As it was, she stumbled backward.

Hugh waded to shore, pulled an envelope from his back pocket, and handed it to Nadia. "Here you go. Instructions are in there on the rules of the game. I'll be back in a week to pick you up." He wasted no time untying the plane, turning it around, and hopping aboard.

They watched, standing in a line, as Hugh took off. Tern wondered if they were all thinking the same thing.

Just where the hell were they, and what would they do if he didn't come back?

CHAPTER TWO

"Well," Mac said, hitching up his backpack on brick-like shoulders and grabbing his rifle. "The day isn't getting any younger. I suggest we make camp and cook up some grub before we tear open those instructions."

They gathered their gear and headed toward the base camp a few hundred yards from the lake. The spot was breathtaking. Grasses so green it hurt Tern's eyes to look at them were intermixed with wildflowers of blue bells, forget-me-nots, brook mint, and cowslips. The air was clean and crisp. Rejuvenating.

She dragged in a deep breath and slowly let it out. The sun beat down with teasing fingers, tempting her to shed her jacket. She'd been locked up too long in her shop this season getting ready for the tourists. It was actually unheard of for her to take time off during the summer. It was her money-making season, but she had a good crew and she badly needed the break from commitments and responsibilities.

The camp consisted of three small log cabins built in a half moon. Tern and Nadia entered the first cabin, while the men carried their gear into the remaining ones. The small space housed two cots each, a shelf, hooks for clothes, and an end table between the cots. The bare necessities. It caused a smile to spread over Tern's face, while Nadia frowned.

"This is it?" she asked, scanning the small space as though some modern day amenities would suddenly appear.

"Did you expect maid service?"

"Running water would have been nice."

"There's a pristine lake out front." Tern gestured to the view out the door she'd left propped open for air and light. The little cabin only sported a tiny window, which wasn't able to brighten the dark, rough-honed log interior.

"You're enjoying this, aren't you?"

"God, yes." Tern rolled out her sleeping bag on one of the cots and stretched out on it. "I didn't realize how badly I needed to get out of town until we got here." She turned her head to look at Nadia, who fought to untie her sleeping bag. "Thanks for talking me into coming."

"Don't thank me yet," Nadia mumbled. "We still need to find a bathroom."

"I'm sure there's an outhouse in back of the cabins."

"Eww, seriously?" Her mouth dropped open.

"They said extreme backcountry. Be grateful there are cabins." Tern laughed at Nadia's staggered expression. "Come on, let's unpack and get something to eat." She sat up and opened her backpack. Unpacking her GPS, clothes, toiletries, extra pair of shoes, and pistol, she noticed things missing. Besides her stuff was always more organized than this. "Nadia, do you have everything you packed?"

"Hmm…" Nadia lifted her head from reading the back of one of the many steamy romance novels she was never without. "What?"

"It looks like someone rifled through my pack. I'm missing my sat phone, M&M's, moose jerky. All the food I brought." Tern frowned.

Nadia dropped the book onto her cot and rummaged through her own backpack. "What the hell. My stuff's missing, too, including my waterproof matches and the goodies I packed."

Lucky knocked on the outside of the cabin. "Hey, the old man's called a meeting."

A shiver of unease settled into her bones. Tern looked at Nadia as they silently followed Lucky to where the men stood around a dug out fire pit with log seating circling the area.

"Your things have been gone through too?" Tern asked.

"Seems to be the case with all of us," Gage said, his jaw hard, eyes narrowed.

The same was murmured around the empty fire pit.

"My tool kit was taken, along with the MREs I'd packed," Robert said.

"Didn't the invite say food would be provided?" Lucky asked. "Aren't you guys jumping to conclusions? Maybe our packs were rifled through because part of the competition is about us finding food in the caches."

"I think it's damn suspicious that all our emergency supplies were taken," Gage pointed out. "Including cell and satellite phones and Mac's two-way radios."

"Why take the cell phones?" Tern asked. It wasn't like they'd work up here anyway.

"Those of you who brought weapons were left with them," Lucky argued. "I think it's leveled the playing field."

"I suggest we start a fire," Mac said. "The temperature is going to drop fast, once the sun settles over those peaks. We'd better do an inventory of what we've been left with. Was anyone left with matches or a lighter?"

"My matches were taken," Nadia said in a small voice and a few of the men shook their heads.

"I've got a lighter." Robert reached into the front pocket of his jeans. "Gave up the smokes months ago, but can't seem to give up carrying the lighter." He looked at Tern as he informed the group of this little personal fact. Another of her issues about him had been the cigarettes.

Gage broke the uncomfortable silence. "I'll gather some firewood." He headed for the trees, his hands flexing into fists as though he had a problem with Tern's history with Robert. She'd been upfront with Gage when they'd been together. He knew about Robert, and the rest. She'd been an open book, and had shared everything with him, but realized now how much she didn't know about Gage and his past relationships.

"Good idea," Mac said. "I suggest we all do the same."

Tern and Nadia hiked down to the lake to gather what they could find along the bank and Tern tried to shut the door on rehashing her failed relationship with Gage. She'd spent too much time questioning what she'd done wrong in the past months. For some reason, he hadn't wanted anything to do with her. It was his issue, not hers. She just wished she could stop caring.

They returned with enough dry wood to feed a fire throughout the night. Robert started a nice blaze with the dried spruce moss Gage had brought back with the wood he'd gathered. Soon a pleasant snap and crackle provided a comforting song to the breeze tickling the coin leaves of the birch trees.

Tern took a seat, reaching her hands out to the flames. She'd put her jacket back on as the temperature had indeed dropped with the sun. While not setting this close to the Arctic Circle, it had dipped just below the high peaks of the mountains surrounding them. The breeze wafting off the glacier to the north plunged the temperature twenty degrees cooler. They were in for a cold night.

One by one the players of the game took seats on the stumps. Nadia sat next to Tern, Lucky close on Nadia's left. Robert on Tern's right while Mac sat across and Gage remained standing, whittling a piece of diamond willow, as though needing to kept himself slightly separated from the party.

"This is much better," Nadia said, moving her feet closer to the heat of the fire. "But what are we going to do about food? I'm starved."

"Nadia, let me see the envelope the pilot gave you," Mac asked.

"Oh, right. I almost forgot about the game with all our stuff pilfered." Nadia jumped up and rushed to their cabin, returning quickly, and handing the envelope to Mac.

He opened it with a slice of his knife, bending the blade back into its case and slipping it into the scabbard on his belt. He shook out the folded pages and scanned them. "Well, it seems Lucky was right. We aren't just to have a race against each other to find the geocaches, but finding them will aid in our survival." He passed the pages around the group.

"What?" Nadia jumped to her feet. "There isn't any food?"

"Doesn't seem like it. We either catch what we eat or start searching for the geocaches and hope they have the supplies these pages promise."

"How the hell is this a competition?" Robert asked, a scowl on his face.

"It's a test of our survival skills," Mac said, not looking unhappy about the prospect.

"That isn't what we signed up for," Gage added, though he didn't seem adverse to the challenge presented either. One of the things that had attracted Tern to Gage in the first place was his similarity to Mac in the way he thought through problems and took charge if need be.

"We knew this was an extreme competition," Mac said. "We all agreed by showing up to this little party."

"I'm here to prove I'm the best geocacher in the state," Lucky said. "That's what I signed up for."

"Is there any food at all?" Nadia asked.

"By the looks of the rules, we aren't going to eat until we locate a few geocaches," Mac said. "It's getting late. I suggest we spilt into pairs. There'll be protection against the unfriendlies if we stay in numbers. Tern, you pair up with me—"

"What?" Robert scoffed. "No way do the old man and the broad get to pair up."

"*Broad?* Really?" Tern asked. "Talk like that is going to get you hurt."

"I'd love you to try it, babe." Robert cocked his brow at her in challenge, then turned back to Mac. "And who the fuck put you in charge?"

"Age and wisdom, you little shit." Mac stood over Robert, who at least had the survival instincts to back down. "Now—"

"The little shit has a point," Gage interrupted. "No offense, Mac, but you're older and the women are weaker—"

"Hey," Tern said.

Gage ignored her objection and continued, "We should keep the strength ratio as close to even as we can for protection."

"Draw names," Lucky said. "Luck of the draw."

"I'll get some paper and a pen." Nadia once again rushed back to their cabin. She returned, wrote everyone's name on a piece of paper and tore them into slips. "Gage, can I borrow your hat?"

Gage took off his ball cap and handed it to her. Nadia put the names into the cap and one by one drew out a name.

"Robert with Mac." She tossed the names into the fire and glanced around waiting for objections; when no one said anything she drew again. "Lucky with, oh, me." She smiled at Lucky, and then faced Tern. "I guess that leaves you and Gage." She mouthed a sorry.

Sorry didn't begin to cover it.

Tern couldn't look at Gage, but felt his irritation from behind her where he'd waited for the return of his hat. Of all the people to be paired up with, Gage was her last choice. Everything had gone wrong since she'd entered the hangar this afternoon.

"All right then," Mac said. "Let's divide up and see what we can find. Does everyone have a weapon? Good. Fire three shots with a full second between each shot if you get into trouble." He motioned with the paper that had the geocache coordinates on them. "Leroy, you and Nadia head south over that hill. Tern, since you're more mountain goat than human, you and Gage head north. By these coordinates, looks as though you might have some ice to navigate. Be careful. Robert and I will head west. I suggest we only give ourselves two hours.

Find what you can in that time frame, then reconvene back here." He looked at each of them in turn. "Got it?"

"I need a minute." Tern grabbed Nadia's arm and dragged her toward their cabin. "What the hell was that all about?"

"What?" Nadia wrenched her arm free.

"Pairing me up with Gage? You know he's the last man I want to spend time with."

"Sweetie, it was the luck of the draw." Nadia ignored Tern's scoff. "You need to find out what happened between the two of you anyway. And now you have some time alone. You should thank me."

"No way." Tern folded her arms over her chest as if that would help protect her heart. "If he couldn't tell me then, I don't want to hear it now."

"Yes, you do. It's been eating you up inside." Nadia cocked a hip. "Ever think that maybe this is fate?"

"Fate isn't this sick."

"Oh, I don't know. It paired me with Lucky." A smile she tried to hide gave her away.

"As if that wasn't who you wanted to be with anyway."

She shrugged. "He's the most fun of the bunch. There's an unfair ratio of men to women, and since they've all had a taste of you, it's up to me to protect myself from being passed around," she said, tongue in cheek.

"You bitch."

Nadia laughed. "Come on, get over it, and let's have some fun. Think of the havoc you can cause Gage. Get back at him for his mistreatment of you."

"Right."

"Hey, you wouldn't mind if Lucky and I hooked up, would you?"

"Uh…" Nadia and Lucky? He'd break her heart. "Be careful, Nadia. He isn't the kind of man who sticks around."

"My favorite. Use 'em and abuse 'em." Nadia gave a sly smile. "Time for the games to begin."

Tern hopped onto a smooth boulder, one of many that had been spat out by the glacier. The chill coming off the ice sank its teeth into her every time she stopped to catch her breath. As long as she kept moving the cold didn't bite too deep.

The glacier nestled in a valley of black spruce with craggy outcropping. The crystal clearness of the lake lay below, topped by a sky so azure it was almost white. Not even a jet stream marred the translucent sky. It felt as though if she focused just enough, she'd be able to catch a glimpse into heaven.

The only thing to ruin this moment was the man trailing behind her. They'd only spoken a few words on the hike toward the glacier. Nothing that wasn't absolutely necessary. Gage cocked the shotgun again.

"How many times do you need to check that thing? It isn't like the bullets are going to disappear."

"I don't like this."

"You could have stayed in camp."

"That's not what I meant. This whole set up. It doesn't feel right. Having no contact with the outside world concerns me. What if someone gets hurt? A week can be a long time to wait for help to arrive."

"Afraid of a little adventure?" Though she shared his concerns, she couldn't help taunting him.

"I'm not afraid."

She turned and gave him a long look. He'd been afraid of her.

"I'm not afraid of you either," he said, reading her correctly.

"Riiight." Like he would have agreed to this 'little adventure' if he'd known she was going to be along. She dismissed him and started climbing again, her feet sliding to a hard stop when he grabbed her arm and swiveled her to face him.

"I am not afraid of you," he repeated.

She studied him. His eyes flashed bright green with golden specks that resembled flames. She moved in closer and laid her hand on his chest. His heart hammered under her palm, and he swallowed.

"You're so afraid of me you can't stand it," she whispered, slinking closer, until their bodies touched from breasts to thighs. His eyes smoldered and his nostrils flared. "You want to do wicked things with me, but you're scared to death of what I make you feel." She let that sink in before she stepped back.

"Don't worry, Gage, you're safe from me. A man dumps me like you did and there isn't anything more I want from him." She left, hoping his mouth gaped open as he salivated after her. She almost turned back to relish his expression, but knew she'd lose ground if she did. The geocache had to be around here somewhere. While the GPS coordinates got them close to the cache, it didn't put them on top of one.

They needed to find it before she did something else stupid.

Stupid or not, she'd enjoyed messing with Gage, in a twisted sort of pleasure. Served the deadbeat right. Six months she'd waited for him. And nothing. She was disappointed in herself that she still gave a damn. She should have been able to turn off her feelings after the way he'd treated her. But she'd never been in love so deep before.

Tern mentally shook herself and concentrated on finding the cache. The light bouncing off the glacier hurt her eyes. She reached into her front pocket, where she'd stored her sunglasses when they'd been in the darkness of the trees, and put them on. The shades cut the rays of the sun and allowed her to see the sharp corner of something square. As far as she knew, Mother Nature hadn't gotten around to perfecting the square.

She hiked up a few more feet and knelt down on the icy crust. The coldness melted into her cargo pants. Someone had chipped a small cavity in the ice and set a five gallon cooler into it. She dug around the edges and pulled the cooler free. Pivoting the handle, which acted as a lock, she opened the top.

Moose steaks, smoked salmon, many different kinds of cheeses, and a few bottles of wine. Hot damn. Her mouth watered. Whoever was running this game was one smart cookie. Encasing the cooler in the ice of the glacier kept the food from spoiling and animals from sniffing it out. She liked the way he thought and couldn't wait to sink her teeth into one of the steaks.

"What did you find?" Gage's tall shadow fell over her.

"The mother lode." She shared a real smile with him this time. When he returned it and held out a hand to help her up, her traitorous heart flipped-flopped. "You're cooking tonight."

"It'd be my pleasure." He pulled her to her feet and kept pulling until she was pressed up against him. "And you're right. You scare the shit out of me." His hand came up and framed her face, the other anchored behind her back keeping her close. "But I scare you too."

Before she could protest, his lips seared hers. Heat erupted between them and flushed her body with enough warmth to melt the glacier they stood precariously on.

Oh God, she'd missed him. The way their bodies naturally curved together, the way her insides liquefied in readiness for him, and the way his body hardened to steel. She'd loved his body, the way it was roped with muscle, how his strength made her feel feminine and protected. She'd loved lavishing attention on his body for hours on those lazy days when they didn't get out of bed. Her fingers itched to touch his skin again, feel his flesh hot under hers as he—

"I'm not the only one who wants to do wicked things," he murmured, his voice husky with arrogance. He nipped the skin below her ear, and licked the sting.

Her fingers curled into his shirt for a moment, and then she pushed him away. He slipped on the ice and fell on his ass at her feet. She stood over him, part of her enjoying the view, the other part already missing the heat of his hands.

"The wicked things I want to do involve sharp implements." She brushed her hands over her clothes as though that would erase his touch and how he made her feel. "I found the cache. *You* can carry it back to camp."

Trying to look as if she wasn't running away, Tern took her time and carefully watched her footing as she descended the ice. She could hear Gage cursing behind her as he struggled with the cooler and his slippery toehold on the glacier.

Served him right for putting the moves on her, like he had to disprove her earlier statements. There was no way in hell she was afraid of him.

A shiver caught her by surprise.

CHAPTER THREE

There was nothing that put people at ease like a full belly. Excitement about the game peppered the talk over the perfectly sizzled steaks Gage had cooked in the cast-iron skillet that had been found in one of the cabins, along with cooking utensils and plates. Mac and Robert had brought back olive oil, spices, steak sauce, ketchup, and mustard from their located cache.

Nadia and Lucky had found a package of dried eggs, beans, rice, flour, canned butter, and evaporated milk along with a large tin of coffee. Tern used the knowledge she'd gained from her Athabascan grandmother to gather the young leaves of soldier's herb, dandelion, fireweed, and lamb's-quarter for a salad. A splash of white wine mixed with a few tablespoons of olive oil made a very tasty dressing for the greens.

Yes, the group was feeling mighty full and content.

Tern had done her best to ignore Gage. Hard to do with how hungry she was. She'd eaten every morsel on her plate and would have gone for seconds if there hadn't been talk of steak and eggs for breakfast. If she were honest, what she really wanted was to go back for seconds on that kiss Gage had snuck in earlier.

The hunger gnawing at her wouldn't be satiated with food.

To get her mind off Gage, she helped Mac secure the perishable food in the cooler and strung it up a tree outside of camp to keep animals from helping themselves. The fire banked, it was decided that they should head to bed and get an early start in the morning.

Each of the caches they'd found had instructions for the next day's challenge.

Nadia pulled Tern aside and whispered that she'd be late coming to bed, and ran giggling behind Lucky Leroy Morgan, who was living up to his nickname. They chased each other into the cover of the trees.

While Tern had said that it wouldn't bother her if Nadia hooked up with Lucky, there was still a pang of something that was hard to identify.

Mac shook his head at them and waved to the rest as he headed to the cabin he shared with Robert. Tern stood and stretched out the kinks in her back and shoulders, slowly lowering her arms as both Robert and Gage's eyes were glued to her movements.

"'Night," she murmured and headed toward her cabin. But once inside, she didn't want to stay. Whether it was the never ending daylight this close to the North Pole, or the freedom to roam—one pleasure she hadn't given into in a long time—there was no way she was sleeping.

The hike up the glacier hadn't worn her out. If anything it had invigorated her. Some of that might be blamed on the time she'd spend with Gage, though torture wouldn't get her to admit it.

She waited until Robert and Gage were no longer sitting around the dying embers, and then grabbed her loaded pistol in its holster and slipped it to her belt, donned a jacket, and headed out.

The temperature had dropped into the fifties, cold enough that the mosquitoes would be bunkered under leaves and not bothering her. She strolled toward the lake where a loon warbled, calling to its mate. She waited, listened, and then smiled as the mate answered.

The night was still, the lake smooth, the sky as clear and crisp as it had been all day. She ambled along, picking a few forget-me-nots, which she wound in her hair as she wandered along the shore.

This was her native soil. Her nomadic ancestors had migrated across this land for thousands of years, taking advantage of the caribou, the moose, and the mighty salmon, and giving back to the spirit gods in thanks for their bounty. She lay on the sand, leaned against a weather-worn log, stretched out her legs, and closed her eyes as she took in the sounds and smells of her homeland.

The fast growth of plants and flowers during the long summer days gave a spicy sweetness to the air as winter had finally shed its heavy cloak. Something small rustled in the bushes, but it didn't concern her. Probably a fox or porcupine. The loons called to each other again, followed by the cooing of a pair of chickadees high within the birch trees.

A new smell joined the mix, faint on wood smoke, sharp on pine, and heavy on musk.

Man.

She opened her eyes and looked straight into Gage's.

Gage had ventured toward the lake to wash up after the long day. Though he hadn't lingered in the glacial-fed water. He was headed back when he'd come around a bend and found her.

Tern.

The woman who haunted him. Kept him up more nights than he wanted to admit.

Reclined against a log, bleached white from the elements, her long legs were stretched out in front of her, ankles crossed. Her face lifted to the heavens, thick dark hair, the color of raven's wings with hints of fire within its depths, fell behind her. A serene smile played upon her lips as though she were the keeper of secrets. Her exotic almond-shaped eyes were closed. Her left brow bisected with a scar that she'd received as a child, gave her a rakish appearance that was damn right challenging.

He should leave, now before she realized he was here, but he couldn't move as he drank her in.

Christ, he craved her.

He'd purposely stayed away all these months. Though at the moment, he couldn't remember why. Not when he wanted to sink to his knees, gather her up into his arms, and bury his face in her hair. Hair that smelled of fireweed and rosehips and drove him to distraction.

The taste he'd had of her this afternoon had only left him starving for more. He should give up on this game and think seriously of hiking his way out of here. But 'here' was so far away from any part of Alaska that he'd ever been to, and it could be weeks before he stumbled upon another human being.

He was stuck. Stuck with Tern. And stuck with the other men who had been important in her life. Maybe still were. The thought twisted his insides.

Tern opened her eyes and looked directly at him. A sharp stab of desire stole his breath. She'd always had this otherworldly sense about her that had sometimes freaked him out. Like now. She didn't blink, didn't act surprised to see him standing there staring down at her. It was like she'd known he was there before she opened her eyes.

"Gage," she greeted him in that sexy come-and-get-me voice. It had undertones that sent blood pulsing to his nether regions. Just like that first time he'd seen her. She'd been behind the counter in her shop, head down, a black curtain of hair covering her face as she'd studied an invoice or something. Then she'd raised her head and looked straight at him, welcomed him into her world, and he'd fallen right then and there.

Shit, he wasn't strong enough to resist her tonight after fighting off her allure all day. "I thought you went to bed," he said, the statement coming out like an accusation.

"Nope."

Just the one word. Those mystical eyes of hers toured his body, from his damp hair, probably still in spikes from being rubbed dry with the towel hanging loose in his hand, to the clean clothes he'd donned after his cold dip. He sure as hell didn't feel the effects of the cold now. He was back to the state of arousal that had drained the smarts out of his brain all day.

"What the hell do you want from me?" he snapped.

"Nothing."

"Nothing? It didn't feel like 'nothing' on the glacier when you taunted me."

"Whatever." She had the audacity to yawn.

"Am I boring you?"

"Yes." She stretched and rolled to her feet in a movement so sensual that it had him clenching his hands on his towel to help remind him to keep them off her.

He wanted to throw down his towel, grab her, and then he'd—

Oh, hell, what was he doing? After all the time he'd forced himself to stay away, worked to get her out of his system, how did she still get to him so easily?

"You left, Gage. We're over." She swept a strand of hair from her face, and he had the feeling that she'd like to sweep him away just as easily. "So what do you want?"

He didn't know what he wanted and that had his temper spiking. "Someone else already warming your bed, sweetheart?" He should shut up and leave. "You sure don't waste a lot of time, do you?"

"Fuck you, Fallon." Hot color slashed across her sharp cheekbones. She moved to brush past him, and he reached out and seized her arm.

"Sorry, I didn't mean that."

She stared at him, stared right through to his soul. "Yes, you did." She glanced down at his hand shackled around her forearm. "Let go."

He tightened his hold and she must have read his intent for she said, "I'm not yours to grab any longer."

Frustration ate at him. He wanted to haul her into his arms, kiss away that shuttered look that his angry words had caused to fall. But then to invite her back into his life, when he'd purposely done everything he could to kick her out of it, would undermine the last six months of hell.

He slowly released her, while her bewitching eyes took in more than he wanted her to see.

"For the record," she said, "we aren't together. What I do with my life and who I have sex with is none of your business. You chose to walk away. Now stay away." She gave him one last long stare before giving him her back.

Watching her stride away from him, knowing that he'd severed his chances with her, should have reassured him, but it made that hole in his chest where his heart had been ache in a way no bandage would ease.

No woman made him ache like Tern had, did. He'd never had a relationship, that wasn't made clear upfront, this was casual, no expectations. Yet each time he'd tried to convey that to Tern he couldn't get the words past his lips as they seemed like lies. He wasn't proud that he'd let their involvement go until the situation in his own life forced his hand. But he could have called, explained, rather than not do anything.

Had he made the right choices six months ago? Or had he royally fucked up his life?

Tern entered her cabin to find Robert waiting for her.

What the hell was this? Old lovers' week?

"What do you want, Robert?" She tossed her jacket onto her bunk. Robert had made himself comfortable on Nadia's cot while he'd waited for her.

"What's going on between you and Fallon? I thought that was over."

"None of your damn business."

He rubbed the back of his neck. "Listen, Tern. You know how much I care about you. Hell, I asked you to marry me. I still want that."

"Stop right there." She held her hand up. "We've been over this. I'm not the right woman for you, and waiting around for me to change my mind isn't going to happen."

"We were good for each other." He stood and reached for her, his hands gripping her shoulders. "I know you want a family. Chloe loves you. You know I'd love to have more children with you as their mother."

The mention of his six-year-old daughter had her softening her tone. "I love Chloe too. You know that. I'm there for her. But marriage between us wouldn't work, Robert."

"Why not?"

"I don't want to rehash this." *Why, oh why, had she gotten on that damn plane?*

She saw his intention but didn't stop the kiss. He tried to coax a physical response from her, but it wasn't there. He tightened his hold on her shoulders, until his fingers bit into her skin, and pressed his body against hers.

"Damn it, Tern." He groaned. "Why can't you care for me?"

Regret for what wasn't there had her framing his face with her hands. "I'm sorry, Robert. I can't force feelings that aren't there."

He dropped his forehead to rest against hers. "But I love you."

"No, you don't," she said gently. "You love the thought of us. You've got to let it go."

He sighed heavily. "It's Fallon, isn't it? You're in love with him."

She stiffened and moved out of his arms. "No."

He gave a bark of laughter that held no humor. "You're in the same place I am, aren't you?" He rubbed the back of his neck again, a habit of his that she used to find endearing. "It sucks to be here."

"You've nailed it."

He shook his head. "We make so much sense together."

"I know, but you can't force what isn't there."

"I'm not giving up." His eyes met hers, and he hardened his jaw. "Get Fallon out of your system."

Oh, hell. "Don't wait for me, Robert. You need to look elsewhere."

He opened his mouth to object when the door burst open. Nadia fell in looking flushed and clearly used, a smile of supreme satisfaction on her face. "Oh, sorry." She turned back to look at the door. "You're supposed to hang something on the knob when you're entertaining."

"Robert was just leaving." Tern tried to stamp down the jealousy poking at her over Nadia's satisfied expression. Since she'd been with Lucky, herself, she knew firsthand how Nadia felt. Maybe she should have taken Gage by the lake shore. Use and abuse him like Nadia planned with Lucky. Though with Tern, since she still cared more than she wanted to admit for the jerk, she'd be the one who ended up used and abused.

Robert glanced between the women, offered a mumbled, "goodnight," and left the small cabin that had gotten considerably smaller with the three of them crowding it. The door closed quietly behind him.

Nadia waited a few beats, giving Robert time to walk out of hearing distance before she whispered, "What the hell is going on? I thought for sure you'd give Gage another run before *Robert.*"

"No one is getting 'another run.' They're all history." She gestured wide with her arms to include all the men in camp. "I'm off men."

"Okay, then." Nadia cocked a knowing brow. "Finally want to try experimenting with women?"

Tern threw a pillow at her, and Nadia giggled. The sound was carefree, making that jealousy monster snap its teeth.

"Why didn't you ever tell me how focused Lucky was? Man, he had me screaming to the heavens more than once." Nadia changed into her silk pajamas.

In the mood Tern was in, the last thing she wanted to talk about was how great Lucky had been in the sack. It had been too long since she'd screamed to the heavens herself. "Don't get too invested in him. I don't want to see you hurt."

A shutter passed over Nadia's eyes. "What makes you think he'd be the one to hurt me?"

"He isn't in it for the long haul."

"Maybe neither am I."

Tern wisely held her tongue. Every relationship Nadia had entered into had been with wedding bells ringing in the background. She didn't do causal. If anything, she was so committed to the men that they ran off scared. "Just be careful, okay?"

"Don't worry so much. Besides, if one of us needs to worry, it's you. What was Robert doing in here?"

"I don't want to get into it."

"What about Gage? How was the trek up the glacier today?"

"Cold." No point in adding the searing kiss they'd shared on that piece of ice. "Let's try and get some sleep. It's been a long day."

But when she was zipped up into her sleeping bag, sleep was the last thing coming her way. Silence settled over the camp, and all that could be heard was the repeating 'who-who' of an owl.

She wished she had an answer.

CHAPTER FOUR

Tern was the first one awake the next morning. She'd given up the pretense of sleeping and silently snuck out of the cabin in the wee hours of the morning and crept back down toward the lake to wash. When she'd been there the night before, she'd caught a whiff of sulfur and decided to investigate. Sure enough, a half mile or so west of the lake was a pocket of hot springs. The interior of Alaska was pitted with thermal activity. She tested the water for heat with a long stem of pootschki—a member of the parsnip family which made an okay celery substitute in soups and stews. Stripping off her clothes, she slowly waded into water just this side of scorching. It was heaven to relax and let the heat burn off the stress and unrest of the day before. When she started to feel like her insides were beginning to boil, she quickly washed, dressed, and hiked back to camp with renewed energy.

Mac was already up as she knew he'd be. The man might be older than the rest of them, but that didn't mean anyone was going to get the jump on him.

"Morning," she greeted.

He paused in pouring a cup of coffee, the strong, dark smell enticing her closer. "How do you do it?" he asked.

She raised her brow in question.

"Look so fresh and inviting all the way out here?"

"Like I'm going to give away my secrets. You don't look too bad yourself." She admired his rugged appearance—salt-and-pepper hair in a military cut, fresh stubble soon to be a beard, and laugh lines crinkling around steel-gray eyes. Not many men could roll out of a cot and look as sexy as he did in the morning.

She took the cup of coffee he poured her, reaching for the sugar and evaporated milk he'd set out for those who needed to dilute the strong brew. "How'd you sleep?" she asked.

"I've had better nights. Doesn't help that Robert is mooning over you. Damn, gal, does every man fall under your spell?"

Gage obviously hadn't. She ignored the question and asked one instead, "Why the rough night?"

"Something doesn't feel right about this setup. I can't place my finger on it. But I'm uneasy." He sipped his black coffee.

Gage had said almost the same thing yesterday. She took a sip of her coffee and held back the wince as the bitter concoction hit the back of her throat and burned its way down into her unsuspecting stomach. One cup of Mac's coffee would erase her sleepless night. "How so?"

"Do you realize how easy this situation can turn into a survival game?"

"Anywhere you go in Alaska can turn into a survival game."

"True, but I think we might be tested more than we signed up for." He sipped his coffee again. "It's too much of a coincidence, all these men and you as the common dominator. You *know* what I think of coincidences."

"Yeah, but I did introduce all of you to geocaching."

"I want to know who the mystery person is behind this expedition. He clearly knows all of us. Or at least you. Any ideas?"

"Not a one. I've racked my brain."

"Might want to rack it again."

"I'll do that."

Mac took a deep sip of his coffee. "Seriously, are these idiots really in your level of found caches? Besides, me, of course."

She bit back a smile. "Lucky, definitely. Gage can hold his own against you, but he falls short of me." In many ways, it seemed. "Nadia and Robert I'd still consider amateurs, but you didn't hear me say that."

Mac nodded as though he'd already come to the same conclusions. "You have any enemies?"

She scoffed. "Are you serious?"

"As a rutting moose." His piercing steel eyes met hers and had her sobering fast.

She swallowed and put aside the coffee, her stomach suddenly pitchy. "No, Mac. Not that I know of."

"Rack your brain for that too." He refilled his cup. "Like I said, something doesn't feel right."

The rest of the group eventually woke, sauntering toward the fire pit looking for coffee and something to eat. Mac rehydrated eggs with boiled water from the lake and scrambled a pan's worth, adding in cheese and cubes of steak. Tern dug up some Hedysarum alpinum, better known as Eskimo potatoes, boiled and served them with the steak and eggs, and made a poor man's biscuit out of the flour.

Gage silently studied her under his brows, while Robert tried to engage her in conversation. She ignored them both. Robert eventually wandered off toward the lake, but Gage continued his scrutiny. Lucky and Nadia were cozy as doves while they ate, and Tern felt a pang every time she looked at them. It hadn't been long ago that she'd had that kind of connection with a man. And no matter how many times she told herself different, she still wanted Gage. Wanted that intimacy they'd shared, the rapport, the promised future. The reality of it pissed her off and had her scouring the pan until its reflection had the power to blind someone.

Mac came up behind her after everyone had taken off to do whatever they needed to do to get ready for the day. "Woman, you'd better figure out what you're going to do about him."

"Shit. You're kidding me."

"Yep, pretty damn obvious." He gave her a pathetic look. "Give me that pan before you scrub a hole in it." He took it out of her hands. "Take a walk. Shake it off." Mac glanced at his watch. "Meet back here in thirty."

"You running a drill camp here?"

"All you nitwits would be lost without me." He smiled and ruffled her hair. "Now, get."

"Yes, sir." She saluted.

"Smartass."

Laughing and feeling more herself, Tern gladly handed KP duty over to Mac.

Since Robert had ventured toward the lake, and she didn't want a repeat of last night, she headed for the hills. Mac's comment yesterday of her being more mountain goat than human wasn't all in jest. It was one of the things that had attracted her to Lucky Leroy. He'd shown her some amazing views in the time they'd spent together. Why couldn't she have been satisfied with him and what he offered? Life would have been one wild ride. But then she knew herself well enough to know she was too set in her ways. She wanted roots, family, and someday grandkids to tell tall tales to.

The birch and the diamond willow thickened, and she had to find a way around them on what looked like a bear trail. She kept her eyes open and made noise as she crashed through the brush. Being on a thirty minute time table, she didn't venture too far from camp, but couldn't resist climbing the rock cropping that presented itself.

She found Lucky at the top, meditating. "Should have known you'd be up here."

Sitting in lotus position, Lucky opened his eyes. "Hey, babe." He smiled and nodded to the space next to him. "Take a load off."

Lucky had a strong belief in daily meditation. What the hell, it could be just what she needed. She sat, copying Lucky, and closed her eyes. He began to hum and softly chant. Years ago when he'd climbed the Himalayas, he'd spent a winter with the Tibetan monks and embraced Buddhism. She let his soft, soothing sounds clear her mind.

The slight breeze was enough to discourage the mosquitoes and carried the sharp scent of spruce. She calmed and felt one with the mountain, as though she could hear the sap running through the trunks of the birch, the heartbeat of the earth, the breathing of the air as it traveled over the great land.

For the first time in days she felt a measure of peace.

"Better?" Lucky asked.

She opened her eyes, and the scene that greeted had her catching her breath. They were high above the treetops, and the view went as far as the eye could see.

"Yes," she breathed the word. "That's got to be the Yukon River down there, don't you think?"

"Don't know. Everything pales with you sitting next to me." The breeze ruffled his sun-bleached hair around his heavily tanned face. He never stayed indoors if he could help it.

"Aren't you with Nadia?" she asked.

"For now. She's fun I'll say that much for her." He lifted a brow that suggested they could pick up where they left off, all she had to do was give the word.

Why was it that the men she didn't want were willing to be with her, but not the *one* man she *did* want? Fate had a perverse sense of humor.

Lucky stood and stretched. "Ready for me to beat your pants off in this competition?"

"In your dreams." She was glad he'd relaxed the atmosphere between them. She stood, feeling the stretch of muscles that hadn't been pretzeled in a while. When she got back to Fairbanks, she needed to take up yoga again. "Mac wanted us back in thirty."

Lucky grimaced. "Don't see why the old man should be in charge."

"Because he's earned it."

Mac was a former Ranger for the military. SEALs listened when he spoke. None of that would impress Lucky as he didn't believe in using military force. In his opinion, everyone should sit in a circle, hold hands, chant, and all would be right in the world.

They hiked back to camp. A shadow passed over Nadia's face when she saw them exit the forest together.

Oh, come on. Nadia had to know nothing had been going on between her and Lucky.

"Good, you're here." Mac checked his watch.

Apparently she'd made it in time, because he didn't knock her for being late. She took a seat next to Nadia around the fire pit.

Nadia wasn't the only one sending her daggers. Gage sat across from her, and the heat coming from his gaze rivaled the fire smoldering in the middle of the circle.

There was at least one fire she could douse right away. She leaned closer to Nadia, and in a low voice said, "I came across Lucky and walked back to camp with him. That's all."

As quick as the shadow had darkened Nadia's face, it cleared. "I never should have thought any different. I'm sorry."

"Nothing to be sorry for."

Lucky sat down on the other side of Nadia after refilling his cup of coffee. "Babe," he greeted Nadia, running his hand over her shoulders.

Nadia reached over and placed her hand on his knee.

Seemed all was right between them. Tern glanced again toward Gage whose expression was still hotter than coals. To hell with him. He had no right laying claim. Not when he'd thrown her away.

Robert settled in, and Mac began. "As you know, we had instructions in the caches we found yesterday." He held up the GPS coordinates typed on pieces of paper. "Even though they are addressed to individuals, I suggest we stay in teams, like yesterday, to find each of them."

"Give me a break, old man," Robert said, rising to his feet. "What the hell kind of competition is this if we stay in teams?"

"One that you'll live through." Mac didn't back down.

"We're armed, and we aren't novices. Quit mothering."

"Listen you little pissant, I'm not losing anyone on my watch." Mac shook his head when Tern opened her mouth to help dispel the argument. "Call it a gut feeling. Besides, our targets are much farther away from camp. Give me this today. We'll reassess the situation tomorrow."

Robert swept a glance over the group and shook his head. When no one jumped in to help him argue his case, he muttered, "Whatever."

Mac handed out the GPS coordinates. "It doesn't need to be said, but I'll say it anyway. Watch out for bears. This early in the season, they're still hungry from hibernating. Remember, three shots, followed by a full second between each shot if you get into trouble."

They disbanded after filling up water bottles and dividing what food they could take along for snacks, which wasn't more than a few slices of cheese, smoked salmon, and biscuits for each person. One day and they were already running low on rations. Tern hoped the geocaches had more food or this high-tech treasure hunt would turn into an actual hunting party.

Gage entered their first coordinate into his GPS, and while it did its thinking, Tern got lost in the quiet and peacefulness of the scenery. Regardless that she had to spend the day with Gage at her side, she also got to spend it outdoors in God's playground. She raised her face to the sun and breathed deep, slowly releasing her troubles into the universe. Lucky would approve.

The purity of the air, with the heat of the summer sun put her in a place so perfect that she suddenly didn't mind the company she was forced to keep. Not when she got to do what she loved.

"Ready?" Gage asked.

"Hmm." She nodded and gave him a smile that had him doing a double-take. The wattage of her smile had always served her well, and she shone it on him just because she could. "Lead the way." She gestured for him to go ahead. He narrowed his eyes, and it seemed he was going to object, but then what did he have to object to? Having come to the same conclusion, he turned and traipsed into the trees.

Under the canopy of the forest it was considerably warmer. The humidity suggested they might see rain before the day was through. The breeze was absent, and after a mile, Tern took a moment as Gage hiked ahead to shimmy out of her backpack and shed her jacket, tying it around her waist. Chances were she'd need it again when she'd least expect to. Weather in Alaska was unpredictable. She'd seen it snow on days that had begun as warm as today.

When she started again, Gage was out of sight. She stepped up her pace and went around a rock cropping to find Gage charging toward her.

"What the hell are you doing? You don't stop without letting me know."

"I would have caught up." She wasn't a child.

"I turned around and you're gone. Do you have any idea how fast you can get lost out here?"

She held up her GPS. "The last thing I'm worried about is getting lost."

His face reddened. "Just stay behind me, damn it. And if you need to stop, let me know."

The man needed a meditation session with Lucky. Sure couldn't hurt his mood.

Thirty minutes had passed without them exchanging any conversation. This was getting ridiculous. They were no longer lovers, but there'd been more about Gage that Tern had liked than just his talents in the sack. He was very intelligent, and she hadn't found a subject he couldn't debate. She'd enjoyed how he'd challenged her, not just physically, but mentally as well. So they could be civil, at least for the remainder of the week.

"So, what have you been up to since I last saw you?" she asked. If he said he'd gotten married she was going to kill him.

"Work," he bit out and trudged up the slick grassy embankment, interspersed with thinning birch trees as they gained altitude.

"That's it?" She scampered up behind him on nimble feet, ignoring the hand he'd held out to help. Her breathing was only slightly increased, while Gage seemed to struggle.

Her gaze journeyed down his body. "Work been keeping you behind a desk?"

"No." He scowled.

"What happened to that grant you were working on? Did you get it?"

"Yes."

"So…you went to Iceland?" Without me, she wanted to add, but didn't. They'd talked of her going with him for part of the time he'd be over there studying the aurora during the spring if the grant went through. Was that where he'd been all this time? "How was it?"

"Cold."

"That's it?"

"And greener than you'd expect," he grudgingly added. "We'll break after we navigate the top of the ridge."

"I'm okay to continue on, but if you need to break, it's fine by me." She didn't understand this sudden need to provoke him, but she couldn't seem to stop it either.

He grumbled something under his breath that she didn't catch and was smart enough not to ask him to repeat. Her good mood was messing with his, making his dark and dangerous. Not that it stopped her from whistling just for the hell of it. She almost choked on a laugh when he sent her a threatening look that was supposed to shut her up.

Like that was going to happen.

Storm clouds brewed over the mountain peak they climbed, but they didn't compare to the storm reflected in Gage's eyes. If she were smart, she'd find cover.

Her self-preservation instincts seemed to be absent as she attempted to engage him in more conversation. "Aidan and Raven got married." And she'd had to go to the wedding stag as he'd been her date.

"How are they?" he asked, a tentative note to his voice.

So insanely in love and giddy with their new life together that it was hard to be around them for long. "Very happy. Aidan asks about you." Almost every time she saw him.

He grunted something she couldn't make out.

When she'd introduced Gage to Aidan it was almost embarrassing how star-struck Gage had been. He'd had a total fan moment when he found out that the man Tern's sister was engaged to was none other than the graphic novelist Aidan Harte. It might be stereotypical of scientists to be obsessed with comic books and their characters, but Gage fell into that category. Aidan, likewise, had connected with Gage on a scientific and philosophical level, and they'd quickly developed quite a bromance that never failed to entertain Tern and Raven.

Tern had thought for sure Gage would put in an appearance at the wedding, for Aidan if not for her. But he hadn't.

She started whistling again, hoping to return to her previous mood, before her tumble down heartache hill.

"Stop whistling," Gage barked, his temper obviously blacker now than before.

Was he feeling guilty? Good. "What's wrong with you? Didn't you get a good night's sleep?"

He grumbled again, and the wind took his words. This time she was going to hear what he had to say.

"What'd you say?"

He turned fully to look at her. "How the hell was I going to get any sleep with you two doors down?"

Whoa. She hadn't expected that. And just for kicks, because she was enjoying his foul mood so much, she said, "Didn't stop me. Slept like a baby," she lied.

He growled. Actually *growled* at her. The sound was so unexpected that she laughed. His look turned darker.

The sound caught in her throat when he grabbed and shook her. "Damn you." His eyes were hot, his jaw clenched tight as though he struggled with something life-altering. "Why the hell did I have to see you again?" He cursed, yanked her close, and slanted his mouth over hers with so much pressure she couldn't object. He held her tight enough that she couldn't move, but everything inside her responded. Her synapses fired so fast that jolts of sexual energy sent her nerve endings into overload, melting the many reasons she should object.

51

He tore her backpack off her shoulders, held her flush against him as he struggled out of his with one arm and then the other. His hands were up and under her t-shirt, freeing her breasts, grabbing, molding. Another growl sounded from deep within his chest, the vibrations traveling upward. Her moan answered him, and her hands went on a grab fest of their own. Suddenly her feet dangled above the ground. Gage hiked her backward, bracing her body against a tree.

His eyes bored into hers, and he reached for the button on her cargo pants.

"Gage—" She didn't know if she was going to protest or tell him to hurry.

"Shut up," he said, kneeing her legs apart. "Just shut the fuck up." He kissed her again, desperate and damned determined, igniting the same reactions deep inside her.

Too far gone for reason to raise its ugly head, Tern kissed him back, biting his lip, clawing his back with her nails in her own desperation to punish him for waiting so long, for leaving her without a word. For making her fall in love with him in the first place.

His mouth left hers to trail stinging bites down her neck. Hands rough, he yanked down her pants as he kissed down her stomach. He unlaced her boots and tugged them off, and then his mouth devoured her. A hoarse cry escaped her throat.

She couldn't breathe. Pleasure overwhelmed, stabbed too hard, too fast as his tongue swept over her, in her. A rough sound, very wild and primal, vibrated from him into her and she almost splintered apart.

He cursed, stood, and freed himself. Hitching her legs around his hips, he plunged deep within her.

She gasped from the suddenness of having him inside her, her body clenching in an attempt to adjust. He didn't give her time, started driving in and out, in and out, thrusting with deep, hard, fast strokes. He gave no quarter, took everything from her and demanded she give him more.

She came apart, hard and quick, her cries startling the birds above them.

Her eyes met his, and he smiled. A predatory smile filled with arrogance and satisfaction. She pushed at his shoulders, and he pushed back with his body, nailing her to the tree. He shook his head. "I'm not done." Then he started to move again.

Her body betrayed her again, taking over her mind as sensations seduced and stupefied her into giving all that his body demanded of hers.

She came again, shuddering around him, leaving marks in his skin with her teeth, her nails. Her climax forced the onslaught of his. He groaned, the sound morphing into a strangled shout as his body emptied deep inside hers.

His head dropped in defeat onto her shoulder. His chest heaved and his heart hammered against hers. She gasped for breath, for reason.

The reality of what she'd allowed to happen—as if she'd had much of a choice—began to show itself physically.

She shoved at his shoulders. This time he stepped back, and her body wept from the absence of his. Her legs trembled, and she was grateful for the tree at her back. Though she'd be feeling the pounding she'd taken against the tree for days.

"You didn't use a condom," she accused. She had many accusations to make. She felt used and abused and almost laughed at the irony, but swallowed it in case the sound came out more as a sob.

He stared at her in shock. Whether it was the shock of not using protection, or the shock of what they'd just done, she couldn't tell.

"Didn't have one." He yanked up his pants. "*Christ*, didn't even think."

"Yeah, a lot of that going around," she muttered under her breath.

"You still on the pill?" He held his breath while he waited for her answer.

She wanted to make him sweat, but couldn't mess with him over something so important. "Yes." But that didn't help the uncomfortable situation she was in currently. It was a long hike back to camp and the hot springs.

He tore open the zipper on his backpack, produced a bandana, and wetted it with water from his water bottle. "Here."

She took it and moved away from him to clean up, and then adjusted her clothing, trying to gather her scattered thoughts and feelings while lacing and buttoning up. The torn clothes were easier to fix. Her jacket had stayed tied around her waist while he'd ripped the buttons off her shirt. She made a knot with the ends of the shirt, glad she was wearing a sports bra. If someone didn't look too close, the bra would hopefully look like an undershirt.

When she turned back to Gage, he looked as shell-shocked and battered as she felt.

He reached out a hand. "Listen, Tern—"

A gun shot rang out, followed by another, and then another.

CHAPTER FIVE

Tern and Gage crashed through the trees and found everyone gathered around the middle of camp.

Everyone except Nadia.

"Where's Nadia," Tern gasped out past heaving breaths. They'd run the distance to camp as fast as they could.

"We don't know," Mac answered, his breathing hard. He and Robert must have just arrived too.

"What do you mean *you don't know?*" Alarm sent a shiver over her sweaty body. Tern arrowed in on Lucky. "Where the hell is Nadia?"

"One minute she was right behind me, the next she was gone." Lucky said. "When I couldn't find any sign of her, I came back to camp hoping she'd returned. When she wasn't here, I fired off the warning."

"I suggest we head back to the last spot you remember seeing her," Mac said, already hitching his rifle onto his shoulder.

They moved toward the direction Lucky and Nadia had taken just as Nadia stumbled out of the trees.

Blood trickled down the side of her face and soaked her shirt. "You asshole," she rasped at Lucky, wincing and grabbing the side of her bleeding head. She gestured to the woods, wavering on her feet. "You left me out there. *Alone.*"

Tern reached Nadia first, wrapping an arm around her to keep her on her feet. Gage was suddenly at Nadia's other side. They helped her to the stumps around the fire pit.

"What happened?" Tern asked, as they lowered her to a sitting position. She held Nadia steady while Gage handed her his water bottle.

Nadia took a long drink, shutting her eyes and then slowly blinked them open. "Someone pushed me."

Tern shared a look with the men hovering around them. "Are you sure you were pushed?"

Nadia went to nod then seemed to think better of it. Pain shimmered in her eyes. She gestured at Lucky who had the decency to look guilty. "I was hiking behind this dingbat. I told him to slow down. And then suddenly someone grabbed my pack from behind and flung me down the side of the mountain." She closed her eyes and held her head in both hands. "I must have blacked out. It was hell getting back here."

Robert moistened a t-shirt he'd pulled out of his pack and knelt down in front of Nadia. Gently he wiped at the blood drying on her face and neck. "It seems to have quit bleeding," he said. "Head wounds are a bitch. I'm sure it looks worse than it is."

"Are you hurt anywhere else?" Gage asked.

Nadia slowly swiveled her head toward Gage as though just noticing him for the first time. "I don't…think so." She turned her hands over. The palms were scuffed up, the skin torn, with bits of dirt imbedded in the wounds. "I think I'd better lie down." Her head rolled on her shoulders and she slumped, unconscious.

Gage caught her in his arms before she hit the ground, picking up her small hundred and twenty pound frame. She seemed more fragile than normal in his muscled arms. "Let's get her to her bed."

Tern rushed to lead the way to their cabin, flinging open the door ahead of Gage. He turned sideways to enter the cabin, and gently laid Nadia on the cot Tern indicated.

Robert had followed them in, while Lucky and Mac stayed just outside the door. Robert knelt beside the bed and continued to clean the wound. "Tern, in my pack is a small first aid kit."

"On it." Tern hurried out of the cabin but didn't miss the look the men shared. She quickly found the first aid kit and returned. The blood on Nadia's face was gone, revealing a huge goose egg.

"Oh, God." Tern gasped.

Gage stepped toward her as though to comfort, but stopped, and shoved his hands in his front pockets instead. "Swelling's a good thing."

"He's right," Robert said. "I'd be more worried if there wasn't any." He took the first aid kit from Tern. "Thanks."

"What can I do to help?" she asked, suddenly feeling at a loss of what to do. She needed to be busy or else the things battering the closed door in her mind were going to crash through.

"Help me get her out of these," Robert said. "When she wakes up, the last thing she's going to want to see is her bloody clothes."

Gage took that as his cue to leave. "I'll be outside if there's anything you need." He spoke to Tern but Robert answered him.

"We need more water. Hot water."

"You got it." One last look at Tern, and Gage left them alone.

Tern heard the murmured voices of Mac and Lucky join in with Gage's. Mac's uneasiness this morning came back to haunt her.

Tern worked on unlacing Nadia's hiking boots first and then she and Robert carefully changed her out of her dirty and blood-stained clothes into a pair of warm, comfy sweats and loose t-shirt with the UAF Nanooks on the front. They didn't speak until after Gage brought them warm water and they washed the evidence of Nadia's fall away.

"She's going to have some bruises," Robert commented, pointing to Nadia's scratched arms and the tops of her legs. "Must have been one hell of tumble. No sign of anything broken. She's damn lucky."

"Do you think she was really pushed?" Tern finally asked the question that was foremost in her mind.

Robert shrugged. "I don't know. I haven't seen signs of anyone else about. But I highly doubt she'd have tossed herself over the mountainside. Maybe her backpack snagged on a tree limb and caught her off balance? She could have overcorrected and fell."

"I like that explanation much better."

"Not what happened," Nadia muttered, her eyes still closed. "I was pushed."

"Nadia, how do you feel?" Tern knelt next to the bed.

"Crappy."

"Will she be okay?" Tern asked. Robert had worked as an EMT for a time before he'd gone into business for himself and opened a Sporting Goods store. Tern didn't know what she'd do if something happened to Nadia. She was like one of her sisters.

Nadia moaned and swore as he checked her eyes and vitals. "She's going to have one hell of a headache—"

"Already do. Shh," Nadia whispered.

"—and be sore for a couple of days." He gave Tern a reassuring smile. "Lucky's the one I'm worried about."

"Yeah," Tern agreed. "He'd better head for high ground."

"Might want to give him a heads up," Nadia said.

"We'll be outside if you need anything," Tern said.

"Got any tequila?"

"No alcohol until we know you're out of the woods." Robert said.

"Funny, doc," Nadia said.

Tern and Robert made Nadia as comfortable as they could, and then joined the stoic men gathered around the fire that one of them had started. It was maybe mid-afternoon by her best guess. Seemed as though more time than that had passed since they'd all sat around enjoying breakfast.

Gage's eyes captured hers and she was the first to look away. She'd taken a tumble along with Nadia. Only hers was along the line of stupidity.

"Did anyone get to their caches before the warning shots?" Mac asked.

Lucky reached into his pocket. "This was all that was in the one we found before Nadia…" He handed over a box of matches to Mac. "There's a note inside you don't want to miss."

Mac opened the matchbox and took out a piece of paper. "No matches. Rob, I hope you have a lot of fuel in that lighter of yours." He dropped the empty box into the fire and unfolded the note. Whatever was written on it had Mac's face turning to stone. "Another GPS coordinate and a message." He glanced around the group, and then turned back to the note. *"Reveal your secrets or suffer the consequences."*

Silence followed the statement.

Mac reached into his pocket, pulled out another piece of paper, and passed it around. "This is what Robert and I found."

There is a murderer among you.

CHAPTER SIX

"What the hell kind of joke is this?" Gage asked, his voice hoarse. He had to work hard to swallow.

"If Nadia *was* pushed, it's no joke," Lucky said.

The message had been typed with a computer on generic white paper, giving no clue as to who had written it. With no choice, Gage handed the note to Tern while dread writhed inside him.

"Who would go through this kind of effort?" Robert continued. "The caches we've found so far weren't set by an amateur. This took planning."

"Which is why I'm concerned. From day one this game hasn't run like a competition," Mac said.

"Only because you declared that we break into teams," Robert said, flip-flopping his argument. "Maybe you're the one who's set this up."

"What do you think would've happened to Nadia today if she hadn't been part of a team?" Mac demanded.

"Maybe being with Lucky wasn't so *lucky*," Robert said. "*He* could have pushed her. Did anyone think of that?"

"Hey!" Lucky said. "Wait a damn minute."

"Lucky is a Buddhist." Tern jumped to his defense. "He wouldn't hurt a fly."

"Thanks, Tern," Lucky mumbled.

"What about you, Tern?" Robert taunted. "I don't know these guys from Adam. But we've all *known* you."

"Are you really going to go there?" Tern asked, her body going still.

"I hate to say this, but Robert has a point," Gage said. Even though part of him wanted to pull her into his arms and protect her from the anger and blame coming off Robert. It was way past time this was addressed. "The only thing we have in common is you."

"I was with *you*, remember." Hurt simmered in her dark eyes for a minute before she blinked it away.

Like he'd ever forget. The taste of her, the feel of her under his hands as his body took hers, and was lost within her soft heat. Lost was a good word to describe him right now. He shouldn't have made love to her. Who was he kidding? He hadn't made love to her, what they'd had was a fast fuck against a tree. He hadn't shown her any affection, his need for her too raw, too animalistic. He had a lot to ask her forgiveness for.

"All I said is that you are the common denominator," Gage said. "In order to figure out what we're dealing with, we're going to have to look at our relationships with you." Her relationships with these other men ate at him. They'd held her, had also known the ecstasy of being in her arms.

Tern glanced from Robert to Mac and then to Lucky. She ended with him. "You think I'm some sort of a black widow, and I'm after killing the men I've slept with?" She said it as a kind of joke as if hoping to dispel the thickening atmosphere.

If anything, it darkened the mood further. "Oh, come on. What would I have to gain?"

"Who's to say you have to gain anything," Robert said. "You've proven to be fickle before. Remember that night you were with me but went home with him?" He pointed to Lucky.

"Why you son of a bitch." Tern jumped to her feet.

"Tern, sit down," Mac barked. "Robert, apologize."

"The hell I will."

"Enough," Gage said. "This isn't getting us anywhere." Tern sat, but Robert folded his arms across his chest, a smug look on his face. He'd been waiting to drop that bomb, Gage thought.

"Tern, what did you and Gage find in your cache?" Mac asked.

Tern's face flamed and she dropped her head as if hoping her hair would hide her reaction.

"The gunshots interrupted us before the cache was located," Gage answered for her. "I'll head back up there."

"Not alone." Mac grabbed his shotgun. "Wait until I get back with Leroy and then I'll go with you."

"What?" Lucky raised his head. He'd seemed to have meditated out most of the conversation. "Where are we going?"

"I need to see where you lost Nadia. I want to look around, see if there's evidence of her being pushed." Mac double-checked the shells in his shotgun, snapping it shut with a flick of his wrist. "We need to find some clues on who's setting us up. Robert, you and Gage stay here and keep an eye out." It went unsaid that he meant protect the women.

Tern crossed her legs, obviously resenting the implication that she and Nadia couldn't take care of themselves, but she kept her mouth shut.

Mac and Lucky left. Robert regarded Tern with open suspicion.

"Oh, to hell with this." Tern stood and stomped off toward her cabin.

Gage looked at Robert. "You're an asshole. I bet it didn't take her long to figure that out and dump your ass." He got up and followed Tern. She emerged from the cabin almost as quickly as she'd entered, holding a change of clothes and a bag of toiletries.

"Where are you going?"

"I thought it was obvious." She held up the items bundled in her arms.

"You heard Mac. You aren't going anywhere alone."

"Listen, I've done a fair job of squashing the reality of what we did earlier. In order to keep up the pretense, I need to wash off your scent."

He grabbed her arm as she tried to push past him. "Not alone."

"Let go of me." She waited until he released her. "Gage, get this clear, you don't have any rights to me. If I want to wash, I'm going to wash. If I want to sleep with every man here, that's what I'm going to do."

"Try it." Gage stepped closer, his chest brushing hers. She sucked in a startled breath, but didn't step back. "You make one sexual move toward any one of them and you'll wish you hadn't."

"You left, throwing away any rights you had toward me." Her voice broke and the pain in her eyes had him wanting to hold her, beg her forgiveness for what he'd done six months ago and how he'd treated her today. But he couldn't.

She was right. She was no longer his to lay claim to. And when she found out why he'd left, she'd look at him with contempt as well as with the pain he'd caused her. "Tern—"

"Leave. Me. Alone."

"I can't." He hardened his jaw. "Not until the threat has been neutralized."

"If you don't give me some space, I'll be the biggest threat you've ever come across."

He watched her stomp away, giving her about twenty paces before he followed. No way was he leaving her unprotected if there was a threat waiting out there. He had a lot to think about with what had happened between them today. His plan to stay away from her until he'd worked her out of his system was obviously a fool's plan. She'd been able to push all his buttons today until he'd lost control. They should talk about what happened, but he didn't think she was open for conversation right now and he didn't know what to say.

Tern returned to camp, clean, but still in a foul mood. She hadn't been able to relax in the hot spring during her scrub fest. Not with Gage standing guard a few feet away in the bushes. The man needed to take lessons from Mac. Covert he was not. She hoped he'd enjoyed the view.

Gage entered camp a few minutes after her, making it look as though they'd planned a clandestine affair. Robert glared at her. She ignored him, too, and escaped inside her cabin.

Nadia was still sleeping. Tern nudged her until she responded and then let her fall back to sleep. She took more time than needed to put away her bathing supplies, braid her wet hair, disposing of her dirty clothes and torn underwear in the laundry bag. She even took time to straighten the cabin. She'd thought about grabbing one of Nadia's books, but her empty stomach sent her back out with the men. Plus, she wasn't in the mood for a romance novel.

Not when she wanted to maim someone.

Gage was the first one she saw. Why couldn't the man take himself off somewhere? She needed a break from his wary eyes.

"Let's make lunch." The men would think better on a full stomach too. Food might do all their tempers some good and besides, Mac and Lucky would be ravenous when they returned.

"What's left to eat?" Robert's tone had a whine in it that made her want to slap him.

"There's rice, remember," Tern said. "We still have the smoked salmon. I suggest we get the rice going, and I'll take a stroll around to see what else I can add." That would keep him busy and not brooding like he was doing now. Brooding wasn't going to help any of them.

He scoffed. "I don't know how to cook rice."

"Well, here's your chance to learn. Two parts water to one part rice. Simmer. Don't boil." Just because she knew her way around a campfire didn't mean all the cooking chores were going to fall to her.

Tern headed toward the forest.

"Where do you think you're going now?" Gage called.

"Let's not do this again." Did he have a death wish? "I'm going to gather more food for dinner."

"Stay in view of camp and make it quick."

She bit back a retort. This overprotective crap was getting old, fast. Taking orders was an exercise she didn't subscribe to.

Tern concentrated on picking greens for a salad, staying in view of camp. Finding a thicket of willows, she freed her pocketknife from the scabbard on her belt and cut strips of bark. With her supplies bundled in the pouch she'd made from hiking up her shirt, she headed back to camp. She felt the searing flick of Gage's glance over her exposed midriff.

She hitched her shirt higher and hoped the sight of her abs tormented the hell out him. She wanted him tied in knots, plagued with thoughts of her as she'd been these last months about him. It was childish and didn't help the situation, but there it was.

The rice was in the pan, boiling over hot flames when she returned. Again using her shirt, she grabbed the handle and pulled the pot back over coals and not flames. Robert gave her a guilty look.

Did men mess up instructions on purpose so women wouldn't ask for their help?

She added more water to the rice since too much of it had boiled off rather than soaked in. Once the rice was cooked, she added bits of smoked salmon and then stirred in the remainder of the cheese, making a casserole of sorts. Her stomach rumbled. It wasn't a meal you'd find in a restaurant or even in her kitchen, but it smelled good, and she was happy with the results. She served it up to the quiet group, along with the wild green salad. Before eating herself, she checked on Nadia, who was still sleeping, her breathing even and pulse steady.

Mac and Lucky returned with Nadia's backpack.

Both Robert and Gage stood as though at attention for their next orders. Lucky seemed more upset than when he'd left.

"How's Nadia?" he asked, voice full of remorse and worry.

"Still sleeping," Tern replied. "I've made something to eat."

"I'm not hungry." Lucky turned toward Nadia's cabin, while Mac dropped the backpack and took a seat on one of the stumps.

"What've you got?" Mac asked.

Tern dished him up the salmon and rice, and he dug in.

Robert and Gage gathered around Mac, waiting. Once Mac shoveled in a few heaping bites, he started to talk. "Found her pack down an embankment, choked with trees. If it wasn't for the neon strip of orange, I wouldn't have seen it. Leroy made the right choice in returning to camp for help. With her knocked out, and no sounds to help him locate her, he wouldn't have seen her."

He shoveled in a few more bites and then resumed. "I didn't see any sign of someone else, but then Lucky had trampled the area, contaminating any tracks left by anyone besides the two of them. The section was so wooded there's no way to tell if she was pushed or her pack was snagged."

Tern didn't like the suspicions radiating off him. "What are you thinking?"

He glanced at everyone. "There's either someone among us setting us up, or out there waiting and watching for an opportunity."

"Opportunity for what?" Tern asked, even though she was afraid she knew.

"That's what we'd better figure out."

Mac finished eating and then he and Gage took off for the geocache Tern and Gage hadn't found earlier. Hopefully, there would be more clues in it to point to what was going on.

Nadia stumbled out of their cabin with Lucky's help. Tern rushed over while Robert kept watch, propped against his cabin with his rifle lying crosswise on his lap.

"How are you feeling?" Tern asked, her gaze roving over Nadia. Her face was pale, the swelling around the cut already turning black and blue.

"Remember that car wreck I was in two years ago?" Nadia grumbled. Tern nodded. "A lot like that."

Tern supported one arm, and with Lucky on Nadia's other side, they helped her over to the snapping campfire.

"Do we have any drugs?"

"I made you some tea," Tern said. "It should help with the aches and pains." Tern poured the willow tea in a cup and cautiously handed it to Nadia. "It's hot, so be careful."

Nadia sipped and grimaced. "Ugh. This is gross."

"Yes, but it will help your headache."

"I think I'd rather deal with the headache."

"Is there anything else I can get you?" Lucky asked, hovering at her side.

"Unless you have chocolate, I don't want to see you right now," Nadia said.

Lucky dropped his head. "I'm really sorry, Nadia." He shuffled off toward his cabin.

"You were a little hard on him," Tern said, watching Lucky scuff his way across the camp. "This wasn't his fault."

"He should never have left me out there. I don't want to talk about him. I heard fighting earlier. What happened between you and Gage?"

"Heard that, did you?"

"I don't know what was real and what I dreamt." She took another sip, her face contorting from the bitterness, but she swallowed. "Clear it up for me."

Tern brought her up to speed with the blame game earlier, then leaned in after searching the camp for anyone listening, and told Nadia what had happened between her and Gage on their geocaching trek.

"Holy shit." Nadia sat stunned. "I bet you wished you could trade me places."

Tern regarded Nadia's bump on the head. "Doubt you'd want to be in my shoes though."

"I don't know. The sex sounded really hot."

Tern didn't want to remember, but was afraid she'd never forget.

Mac and Gage entered camp. Anger and apprehension drifted off them in waves. Mac called the group together.

"Give me a minute to talk to Tern first," Gage began.

Mac shook his head. "Need to see everyone's reaction to the news." He stared at Tern. "Especially hers."

CHAPTER SEVEN

"Tern." Gage grabbed her hand. "I need to talk to you. Alone."

"No one is going anywhere," Mac said. "Robert, get Leroy out here. Gage, take a seat. Nadia, glad to see you up and about."

"What's going on?" Nadia looked at Tern.

Tern shook her head, but she had a bad feeling. She should have listened to that feeling when it had slithered over her skin at the hangar in Fairbanks. Her grandmother, Coho, had always advised to heed the warnings of her ancestral spirits. She pulled on Gage's grip. He tightened his hold as though trying to telegraph something before releasing her.

Robert and Lucky joined the group. Everyone had taken a stump except Mac. He leaned his .30-06 butt down on the ground against a log, reached into his breast pocket and pulled out newspaper articles.

"We found news clippings on everyone except Tern." He observed Tern. "I think it's safe to say we are all here because of you."

A chill snaked up her spine. "News clippings? Why?"

"We'd better hurry and figure out why." Mac clenched his jaw and glanced down at the newspapers. "Before we start, just know that we all have secrets. None of us are saints."

"What the fuck is in those?" Robert rose to his feet.

"Our deepest and darkest."

"I'm not staying here for this." Robert backed up a few steps.

"Really, Robert, where are you going to go?" Lucky asked.

Robert looked frantically around and cursed again. "Burn 'em." He pointed to what Mac held in his hand. "Right now, toss them in the fire."

"Gage and I already know what's in these," Mac said. "The rest of you need to be aware of what we're up against."

"Bullshit," Robert huffed. "This is a sick game."

"One that almost got me killed this afternoon," Nadia said. "I don't want to hear what's in those any more than you do. But whoever's pulling the strings does."

"So, we're going to blindly obey the son of a bitch?" Lucky asked, joining with Robert.

"You have a better idea?" Nadia asked.

"Yeah," Lucky said. "We can pack up and walk out of here." He glanced around the group.

"I'm in agreement," Robert said. "Burn the newspapers and let's leave. None of us signed up for this."

"I'm not in any condition to hike out of here," Nadia said, raising her hand to her head. "I vote for the big reveal and playing out the game until the plane shows back up."

"That's five days away," Gage quietly reminded everyone.

"How long will it take to hike out?" Nadia asked. "Get real. We might as well put a bullet in our heads right now."

"Okay, none of that kind of talk," Tern said.

"Nadia's right," Mac said. "We're a good fifty to a hundred miles from any village. If there's someone out there lying in wait, we're better equipped to stay here and defend ourselves. If one of us is the culprit, best to stay and keep an eye on everyone."

"What about that trash?" Robert gestured to the news clippings. "I still vote we destroy them and refuse to play."

"What are you afraid of, Robert?" Nadia asked.

"None of your goddamn business." He tightened his lips.

"Actually, it is her business." Mac regarded the group. "For whatever reason, we're all here, which means we need to know what's in these news articles. Whoever set this 'competition' up went through a lot of time investigating us. We need to know what he knows. It's the only way to get to the bottom of this." Mac drew in a deep breath. "I'll go first." He held Tern's gaze for a moment before glancing at the others. "Remember, every story has two sides."

When he began it was like he was lost in some dark place, reliving a nightmarish past. He passed the copy of the article around. "My wife was killed because of me. After I left the Rangers, I worked intelligence for the government. Shannon was kidnapped and used as leverage to try and get me to turn traitor against my country." His voice failed him, and he took a minute. "You'll notice the newspapers painted a different picture of her death. Make your own judgments."

Gage passed Tern the article.

The headline read: *Decorated US Army Ranger's Wife Tortured and Killed.*

The article went into depth on how Mac refused to give into the kidnappers' demands, and his wife was murdered. Rather than concentrate on the supreme sacrifice that Mac had made for his country, the journalist had focused on the inhumanity of the man who would forfeit the life of his wife. It painted Mac and the military in a harsh, callous light.

Tern didn't read any further, and handed it to Nadia. Why hadn't he confided in her? This explained so much of why he refused to commit to her. She stood and walked over to him, her hand resting on his forearm. "This is the why?"

He nodded and lightly cupped her cheek. "I couldn't put another person I loved in harm's way."

"You could have told me. I would have understood."

"You would have talked me into marrying you."

She gave him a sad smile. "Probably."

"Which is why I couldn't risk it." He cupped her face and kissed her cheek. "Better have a seat, love. There are more punches to come."

She returned to her seat, catching Gage's narrowed stare.

"Anyone want to volunteer to go next?" Mac asked. There was a lot of squirming, except for Gage who sat like a stone, hands clasped loosely between his knees, while he stared into the flames.

"Make no mistake, we'll be diving deep into these." Mac waved the evidence in his hand. "For whatever reason, they have something to do with why we are all here."

"I'll go," Nadia said. "If it's what I think it is, Tern is already aware of it." She held out her hand and took the article from Mac. A quick glance had her rolling her lips as though fighting back tears. She lowered her head and began to speak in words barely above a whisper. "I was babysitting. Sometime during the evening my sister fell between her mattress and the frame of her bunk bed. I never heard her as she was strangled." Nadia swallowed and cleared her throat. "She died. I was fourteen. She was only three."

Tern put a comforting arm around her. Nadia leaned heavily against her as though the telling had taken whatever spunk she had left.

"This is ridiculous, Mac," Tern said. "What is any of this going to accomplish?"

"Until we can figure something else out, it will relax the person who brought us together into thinking we're complying," Mac said. "Besides, I prefer knowing what the guy has on all of us. Knowledge is power."

"This is a bunch of shit," Robert said, tossing a stick into the fire. "There is nothing that has been revealed that helps us figure out anything. What does your wife's death have to do with this? Nadia's little sister? It's all fucking bullshit."

"It speaks to character," Mac said. "We're made up of our experiences. They are the fires that forge who we are. What are you made of, Robert? Or should we call you Wyatt?" Mac stood impassable, his thick muscled arms crossed over his chest, the stern, tightness of his face speaking louder than words. The warrior was in charge, and Robert must have recognized that there was no way out of this particular game.

Robert's skin blanched. "Fine. Let me see that." He took the offered printed page, glanced at it. His shoulders dropping. "I was seventeen. It was fifteen years ago. Road conditions were bad, ice fog was thick. I never saw the other car."

"What happened?" Tern asked when he paused long enough to make her think he wasn't going to finish.

"We'd been drinking, okay. We were fucking teenagers. I was driving. I was the only one who survived. The others were killed."

"How many others?" Nadia asked.

"I did the time, okay. Plead guilty to vehicular homicide."

"Finish it, Robert," Mac said.

"Three, okay. My girlfriend, my best friend, and his date. It was prom. We'd decided to double."

"Any reason for anyone to still want justice?" Mac asked. "Family members of the ones killed?"

"It happened in Minnesota. As soon as I got out of juvie, I changed my name and headed north. As far as I know, nobody has a clue I'm here."

"Someone does," Mac said. "Pass the picture around."

Reluctantly, Robert did.

The picture accompanying the articled showed a hunk of twisted metal wrapped around a tree with the headline, *Drunken Teen Slays Friends.* Tern's stomach sickened as she passed the newspaper clipping back to Robert. He stared at the paper before crumpling it in his hand. "Who the fuck is doing this?" His voice broke. He stood and stomped a few steps away, giving the group his back.

Silence settled over the camp until Lucky spoke, his tone subdued, "I killed my best friend too."

Robert slowly swiveled around and stared at Lucky as he continued. "We were climbing the north face of Monte Blanc. Wicked granite walls." He paused, breathing deep as though gaining courage to continue. "The rigging broke. I'd checked all the gear the night before. Everything seemed fine. But…it didn't matter in the end. Hansen was dead."

"This is ridiculous," Tern said. "These incidents are all tragic accidents."

"Maybe if I had double, triple checked the gear, I could have saved him. It was my responsibility. It was my gear. I'd talked him into the climb. He wasn't as experienced as I was. He trusted me, and it got him killed."

"That's enough." Tern jumped to her feet. "Accidents happen."

"Mine was no accident," Gage said, a finality in his voice.

Tern slowly sank back onto the stump, her heart thudding in her chest. She didn't want to hear this. Didn't want to know what Gage had hidden from her. This whole game, the big reveal, had been building to what Gage had kept from her.

"I killed my brother-in-law," he said. "And if I could, I'd kill him again."

CHAPTER EIGHT

"Want to know where I went six months ago?" Gage asked, almost daring Tern to ask. "Jail, on murder charges."

Silence cut the group. It was like someone had pushed the mute button on the remote. Even the chickadees, high up in the birch branches, ceased their chirping. Either that or Tern's hearing refused to take in the conviction of his words.

He couldn't have killed someone.

The man she'd loved wasn't a murderer. Besides, if he had killed this brother-in-law, he'd be in prison, not free and here with them now. There had to be more to the story. It was a struggle, but Tern found her voice. "Tell us."

Gage arrowed in on her, the fire in his eyes making her uncomfortable. She wanted to look away but couldn't.

He started to speak, fast, as though regurgitating what happened. "My brother-in-law beat the shit out of my sister. Apparently, he'd been doing it for years, but no one informed me until she was hospitalized. They didn't know if she was going to live through it. Mitch had beaten her within an inch of her life. Broken ribs, collapsed lung, left her blind in one eye, and caused her to miscarry her pregnancy of five months.

Jury's still out on whether she'll be able to have any more kids. She refused to press charges, said she'd fallen down the stairs. Something had to be done. So I flew back home to New Mexico and confronted Mitch, told him to leave. He wasn't going to be within a hundred feet of my sister ever again. We got into it. He pulled a knife and I killed him."

Tern's heart clenched at the pain and powerless rage in Gage's voice. "Why didn't you call me?" she asked.

"I couldn't call you from jail. Tern, I *never* wanted you to know what I had done."

Silence once again smothered like a blanket over the group. What did she say to that? She wanted more information, like how was he released? Was there a trial still pending? Would she lose him again, this time for life as he served out a murder sentence?

"Okay, time to move on."

Wait? She wasn't ready to move on. She couldn't process everything that Gage had said.

Mac continued, "We know what this psycho is using against us. Does anyone have anything else to add?" Everyone looked at each other but didn't say anything. "From what I can tell this whole thing has been orchestrated around Tern. So, Tern, what's your verdict?"

"None of this means anything," she said. "*None* of it changes how I feel. I still care for everyone the same." Why hadn't Gage trusted in her?

Gage lifted his head, his eyes focused on her.

"I knew about Nadia's past and I'm not naive enough to assume that all of you are perfect. I don't understand what was to gain by this exercise."

"Probably trying to pit us against each other," Robert said, calmer now. "We just found out that we're stuck with a bunch of people capable of murder." He nodded at Gage.

"Given the right motivation, everyone is capable of killing someone," Gage said.

"I don't know about you guys, but I could use a breather," Nadia said. Tern silently agreed.

"I could use a drink," Lucky said attempting to joke until he caught the look in Robert's eyes. "Sorry, bad taste."

"I suggest we figure a way to get out of here," Robert said. "I'm not going to be used like a pawn in some psychotic fuck's game."

"This was supposed to be fun," Lucky said. "I'm not enjoying myself at all. Anyone else?"

There were a few grunts of agreement.

"We need to hike out of here tomorrow morning, first light," Lucky said. "The Yukon River is below us. There is bound to be traffic this time of year. Fishing, tourists, supplies headed up river. We hike down, walk along the bank until we run into someone. Chances are we might get some cell service."

"Except our cell phones were taken, remember?" Nadia reminded. "I think we should stay put. The plane is going to be here in a few days—"

"We can't be sure of that," Lucky said.

"Who's to say if we leave, we won't run into more problems?" Nadia pointed out.

"We're sitting ducks here," he returned.

"With water and food—"

"We're almost out of food," Lucky said.

"Enough," Mac interrupted. "Let's put it to a vote. All in favor of hiking out of here come morning raise their hand."

One by one everyone's hand rose except Nadia's.

"I have a real bad feeling about this," Nadia whispered, wrapping her arms around her as though in a hug.

"Majority rules," Mac said. "We hike out of here in the morning. Until then, I suggest we hunt up some food." He regarded Robert. "Rob, from what I've heard, you know your way around a bird hunt. Care to come along?"

"What the hell." Robert grabbed his rifle and followed Mac.

"I'll gather some more water," Gage said, heading toward the lake after a quick stop for the bucket they'd found yesterday in one of the cabins.

Good, that would keep them all out of Tern's hair for a bit so she could think.

"I'm going to lie back down," Nadia said, holding her head. "I've got a killer headache."

"Want some company?" Lucky asked with concern in his voice.

"No." Nadia wobbled to her feet. Tern rushed to help along with Lucky, but Nadia pulled her arm from his grasp.

"Nadia, I'm really sorry," Lucky said, the need to help warred in his expression.

"Lucky, let her be for now." Tern shared a look with him. He nodded, and turned his attention to building up the fire.

Tern and Nadia didn't speak until they were inside their cabin. Tern helped her lay down on the cot. "You were a little rough on him, weren't you?"

"He left me for dead, Tern."

"He left to get help." Tern sat on the edge of her bunk. "I can understand how you are hurt and angry, but he did the right thing. Can't you tell how upset and worried about you he is?"

Something passed over Nadia's expression, but she put up a hand to cover her eyes. "Tern, I'm sorry. I'm not handling this well. I know he's worried, I just hurt too bad to care about what he is going through. Do you mind? I just want to rest?"

"Sure, hon." Tern stood and patted Nadia's shoulder. "You're right. Rest, I'll talk to Lucky."

"Thanks." Nadia sighed and shut her eyes in obvious relief.

Tern headed back to the campfire to find Lucky gone and Gage returning with a bucket of water.

"Have you seen Lucky?" she asked him.

"I passed him on the way up here. He said something about picking wildflowers by the lake." Gage set down the bucket, whipping his hands on his jeans, and seemed like he needed to find something else to do. He glanced around the campsite. "Where's Nadia?"

"Lying down."

He swallowed, and she recognized the hunger in his gaze. Oh, no. She didn't know if she was ready to revisit their earlier stupidity or what she'd learned afterward.

"Tern—"

"I've got things I need to gather for dinner." She swiveled and started walking toward the cover of the trees. Gage followed her. She swiveled on her heel. "What are you doing?"

"Going with you," Gage said. "It's not a good idea for you to be alone."

"I have a gun with me. I don't need you." A flicker of pain crossed his face, but it was gone so fast she thought she'd imagined it.

"Whether you need me or not, you've got me."

For how long? He'd left her before. Granted, he was in jail. Oh God. Jail.

"We need to talk. I understand that you don't want to right now. I never wanted you to find out what happened, why I'd left."

But he was okay with letting her think he didn't care enough about her to call, trusting her to be there for him?

"Tern, I can't ignore what happened between us earlier. For six months, I've tried to forget you. It didn't work."

"So what? You're saying you want to pick up where we left off?"

"Maybe. No. I'm not sure. Hell, I don't know what I want. You confuse the hell out of me, Tern."

She was too raw dealing with what had happened between them earlier to take a stab at helping him. Hell, she was confused too. And angry. Really angry, the kind of anger fueled by hurt. "Let me make it easy for you. No. No picking up where we left off. There."

"I wasn't the only one who lost it out there. You were just as into me as I was you."

"So I fell off the wagon. Doesn't mean I'm staying off." She moved to leave him.

He grabbed her arm, bringing her to a halt. "There is still something between us."

"Actually, I think we got that 'something' out of our system." She glanced down at her arm. "It's getting old telling you to let go of me. I'm not your property and one fast—whatever that was—against a tree doesn't make up for being ignored for six months."

He let her go.

She took a few steps and suddenly turned back to face him. "Did you really go to Iceland this spring?" Had he lied to her on their hike earlier, as well as keeping that he'd been in jail from her?

"Yes. I went. I was released in time to fulfill my commitment to the University."

Oh, so he could fill those commitments but not any that he'd made to her. Actually he hadn't made her any commitments. Was she nothing more to him than a woman he'd hooked up with for a while? "Why did you come on this competition anyway?"

"I don't know." He glanced away into the forest.

"Don't know or don't want to tell me?"

"Both." This time he met her stare.

What was she supposed to do with that? She turned to gather more plants and tried to gather her emotions at the same time. He'd stirred up a beehive's worth of hurt feelings and rejection. She'd done her best to ignore him as he watched her scour the forest floor for edible plants. Too many things had happened today.

After collecting enough greens to supplement their meal, she headed back toward the clearing and Gage.

He looked skeptical at what she'd picked from nature's pantry, but the wild puffball mushrooms would be delicious sautéed with butter and some of the leftover wine.

"Don't be so cynical," she said. "If we don't find more food, you'll be thankful for what I can pick in the forest."

"Any of this going to kill us?" He motioned to the puffball mushrooms, which when dried out and stepped on made a puff of dust that seemed anything but appetizing. Young kids had fun hunting them out and stomping on them since they were like a nature fart. But these were picked while they were still moist and young.

"I could poison you with my knowledge," she couldn't help interjecting. Let him be a little worried. "I guess you'll just have to trust that I won't."

He let the trust comment go. "How'd you learn all this? I thought you studied marketing and business in college?"

"Not everything is learned in school. My grandmother taught me. She, in turn, was taught by her mother, who was taught by her mother. The knowledge has been passed down through the women in my family for thousands of years," she said with pride. Pride of her heritage, her race, and the long line of strong women she'd come from.

"I had no idea."

"There's a lot about me you don't know." He would have had to stick around in order to find out.

"We're getting low on firewood. I'm going to go and find some more." Without a sound, he was gone.

He was good at leaving, she'd give him that.

CHAPTER NINE

Mac and Robert had found a covey of ptarmigans and brought back two plump birds for her to cook. Tern butchered the already dressed-out birds and coated them in flour and set them to fry in oil. The grate over the fire had a pan of rice, the ptarmigan, and more willow tea for Nadia boiling away. It was a balancing act finding the hotspots and the not-so-hot ones over the banked coals.

Her optimism began to return as she cut up the puffball mushrooms and added them to the skillet with the ptarmigan. Pouring the remainder of the wine over the top, she covered the pan, and let the ingredients simmer. The rich savory smells started her stomach to rumbling.

Mac sat studying a map on his GPS, most likely figuring out the safest way down the mountain. His bifocals looked very distinguished on his chiseled and weathered face. Kind of Indiana Jonesish. Robert lay in the soft grasses, by all accounts napping the late afternoon away, but he wasn't sleeping. She'd seen him do this before. He seemed unimposing, but in truth, he was cataloging everything around him. People said and did things in front of those who they deemed were asleep.

She'd learned this about him the hard way.

He'd overheard a private conversation between her and her sister Raven, and found out things she'd wished he didn't know about her family. She'd invited him over for a family dinner, and he'd pretended to 'rest' later on the couch. The man was sneaky as a wolverine. She hadn't been able to trust that his attentions toward her were honest now that he knew she and her family had millions in gold.

Lucky had returned to camp clutching a fistful of wildflowers and went into the cabin to watch over Nadia who was still down for the count. Gage continued to gather firewood. If he kept it up, they'd soon have enough to make it through the winter.

"Tern?" Mac stood, stretching out the kinks.

"Hmm?"

He glanced at Robert and then tilted his head in the direction of the lake. She wasn't the only one who knew Robert pretended to sleep.

She glanced down at the dinner she was cooking and moved all the pans to the outside of the heat where they would to be kept warm but not too hot. She wiped her hands and followed Mac. Gage stopped and watched them leave, his arms loaded down with wood.

"Gage, keep an eye on the food, would you?" Tern didn't wait for his answer. His scowl was answer enough. He didn't like seeing her with Mac.

"Sweetcakes, you're tearing that man up." Mac chuckled, wrapping an arm around her shoulders. "Wanta give him something to stew over?"

"Aren't you too old for games?" Tern liked the feel of his arm across her shoulders, though. She leaned her head into the crook of his arm, feeling safe and protected.

"One thing you need to learn about men, we're never too old for games. Especially when they involve a beautiful woman."

"Are you flirting with me?" She leaned back to look into his eyes. They twinkled down at her.

"Would I do that?"

"Yes."

He threw his head back on a booming laugh that would be heard back at the campsite. No doubt both Robert and Gage heard it.

"Just what are you up to?"

He smiled at her. "That's one thing I loved about you. Nobody pulls the wool over your eyes." He guided her farther away along the lake's edge to an outcropping of spruce dipping their roots into the rich, glacial-fed water. "Gage is being an idiot."

"What? You playing matchmaker now?"

"Hell, no. But pointing out when a man is being particularly stupid is just too much fun to pass up. Now, I need information on everyone here." His teasing manner dropped like a stage curtain. He guided her to a boulder and motioned for her to take a seat. He remained standing, propping his booted-foot on a log, and leaned forward. "Keep your voice low in case one of them decides to lurk. I think I'll hear anyone who comes up, but you never know." He glanced around the area.

"Mac, you're worrying me with all this cloak and dagger stuff." Indeed her heart was skipping a few beats faster like they had jogged to this place rather than the leisurely stroll they'd taken.

"Good. I want you to stay on your toes. Anything out of the ordinary—right, what's not out of the ordinary here," he said at her sardonic expression. "Does anything concern or worry you about our players back there?"

"*Everything* about the big reveal we just had."

"What else?"

"Does there have to be more? Please, don't let there be more."

He flicked the end of her nose. "Damn, but you're fetching."

She placed a hand on his leg and leaned toward him. "Not fetching enough for some."

"We've been over that."

"You're the one who broke off our relationship. You know I didn't want it to end." In fact, she'd cried and begged him not to leave her. Now that she knew what happened to his wife, she wanted to talk about the things they hadn't.

"Love, I'm not the man for you." He gave a deep sigh. "I was filling a role for you, one that I will continue too as long as you need me."

"Not that father figure crap again." She went to stand.

He pushed her back onto the boulder. "I'm twenty years older than you. I'm not hero material or," he continued when she went to interrupt, "willing to father more children. You know deep down you would've resented me for making you give up being a mother. You'll make a great mother someday. Probably reproduce with that idiot back at camp."

"Hey, we aren't together."

"Like you weren't this afternoon?" He cocked a brow in question and then chuckled at the blush that heated her face.

Tern looked down at the pebbled ground and tried not to squirm. "What gave us away?"

"Not important. What I need to know is what kind of dirt you can give me on our campmates."

Mac took a seat on the log kitty-corner from her boulder. Legs spread, he rested his elbows on his knees, his hands clasped loosely in front.

"Are you serious?" Tern asked. "Do you suspect one of them?"

"Help me rule them out."

"Okay." She swallowed. "Who do you want to start with?"

"Lucky Leroy Morgan. And none of that shit that he's a Buddhist and wouldn't hurt a fly. Like Gage already mentioned, any man, or woman, could kill given the right motivation."

"You want to know what could motivate Lucky to kill?" She had trouble wrapping her brain around this.

"Or be passionate enough about something that he would go through these lengths to put into motion this geocache competition."

She thought long and hard. "I don't see how he could. He just returned from climbing the Andes. Whoever did this would have to have means and opportunity. Lucky is always broke, and when would he have had the time?"

"We both know that you aren't a poor woman. Could he be after your money?"

"No. The reason Lucky is always broke is because he has no need of money. He seriously doesn't care about things like that. And you've seen him. People love him. He's taken in all over the world. No matter where he is, what mountain he feels he needs to climb, people cheer him on. I don't see anyone holding a grudge against him or vice versa."

"Why did you break up with him?"

"Because I needed more stability in my life, but there is still a big part of me that loves him. While he has these faults, he'd die for all of us here. He wouldn't even think twice about it."

Mac nodded, taking in the information. "Nadia. Tell me about her. How long have you known her? What type of relationship do you have?"

"Mac, I don't like this. I don't want to think of my best friend, or the men I've been with, in the way you're asking me to."

"Humor me. It might end this without anyone getting hurt."

"You really think we're in danger?"

"Yes."

She sucked in a breath and stared into his unwavering eyes. "Okay. I met Nadia in college, did all the stupid stuff that college kids do. She got serious with an old professor of mine, got really wrapped up with him, and we kind of lost touch. Years later, she came into the shop, and we got to reminiscing. We've been friends ever since."

"How long?"

"I don't know. A few years ago."

"Tell me about her."

"Well, you already know about the sister who died. She was an only child originally. Her mother died when she was young, and her dad remarried and had her little sister. The marriage didn't last after the girl's death. It's just been her and her father since then. She works at the University in the math department.

She's got tenure and is a professor. What else do you want to know?"

"Relationships?"

"Nothing serious. She has trouble in that department, but then don't we all," Tern added under her breath, but Mac caught it.

"Don't sell yourself short. Your time will come. Back to Nadia. Any trouble?"

"No, not really. We have fun together. We laugh, hang out, talk on the phone, shop, do each other's hair. What do you want?"

"I'm not sure. Tell me about Robert."

"Single parent, and yes, he's a good parent. He's great with his little girl, Chloe. His wife died of cancer when Chloe was two. He owns his own business, is involved in the community. Likes to hunt, fish, all the things most men in Alaska like."

"Why didn't you marry him?"

"Dang it, Mac. Why do we need to go into that?"

"Motivation, love. Now give it up."

She huffed out a breath. "He's too clingy, I guess you could say. I couldn't go anywhere without him needing to know where and why and with whom. It got old. Plus, the chemistry while in the beginning was okay, by the end it was forced."

"You stuck it out for his kid."

She nodded. "I fell in love with her, and no matter how much I tried, I couldn't love Robert. He's too controlling, and—" She broke off the rest of what she was going to say because she didn't like where her thought process took her.

"And?"

Of course, Mac wasn't going to let it go. "He knows about the gold."

"Ahh." Mac stood. "Does Nadia?"

"No."

"Gage?"

"No. You know I don't like people to know since they treat me differently."

"Does Gage know the story behind your father's death?"

"We never got that far." Tern looked down at her hands. She really needed a manicure. It was easier to concentrate on that than the past and all she and her family had lost at the hands of a killer.

"How far did you and Gage get?"

"I thought I loved him. He didn't feel the same."

"What happened?"

"No. No, I'm not getting into it. All you need to know is that he left, and I haven't seen him in six months."

"Did he have opportunity to set this up?"

"I don't know. You know as much as I do of where he's been. I haven't talked to him, or seen him. Nothing in six months, okay."

"It's all right, Tern. Settle down."

"Don't do that. You started this. Don't get all 'adult' on me when it makes me upset."

"Fine."

"Plus, Gage doesn't have any motivation to do all this. Why would he? *He* left *me*, remember."

"Then we need to look at the rest of your life. People you might have upset, unwittingly. Someone who is jealous of you."

"I can't do this anymore, Mac." Her hold on her emotions was tenuous at best. If he kept chipping away at her, making her think things she couldn't comprehend about the people she loved, she was going to break apart.

"All right, we'll take a break. But I need you to be thinking who in your life, either someone here, or someone back in Fairbanks, who might—and I don't care how ridiculous you think it sounds—have set this up. I think you're in real danger here, Tern."

Of course, the first person Tern saw when she and Mac returned to camp was Gage. His gaze held hers until she had to look away, but not before she caught the tightening of his jaw and narrowing of his eyes. Nadia had emerged from the cabin and sat around the campfire looking pale and tired. Lucky fidgeted around her and seemed to be pissing her off.

"Where's Robert?" Mac asked.

Gage nodded his head toward the cabin. "Taking a nap."

"Still?" Mac lowered his rifle to rest at his feet as he took a seat by Gage.

Gage shrugged, looked from Mac to Tern and then into the flames he was poking with a stick. He must have moved the pans farther away from the heat of the fire that he'd built up to combat the lower temperature.

She pulled her sleeve on her hoodie down over her hand, using it as a sort of hot pad and took off the lid to the ptarmigan. She needed to thank Gage for watching over the meal. The bird was ready to serve, and since she'd been gone so long with Mac it could have been overcooked and then inedible. They didn't have the luxury of heading down to the corner market or calling for takeout if dinner was ruined.

"Is that all there is?" Lucky asked, peering over her shoulder.

"I have some greens that I gathered, and a little leftover rice." Lucky's vegetarian diet was going to suffer. There weren't any protein substitutes handy. He'd have to go to the source in order to keep his strength up.

"Any cheese left?"

"Sorry, no. We ate the last of that for lunch. I know this goes against your beliefs, but you'll need to compromise if we're going to hike out of here."

"Bad idea," Nadia spoke up. "We really need to stay here. I can't hike down the mountain. Not with this humongous headache."

Tern and Mac shared a look. Mac obviously had taken in Nadia's pallor and sunken eyes and thought the same thing she had.

"You're right, Nadia," Mac said. "We'll give you another day to rest and then reassess the situation."

"What?" Lucky asked. "Listen, we need to leave tomorrow. The sooner we get back to civilization, and some tofu, the better."

"The rest of us can find food with what we can hunt," Mac said. "But if you're going to stick to plant food, Leroy, you won't make it out of here."

Tern could feel an argument heating up between the-meat-and-potatoes kind of guy and tofu-and-nut kind. "Mac, would you fetch Robert so we can eat? The food is ready."

Mac wanted to stay and drill into Lucky the stupidity of his choices, but he grabbed his rifle and trekked to the cabin to get Robert.

"Nice save," Gage commented, giving her a small smile.

"Thanks." Tern didn't like the way he was looking at her. It was like before, when she'd thought he loved her, wanted to be with her forever. All soft and appreciative with a hint of I-can't-wait-to-get-you-naked. He must have realized it, because he tightened his lips and stood, putting distance between them.

Mac returned to the group. "Robert's gone."

Chapter Ten

"Gone?" Tern asked, rising to her feet. "What do you mean Robert's gone?"

"As in not in his cabin." Mac turned to the three who had been in camp while she and Mac had been down by the lake.

"Did anyone see him leave? Head to the latrine?"

Nadia shook her head and then had to grab it. "No," she muttered, her voice clenched with pain. "I'd just gotten out here before you two showed. I haven't seen Robert since before I laid down."

"I was watching over Nadia," Lucky added.

They all turned to Gage. "Hey, I didn't do anything to him. After you two headed down to the lake, he headed toward the cabin. If he left, I never heard or saw him." His tone clearly said he wouldn't miss the man either.

"Shit," Mac said. "I told everyone not to leave camp and never to go anywhere alone."

"Which is probably why he left." Tern laid a comforting hand on Mac's arm. The muscles under her fingers were tense and bunched. "He doesn't like taking orders."

"Well, pissy for him. He's going to get himself killed." Mac swept the clearing with his eagle eyes. "No one's got his back out there. If there is someone pulling the strings, he's on his own."

"Unless, he's the puppet master," Gage said.

Nadia sucked in her breath, a hand covering her mouth.

"Oh, come on," Tern scoffed. "Robert wouldn't be behind this. He has a daughter."

"So did Ted Bundy," Nadia said.

"She's got a point," Lucky said. "Just because Robert has a little girl doesn't mean he isn't a killer. He admitted to killing his friends in high school."

"It was an accident," Tern reminded. "One that you had the misfortune to experience yourself."

"He'd admitted to drinking," Lucky said.

"Drinking and driving, while stupid on so many levels, is not premeditated."

"Might as well be if you ask me," Lucky muttered.

"All right, enough," Gage said. "Are we going to go after him?"

"We have no idea what direction he went," Lucky said. "I've seen what happens when people go off searching for some idiot in a horror movie." He ran his finger across his throat.

This was starting to feel like a horror movie.

"There he is!" Tern pointed with relief at Robert as he came out of the trees, carrying a white bucket by the handle.

Everyone started talking at once, except Mac. Robert entered the circle around the campfire.

"You are a fucking dumbass," Mac said. "What were you thinking of heading out there alone?" Mac pointed to the dark forest that Robert had emerged from. "You have a daughter. You have no business risking your life."

"Back off, old man." Robert looked at the rest of the worried faces and settled on Tern's. "I went looking for another of the caches listed. Sweetheart, you gotta see what I found." He set the bucket down. It was a standard five gallon bucket that someone would store flour or sugar in.

Robert popped the lid off.

Tern gasped as the contents were exposed.

CHAPTER ELEVEN

Tern squealed. Chocolate. Better than that, Almond Joys. Coconut and almonds drenched in chocolate. She reached her hand into the bucket to grab a candy bar.

"Stop!" Mac barked. "Don't touch them. They could have been tampered with." He reached for the bucket. "Hand me that."

"Oh, come on," Robert scoffed. "You seriously going to inspect a bunch of Almond Joys, like a *parent* with a bag of Halloween candy?"

"Yes." Mac's glare dared Robert to argue with him. "And what the hell were you thinking, leaving camp *alone* when I gave everyone orders not to?"

"Last I knew I had rights, and you have no right to order me shit."

Mac clenched his fist around the handle of the bucket. Any minute now he was going to haul off and plant it in Robert's face. Tern thought he was justified and took a step back.

"This isn't helping anything." Gage was the voice of reason. "Robert, you're being an ass. Mac, inspect that candy because if it's fine, I want a few."

"Me too," Lucky said, licking his lips. "And I don't even like coconut."

"I'd kill for some chocolate," Nadia added, smiling in obvious anticipation.

Tern was glad to see Nadia crack a smile. The tension between Robert and Mac lessened a tad, though she knew any spark would light it up again.

Mac dumped out the chocolate bars onto the rough, makeshift table they'd been using to prepare food, and carefully inspected each commercially wrapped candy bar. While he did that, Tern served up dinner to the rest, hoping that feeding Robert would also help soothe his temper.

"Wow, Tern." Gage swallowed a bite of her ptarmigan. "This is five-star restaurant quality."

"Uhmm…thanks," she mumbled, not knowing how to take the compliment when they'd been slinging barbs at each other most of the time. She was much more comfortable in that role than one of appreciation. If he started being nice to her now, she'd be a goner, and she hated women who fell back into love with deadbeats.

"It *is* really good," Nadia added, her color looking better.

Tern handed her the mug of willow tea she'd reheated from earlier. "Drink another cup of this."

"Do I have to, Mom?" Nadia asked in whiny child's voice.

"If you want dessert."

Nadia rolled her eyes and then shut them as pain crossed her face. She reached out a shaky hand for the mug. "Gimmie."

Mac sat next to Tern and picked up the plate she'd made for him. She raised brows, and everyone else waited with baited breath for Mac's verdict, except Robert who shoveled food into his mouth and still had a pissed off expression tainting his face.

"The candy seems safe," Mac announced.

"Woohoo," Tern said, with a beaming smile. She'd been too long without chocolate. It hadn't been that long since they'd left Fairbanks, but it seemed like forever.

"I don't like it though," Mac continued.

"Neither do I," Gage added.

"Hell, what *do* the two of you like?" Robert muttered, shaking his head.

"Let's not do this again." Tern set down her plate, no longer hungry. At Gage's expectant look, she handed him her leftovers.

"Am I the only one who hates being ordered around?" Robert scanned the group, settling on Lucky. "What about you, Lucky? You enjoy being bossed around?"

"Listen, dude, don't drag me into your rage."

"Pansy," Robert spat and then addressed Nadia. "Nadia?"

"I've no complaints." She dismissed him by picking up her tea and drinking deep, though the grimace was visible as she choked the bitterness down.

Robert stared at Gage. "You're just a mini Mac, aren't you? Is that what Tern saw in you? A younger version of the old man."

Tern sucked in her breath. Robert wasn't pulling any punches tonight. The idiot was out for blood.

Gage tightened his jaw. His knuckles whitened around the fork clenched in his hand. The comment had obviously hit a nerve. In a way, Robert was right. Gage had a lot of the same qualities that Mac did. What had she been thinking hooking up with Robert in the first place? He was showing his true colors now, instead of what he'd wanted her to see when they'd been dating.

"Seems to me you have a burr up your ass." Gage laid his plate on the ground beside his feet.

"What is this? A pissing contest?" Tern asked. "I've had enough of this. Robert, quit being a jerk. Gage, don't take the bait."

"You tell 'em, girlfriend," Lucky said, shutting up with a murderous stare from Robert.

"I find it interesting, Robert, that you were the one who left camp, alone, and happened to find a geocache that was filled with Tern's favorite candy bar." Mac folded his arms across his chest. "Better start explaining."

Robert now resembled a mouse with his tail caught in the claws of a cat. "What? You think *I* set this up?"

"Did you?" Mac asked.

"Hell, no." Robert glanced at Tern. "Tern, honey, I'd never do anything to hurt you. You gotta know that. I lov—"

"Just explain why you left camp," Gage interrupted.

"When I entered the cabin, on my bunk was the GPS coordinates that we'd found in the previous geocache. I was bored. So I decided to check it out."

"That's convenient," Mac said. "Why did you leave camp without letting anyone know where you were headed? This is Alaska, not Maryland."

Robert huffed a deep breath. "Fine. I wanted to find that damn cache and destroy what was in it."

"Why? Afraid of what else might be inside?"

"Yes, goddamn you." He rubbed the back of his neck. "Why must we know every fucking secret about each other?"

"What else are you hiding?" Gage asked.

"Wouldn't you like to know," Robert shot back.

"Yeah, I would. I'd like to know if the whiny jackass sitting in front of us is the one capable of organizing this farce?"

It was like a tennis match with Tern, Nadia, and Lucky looking from Gage and Mac to Robert as they volleyed accusations at each other.

Where was a referee when you needed one?

"Fuck off," Robert said.

"Yeah, that kind of attitude doesn't endear you to others," Gage said. "Exactly how pissed off are you that Tern left you for me?"

"Do we have to go there?" Tern jumped into the fray.

"You bet we do," Gage said, arrowing a volley at her that had her wanting to duck. "This is about you. Which means it's about your relationships. The most current ones are me and him."

"This is wrong," Tern said.

"And a little fascinating," Nadia added, wide-eyed. "What? It is. Too bad this isn't a reality TV show. We'd make millions."

"Nadia!"

"Sorry." Nadia waved her hand. "Carry on with the drama."

"All right, I'm tired of hammering this to death," Robert said. "I went after the cache to see what damning information was in there, hoping to spare the rest of us. Leave it at that."

"No," Mac said. "I very much doubt you were worried about sparing any of us. What did you want to intercept?"

"Nothing."

None of them bought it. There was more that Robert wanted to keep quiet. What could be worse than what had already been revealed?

"I don't believe you," Mac said. "Right now you are my number one unsub."

"I didn't fucking set this up!" Robert jumped to his feet. "What's it going to take to get you to believe me?"

"Son, you have serious anger management issues," Mac said. "That makes you a loose cannon. Better dial it back or we'll never believe you."

Robert visibly tried to do as Mac suggested, but it was a struggle. Tern knew he had issues, but she was never more happy than now that she'd listened to that little voice inside her which had told her to kick him to the curb. Wish she'd listen to it before she'd gotten on the floatplane.

"I had a drinking problem, all right?" Robert rubbed the back of his neck again. "After I got out of juvie, I had another stint in the joint. I thought that was what was in the geocache. Instead it was full of Tern's favorite candy bars. I thought she'd be thrilled to have me bring that back for her. That's it."

"No, it isn't," Gage said. "Why were you in prison?"

"What? Going to judge me on that when you just got released yourself?"

"Why, Robert?" Mac asked.

"Shit," Robert muttered under his breath. "Statutory rape, okay. She told me she was twenty-one. Hell, I picked her up in a bar. How was I to know she was only sixteen? And that's the fucking lot, okay?" He stomped to his cabin and slammed the door behind him.

"Well," Nadia said. "I don't know about the rest of you, but I seriously need a freaking candy bar."

"Tern," Lucky said, "got a minute?"

"Uh, sure." Tern hated that she took a moment to glance around the campsite before she agreed to leave with Lucky.

Gage and Mac were in deep discussion over one of the GPS, most likely planning the best way to get them all out of here. Nadia had turned in early, still complaining that her head hurt, and Robert sulked inside his cabin.

"What's up?"

"I'm worried about you." He reached out a hand and rubbed it up and down her arm in a comforting, non-sexual caress.

The sincerity in his voice took her back for a moment. "I'm fine."

"I know this is a lot to deal with, and knowing the person you are, I'm sure you're beating yourself up inside."

If he didn't stop he'd have her in tears.

"You're sweet, Lucky. Thanks for thinking of me. But the one I'm worried about is Nadia."

"She's stronger than she looks," he said. "I have no doubt she'll bounce back. But you'll take all that has happened here and internalize it until it poisons you. Come on, mediate with me."

"I really don't feel like it."

"Which is why you need to." He took her hand. "Come on, let's head down to the lake and plug into nature."

What the hell. It wasn't like she had anything else to do to pass the hours until they got to hike out of this place and return home.

"Sure."

"That's my girl."

Hand in hand, they walked to the lake. Tern already felt better, as though Lucky was taking half her load of worries.

"You know, you really need to give Gage another crack at ya."

"What?"

"I saw how you looked after your empty cache run." Lucky wiggled his brows suggestively. "There's a reason you never made it to your cache."

"I don't want to go there."

"Do me a favor and just be open to what could be between the two of you. He might have acted like a dung beetle, but the man is so twisted up with you that he probably can't digest his food."

She scoffed. "Right."

"Seriously, babe. Give him another run. He has some explaining to do, but open your heart. He's a good man, just not a very smart one, regardless of his degrees." He cocked a grin.

She didn't know whether to thank him for his insight or tell him to butt out. Instead she said nothing and copied Lucky's pose. He started her out with yoga that had her muscles screaming and then into a meditation that had her insides singing.

CHAPTER TWELVE

A scream tore Tern from a deep sleep.

She bolted up in bed, glanced over at Nadia's bunk and found it empty. Throwing back the sleeping bag, she ran barefoot for the door.

Nadia stood by the cold ashes of the fire pit, bathed in the crimson rays of the insomniac northern sun. Her hand over her mouth, as though ready to vomit.

Mac rushed out of his cabin, wearing sweats and a t-shirt, rifle at his shoulder ready to shoot something. Robert and Gage hurried to join them, Gage bare-chested and wearing tan cargo pants with the top button undone, and Robert in flannel pajamas dotted with moose.

"What's going on here?" Robert asked.

"Nadia?" Tern inched toward her. Nadia reached out a shaking hand and stepped toward Tern, revealing what her body had been blocking.

Lucky's severed head sat on the stump. His pasty face was frozen in shock, his black soulless eyes frozen open. His mouth caught in a silent death scream. "Play or Die" was carved into the flesh of his forehead.

Tern gasped, her hand coming up to cover her own mouth as tears flooded her eyes. She was not seeing this. She couldn't comprehend what was before her.

A raven gave a death caw from its perch high up in a tree before catching flight. Tern shivered.

"I-I-I found him like t-that." Nadia's tortured words turned into a soul-wrenching moan. "Who would have done such a thing?"

Mac stepped over and laid a hand on Nadia's shoulder, giving her a push toward Tern. "Take Nadia, and return to your cabin."

"No." Tern wasn't going to be treated like the little woman to be protected from all that was unpleasant in the world. Though she badly wanted to run screaming from this place.

Not Lucky.

Not the sweet man who loved life. How could he be dead? Her eyes had to be playing tricks on her. But how could this be a trick if everyone saw what she was seeing?

Mac stared at her for a long moment. "I want you to take Nadia and stay back. Understand?"

Tern gave a jerky nod and took Nadia's arm. They backed out of the way. Nadia's muffled moans answered the silent screams of horror inside her head. They wrapped their arms around each other and tried to offer as much comfort as they could in the awful, gruesome reality.

"I need a camera." Mac glanced at Robert and Gage. Gage was the first to respond. He silently headed to his cabin. Robert hadn't moved. He seemed trapped, his eyes large and opened wide, fixated on what remained of Lucky. Gage returned and handed Mac the camera, who methodically took pictures of

Lucky from every angle. "We need something to put…store his head in."

"The cooler?" Gage suggested. "We can store it in the ice of the glacier and mark it with the GPS for the authorities."

"Good idea." Together they packed the head into the cooler. "Robert?" Mac turned toward Robert. "Robert!"

He jerked free from his trance. "Yeah, what?"

"Stay with the women." Mac handed him a pistol from his waistband, thought better of it and walked over to Tern and offered the weapon to her. "Keep an eye out."

Tern tightened her fingers around the butt of the gun and looked around the clearing. She gave a tight nod.

Gage entered the cabin for his GPS, and then returned to help Mac dispose of what was left of Lucky.

"Guess his luck finally ran out," Robert said, watching the men head out of camp.

"Oh God, you…you bastard." Nadia hauled off and slapped him.

That seemed to break the spell Robert had been under. His hand covered his reddening cheek. "Sorry, I deserved that." He looked around the campsite. "Let's…uh…return to one of the cabins. I don't know about you, but I don't want to look at…that anymore." He pointed to the stump stained in blood.

Stained with Lucky's blood.

Unable to speak over the grief threatening to drown her, Tern led the way to her cabin. Nadia curled up on her bunk into the fetal position while Tern sat at the head of hers and wrapped her arms around her knees. The gun hung in her hand in case she needed to use it. Robert sank onto the foot of her sleeping bag.

"Who would have done something like that?" he asked under his breath.

There was no answer to his question. They sat in stunned silence until Mac and Gage returned. Gage sought her out, his eyes echoing the alarm and concern she felt. They all crowded into the small space of the cabin.

"There's no question, we leave today," Mac said.

"No," Nadia cried, flying out of her fetal position, swinging her legs off the cot. "Didn't you read what that…that bastard wrote on L-Lucky's f-forehead? We can't leave."

"We can't stay," Gage said. "Who knows what this guy's plan is? It would be suicide to stay."

Robert nodded. "Lucky was the one who stressed the most that we hike out of here, and now he's dead."

"Before we decide anything, I want to know everyone's whereabouts during the night," Mac said.

They all looked at each other. Nadia was the first to speak. "What? You think one of *us* did that?"

"Who was the last to see Lucky alive?" Mac ignored her question, glancing at each of them in turn settling on Nadia. "I thought I saw the two of you sneak down to the lake together."

Nadia dropped her gaze to her fingers tearing at the seam of her sleeping bag. "We did. We, uh, made love down by the lake last night." Her words ended on a gasp, and she covered her face in her hands. "We walked back to camp, and he left me at the door of the cabin. He kissed me g-good-night." A sob escaped her as her fingers touched her lips. "He was so sweet, so apologetic for me being hurt yesterday. He felt so responsible. Oh, God, I'm going to miss him." She buried her face in her hands and moaned.

Tern couldn't seem to move. The reality of Lucky's death didn't seem real. He'd been so full of life, up for anything, and so quick to laugh. She couldn't believe it was only last night they'd done yoga on the beach while he tried to talk her into giving Gage another chance.

He'd never climb another mountain, never love again. His chances were over.

"Where's the rest of him?" Gage asked, his jaw taut as though he'd leashed his emotions.

"That's a morbid question," Robert scoffed.

"Yes, and one that needs an answer," Gage said.

"You didn't notice when Lucky returned to your cabin?" Mac asked Gage.

"No. He wasn't there when I went to sleep, and I didn't wake up until I heard Nadia scream. His cot doesn't appear to have been slept in."

"Tern, did you wake when Nadia came in?" Mac asked.

"Sorry, I was exhausted." She hadn't slept the night before and didn't even remember her head hitting the pillow. She looked at Nadia's cot. There was no way to tell now if her cot had been slept in or not.

"What are you implying?" Robert asked Mac. "That one of us had a hand in Lucky's murder?"

The word murder sent a frigid wave of fear flowing through Tern. It *had* been murder. No accident would result in a man's head severed from his body and words carved into his forehead.

What kind of nightmare were they living?

"Either one of us is the murderer or there is someone out there hunting us," Mac said.

"I thought we'd already established that someone besides *us* was pulling the strings," Robert said.

"Had we?" Mac asked with a lift of his brow.

"We'd better look for Lucky's body," Gage said, not liking the prospect of coming across a headless body. Though he doubted it would be worse than putting Lucky's head in a cooler and burying it in a glacier. "His body might give us some clues to who did this to him. Tern, you're with me."

"Now wait a goddamn minute," Robert objected.

"I don't trust any of you right now, and I don't want anything happening to her."

"Which is why she's going with me. There is no way I'd hurt her. I'm in love with her."

So was he. *Oh God.* The truth of it hit him hard. He wasn't trusting her welfare to anyone but him. Especially this pissant.

"I'm not a bone," Tern said. "Nadia and I will go with Mac." She grabbed Nadia's hand. "You and Robert can buddy up."

"Tern," Robert objected.

"Robert," she fired back with a determined lift of her scarred brow, which gave her a much more dangerous look.

He was the first to back down. "This sucks."

"For once I'm in complete agreement," Mac said. "Everything about this sucks. I'll head west with the girls. You two head south. We'll reconvene in an hour. Return in *one* hour. No longer. Synchronize watches. Sure wish I had my two-way radios," he grumbled, matching his watch with Gage's.

Robert rolled his eyes. "I hate all this military bullshit."

"You're an idiot," Gage said. He gave Tern a last look. Grief rippled off her. Her eyes were wide and rimmed in pain. He wanted to take her in his arms and shelter her from all the hurt. Instead he opened the door and called over his shoulder at Robert, "Let's go."

He made a stop at his cabin to pack supplies and double-check his weapon and bullets. Robert did the same. Clipping his GPS onto his belt, he hitched his rifle onto his shoulder, all the while trying not to look at Lucky's empty bunk. While he hadn't hit it off with the man, the only thing he had against him was his history with Tern. If he had met Lucky under different circumstances they probably would've enjoyed sharing a beer. He'd already connected with Mac and now understood the attraction Tern held for him. Robert, on the other hand, was a waste of space. For the life of him, Gage couldn't see why Tern would've hooked up with him.

"You ready?" Robert stood outside the cabin door. He caught sight of Lucky's bunk and blanched.

Gage left the cabin, quietly closing the door behind him. The girls and Mac were also heading out. He was glad to see Tern fully armed, along with Nadia. If Tern couldn't be with him, Mac was the next best choice. He studied Robert. If he were a betting man, Robert would be the one he'd line up for Lucky's murder. But what would Robert have against Lucky other than his connection to Tern?

"Since the women have already left, help me get rid of that." Gage pointed at the blood-stained stump. He didn't want Tern reminded of Lucky's severed head every time she looked at it.

"Where the hell we going to put it?"

The choices of hiding the stump, or a body, were endless in this wilderness. He didn't think he had to point it out. "You allergic to work or something?"

"No. I just don't want to touch the thing."

"And you think I do? I don't want the women reminded of—just help me move the damn thing into the cover of the trees."

"Fine. Whatever."

Gage and Robert hefted the sawed off log into the trees behind the cabins, out of sight, then began their trek south. Gage let Robert take the lead, not wanting the man behind him. Until things changed, he didn't trust Robert. He hated the way the man lusted after Tern, followed her every movement. He was like a dog with his tongue hanging out any time Tern was within sight.

What did that say about him? He basically reacted the same way. Lucky was dead, and he was worrying over the attention another man gave the woman he wanted. He kept his eyes on the woods around them, listening for anyone coming up behind him.

"See anything?" he asked.

"Yeah, trees," Robert replied, his tone full of sarcasm.

"Are you always such a shit?"

Robert stopped and turned. "You want to get into it. I'll oblige."

"I bet you would. You've been after a fight since we got here. Sure you didn't get into it with Lucky and things went too far?"

"I didn't kill him."

"Doubt you would admit it, if you did."

"Do you know what it takes to cut someone's head off?"

"No. Do you?" Gage tightened his hand on the stock of his rifle. "I've hunted. His head could've been cut off after you killed him. We don't know how he died, which is why we're out here looking for his body."

"Feeling pretty confident, being out here with me, if you think I'm the killer." Robert raised a brow.

"You don't scare me. You might have intimidated Lucky, but you won't me."

"I didn't kill him. I'm as freaked as the rest of you."

"Then quit being an ass, and help look for blood or tissue. Some sign that the killer carried Lucky's head back this way."

Robert swallowed as though he fought the need to throw up. Good. Gage hoped the man did throw up. He doubted the killer would. Someone who could sever a head off a body was someone dark and evil. Someone who didn't have a conscience.

They hiked for another mile before turning back, staying on Mac's time schedule.

"If the killer came this way, he's got superhuman powers. There's no sign that anyone has been this way in a while."

Thunder boomed over their heads. The temperature had been dropping steadily since they'd left camp.

Gage regarded the boiling black skies above the tops of the trees. "If we don't find some sign soon, we aren't going to once that storm arrives."

They doubled their time returning to camp and found Mac and the girls already there.

"Anything?" Gage asked.

"Nope," Mac responded. Tern and Nadia sat huddled together, their shoulders touching. They were pale with bright spots of wind-blown color on their cheeks.

"Let's cover the other directions, but we'd better hurry. I don't want to get caught in the storm." Mac glanced up at the sky. "I don't like the looks of those clouds."

They might get snow out of the storm by the looks of the thunderheads. The temperature had dropped even more. They were close to the Arctic Circle. It wasn't unheard of for the weather to turn and dump serious snow fall in the mountains all summer long.

Robert was quiet this time as they both concentrated on looking for blood drops and disturbances in the soil. Anything that would give them a clue as to what had happened to the rest of Lucky.

Robert jerked to a halt. "There." He pointed, not venturing farther. "Something's wrong with…that."

That was a bed of grasses bent and broken like a bear had laid down and taken a snooze, but the difference was that instead of a crushed mat of vegetation, blood lay everywhere, spraying in an arch on the trees, around the grasses, staining bluebells and buttercups. But no body. Lucky had died here, that was certain, but what the hell had happened to the rest of him?

"Animals must have dragged him off." Robert once again pointed to an area not ten feet in front of them where a thick blood trail disappeared into the brush. "I'm not wrestling a bear for what's left of the guy."

Gage dragged a hand through his hair. The wind blew in huge gusts, and a few heavy drops of rain knifed at his exposed skin. "Let's head back. There isn't any more we can do."

"Hallelujah. Finally, something that makes some sense. I want cover before this bitch of a storm hits us."

"Mark the spot on the GPS while I snap some pictures for the authorities."

"Better make it quick." Robert grabbed his GPS while Gage took pictures. They hot-footed it back to camp, this time beating Mac and the girls.

A shiver of fear skittered through Gage. There might be a killer out there stalking Tern, Nadia, and Mac. They should have all stayed together.

One of them was dead. One of them could be the killer. All of them had been responsible for the death of someone else. Except Tern. Did one of the remaining caches out there reveal something about Tern that none of them knew?

Could she have killed Lucky?

Good Christ, what was he thinking? No way did he believe for a moment that Tern could have killed Lucky. It was just the uncertainty of everything and not being in control of anything. He knew her. Loved her. But he'd seen how love ruined lives.

"Are you just going to stand out here in the rain?" Robert poked his head out of his cabin.

"I'm waiting for Mac and the girls."

"You can't wait inside where it's dry?"

"Do you only think of yourself?"

"You want to hike after them?" Sarcasm dripped like syrup from his lips. "They're with Ranger Mac. He's invincible."

Rain started to slash sideways, and the wind gusted in bursts and eddies, tossing his hair and stinging his cheeks. Still there was no sign of them. He glanced at his watch. They should have been back by now. What if the killer had laid in wait? He never should have let Tern out of his sight.

He caught a sound on the wind. It was like nature laughed at him, taunted him. Then he caught sight of Tern. Her hair reflected the light, like raven wings on fire. The relief of seeing her safe and whole almost had him rushing toward her, wanting to haul her into his arms and bury his face in her hair.

"Tell me you found him?" Mac asked.

Gage broadened his focus from Tern to see a very cold Nadia and a frustrated Mac. "No." Gage looked at the women and tried to send a message to Mac that he'd like to talk to him alone.

"Out with it, Gage," Tern said, tightening her lips as though preparing herself.

"We didn't find Lucky, but we did find where he was killed."

"Animals?" Mac asked.

He nodded. "Looks like."

"Pictures?"

"Got 'em."

"Let me see." Mac held his hand out for the camera.

"Why don't we get out of the weather first?" Gage indicated Nadia, who shivered with enough force to rattle her teeth.

"Where's Robert?"

"Your cabin."

"I'm sure he's lonely. Why don't we join him?" There certainly was no love lost between Mac and Robert.

"Let me get Nadia something dry and warmer to wear," Tern said.

Mac ushered Nadia in out of the cold, and Gage followed Tern into her cabin. She didn't hear him and jumped when he laid a hand on her shoulder.

"Sorry, I didn't mean to scare you. I just wanted to know if you were okay."

Her eyes flickered up and met his, the dark depths reflecting grief so deep he felt it inside himself. "Lucky is dead because of me."

"You can't blame yourself."

"Who else is there?"

"The man who killed him."

"But who is that and why? Who hates me so much that they killed a man who wouldn't have hurt anyone?"

"I don't know, but we'll find out."

"And what about the rest of you? You're all at risk, and I don't understand any of it."

He reached out and pulled her into his arms. Her head nuzzled into his shoulder. She fit so perfectly in his arms. He'd wanted to pull her into his arms since they'd discovered Lucky this morning. Keep her there where no one could get close enough to hurt her. "We'll figure this out and punish whoever did this."

She nodded, took a stuttering breath, and shifted away from him. He let her go, part relieved that she was no longer so close to him and part mourning her loss. Tern gathered Nadia's sleeping bag into a huge ball in front of her, like she was clutching a pillow. He opened the door to the cabin, and both of them braved the freak storm. It felt more like October than June.

They ran to Robert and Mac's cabin, the wind blowing them into the small space when they opened the door. Gage had to struggle to latch the door behind them. Nadia sat on the end of Robert's bunk, her body quaking. Tern quickly unzipped the sleeping bag and added it to the covers already around her shoulders.

"T-thanks," she mumbled through chattering teeth.

Tern crawled under the sleeping bag too, hoping her body heat would warm Nadia faster. Robert was like stone, sitting unresponsive while Mac held his hand out for Gage's camera. Gage took a seat and waited while Mac viewed the gruesome images.

After a period of time, Mac looked up. "Not a lot to go on. I'd like to see the actual spot when the weather improves. Though with it screaming out there like this I don't think there will be a lot of evidence left."

"We need to leave this place," Robert said.

"We can't leave," Gage said. "Not today. It would be suicide to try and hike down to the river in this weather." He gestured to Nadia. "She's already too cold, and with her head injury, she wouldn't make it."

"W-we need to play the g-game," Nadia said, stuttering as her body shook in an effort to warm itself. "If we d-don't, he'll kill us t-too."

Tern wrapped Nadia in her arms. Nadia laid her head on Tern's shoulder.

"We gotta eat," Robert said. "None of us ate breakfast."

"I'm not hungry," Tern said.

"We've got to keep up our strength," Mac said. "Is there any food easy to get to?"

"The candy bars that Robert found," Tern said. "Other than that, we need to hunt. I'd saved some rice and biscuits for Lucky since he—"

"But they would need to be cooked?" Gage interrupted.

"We need to do something," Robert said, standing. "We can't sit here waiting for a killer to come and get us."

"Chances are whoever killed Lucky is somewhere dry and warm and will stay that way," Gage said.

"Then shouldn't we take advantage of the bad weather and hike out of here?" Tern asked.

"Not if the risk of doing so is too great, and I think it is," Mac said.

"The cold doesn't bother me," Tern said, disengaging herself from Nadia. "I don't mind going out there and cooking some rice and see what I can do with the flour that's left."

"I'll go with you," Gage said.

"So will I," Mac said.

"I guess, I'll stay here with Nadia and make sure she gets warmed up," Robert said.

"You okay with that?" Tern asked Nadia.

Nadia nodded her head. "I'm really t-tired."

"I'll boil some water and make some coffee. It'll warm you up."

"S-sounds great."

"Sure does," Robert agreed.

Gage stood and went to the door. He opened it and swore. "Guys. We've got more problems."

CHAPTER THIRTEEN

Tern peeked over Gage's shoulder. The campsite was blanketed in snow. The rain had turned into a blizzard.

"Well, this complicates things," Mac said from behind her.

"S-snow?" Nadia whined. "Are you f-freaking kidding me?" She huddled deeper into the sleeping bag. "Let me k-know when summer r-returns."

"The day isn't getting any younger," Mac said venturing into the cold.

"Wished I had packed my snow gear," Gage said. "Tern, you stay. I don't want you getting cold."

"I was bred for weather like this." She nudged him with her shoulder and pushed past him out into the blizzard. The wind cut like knives, making a liar out of her as she wrapped the edges of her jacket tightly around her. While winter didn't normally bother her much—she always loved that first snowfall of the season—having a blizzard in the middle of June threw even her off balance. People died in conditions like this. Alaska's wild whims had killed many in the past and would claim many more in the future.

Would they be among this year's statistics?

She hurried to the cache they had strung up a tree to keep animals from helping themselves, while Gage and Mac worked on getting a fire started. Luckily, one of them had the foresight to stack wood under cover, so that some of what Gage gathered the day before was dry enough to burn.

A blaze cracked and danced erratically in the gusting, snow-swirling wind. Gage kept pilling on more wood. Tern did her best to shield herself by turning her back to the wind and mixing biscuits that she doubted would taste very good, but then she had the idea to break up pieces of the Almond Joys into the dough. Necessity was the mother of invention. It didn't really matter what they ate or how it tasted, as long as they had something to fill their bellies.

Gage had rice simmering over the flames he continued to feed. Mac had been fairly quiet as he made coffee, pouring her a mug as she dropped globs of biscuits onto the cast-iron pan. She took a fortifying sip, for once grateful for the strength of his coffee. They were all quiet, seeming to just get through the effort of making food while being bullied by the elements. No one spoke of Lucky or the missing log his head had been displayed on. She was glad for whomever had removed it, probably Gage. Robert wouldn't have given a thought to how she'd feel seeing the horrific reminder of Lucky's tragic end.

She handed Gage a hot biscuit, added a helping of rice, and then piled a plate high for Mac. Before serving herself, she made plates for Nadia and Robert. It was the least she could do for Robert since the man had taken over for her with Nadia. While she loved Nadia, it irritated her sometimes when Nadia turned drama queen. Yes, she understood that Nadia was upset over Lucky, they all were, but just because she'd currently been sleeping with him, didn't make her grief more important than the rest of theirs.

Or hers.

Tern had been the closest to Lucky. She'd had a relationship with the man that had lasted years. While their romantic relationship had only spanned six or seven months, they'd frequently gotten together when he was in town and she wasn't involved with someone else. Except for that time when he had found her in the *Howling Dog Saloon,* and she'd been so upset with Robert and his poutiness that she had looked at Lucky as 'manna from heaven' and escaped with him. She hadn't seen Lucky in almost a year, and there he was, blond hair flowing around his collar, sunburned cheeks from whatever mountain range he'd just conquered, with a smile that promised to make all her wishes come true. And that night he'd done a damn good job of trying to fulfill her every wish.

The morning after had come with all sorts of regrets. She'd never cheated on anyone before, and didn't like that she had felt so trapped with Robert that she'd done something so drastic. It was obviously the universe waking her up and telling her she didn't belong with Robert. By that afternoon she was a free spirit, but hated that she'd broken Robert's heart. The hardest part was telling Chloe why she would no longer be dating her dad. She'd given the little girl her cell phone number and told her to call any time she needed anything.

Lucky had flown off again to parts unconquered by man, and she hadn't seen him until she'd walked into the hangar a few days ago.

Wiping away a tear she hadn't realized she'd shed, she picked up the two plates she'd prepared for Robert and Nadia and headed toward the cabin. Out of the corner of her eye, she saw Gage stand and follow her. She hadn't asked him to, but he was there to help open the door for her anyway. He was also there to steady her when she caught sight of Nadia, naked and straddling Robert, riding him to climax.

"Holy shit!" Tern almost dropped the plates she carried. If it wasn't for Gage who caught them, she would have. "What the hell are you doing?"

Nadia screeched, and scrambled off Robert, grabbing her sleeping bag that had fallen on the floor, using it to cover herself.

"Fuck," Robert muttered grabbing for the closest cover, which turned out to be Nadia's shirt, to cover his large erection. "You could have knocked." He arrowed a frustrated glare in Tern's direction.

"Why would we?" Gage said. "You were supposed to make sure Nadia warmed up. That didn't mean take advantage of her."

Tern set the dishes down on the dresser and rushed to sit next to Nadia. She was going to kill Robert. She cautiously put an arm around her friend's shoulders. "Are you okay?"

Nadia jerked her head but couldn't meet Tern's eyes.

"You're a bastard," Gage said to Robert.

"Me? I didn't take advantage of her. *She* took advantage of me."

"Oh, come on," Tern said. "Why would she do that?"

"Hey, just because you threw me away doesn't mean that I don't have a lot to offer a woman," Robert grumbled, adjusting himself.

Nadia buried her head in the folds of the sleeping bag. "I'm so ashamed. I don't know what happened."

Tern swallowed the accusing words that Lucky hadn't been dead that long.

Nadia continued with her whining, "I don't know why I let this happen. It didn't mean anything, Tern. I hope you aren't mad at me." She blinked her eyes up at Tern, her expression full of guilt and shame.

"No, Nadia, I'm not mad at you. I'm mad at Robert." She narrowed her eyes at him.

"Hey," Robert objected.

"Whether she took 'advantage' of you or not, you knew what you were doing. What about all that crap about still being in love with me? Huh? Guess that was a bunch of bullshit."

"Like you were ever going to come back to me with *him* around." Robert jerked his thumb at Gage.

"Got that right, asshole," Gage added.

"Gage, this is hardly the time for that."

He let his smile shine through.

The door swung opened and Mac entered. "What's taking you guys…oh. Hell, you never know from one minute to the next what's going to happen on this competition of ours." Mac threw Robert the rest of his clothes that had been tossed on the floor. "Get dressed. We have visitors."

"The plane?" Nadia gasped, her eyes wide with surprise.

"No. Wolves."

CHAPTER FOURTEEN

"Seriously?" Tern swiveled for the door.

"You aren't going out there." Gage grabbed her arm and kept her from running out.

"I'm not going to miss the opportunity to see wolves in the wild. Where's my camera? My nephew Fox would love to see this."

"Tern, love," Mac said. "These wolves are probably the ones that helped dispose of Lucky's body. Most likely they followed the scent of his blood and decided to steal into camp. They aren't to be messed with."

Tern swallowed over the picture Mac had just drawn for her. "I'm not ignorant of the kind of predators they are. I wanted to see them, not pet them."

"Could have fooled me," Gage muttered.

"Enough gabbing," Robert said, who was finally dressed. "We need to declare this camp our territory or the wolves will take it over." Robert grabbed his gun.

"He's right," Mac said. "We've got to show them who the alphas are around here." He nodded at Gage and Robert. "Girls, stay here."

He opened the door and the three men walked out.

"*Girls?*" Tern repeated. She was getting sick of that. "Are you serious?"

Apparently. The door shut behind them, not letting her catch a glimpse of their visitors. Tern had her hand on the knob, twisting it when Nadia clutched her arm.

"Tern, please don't go out there."

"But, Nadia—"

"Please, I just had sex with Robert. Doesn't that bother you?"

Tern had trouble switching gears. Did it bother her? Kinda. Yes. No, not really. "Nadia, I understand why you did it. You're upset over Lucky and you needed to feel alive." Not something she'd ever think to do, she hoped, but it fell under Psych 101 stuff.

Nadia nodded. "Yeah, that must have been it. I'm sorry. It just sort of…happened."

Just stay away from Gage, Tern wanted to threaten, but because the need to say it was so strong, she stayed quiet.

There was a repeat of a rifle being fired.

"That's it. I'm not waiting inside here like a kid." Tern swung open the door and almost took a step back.

The men were facing off a pack of wolves. Wolves that didn't seem intimidated by their 'alpha stance' or sound of the rifle going off.

There were seven timber wolves in all. The one in front— black with tips of gray, his eyes obsidian pools—was gorgeous, and obviously in charge. Tern would have made a dive into Robert's stuff, looking for a camera, if not for the fact that the wolves weren't budging from their position. They continued their face off with the men. Gage and Mac raised their hands and hollered, but didn't seem to impress the wolves one bit. In fact, the wolves advanced farther into camp, snarling, their black gum contrasting against white sharp teeth.

Mac fired a warning shot right in front of the leader, who had the smarts to back up and reevaluate. There was growling and lots of teeth gashing. The hair on the back of Tern's neck rose until finally the alpha wolf howled what sounded like an expletive in wolf speak, and then loped off into the trees, followed by his pack.

One minute they were there, the next it was like they'd vanished into the waves of blowing snow. The only sign was the trail of large paw prints left behind, but as the seconds ticked by, they were quickly covered up too.

"Damn, but that was nerve-wracking," Robert said, dashing into the cabin. Gage and Mac followed at a slower more watchful pace.

Gage shook the snow from his hair as he entered the small space. He stared at Tern as if the wild from the wolves had seeped into him. The fire reflected in his eyes suddenly heated her from the inside out. Tern could see he wanted to grab her and take her. She banked the answering spark simmering inside her and glanced down at the rough plank floor.

"We really need to get out of here." Mac sat on the bunk, resting the butt of his rifle between his legs.

"We can't leave," Nadia whined once again, curling under the sleeping bag.

Tern couldn't remember with all that had been happening if Nadia had dressed yet.

"Nadia, I'm not getting into this with you again," Mac said. "We leave in the morning. Snow or not, we can't stay here."

"If we leave we'll end up like Lucky." She clutched the sleeping bag tighter around her.

"How do you know that?"

"Lucky complained the loudest yesterday," she added. "The killer must have been listening, I guess. I don't know. I don't want to hike out of here in the snow, and Lord knows what else we'll encounter. Wolves are out there. The plane will be here in four days. We're armed. You could have shot those wolves. Why can't we wait it out?"

"For the very fact that we already have one dead body," Mac said. "Either the killer is in this room, or he's waiting for us out there and planning his next move."

"But—"

"Drop it, Nadia. We leave in the morning." Mac eyed everyone else in the room. "Anyone else have anything to add?"

"Yeah, any ideas on what are we going to do today?" Robert asked.

"The weather's already decided that," Mac said. "I suggest we stand watch in shifts, rest and pack up. Gage and I have already mapped the route out of here. It goes without saying that no one is to be alone. Even on watch, I want teams. I don't trust anyone. And neither should you."

"Damn, old man, a bit paranoid?" Robert asked.

"You saw Lucky this morning. You want to be next?"

Robert gulped. "No."

"Then better heed my advice. I know a thing or two about protection. Now, since you and Nadia are getting along so famously, you two can take the first watch."

"I don't want to go first. I just got warmed up," Nadia complained.

It showed the maturity of the group, or the shock of one of them dead, that no one commented on how Nadia had gotten all 'warmed up', Tern thought.

"Dress accordingly," Mac said with no room for further argument in his voice. He lay down on his bunk and draped his forearm over his eyes. "Holler if you need back up."

Gage stood. "Tern, I'd like to talk to you."

Since she didn't want to spend any more time around Robert or Nadia—still trying to get the image of them humping each other out of her head—she followed Gage to his cabin. She entered behind him, stomping snow off her boots, and came up quick when she realized that Gage and Lucky had been sharing a cabin.

True to form, Lucky's clothes were everywhere. He had always kept his hiking gear organized and clean, but not his personal items. She slowly walked over to his bunk and picked up one of his fallen flannel shirts. She clutched it in her hands and brought it to her nose, dragging his scent inside her.

God, she was going to miss him. Tears snuck up on her and settled in her throat. She hugged Lucky's shirt to her chest and slowly dropped onto his bunk.

"You okay?" Gage asked.

She nodded unable to get words passed the emotions clogging her throat.

"I'm sorry, Tern. I should have thought of how seeing Lucky's things would affect you before bringing you in here."

"Why did you bring me here?" Please tell me it wasn't to follow up on the heated look they had shared earlier. She couldn't get intimate with Gage. Not now. She believed in life after death, spirits, and at the moment she could swear Lucky was in the room with them. "Who killed him, Gage? Who would have done something like that to him, of all people?"

"I don't know." He fisted his hands. "I wish to God I did. But until we do know, please don't leave my sight."

She paused before responding. "What?"

He knelt in front of her and took her hands in his. "When we were looking for Lucky's body, I couldn't stop worrying about whether you were safe or not. Tern, I couldn't handle anything happening to you."

"Let me get this straight. You don't want me out of your sight, but you don't want me."

"I want you, Tern. But I can't have you."

Well that made a lot of sense. "Why?"

Gage glanced away.

"Don't pull that shit. I can't take it right now." She yanked her hands free and grabbed the collar of Gage's jacket, getting right in his face. "*You* left and never explained why. I get it that you were in jail, but why wasn't I important enough for you to call? I thought we'd shared something special."

"We did." He ran shaky fingers through his hair. "I don't want to get into it."

"Too damn bad. You're going to. Right now, right here. You are finally going to admit what the hell went wrong. What did I do that scared you off?"

"Damn it, Tern." He covered her hands on his collar of his jacket. "You made me love you, okay? There you have it. Shit." He yanked out of her grasp and stood.

"Excuse me? Why is loving me so horrible?" She got to her feet, too, not liking him glaring down at her from his full height.

"I don't want to love you. And you, you're...*too much.*"

"Huh?"

"You're too much for me," he repeated. "Too much woman, too much of everything. If I hadn't cared so much, being with you wouldn't be that big of an issue. I've made it clear up front with every woman I've been with that it was casual, no strings. When I tried to tell you the same thing, I couldn't get the words out right. And then you would go and do something sexy and my brain would melt."

"You aren't making any sense." Didn't make his words hurt less, though.

"I know." He dropped onto his bunk, stared at the floor for a few minutes and then finally met her eyes. "Take a seat. Please."

Tern sat. He'd said please and besides, her legs were barely holding her up with the shock that he, on one hand *loved* her, and on the other didn't want to be with her.

"I never told you about my mother."

Why did it always go back to the mother?

He seemed to take forever as he struggled with his thoughts. She'd got caught up in the chinking pattern between the logs of the cabin by the time he finally spoke.

"My father was an asshole and my mother loved him to distraction. She not only loved him, but in a way, became enslaved by him. It didn't matter what my father did, she forgave him. If he spent all the money, slept with other women, beat the shit out of her and us, she always forgave him." He started shaking his head as though he couldn't believe what his mother had tolerated. "Even though he ran off with our neighbor when I was sixteen, she's still waiting for him to return to her today. Even prays for it. If he did show up on her doorstep after all these years, I'd have no doubt she'd take him back. Probably wouldn't even ask for an apology.

"My sister, Rebecca…" He stopped and cleared his throat before starting again. "When I showed up and found her in the hospital, beaten, bloody, and childless, she *begged me* not to hurt Mitch. He'd almost killed her. There was no grieving for her baby. All she was worried about was her asshole of a husband."

Tern started to see the pattern he was drawing out for her and didn't like the direction he seemed to be taking.

"When Rebecca came home from the hospital, I left to pick up her prescriptions. Mitch showed up. I think he was watching the house. When I returned, he was inside and Rebecca was attempting to cook him dinner. He'd already hit her once, I didn't give him a chance to hit her again. You know the rest. While the court threw out the case, labeling his death self-defense, Rebecca never wants to see me again. I saved her life and she blames me for killing her husband." He rubbed the sides of his stubbled face. "I won't love like that. I can't be obsessed with you and that's where I'm headed. I have to stop loving you, Tern, before loving you ruins me."

CHAPTER FIFTEEN

I have to stop loving you before loving you ruins me.

Wow. What did she do with that?

She sat there on Lucky's bunk feeling like Gage had plunged her into the glacial lake and then held her under. It was hard to catch her breath, if breathing were even possible with her heart ripped out. She loved Gage. Loved him like she'd never cared for another man. That was why his leaving had hurt so badly. She'd take that hurt tenfold over the kind of pain she felt now. How did she comprehend that the man she loved, returned her love, but refused to give into his feelings because he thought she would ruin him?

There was nowhere to go with that.

The situation was impossible, unbelievable, and seriously fucked up. He needed counseling. Hell, so did she right now. How she wished her sister, Raven, were here to talk with. No, she wished she were home, in the bosom of her family with Raven advising her on what to do.

Why oh why had she gotten on that plane?

"Well…I guess there isn't anything else to say." She raised her eyes to his, knowing he would see the pain swimming in hers but didn't care. Would she ever care about anything ever again?

He sucked in his breath. "Don't. Don't look at me like that."

"Like what? Like you just ripped out my heart? I've never lied to you, Gage. I fell hard for you. You knew that. Twice now, you've put a knife in my heart." She stood on wobbly legs. She wanted to slink away and lick her wounds, but didn't know if she had the power to do so.

"Tern—"

She held her hands up in a show of surrender. "No more. It's best if I leave now." Before she gave into the tears she'd strangled in her throat. She needed time to fortify her defenses. She'd had good defenses in place.

When had they crumbled?

Not yesterday when they'd gone at each other like wild animals in heat, though that had helped chip away at the foundation. Lucky's death had weakened them more, allowing an opening. She looked at Gage for reassurance of some sort, and she knew better than to depend on him.

Maybe she shouldn't have been so hard on Nadia and Robert needing human contact. Death did strange things to people. And up here in the Arctic away from everyone, with their lives on the line, explained why she had let Gage get close a second time.

But never again.

The cold hit her with icy fingers as she stumbled out of Gage's cabin. She welcomed it, unzipped her jacket and let the cold sink in. The frigid air relieved her burning lungs and froze any tears begging to fall.

Nadia and Robert were huddled around the campfire. Robert was giving Nadia those sexy, hooded looks he used to send her way. Would she ever find someone who could return her love in the way she needed, believed she deserved?

What did any of it matter now?

Lucky was dead, there was a thick blanket of snow covering the June meadow, and someone was out to murder them. As problems went, those were pretty damn serious. What did her relationship issues matter next to them?

Nadia glanced up and saw Tern. "Want a cup of coffee?" She raised the coffeepot for emphasis.

"Sure." Tern sat around the blazing fire and took the cup Nadia poured for her, cradling it between her hands. It was warm, but the expected comfort didn't come.

"You okay?" Nadia asked.

"Yeah." She took a sip and relished the burn of the hot liquid searing a path down her throat. At least she felt that.

"Where's Gage?" Nadia asked.

"Who cares?"

"You two have a tiff?" Robert asked, putting an emphasis on 'tiff'.

"Robert," Nadia scolded, "can't you see she's hurting?"

"Sorry," he grumbled and drank his coffee.

"Want to talk about it?" Nadia asked, reaching out and covering Tern's knee with her hand.

Yes, she did want to talk about it, but did she want to talk to Nadia? She wanted her sister. Raven would know what to do, or she'd say the perfect thing to make Tern feel better. Besides, she couldn't talk to Nadia with Robert in hearing range.

"I'm okay. I think I'll try and lay down for a while before I need to relieve the two of you."

"Some sleep would probably help," Nadia agreed, her tone seemed relieved that Tern didn't want to talk. Did she want

Tern to leave her alone so she could spend time alone with Robert?

Regardless, Tern was through with them all. While she and Nadia had been friends for years, they had never spent this kind of time together. Maybe they weren't the kind of friends who did well cooped up for too long. Seeing her jump from Lucky's bed to Robert's so fast was more than a bit disconcerting.

A beam of sunlight sliced through the gray clouds, creating a luminous conduit into the heavens. For a moment, Tern caught her breath at the beauty of it. A moose lumbered out of the trees and drank from the lake. The multi-hued blues of the glacier in the background was sharp in contrast. She felt as though Lucky were shining down on her. What was it like in heaven for him? Were there mountains to climb? She hoped for him there were. God wouldn't be so cruel as to not have the things they enjoyed on earth absent in heaven, would he?

The thought cleared her mind a bit until she turned and caught Gage watching her from the doorway of his cabin. How long had he been standing there? And why? He'd told her that even though he cared for her, he wouldn't allow himself to follow up on his feelings.

The storm was lying down, the sun getting stronger as it burned off the clouds. Good, she didn't relish a night of trying to sleep with the temperature dropping below zero and no way to heat the cabins. She hadn't brought her subzero sleeping bag along.

She turned her back on Gage and walked into Mac's cabin. He was the only man she was willing to tolerate at the moment, and she couldn't face being alone right now.

"Hey," he greeted as she entered. "They driving you nuts?"

"You could say that. Mind if I crash in here with you."

"As long as you don't snore."

"I don't snore."

"You have."

She dropped down onto Robert's bunk and remembered him and Nadia having sex here. She jumped up, and Mac laughed.

"Just remembered the last occupants?"

"I need a hot shower. Scathing hot." She wiped at her clothes as though she had picked up some residual sex cooties. "Hey, want to head to the hot pots with me?"

"The minute you walked into this cabin, I knew you were going to talk me out of my clothes in some fashion." Mac pulled himself up and swung his legs over. "Beats taking a nap." He grabbed his rifle. "I don't have swimming trunks."

"I've already seen what you've got."

"Does that mean we're both going commando?" He wiggled his brows.

She attempted to answer his teasing smile, but fell short with the sound of a roar that had the hairs on the back of her neck standing at attention.

Mac rushed for the door, pushing Tern behind him. "Stay back."

Like that was going to happen. She followed right behind Mac. Gage had the butt of his rifle tight against his shoulder. Robert was in the same stance. Even Nadia had her pistol clenched in a two-handed grip.

A big grizzly raised its muzzle and sniffed the air. Gage fired a shot before its feet. The lumbering bear just roared again.

"Every damn animal is following Lucky's scent back to camp." Mac picked up a rock and threw it at the bear. It hit the muscled mass of terror in the face and had a greater effect on scaring off the predator than the noise of the gunshot. The bear lumbered away to the edge of the tree line, where it stopped and looked back. After a long stare, it ambled off as though not fearing them one bit and was already planning its return.

"We're going to be fighting off predators all day," Gage said.

"Another reason we need to get out of Dodge," Mac muttered. "Maybe we'll get lucky and the SOB who invited us all here will get taken out by the wolves or the grizzlies." Mac looked at Tern. "Still want to head to the hot springs?"

"Maybe not. I don't relish the idea of fighting off animals in my birthday suit."

Mac nodded. "We'd better be extra vigilant. Besides, I'm hungry. Probably should have shot that bear so we had something for dinner."

"How about we try fishing instead?"

"Sure, got any fishing supplies?" Robert asked, sarcastic as always.

"I wonder how my ancestors fished these waters without a pole and a three hundred dollar reel?"

"What? You going to fish like your ancestors?" Robert scoffed. "Going to spear us some dinner, Native?"

"I'd shut up if I were you," Gage said.

"Tell you what, Robert" Tern said. "You gut and cook whatever I catch."

"Not a problem."

"And clean up."

"What if you don't catch anything? What do I get then?"

"Free babysitting for a year."

"You're on." He snickered. "Don't fall in."

"How the hell did you ever go out with him?" Gage asked with obvious astonishment.

"I'd like the answer to that one too," Mac said.

"You have to meet his little girl. She makes him look damn attractive."

Tern entered her cabin and grabbed her knife. She then went into Lucky and Gage's cabin and rummaged through Lucky's climbing gear, finding a nylon rope. She cut the sealed end so the nylon would fray and unraveled ten feet or so. Then she tied the nylon thread to the end of her knife and headed for the lake.

Mac and Gage followed her, both men armed. It was like being flanked by bodyguards. Nadia and Robert stayed behind to feed the fire and who knew what else. She heard Nadia's giggle and the rumbling timber of Robert's voice. They were sure getting cozy.

Along the shore of the lake the threesome walked, Tern wishing Gage had stayed behind. But then she didn't blame him for not wanting to stay with Robert and Nadia gushing sickeningly over each other.

The lake was so clear she could see straight to the bottom. Pebbles sparkled back at her like a scattering of jewels. A shadow would flicker past every so often and flit away. The lake had a healthy population of arctic graylings. Tern climbed onto a bunch of boulders that were half-submerged in the lake and waited.

"Are you planning on stabbing the fish?" Gage asked.

"Shh," Tern admonished.

"I take it she never showed you this trick," Mac murmured under his breath.

"Shh," Tern said again.

They finally hushed and she stood still, becoming part of the landscape until the fish flickered closer to the presumed safety of the rock outcropping. Tern left them to swim, getting used to her shadow, their smooth water ballet calming her as she watched and aimed. She let her knife fly. It sank into the water with deadly precision, slicing through the hard gills of the fish to the hilt, keeping the blade stuck enough that she could pull the fish to the surface with the nylon thread she'd tied to the handle.

"Now that was slick," Gage said.

"Damnedest thing I ever did see," Mac said. "Still can't copy it even with the years I've practiced."

"It helps to be 'native'," Tern said, tongue in cheek. And to have learned from the best of teachers, her Uncle Pike. He'd taught them all to fish like this on the banks of the Chatanika, Chena, Yukon, and the Kuskokwim Rivers. Since her father had died, Pike had taken over the teachings her father would have imparted. There had been many summer days and nights learning the art of spearing fish for dinner. You learned fast when you didn't eat unless you were successful.

Mac chuckled and Gage smiled at her, until he realized what he was doing and the smile disappeared.

She turned away, hiding her hurt. She grabbed the fish by the head and pulled out her knife, tossing the Arctic grayling toward the men. Then she resumed her stance and waited for the next one to swim into her kill zone.

CHAPTER SIXTEEN

They returned to camp with four fat arctic graylings. Gage was in awe at the patience and skill Tern had displayed.

The midnight sun had returned and the blizzard was history, like it had never happened. Gage wished Lucky's death could be erased as easily, and the blundering way he'd tried to explain to Tern why they couldn't be together. He'd sure as hell had botched that one.

The surprise on Robert's face when they placed the graylings at his feet was priceless. The dumbass was wise enough not to comment. He just grabbed his knife and began filleting the fish.

"Save me the eyeballs, would you?" Tern said. "Us natives love our eyeball soup."

Mac snickered, taking a stump near the fire.

"I'm going to gather some herbs for cooking the fish," Tern said. "Mac, want to join me?"

"Gage, go with her. There're some things I need to take care of in order to be ready for tomorrow's trek."

The bottom of Gage's stomach dropped out. Being alone with Tern again would pierce what was left of his heart. He needed some kind of buffer, but to make an issue of it would bring more attention than either of them wanted.

Tern must have felt the same, for she tightened her hold on her knife and looked from Mac to Gage, her gaze flicking just past him without landing.

Gage grabbed his rifle and waited for her to make the call.

"Nadia?" Tern asked.

Nadia picked up a fish. "I think I'll give Robert a hand." She glanced at the trees, worrying her lip. "With all the wild animals roaming about, I'd rather stay here in camp."

"Let's make this quick," Tern mumbled under her breath.

"Lead the way," Gage said.

"Don't venture far," Mac hollered after them.

Tern led him back toward the lake. They didn't talk. Tern stomped, obviously angry and frustrated—not her normal, graceful swagger. Watching her took him back to yesterday and the unruly way they'd gone at each other. He'd been the one angry and frustrated then.

Had that only been yesterday?

The last thing he needed was to have those memories return now.

She suddenly stopped and he almost ran into the back of her. She swiveled and glared at him. "Stop it."

"Stop what?" he asked.

"Watching my butt. Unless you want to end up on yours, pay attention to something else."

She turned around and stomped off again and he had to scramble to catch up.

"Sorry," he mumbled.

"You ought to be. One minute loving me is ruining you, and the next you're ogling me. Make up your damn mind."

He grabbed her arm and yanked her to a halt. "I can't. I can't stop looking at you, wanting you. This is why I stay away from you. If I hadn't decided to answer the invite to this farce of a competition, you would never have seen me again."

"Bullshit." She stepped closer until she was right in his face. "You are so full of bullshit."

He could smell her, fireweed and wild roses. His nostrils flared and his hands tightened around her bicep.

"You decided to come on this geocache *because* you knew I'd be here."

He scoffed, though the sound came off weak to his ears too.

Tern leaned in, becoming flush with him breast to chest. "You wanted to be with me. Living without me was killing you. Why don't you be honest with yourself for once?"

Frustration and something darker, edgier boiled to the surface. His arms banded around her, yanking her closer against him. He kissed her hard, pushing into her mouth, tangling his tongue with hers, groaning from the feel of her, the taste of her.

She was right. Everything about her, he'd missed. It was driving him senseless, causing him to do irrational things. How could one woman have this kind of power over him? He was a scientist. He should be able to compartmentalize, make decisions based on thinking, not what pumped through his heart. But no matter what his head demanded, he physically didn't have it in him to stay away.

"I give up, you win," he said.

"You give up? I've beaten you into wanting me, loving me? No, I don't think so." She pushed him away.

He gave her a warning growl as he reached for her again.

She slapped at his hands. "Don't even think about it." She looked him up and down and the sting in her stare started to penetrate the fog encasing him. "You aren't man enough to be with me."

Her words slapped him back harder and more effectively than any blows she could have landed.

"My love doesn't ruin a man. If anything, it will make him more of a man." One last look full of fury and lined with his own aching need, her hair flipped him good-bye as she stomped away from him.

He stood dumb stuck for a minute before slowly following. Her words reverberated around in his mind like a Ferris wheel on warp speed. Around and around they went, bruising and mashing all he thought he believed.

He didn't want her, yet…he *wanted* her so much it scared him. He was torn between what he was driven to do, and the logical part of him that had spent months deciding what he ought to do.

Right now, the drive to twist his hand in her long mane of hair, pull her head back, and kiss his way down her exposed neck was almost his undoing. His hands itched to pick her up and carry her to a soft grassy place where he'd take the rest of her body. He'd pushed her away when he knew she loved him. He'd hurt her and he was an ass for wavering back and forth with her emotions like this. But knowing all that didn't seem to help this…yearning. It was primal and made him no different than the wild animals.

He adjusted the erection that rubbed behind the zipper of his pants. Not that it did any good when she bent over and ripped plants out of the ground. If he had only kept his mouth shut, he'd be inside her right now. His hands would be clenched around those hips, thrusting deep within her caressing warmth. And she'd hate him even more than she already did afterward.

"Here, carry this." She slapped a stalk of something with a sharp lemon-bay leaf smell across his chest. Then she went on to harvest other plants from the bank of the lake.

How did she know what would feed them? She'd told him her grandmother had taught her, but what if she was wrong about a certain plant? What if she made them sick? He'd seen *Into the Wild*.

He opened his mouth again and then decided to keep it shut at the last second. Look at what he had already done not thinking before he thought it through. So he bit his tongue and just took whatever she threw at him without comment, letting her spank him with the wet weeds from the lake.

They hiked back to camp, his arms laden with what looked like weeds to him. Tern, in full drill sergeant mode, proceeded to tell Robert how to cook and season the fish with the plants she took from Gage's muddy arms.

Robert went to speak, and Gage sent him a warning look. He picked up the vibe, showing he was smarter than Gage would have given him credit for, and buttoned his mouth, nodding at the appropriate times. Finished with her instructions, Tern left them to do as she ordered.

"I think I'll go have a chat with her," Nadia said, getting up from where she'd been helping Robert fillet the fish. She gave Gage an irritated look as she passed by him.

"What did you do to her?" Robert asked, when the women were safely installed in their cabin. "She's on the warpath."

"Stay out of it." The last person he would confide in was one of Tern's former lovers.

"Did you at least pay attention when she told me how to use all this stuff?" Robert gestured to the pile of greens and roots laid out in front of him.

Yeah, they were up a creek.

"What's the deal?" Nadia asked, shadowing Tern into their cabin.

Tern tossed clothes into her backpack and wished Nadia had remained with the men. What she wouldn't give to have a freaking timeout.

"What happened between you and Gage out there? Don't tell me you went at each other again?"

"Not in the way you're thinking." Tern blew out a deep breath. She didn't want to talk about what went down between her and Gage. She'd be fine never thinking of him again. It hurt too much. "Can we not do this?"

Nadia fell back and dropped her gaze. "Okay, well...I wanted to talk to you about Robert."

She didn't have time for Nadia's hurt feelings, not when hers were bleeding. She did a mental sigh. Talking about Robert wasn't as bad as talking about Gage. "What about him?"

"Well, you did interrupt us in a very private moment. I wanted to know how you were feeling about it? Feeling about me?"

With everything going on she hadn't really cared, but Nadia wouldn't take well to that. She asked a question of her own. "I thought you were crazy about Lucky?"

"I was." She ran a hand through her hair. "I hadn't meant for it to happen. I was so cold and upset, and he offered to hold me. The next thing I knew we were...you know." She shrugged, dropping her gaze again, and working the zipper up and down on her hoodie. "I hope you don't think less of me because of it. If it makes you feel better, neither one of us actually...finished."

Way more information than she wanted. "People tend to do things out of character when they experience a death." She'd done her fair share. "Let's just forget about it."

"That has got to be it. So tell me, did you and Gage get it on then. Come on, give." Nadia curled up on her cot like she was preparing for some serious girl talk. But Tern wasn't in the mood. All she wanted was to be alone.

"Nothing happened between us," she repeated, the ability not to gash her teeth straining the muscles in her jaw. The start of a headache materialized.

"You can tell me. Give a little, girlfriend."

"Nadia, I can't do this. I'm not good company and what's between Gage and I is too...raw to talk about right now."

"Oh, sure, hon. I understand." Nadia stood, her expression crestfallen. "You rest and if you need to talk later, I'll be here." Nadia opened the door to leave the cabin.

Tern knew she'd hurt her feelings again, but couldn't find in herself to care right now.

"I'll come and get you when dinner is ready. Until then, try not to think too much about what happened between you and Gage. Things have a way of working themselves out."

Right. And tomorrow she'd wake up and all of this would be a dream. Lucky would still be alive and Gage never would've reentered her life.

"Where's Mac?" Gage asked. How much water per measure of rice had Tern told them yesterday? One part rice, one part water? No, that didn't sound right. Two parts rice, one part water? Oh, hell. He grabbed the bag of rice and flipped it over to read the instructions on the back.

"I haven't seen Mac since you guys came back from fishing. The old man must have needed a nap." Robert snickered while dredging the fish in flour mixed with the herbs Tern had gathered, and carefully laid it in the pan sizzling with melted butter.

"Has anyone checked on him?"

"I'm not his babysitter."

"Robert, Lucky was killed. We don't know who the killer is. What if he got to Mac?"

"Fine. Go check on the old man if you want. He's gotta be all right. He'd be one hard asshole to kill."

"Who would?" Nadia asked, joining them and hitching up on one of the stumps.

"Tern okay?" Gage asked.

Nadia shrugged. "I don't know. She wanted to be alone."

And away from him. Gage looked down at the bag of forgotten rice in his hands. Tern not wanting to be around him shouldn't bother him. That was what he wanted. Needed. Then why did it make him feel empty inside? He measured water and rice into a pan and set it on the coals.

"So who would be hard to kill?" Nadia asked again, hooking a knee with her arms as she rocked on the stump.

"Mac," Robert said, picking up a stalk of something that Tern had picked. "Do you remember what she wanted me to do with this?"

"Uh…chop it and cook it?" Gage said.

151

"I thought that was what I was supposed to do with this one?" He held up another leafy plant.

"Wasn't that supposed to go in the fish stock?" Gage suggested.

"Right. The fish eye soup." He shuddered. "The woman's got some weird tastes."

"She's the reason we get to eat."

"Why would Mac be so hard to kill?" Nadia asked, once again bring the subject back around.

"Mac's a former Ranger," Gage said. "They're worse than Marines and SEALs put together."

"Yeah, but under the right circumstances, anyone can be killed," Robert said, adding the chopped whatever to the stockpot of fish eyes and bones.

"Why are we talking about this?" Gage asked, the subject matter not sitting well with him. He glanced at Nadia. "Why you so interested?"

"I don't know." Nadia shrugged. "Curious, I guess. I never thought someone could get the jump on Lucky either. I guess that's why I was wondering."

"I'd think Lucky would be easy to take out," Robert said. He flushed when all eyes focused on him. "I mean, he is, *was*, kind of a space cadet. It wouldn't be hard to distract him, is all I'm saying. The man thought more with his dick than his brain."

"Not a nice thing to say about a man who isn't here to defend himself," Gage said.

"I never said I liked the guy."

"Tern left you for him, if I remember right," Gage couldn't help baiting. Could Robert have murdered Lucky out of jealousy? Had this whole geocaching charade be motivated by something so petty as jealousy?

"I know what you're thinking and I didn't kill him."

"Your alibi sucks."

"So does yours."

"All right, guys," Nadia said. "This pissing match is going to spoil dinner. Might want to check the rice, Gage, and Robert, time to turn the fish."

"Nadia, why don't you watch the rice?" Gage said. "I need some fresh air." He stood and walked away, knowing he was damn close to taking Robert down. The man was a fucking asshole.

Gage decided to check on Mac, and tell him dinner was almost ready. He knocked on the cabin door. "Mac, its Gage." There was no answer. "Mac?" Gage turned the knob and pushed the wooden door in.

The cabin was empty.

CHAPTER SEVENTEEN

"Where's Mac?" Gage hollered at Nadia and Robert. Neither one looked concerned.

"He's probably taking a shit," Robert said.

Why hadn't the killer taken out Robert instead of Lucky? At least Lucky was fun. Robert was useless.

"Check Tern's cabin," Nadia said.

Gage headed to Tern's cabin and knocked on the door, this time not waiting for an invitation. He opened the door and entered.

There were Tern and Mac, lying together on her cot. Mac holding Tern in his arms. Tern struggled to sit up and wipe tears from her face.

"What's going on?" Gage asked. The tears on Tern's face had his insides clenching. "Are you okay?"

Tern nodded. "Just upset over Lucky."

Of course she would be. But why hadn't she sought comfort in his arms instead of Mac's? *You're just as much of a fucking idiot as Robert. She tried and you pushed her away.*

"Dinner's ready," Gage said, at a loss of what else to say.

Mac inclined his head. "We'll be there in a minute."

Gage took another look at Tern, but she'd hidden her face in the crook of Mac's shoulder. Both his arms were wrapped around her, their legs comfortably resting alongside each other, stocking feet touching.

He wanted to rip them apart. Had this situation brought them closer together? Now that he had pushed her completely away, would she turn to Mac again? Of course she would. She had. He was seeing it with his own eyes and couldn't look at it any longer. He shut the door behind him, dragging in deep breaths that failed to fill his lungs.

Gage had no rights to Tern and he respected Mac. He should be glad the man was there for her, since obviously he couldn't be. He'd gone far enough to tell her she wasn't worth loving and then tried to make the moves on her later. He was the asshole. At least Robert didn't pretend to be something he wasn't.

What did he really want from Tern? He'd thought he'd known. Nothing. But nothing wasn't even close to what he needed. The reality of how much he'd fucked up his life came crashing down on him.

Dinner was surprisingly good, Tern thought. Robert did a fair job even though he'd messed up her instructions. Oh, well, nothing like trying something new. They ate, all of them too hungry to converse over dinner. The four graylings disappeared quickly followed by the slightly crunchy rice. They broke out the Almond Joys for dessert, and then Nadia helped Robert clean up. She also made a pot of coffee and poured everyone a cup. After warming enough to melt the snow, the temperature had dropped again, but the sky was clear and without threat of snow. The fire crackled soothingly, and Tern got lost gazing into the dancing flames.

"I could hike out of here on my own, while the rest of you stay here in camp," Mac said.

"No," Nadia said, her hair swinging around her face as she shook her head. "Haven't you ever watched a horror movie? Once the characters spilt up, they're massacred one by one."

"I'll move faster alone," Mac said.

"Nadia's right," Tern said. She didn't want Mac out of her sight. Not only did she feel safer with him around, she didn't want anything to happen to him either. She didn't want anything happening to any of them. It hurt so much to know that Lucky had been killed because of her. "There's safety in numbers, Mac. Plus, how would we know if something happened to you?"

"We stay together," Gage said. "We're stronger as a group, and if one of us is the killer, I'd rather have them close, you know what I mean?" He took turns glancing at each one of them.

"It's settled then," Mac said. "We leave first thing in the morning."

"I still want to go on the record that we should wait until the plane returns," Nadia said.

They all looked at her and then back to Mac. Mac tightened his lips. "Pack only what you can carry. Leave the rest."

"Are you seriously thinking this through?" Nadia protested. She gestured to the lake and surrounding forests. "We have fish here. There could be more food in the caches we have yet to find."

"They could also be traps," Gage said.

"The Almond Joys I found were okay," Robert mumbled.

"Do we have to argue about this again?" Gage said. "We're out of here. Lucky's been killed. We aren't staying. The authorities need to be notified. The sooner the better."

Mac nodded. "I suggest we get an early night." He yawned.

Tern had to cover her mouth as Mac's yawn sparked hers. "I'm with you. It's been a long day." Horrific. One she'd like to forget as quickly as possible.

"Who's on first watch?" Robert asked.

"Mac and I," Gage said. "Robert, get a few hours sleep, and then I'll switch with you. Nadia, you're with Robert in four hours. Then Tern and I will have a go."

What did he mean by that?

"Got it." Robert stood and stretched. "I'm beat."

"I need to hit the latrine," Mac said, narrowing his stare back and forth between Tern and Gage. He'd picked up what Gage had said too. "I'll be back in a few."

Nadia and Robert headed toward their cabins. Tern stayed behind.

"Are you going to be okay?" Tern asked Gage. He'd be on watch the most tonight. She hated this incessant need to ask. It was on the tip of her tongue to offer to take Mac's place on first watch, but she bit it back.

"Get some rest," Gage said. "Tomorrow isn't going to be easy."

Nothing had been easy since they'd gotten here. She was balancing on the edge of an emotional crevasse; just a little push, and she'd tumble over into the abyss.

"Good night then," Tern said.

"'Night, Tern."

Maybe they should take watch in threes. Gage had his rifle and a knife clipped to his belt, and Mac was no slouch in the weapons department. He could kill with just his hands. She didn't doubt that both men could protect themselves, but they didn't know who they were up against.

"Be careful, Gage."

His head popped up when she said the last. He must have thought she'd already left. For a moment his eyes burned her with need. He blinked, and she wondered if she saw only what she wanted to see.

"Don't worry about me, Tern. Get some sleep."

She nodded and turned toward her cabin, entering to find Nadia already in bed, her sleeping bag pulled up under her chin. A small flashlight was tucked into the crook of her shoulder and neck as she cracked the spine on another romance novel.

"Good book?" Tern asked while getting ready for bed.

"Really good." Nadia sighed. "I just love a tortured hero. You'll have to take a gander at this one. You'll love it."

Tern shed her clothes and stepped into her flannel pajamas, glad that she'd packed them. Summers in the arctic weren't for the faint of heart as the blizzard they'd experienced earlier that day attested. Another yawn surprised her. She couldn't remember when she'd been this tired. Climbing into her sleeping bag, Tern zipped up the side. "Wow, I'm beat."

"Me too," Nadia said. "I won't read much longer so the light doesn't bother you."

"Don't worry. I can barely keep my eyes open. Just don't stay up too late. Mac's going to push us tomorrow." Her eyelids felt heavy as though someone had taped them shut. It was even hard to drag a deep breath into her lungs. Her legs turned to tree trunks and her arms felt tied down to the cot.

She had a moment of panic. This wasn't normal exhaustion. Then everything went black.

Chapter Eighteen

Tern struggled to open her eyes. All she could think about was using the bathroom. She felt hungover as she fought with the sleeping bag's zipper and pulled the cover back.

What time was it?

She glanced over at Nadia, who lay there with a book open on her chest. The flashlight had rolled along her shoulder, the batteries probably dead. Since this was normal behavior for Nadia, Tern didn't think much of it until she tried to gather up the book and set it on the night table so it wouldn't fall off onto the floor. Her fingers didn't want to work. It took extra focus to pick up the book and mark the page.

What was wrong with her?

She wavered on her feet, and had to catch herself. It was like she was drunk. She yawned wide enough that she heard her jaw crack in protest. Scratching her head, she slid her feet into shoes and opened the door.

Gage was slumped over on the ground next to a dead fire. There was no sign of Mac.

A raven perched on a stump, meeting Tern's gaze with his beady stare before spreading his wings and flying off.

No, she silently screamed. God, no. *Not Gage.* She rushed over to him, as fast as her stumbling legs would move. Her heart pounded loud in her ears, and she prayed he was all right.

"Gage!" She called his name, her voice coming out as a hoarse shrill. She collapsed next to him, terrified over how cold to the touch he was. She rolled him onto his back and he flopped over like a fish. "Damn it, Gage, if you let anything happen to you, I'll hurt you myself." Making a deal with God, she searched for a pulse in his neck, and crumbled with relief when she found one steady and strong. "Oh, God, Gage." She pounded on his chest. "Don't scare me like that." He didn't respond, which had her heart skipping again. "Gage, come on. This isn't funny."

What was wrong with him? She leaned her head down onto his chest and listened for his heartbeat, even though she'd just checked for his pulse. It was there, thumping away like it didn't have a care in the world. Next, she checked his breathing, short breaths, spaced evenly apart.

He was asleep. But this wasn't regular sleep. He'd been drugged. It was the only thing that explained why he didn't wake when she'd hollered and beat on him.

She'd been drugged, too, she realized. That was why she'd fallen asleep so quickly last night after the horrible day they'd all had. Normally she'd relive the day, wondering what she could have done differently, what she could have said differently. But none of that. She'd dropped right off the planet the minute her head had hit the pillow.

"Come on, Gage." She shook him. "You gotta wake up." How had they been drugged? What about the others? She glanced quickly around the camp. She reached for Gage's rifle and laid it next to her hip within easy reach.

What if whoever had drugged them was watching her right now? Was he getting a kick out of her trying to wake up Gage? What if she couldn't get Gage to wake up?

Oh God. Had the killer given more of the drug to Gage since he was such a big man?

"Goddamn it, Gage," she cried. "Wake up!" She slapped him across his face with her open palm, swearing at the pain. Her hand went numb, but Gage groaned. "Oh thank God. Come on, Gage. Snap out of it."

She hit him again, not as hard as before.

His lids stuttered open and his fuzzy eyes blinked into focus. "Ouch," he mumbled.

"Get up," she said, her voice ringing with panic. She scanned the campsite again. Still nothing. No one else was up either, and that scared the shit out of her. "Please, Gage, you have to get up. We've been drugged. I don't know who or how, but I'm terrified."

He caught on and struggled to sit. "Water," he said.

"Good idea." Water would help dilute whatever was in their system. She stood, moved too quickly, stumbled, and grabbed onto one of the stumps as everything spun like a kaleidoscope. She reached the bucket of lake water they'd boiled for drinking and dipped a cup in it for him. She grabbed a cup for herself and downed it. Carefully, she brought the cup to him. He took it from her and instead of drinking it, splashed the water over his face, and then held the empty out to her. "More," he said.

This time she brought him the bucket, dipping her cup and splashing water on her face. It didn't help as much as she'd hoped. Everything was slower, every thought and action took longer than it should have done.

"Nadia?" Gage asked.

"Sleeping. At least, I think she is." What if Nadia had been given too much of the drug? Gage was struggling to stay conscious. Nadia was much smaller and weighed at least a hundred pounds less than Gage.

"The others?" he asked, rubbing his face.

She bit her lip with worry. "I haven't checked on Robert. Wasn't Mac supposed to be out here with you? I saw you out here—oh God."

"Don't panic. We don't know anything." He crawled toward a log and used it to get on his knees. He stood, shaky as a newborn moose calf. Tern reached out and wrapped her arm around his back. He leaned on her, and she on him, and between the two of them they were able to prop each other up. "Can you grab the rifle?" Gage asked.

"Yeah." Tern reached down and picked it up, almost losing Gage in the process. "Steady."

"Damn, what the hell were we given?"

"I don't know." She just prayed it would work out of their systems fast.

They walked to Mac and Robert's cabin. "Did Robert relieve you on watch?"

"All I remember is you saying goodnight to me, and Mac needing something from his bunk."

They reached the door, turned the knob, and pushed it open. Robert was revealed in the light entering the cabin. He was on his cot, sleeping bag pulled up to his chin, looking a lot like Nadia had when Tern had woken up. His chest rose and fell slowly but steadily.

Tern moved into the cabin to get a look at Mac. His bed was hidden in the shadows. Gage grabbed her arm and pulled her back.

"Don't," he said his voice raspy.

"No." She moaned and pushed at Gage to let her go. In his weakened state, his grip loosened and she stumbled toward Mac, her eyes adjusting to the cabin's dark interior.

Mac lay on his bunk, just like Robert except for the knife sticking out of his chest and the words, "Play or Die" carved into his forehead.

CHAPTER NINETEEN

Tern's tortured cry broke Gage's heart. He'd tried to pull her back when he'd caught the hint of death on the air. But he hadn't been strong enough to spare her. He pulled her into his arms, and turned her so that her face was pressed into his chest and she could no longer see what the bastard had done to Mac.

The sobs wrenching from deep within her soul had tears springing to his eyes. He just held her as her body shook with spasms of pain and grief.

The sounds of torment woke Robert from his drug-induced state. He opened his eyes and stared unseeing at the rafters. Slowly he began to focus. He stared for a few moments at Gage holding Tern as she crumbled in his arms before things seemed to click into place. He struggled to sit up, grabbing onto the log wall to help pull himself into a sitting position. Then he looked over at Mac. His skin blanched as white as birch bark.

Robert swallowed. "He's…"

"Yes," Gage answered passed the lump in his throat.

"How?"

"Near as we can tell, we were drugged."

Robert swallowed again, his scared eyes flicking up to meet Gage's. "Drugged? How?" he asked again. He tossed back the sleeping bag and tried to stand. It took him a few tries before he managed it.

Tern continued to weep in Gage's arms. Her sobs were full of despair and he didn't know how to comfort her so he just held her.

Robert got dressed as quickly as he could manage, looking everywhere but at Mac's dead body. He gestured toward the door. "Can we…"

"Yes. Help me with Tern." Gage knew he couldn't move her by himself in this condition. "Bring your gun." They'd better be prepared for whatever awaited them outside. If Robert were the one killing off this group, now would be the time to take them out. Except for the perfect opportunity when they had all been unconscious. Why hadn't he killed them then?

What game was the killer playing? And for Hell's sake why?

He and Robert carried Tern outside. Gage scanned the open area, trying to see deep within the trees. Nothing seemed out of place.

"Tern's cabin," he said. No way was he staying out here with her grieving, unable to help herself, and him and Robert not up to snuff. "We need to double-check that Nadia's all right."

"Goddamn, what a fucking nightmare," Robert said.

They made quick work of getting Tern back into her cabin. Gage dropped with her onto her cot, cocooning her as best as he could while Robert bent over Nadia, checking her vitals.

"She's breathing fine." He shook her. No response. He shook her again and her head rolled on her shoulders, but still no response. Robert shared a glance that silently said the same thing Gage worried about. What if Nadia had been given too much of the drug? She might be breathing now, but what if the drug had started shutting down her organs? They had to get her to wake up.

"Should we make some coffee?" Robert asked.

"She's got to be awake enough to swallow it."

"Oh, right."

"The lake," Tern murmured, pulling back from Gage and wiping her tears. "We need to get her into the cold water."

Gage looked at her. Sorrow swam thick in her eyes, her face wet with tears. He could see the guilt and grief eating her up inside, but she'd yanked herself back from the brink of despair to help save her friend. What a hell of a woman.

Working together, they unzipped Nadia from her sleeping bag, and stripped her down to her underwear and tank top.

"Tern, you keep watch while Robert and I carry her," Gage instructed.

Tern wiped her nose and stood a little taller. She checked her pistol to make sure it was loaded and did the same to his rifle. Once satisfied, she looped the strap of the rifle over her shoulder and palmed the pistol. "Ready."

"Robert?"

"Ready," he said. His color had returned some with the physical excursion, but he was pale and sickly looking.

Together he and Robert lifted Nadia's slight frame. Tern grabbed the door, checking to see if it was clear before holding it open for them. They hurried, though it seemed like they were working at a snail's pace, down the path toward the lake. Once there, they didn't stop, just continued walking into the frigid, glacial-fed waters.

Needles of pain hit his legs as the cold water washed over him. From the grimace on Robert's face, he was feeling the same. Tern stayed on the bank, her eyes rapidly taking in their surroundings searching for a threat. When they were waist-deep, they lowered Nadia into the water. Panic crawled up his spine when she didn't immediately react. Was she too far gone? Had they lost two members of their group during the night?

Nadia screamed, her arms flaying clumsily to the side and her legs attempting to kick.

"Oh, thank God," Tern said from the bank.

Nadia screamed again and started to struggle, the sound a huge relief to Gage.

"Hold on, Nadia," Gage said. "We got you."

"What the hell is going on?" She shivered, her arms going around him as Robert lost his hold on her squirming, slick body.

"Can you stand?" he asked, his arms aching not to drop her.

She stood in the water and promptly sagged against him. "What's wrong with me?"

"We've been drugged," Robert answered, grabbing her other side. Together, he and Robert maneuvered her to shore. They were all shivering from the cold, but his head had cleared and he welcomed the return of his faculties.

"D-drugged?" Nadia said. "H-how?"

"We don't know," Gage said. "Let's get back to the cabin. I don't like being in the open like this."

They struggled to climb back up the path in their wet clothes while holding and carrying Nadia. She still wasn't able to support herself.

Once back inside Tern's cabin, Gage and Robert lowered Nadia onto her bunk. Tern grabbed a towel and helped Nadia dry off. "I need to help Nadia change her clothes." Tern glanced at both men. "You guys need to get into dry clothes too." Her tone was defeated but she was functioning. Gage didn't want to leave her but saw the wisdom in her words. He took the rifle from her but made sure she had her pistol handy. "If anyone enters this cabin besides us, shoot first and ask questions later."

She nodded.

Robert followed him out. "What are we going to do about…Mac?"

"I need to take another look at him," Gage said, not liking the idea one bit. He'd really connected with Mac. Even though he'd been jealous of that special bond between Mac and Tern, he still liked the guy.

They entered Robert's cabin. Mac was just as they'd found him. Gage's chest constricted and it was hard to breathe.

"What are we going to do with the body?" Robert gestured toward Mac. "We can't leave him like this."

"We'll have to do the same thing we did with Lucky."

"The glacier? Hell, man, that's going to take some serious work."

"We need to preserve the body as best as we can for evidence. Change your clothes."

Gage walked out, scanning the open area of the camp again and still didn't see anything out of order. What he wouldn't give for a face-to-face confrontation with whoever the hell was out there.

He returned after a quick change into dry jeans and t-shirt. He had his camera in hand to help document Mac's murder the best he could. They needed to hike down to the river and locate help. He was following Mac's plan. There was no way they were staying in this death camp another night.

He knocked on Robert's door and identified himself before pushing it opened. He was glad to see Robert with his gun in hand, taking everything as serious as Gage was.

He nodded and propped open the door for more lighting and started taking pictures of Mac, trying to detach himself from the fact that this man had been a friend. For the short few days he'd known him, Gage had recognized a kindred spirit.

He snapped shots from every angle he could think of. Close up shots, far away shots, hoping the troopers could find something on the digital film to give them a clue as to who had murdered him. Gage wanted the person punished to the full extent of the law and then some.

Robert had thankfully stayed quiet during the tedious process. Now he started to ramble.

"Mac was killed while I was sleeping, wasn't he?" Robert didn't wait for answer. "I was right here while it happened and I didn't have a clue."

Or he'd been the son of a bitch who had drugged Mac, killed him, and then drugged himself to make it look like he hadn't done it.

Gage's thoughts must have come across loud and clear to Robert, who shuddered.

"I didn't kill him. No way could I have slept, drugged or not, in the same room with a dead man. No fucking way." He shuddered again. "I'm getting the heebie-jeebies standing here right now."

Gage wanted to tell him to suck it up but he was feeling the same. "Come on. Let's check on the girls. We'll move him later when more of the drug is out of our system."

They left, Gage making a quick sweep of the campsite before venturing out of the cabin. He knocked on the girls' cabin, identified himself, and waited. Tern opened the door. His heart clenched at the despair and grief shadowing her eyes. She looked as though her spirit was broken and it tore at his heart. It also made him angry. He wanted to find whoever was doing this to them—to Tern—and take them out.

He entered with Robert and shut the door behind him. He was glad to see Nadia's color was better. Tern must have told her about Mac. She seemed to be handling it about the same as the rest of them.

Robert took a seat next to Nadia and Gage sat on Tern's cot. "What is the last thing everyone remembers?" Gage asked, starting with Tern.

She wetted her lips and swallowed before beginning. "You were taking first watch with—" She wiped away a few tears and cleared her throat. "I was worried about both of you being alone out there. I wanted to stay but returned to the cabin. I saw Nadia in bed, reading. I think we exchanged a few words."

She dragged a stuttering breath into her lungs and he reached out for her hand to hopefully give her strength. His heart warmed when she returned his squeeze.

"I don't remember much after that. I do remember feeling like my eyes were taped shut and my legs were heavy. Then nothing."

Gage turned to Nadia.

"It was much the same. I was in bed reading but I don't remember putting my book away."

"You didn't," Tern said. "I found you with your book open on your chest. I put your book away."

Gage glanced at Robert.

"Similar experience. I remember Mac saying how tired he was. His yawns were contagious, and I thought it was just because of the day we'd had with Lucky and all. Actually, I had started feeling groggy earlier after eating dinner." He arrowed in on Tern. "Just what was in those plants you had me cook up? Did you drug us?"

"Hold off there, Robert," Gage said.

"There was nothing in the plants I picked that would have hurt us. Besides, I ate everything you did. You sure you didn't add anything to the food since you were the one who cook dinner?"

"Hey," Robert objected.

"It's a valid question."

"Nadia can vouch for me. She helped with dinner and there wasn't anything we cooked that you didn't hand us."

"Then what the hell were we drugged with and how?" Tern asked.

"I have a theory," Gage said. "I think we were given sleeping pills. Strong ones or at least a heavy dose. Mac was a Ranger. There's no way anyone would have gotten the jump on him if he wasn't impaired. The only way to take him out was to incapacitate him."

"Sleeping pills?" Tern swung her gaze to Nadia.

"Oh my goodness." Nadia got up and moved to the dresser. On top was a makeup bag. She grabbed it, sat down and rummaged through the contents. Not finding what she searched for, she upended her bag and dumped out all the contents. "They aren't here." She raised her head and met their eyes. "They're gone. My prescription sleeping pills are gone. Someone took them."

Gage sat back. "That explains the what but not the how."

"The food," Robert said. "We all ate. So how did he get the pills in our food?"

"Or drink?" Tern added. "The water we boiled for drinking. That would explain why we reacted differently. Those who drank more would have gotten a stronger dose."

"The pills would have left a bitter taste in the water," Gage said. "The coffee." He looked at Nadia. "You made the coffee we all drank after dinner."

She reacted as though he'd slapped her and in a way he had. "I just made the coffee like regular. You were all there. One of you guys would have noticed if I had opened a bottle of pills and dropped them in. Get real. And why would I have drugged myself?"

"To throw off suspicion," Gage said.

"All right, cool it." Tern dropped his hand. "Putting the pills in the coffee makes the best sense. We need to look at the coffee grounds. Think about it. How easy would it be to grind up pills into a powder and then mix them in with the grounds? It's brilliant, really."

"Robert?"

"On it." Robert went for the coffee, leaving the cabin door open. He quickly returned and shut the door behind him. "Here." He offered up the tin.

Gage opened it and huffed out an angry breath. "The son of a bitch emptied the container." He showed the sparkly clean tin. There wasn't one coffee ground remaining. "He must have washed this out."

"He's covering his trail," Robert said.

"What now?" Tern asked.

The other two also looked at him. Guess he'd taken over Mac's spot as leader. He dragged in a deep breath as the heavy burden of responsibility settled on his shoulders. "We stick to the plan Mac had mapped out. Let's break camp. Pack only what you can't live without and keep in mind weight. We need to move fast."

"What about Mac?" Tern asked, blinking away tears that had refilled her eyes.

"Robert and I are going to take him up to the glacier and put him next to Lucky."

A smile trembled on her lips. "He wouldn't like that. He didn't have a lot of use for Lucky."

"Their spirits are going to have to come to some sort of understanding." He shared her smile, and then turned to Robert. "Ready?"

"As I'll ever be."

"Wait a minute," Nadia said. "We need to rethink this. Two of us are dead. We need to stay and defend ourselves until the plane gets here. We have water, bathroom facilities, food as long as Tern can continue to spear-fish, and roofs over our heads. We have none of that out there." She gestured to the wilderness, her voice rising.

"Nadia," Gage said, "we've been over this."

"Yeah, with Mac making the decisions. Now you're going to jump right into his shoes and decide for us? We need to think about this again."

"Do the math," Gage said. "We've been here three days and two people are dead. If we wait for the plane, that gives the killer four days to kill the four of us."

"He's got a point," Tern said.

"Of course, you're going to agree with him. You're sleeping with him."

"I am not," Tern said, with a telling blush.

Nadia scoffed.

"Come on, Nadia," Tern stressed her point. "We stay, we're easy targets."

"Unless it's one of us," Nadia said, staring at each of them. "Then we just take the killer along with us."

CHAPTER TWENTY

Tern laid her hand on Gage's forearm. He and Robert had fashioned a type of pack board out of branches and pine tree boughs as a carrier for Mac's body, and were getting ready to put Mac on it and hike up the glacier.

"I need a moment to say good-bye," she said.

Gage stepped back from the door to Mac's cabin. "Do you want me to come in there with you?"

"No, I need to be alone with him," she said, hoping she would be all right when she saw Mac again.

"Just so you know, we haven't touched him yet." Gage tightened his lips. "He still has the knife in his chest. I felt it best not to disturb the body, in order to retain as much evidence as we can for the authorities."

She gave him a jerky nod and reached for the doorknob. His hand covered hers.

"Tern, I didn't want you to have to know this, but the killer cut out his tongue."

She gasped. "Why? Why would he do such a thing?"

"Because he or she didn't like whatever Mac had said."

"She?" Tern realized, for the first time, that they'd been referring to the killer as being a man. But the killer could as easily be a woman except that cutting off someone's head would have taken a lot of strength. Could a woman do that? She couldn't imagine being able to do it herself.

"When you are finished with your good-byes, I'd like a few minutes to talk with you before Robert and I take off."

Once again she nodded. Questions skipped through her mind like pebbles on a pond's surface.

Gage released his hold on her hand and she turned the knob and entered the darkened cabin, shutting the door behind her.

There was an unnatural stillness in the air. Goose bumps rose on her skin and she rubbed her arms. A few steps brought her closer to Mac. He hadn't moved since she'd first seen him this morning. Of course he hadn't moved. He was dead.

It seemed impossible that he was no longer of this earth. He'd been so full of life. Tern slowly lowered herself onto the edge of Robert's cot, clasping her hands in front of her almost in a prayer-like position. She wasn't one who believed in traditional religion. Her Athabascan heritage had a way of messing with that. Like now, she knew she wasn't alone in this room. She'd wondered if she would still feel him or if he'd already moved on. She had her answer in the brushing of icy fingers along her cheek. Tears burned her already cried-out eyes.

"Mac, I wish you could tell me who did this to you." Whoever had killed him did so because of her. She might as well have been the one to plunge the knife into his chest. The room temperature dropped abruptly, and she choked out a laugh, wiping away a tear at the edge of her lashes. "Okay, I'll try not to blame myself. But don't you stay on this plane, Mac. Move on. Find Shannon and be happy."

Many of the Native Alaskan tribes believed that to stay on this plane after death trapped you and kept you from living the next step in your spiritual evolvement. The Northern Lights were believed to be spirits of their ancestors trapped in this realm, turning evil with time and reaching down from the skies to steal souls. Mac believed in God and heaven and that was what she wanted for him.

A peacefulness settled over her, and she knew Mac heeded her advice. "You'll always own a piece of my heart, Addison MacFearson. I love you." She stood, pressed a kiss to her fingers and lightly laid them to his cold lips in a final farewell. She gazed down at him, not seeing the man she knew before her. Mac no longer inhabited this shell. That was all it was— just a shell, a container. One that needed to be preserved for evidence and then made one with the earth again.

Damn, she would miss him.

She turned and walked out of the cabin. Gage waited where she had left him, his eyes full of concern.

"You okay?" he asked.

She wiped away the tears that seemed to be on a constant trickle. "I will be." She shut her eyes as a wave of energy past through her. When she opened them and gazed up at the sky, it was the bluest, clearest sky she'd ever beheld. The sun glinted down and warmed the raised flesh on her arms. They'd need sunscreen today. It was hard to believe it had snowed yesterday.

She returned her attention to Gage. "What did you want to talk to me about?"

He glanced around. Both Robert and Nadia were on guard around the campfire, armed and looking spooked. Breakfast had been the last of the rice and dry biscuits without coffee to swallow them down with. They could all benefit from some caffeine.

"Come with me." Gage took her arm and led her toward his cabin.

Tern wanted to put on the brakes, but to do so would draw more attention to them.

"Drop your head and act like you're grieving," Gage whispered under his breath.

Act? She did what he said, sagging against him for the hell of it. He grunted when her weight hit him, but then he wrapped his arm around her and held her close as they ambled toward his cabin. The friction between their bodies as they moved together had sparks flaring to life.

What the hell was wrong with her? Mac had just been killed, Lucky twenty-four hours before, and her body was sending up sex signals? Was there something to that need to reaffirm that you were still alive? Nadia and Robert had succumbed to it without much of a fight. For a moment, Tern wished she could throw Gage down on his bunk, tear off their clothes, and climb on top of him. That would be too easy, and she didn't want to look back at Mac's death and have orgasms with Gage clouding the memory.

They entered Gage's cabin, Tern coming up short to see all of Lucky's things neatly packed and sitting on the bare cot. Gage must have done it. She was both mad and relieved that he had done so. She should have been the one to have taken care of his belongings, but she hadn't even thought of them.

"Thank you for packing up Lucky's stuff," she murmured, fingering the straps of his well-used backpack.

"You're welcome." Gage ran a hand through hair that had been tousled all morning. "How well do you know Nadia?"

She looked at him stunned for a moment. "Huh?"

"Nadia? How well do you know her?"

"Oh, come on. You can't mean to think…no, I won't even say it. Nadia is not behind this. She could never kill anyone." The idea was preposterous.

"Humor me, okay?"

"No, absolutely not." She turned to leave.

"Tern, listen." He grabbed her arm before she reached the door. "Nadia's pills. She made the coffee. With Mac in a drug-induced sleep, she could have easily snuck in there and killed him."

"Anyone could have stolen those pills out of her bag, crushed them, and hid them in the coffee. You could have made the coffee last night, for that matter, so could I. We've had coffee after dinner every damn night we've been here." Her tone increased with each explanation.

"Lower your voice or they'll hear you."

She wanted to scream that she didn't fucking care. Two people were dead. Two people that she deeply cared for.

"Fine. You want to know about Nadia, ask away." The fastest way through this was obviously Gage's way.

"Has she ever shown any jealousy toward you?"

"What? No. She's my friend."

"Friends can be jealous of each other. She did hook up with Lucky, and then with Robert. Two men you have also been with." This last bit was said through his teeth.

"Who's jealous?" She cocked a brow.

"Yes, I'm jealous. I've been green with it since we left Fairbanks. But I wouldn't kill anyone over jealousy."

Interesting that he said 'over jealousy'. He'd admitted to killing his brother-in-law. Could she trust that he hadn't killed Lucky and Mac?

"Don't look at me like that."

"You brought it up. What would make you kill someone, Gage?"

"We aren't going there."

"Why not? You opened the subject."

"Damn it, Tern. I know what you're doing. You don't want to entertain the idea that Nadia could be responsible."

"Big gold star for you. Of course, I don't want to think my best friend is capable of murdering people who are close to me. Nadia knows everything about me. We've been friends for years. No way could she have done this." It was mind boggling to even contemplate.

"Everyone here is a suspect, even you, Tern. You knew she had those sleeping pills. You had easy access to them too."

His accusations stabbed at her like a dull knife. "You think I could be capable of killing Mac? He was like a father to me."

"I have a hard time wrapping my brain around that since you've slept with him."

She sucked in her breath but it didn't help divert the blow he'd just delivered. "You son of a bitch. You're twisting my words. You have no idea what kind of relationship Mac and I had." She swiveled and swung the door open.

"Tern—"

She whipped around. "Go to hell."

"Tern, shit." He grabbed her arm, bringing her to a halt. He hissed low as not to be overheard. "I don't want to leave you here with Nadia unprotected while Robert and I take care of Mac."

"If she was the killer, I'd choose to spend the afternoon with her rather than you at this point." She yanked her arm out of his hold.

"Is there a problem here?" Robert asked, standing a few feet away, Nadia right behind him. "Tern, you okay?"

"Peachy." She shot Gage one last scathing glare and turned to Nadia. "Let's pack up."

"All of us are going to hike up to the glacier with Mac's body," Gage said through a tightened jaw.

"What?" All three of them answered together.

"It's safer if we stay together, even if one of us is the killer."

"Are you freaking kidding me?" Nadia asked. "I don't want to climb that glacier and then traipse down this mountain. You push us like that and we won't have to worry about a killer taking us out. The trek will." She cocked her head to the side. "Unless that's your plan."

"Don't be an idiot," Gage said, twisting his lips in disgust. "I'm trying to keep us alive."

"Unless you're the killer," she said. "Killing Lucky would have been a piece of cake for you. Heck, even Mac probably wouldn't have stood a chance against you even without being drugged."

"I didn't kill anyone," Gage said.

"Neither did I," Nadia yelled.

"Everyone calm the fuck down," Robert said, moving to stand between Gage and Nadia. "Back up, Nadia. Gage, you too." He gave them a minute to get themselves under control. "If the killer is out there watching us, I'm sure he's laughing his ass off enjoying the spectacle. Holy shit this is twisted." He paused a minute and ran his hand through his hair. "Gage is right. We need to stay together."

"Wait—"

He interrupted Nadia. "I know you don't want to hike up the mountain and then back down it again. Guess what, none of us do. But we're going to. I suggest after depositing Mac with Lucky we head down the mountain, toward one of the geocaches. I've been studying the placement of the caches and there's one in the direction of the river. It will look like we're playing this sick game for whoever is watching. If someone's out there, it will buy us time."

Silence followed Robert's speech.

Tern stepped up, her anger toward Gage still simmering under the surface but enough under control that she saw the wisdom in what Robert had said. "I agree with Robert."

Gage gave a short nod. "It's decided then. We all go with Mac."

It seemed fitting.

"Mac's final decision was for us to hike out of here today," Tern said. "We'll do it in remembrance."

Nadia scoffed and stalked off toward their cabin.

"Give us a few minutes to get ready," Tern said, and then hurried after Nadia. When she entered the cabin, Nadia was tossing things around. None of them were landing in her backpack. "Nadia?"

She swiveled at the sound of Tern's voice, her face a mask of calculation. "He makes me so mad," she spat.

"Who? Robert or Gage?"

"Right now, both of them, I guess." She dropped her head and sank down on her bunk. Her shoulders slumped and all the fight seemed to go out of her. "I'm scared, Tern. I'm scared to leave this place even though we've lost Lucky and Mac." She raised her head and gestured to the outside. "What if the plane returns? Couldn't we wait it out and see rather than leave and maybe encounter something even scarier out there?"

"It comes down to being proactive and not waiting around to see what happens. Like it or not, Robert and Gage are take action kind of men." So were Mac and Lucky. "Robert and Gage won't wait around for a threat to materialize. They're going to face it head on."

"But why do we have to go along?"

"We don't have much of a choice. Besides, I think they're right."

Her lips quirked into a half smile. "That's because you're the same. The take charge, take action kind of person. I wish I were more like that."

"Well, here's your chance."

Nadia sighed. "I just hope it doesn't get me killed next."

CHAPTER TWENTY-ONE

Gage pulled up the edges of Mac's sleeping bag, glad that it was a survival one with the hood. He used duct tape to seal the sleeping bag into a body bag. He'd have a hard time using one in the future without thinking of this moment.

Would he be wrapped in one before this ordeal was over?

Thoughts like that wouldn't get him anywhere he wanted to be.

While he really didn't believe that Tern had anything to do with Lucky and Mac's deaths, she was the catalyst. He'd blurted out those thoughts without thinking, since she'd made him so mad. No woman got under his skin like she did, but then no woman had evoked such passion, love, and contentment either. She made him feel more alive than anyone else.

"Ready?" Robert asked, entering the cabin. "Glad he's covered up. Doesn't seem so creepy, you know?"

For a man who owned his own sporting goods store and hunted everything there was to hunt in the state, you'd think he'd have a better stomach with a dead body. Was it all an act?

"You grab his feet." Gage reached under Mac's stiff shoulders and lifted. Together they carried him out of the cabin and onto the makeshift pack board.

"This is going to be a bitch," Robert said.

Gage hoped he didn't complain the whole time. It had been considerably easier to carry Lucky's head incased in the cooler, up the glacier than Mac's two hundred plus pound frame.

Tern and Nadia joined them. Tern gave Mac's form a grief-stricken look, but held herself together. Nadia averted her gaze and walked alongside Tern. In silence, they left the camping area and cabins, trekking around the north side of the lake to where the glacier dipped its icy toes into the pristine arctic waters.

Gage felt the pull of the pack board on his shoulders and they hadn't even started to climb. He stopped for a moment to catch his breath. Tern stepped up next to him.

"Let me help. Please."

His first objection died in his throat at the emotion in her eyes. He dropped one of the nylon ropes he'd confiscated from Lucky's belongings, and handed it to her. She picked the tie up and braced it over her shoulder. Together they pulled Mac up the ice, covered with six inches or so of new snow from the day before. Robert and Nadia took the end, and the four of them carried Mac to his temporary resting place. They were all breathing hard when Gage motioned for them to stop. The snow created a risk he hadn't counted on. It covered any crevasses in the glacier that had been visible before. He didn't want to hike too far onto the ice in case they encountered one. "Let's dig out the snow and then cover him with it here."

"What about animals?" Robert said.

Gage shot him a look. Did he have to bring up animals in front of Tern? They had no way of chipping into the glacier that deep for a body. A cooler, yes, but not something that would encase a full grown man. "The best we can hope for is the snow keeping him cold and the animals at bay. We don't have tools for anything more permanent."

Gage dropped to his knees and started digging in the snow. Tern knelt to help. Nadia was next to join in, and then finally Robert. Gage couldn't help wondering if it had taken Robert so long because he'd been the one to kill Mac and didn't want to help bury him.

Gage and Robert untied Mac's body from the pack board and laid him in the cold, shallow grave. They made quick work covering him up with the snow and patting it down. Tern had silent tears running down her face. He wanted to comfort her, but didn't know what to say or do. Would anything he'd say help anyway?

"Let's get off the fucking ice," Robert said. "I'm freezing."

"Me too," Nadia added.

"Tern?" Gage asked. She'd make the call when they left and not one minute before she was ready.

She nodded her head. "I already said good-bye. The rest can wait until I get him back home."

"All right then." Gage turned to Robert. "Let's place the pack board over Mac to help mark the spot." He'd already set GPS coordinates for help when they returned with the authorities, but the pack board—if it wasn't moved by scavengers—would help them find Mac easier.

They hiked off the glacier. It was a relief to get off the ice and the cold that seemed to seep into his bones. He consulted his GPS to make sure he led them on the right track, and hoped to hell they were making the right choice by leaving.

"Anyone have anything to eat?" Nadia asked. "I'm starved."

Tern swiveled her pack around and unzipped the front pocket. "All we have are the Almond Joys until we stop and hunt for something else." Tern passed candy bars to everyone.

"I really hate Almond Joys," Nadia muttered, but tore into the chocolate anyway.

"Beggars can't be choosers," Robert said. "I'll take a couple."

"Better string it out," Gage said, taking the candy bar Tern offered him and continued to hike on. "We don't know when we'll eat again."

"What?" Robert scoffed. "So now you're the boss."

Gage stopped. Tern almost ran into him; as it was, he had to make a quick grab at her hips to help steady her. When she had her balance, Gage released her and confronted Robert.

"You got a problem?" Gage asked, getting nose to nose with him.

"Yeah, I do." Robert took a step forward.

"Guys," Tern said. "Please don't."

Robert faced her. "How do we know Gage isn't the one behind this?"

Tern rubbed a hand over her eyes. "Can we stop with the accusations? I can't take any more pointing the finger."

"Hey!" Nadia hollered. "We don't have time for this. Not if there's a killer following. Put your dicks away and let's move on."

Tern choked on a laugh.

"Fine," Robert said, stepping back. "Lead the way."

Gage ground his teeth and moved to the head of the line. They continued down the mountain in silence and entered the darkness of the forest single file. Gage with Tern behind him, then Robert, and then Nadia. Earthly smells of spruce, low bush cranberries, and thick pootschki permeated the air.

They walked for a long time through the forest. There was no trail and they were getting into thicker and thicker undergrowth. It was hard to see where they were stepping. Nadia had fallen more than once by the time Gage announced that they were coming up on the GPS coordinates for the geocache Robert had suggested they search out.

"Look around," Gage said. "Who knows if we'll find it in all this vegetation? We don't even know what size of container to look for. It's probably too much to hope for, but keep an eye out for anything that could indicate whose pulling this off."

They fanned out from the center of the GPS coordinates, keeping in sight of each other. After thirty minutes or so Robert said, "I say we give up and move on."

"What if there's food in the geocache?" Gage asked with a cock of his brow.

Robert conceded the point. They were all hungry. No breakfast, no caffeine, no lunch and late afternoon was fast approaching. The only thing they had to eat was a few Almond Joys. While the candy bars did have almonds, there weren't enough to call it protein. And, physically working the way they were, they needed protein.

"There." Nadia pointed up. "In the tree. What do you think?"

Up in the tree, rigged with a rope and pulley, was a waxed cardboard box, the kind used to wrap fish in. It blended in the treetops with its dark brown, somewhat reflective surface.

Robert located the end of the rope tied to a birch tree. He eased the knot free and gently lowered the box to the ground.

"We should keep the rope, in case we need it later," Gage said, coming to stand over the box with the rest of them.

"I hope to hell there's food in here," Robert said, flipping out his knife to cut the tape keeping the box closed.

They all leaned in as he opened the top.

Nadia gagged and covered her mouth. "Oh, God, I'm going to be sick."

CHAPTER TWENTY-TWO

Inside the box were six dead arctic terns, their beautiful white and black-tipped wings displayed like fans as though still in flight.

Tern stood there in shock. This couldn't be real. What kind of sick bastard could have done this? She swayed and then locked her knees.

The arctic tern was her namesake, her spirit totem.

"Son of a bitch," Gage said, moving over to wrap an arm around Tern.

"This is sick," Robert said, backing away from the grisly contents of the box. "We are dealing with a really sick puppy here."

"You just now getting that idea?" Tern asked. Her voice broke.

"Everyone keep your wits," Gage said. "There might be a note inside—"

"I'm not touching anything in that box," Robert said. "You want to dive in there, be my guest."

"I thought you were a hunter?" Gage scoffed. "Dead animals shouldn't gross you out."

"This is creepy. I don't do creepy." Robert stepped farther back as though the box would explode any moment.

Nadia rejoined them, but stood off to the side. "Sorry, I didn't mean to act like such a girl." She rubbed a hand up and down Tern's arm. "You okay?"

Tern straightened her spine. "I'll have to be." They'd already figured out that this whole invite had to do with her, but this was the most personal evidence of it.

Gage found a stick. At least the birds had been dead long enough not to be mushy, Tern thought. No maggots squirmed around the dead carcasses. They were just dried husks of their former free selves. Gage used the stick to move the birds around.

"Who cares what else is in there?" Robert said. "I say leave it. Even if there was something worth keeping, who would want it?"

"Stop! There." Tern pointed. "Oh no. How?" Her voice failed. She dropped to her knees alongside the box, reached in and carefully picked up the intricate hand-carved ivory arctic tern. Tears choked her as she clutched the little ivory tern to her chest, right over her heart, and began to rock back and forth as tears ran hot and unchecked down her face.

"Tern, honey, what is it?" Gage wrapped both arms around her and held her close to him. "Come on, baby, talk to me."

She heard the worry in his voice but how could she reassure him when her life was so upside down?

Gage picked her up and carried her to a fallen log. "Nadia, cover that up." He sat down and cradled her on his lap. "Tern, tell me what's wrong."

What's wrong? Everything was wrong. So horribly wrong. "This is mine."

"Can you let us see it?"

Carefully, she moved her hands in front of her. Cradled in her palms was her priceless arctic tern, carved in flight, its wings out to catch the wind's kisses–her father's name for thermals. Terns were the foremost migratory bird on the planet, traveling from the Arctic to the Antarctic and back every year. They spent more time in flight than on the ground, which her father had said explained Tern's compulsive need to always be doing something.

"You don't have to catch every meal on the wing. Now sit with your father and tell him all the wondrous things you have discovered today."

God, she missed him.

"It's beautiful," Gage said. "What's it mean?"

"It's mine. I keep it in my bedroom so I can see it every day." She swallowed more tears as they rushed up her throat. "M-my dad carved it for me. It's the most personal item I own." The memories attached to the arctic tern were those of her childhood, before the nightmare started. "Someone broke into my house, stole it, and put it here. What if I never knew what happened to it? I can't lose this." She clutched it to her heart again.

"Who knows this about you?" Gage asked. "Who knows about the tern?"

She lifted her head and looked around. "I don't know." She wanted to curl into the fetal position and cry. Losing Mac today, Lucky yesterday, and now this?

"Tern, snap out of it. Arctic terns are determined, tenacious little creatures. You're the same."

"Gage," Nadia said, "her father made that for her. It's one of the only things left that she has of him."

"Robert, what about you? Did you know?"

"Uh, yeah. I remember her once talking about it, but I seriously didn't get a clue how much it meant to her."

That was because the only thing Robert had been interested in when he was at her house was getting her into bed.

"Tern, you need to remember how many others knew," Gage said.

Her head hurt. So did her heart. She didn't want to do this. Gage must have read what she was thinking.

"The person who killed Mac and Lucky stole the arctic tern from you as a warning. This person can get close to you, has gotten close, and he knows you very well. Your life, our lives depend on you remembering who could have taken this and placed it here."

Gage worried over the pallor of Tern's skin. How much more could she take? He couldn't wait to get his hands around this son of a bitch's throat.

"We need to get out of here," Nadia said, glancing quickly around. "What if the killer is out there waiting, watching the scene unfold?"

"Nadia's right," Robert said.

Gage agreed. Thinking about being watched made his skin crawl. He studied the surrounding forest. This was a bad spot to get caught. They wouldn't see the danger until it was over with. The thick mix of birch and spruce and forest floor vegetation made defending themselves almost impossible. He pulled Tern to her feet and helped steady her.

"Let's move. Robert, take up the rear. I want the girls in the middle for better protection." He eyed Tern warily. She had to bounce out of this. Fast. He needed her on her game, because if the killer got inside her head, the game was over.

He nudged her to move. For a while he had to put her in front of him to prod her forward. As soon as she got the hang of it, he moved to pass and break a faster trail. "Nadia, make sure she doesn't fall behind."

"Got it."

He wanted to push Tern into remembering who could have gotten into her house and taken the bird from her. She obviously hadn't noticed it missing, so the ivory carving hadn't been gone long. Who knew her well enough, and hated her enough, to set this charade of a competition up to kill her? Tern was at the heart of it. Either the killer wanted her dead, or those she cared about dead. He'd bet money they were all marked.

They were prey.

Hours hitched by as they hiked. The birch had begun to thin, and they'd left the spruce behind miles ago.. The terrain was changing and he didn't like it. They would be in the open soon, without the cover of the forest, but then so would the killer.

"I don't like this," Robert hollered from the back, echoing Gage's thoughts.

"There's no other way down without climbing gear."

"I need a break, if you know what I mean," Nadia said.

Living outdoors was more complicated for women. Gage made a note of it. "You'll need to hold it for a bit."

"I need something to eat, or I'm going to drop," Robert said.

Obviously the biggest issue about taking lead was the complaints from the ranks. Did he have to figure it all out for them? The only one not complaining was Tern. She'd yet to comment on anything since they had left that last geocache. He wished she would complain about something. At least make some noise.

Her silence was killing him.

CHAPTER TWENTY-THREE

Tern traipsed behind Gage, automatically placing one foot in front of the other.

Someone had been in her house. When? Why hadn't she noticed her little arctic tern was missing? In a way it was as if by not noticing she'd forgotten her father. She could still remember him placing the little bird in her hand and telling her all the special qualities that terns carried, qualities that he could see in her. His belief in her and her siblings had been absolute. As her beliefs in him had been. Anger at his wasted death stole over her, and had her seeing red.

He'd been killed for treasure. Money plain and simple. Her father had been a geologist and couldn't resist the pull of gold fever. The land in and around Chatanika, where she'd grown up was just thirty or so miles north of Fairbanks. Chatanika had been one of the largest gold finds in the early 1900s. Billions had been mined, dredged, or picked up off the ground back then. Around the late 1950s people pulled out thinking the mining town was dried up. But her father thought he knew better.

He'd been digging for years without ever finding much more than nuggets to put on a chain and hang around her mother's neck. He'd always been good at the 'just because' gifts.

The real treasure had been him.

Tern scrubbed at the tears silently wetting her face. It had been a long time since she'd allowed herself to revisit the memories of that time when everything had been rosy and warm. Then there had been the explosion, the landslide, and the rocks crushing the life from him. All because he'd found the gold and someone had been watching.

Like now. Someone was watching.

But why? She didn't have anything. Yes, she had her share of the gold and was very wealthy in her own right, but that didn't matter. Plus, if something happened to her, the share of the gold would go to her family. Her siblings Raven, Lynx, and Chickadee would split her share.

Who had anything to gain from her death other than them? Her brother and sisters wouldn't be out here hunting her down. They loved her. She was part of a close-knit family. They were all rolling in money, but none of them knew how to live like they were wealthy. So they didn't. No one outside the small circle of friends and family had a clue how much they were worth.

There was Raven's new husband Aidan, whose father had actually killed theirs, but that was another story and fully resolved now. No, there wasn't anyone Tern could think of who would want to harm her or those she loved.

Could this person have targeted her family too? Oh God. She stumbled. What if this demented person had gone after them? What if they were dead?

Damn it, think it through.

Her family had been fine when she'd left on this crazy geocache trip. She'd had dinner with them the night before she left. The trouble had started here. So the killer was here. Most likely one of them.

She glanced at Gage in front of her, cutting a trail through the thick underbrush. Could he have done this?

Six months ago she'd have laughed at the idea of Gage being a killer. Then he'd admitted to killing his brother-in-law. But those were extenuating circumstances. If someone had done to one of her sisters what his brother-in-law had, she wouldn't be surprised at what she could do either.

They'd only heard his side of the story. Had he told them the full truth? She thought she'd known Gage before he'd left her with no word. Did he have a demented side that wanted her to suffer for some unknown reason?

He'd never displayed any reason to hate her. He admitted that he'd stayed away from her was because he was afraid she'd enslave him. Was that enough of a reason to kill her? If in some bizarre way that made sense, it didn't make sense to kill Mac and Lucky.

No, Gage as the killer didn't fit.

But what about Robert? He'd displayed jealousy, and his temper had more control over him than he had over it. He hated Lucky. She hadn't helped there, when their relationship was ending and Lucky had shown up in town.

Robert had been scary with his anger that night. She'd truly been frightened. He'd apologized the next day, but what did that really mean? Weren't his actions the night before more telling of his true nature?

Robert hadn't liked Mac either. He'd complained over Mac taking charge, like he had earlier with Gage. Would that have been enough of a reason to kill Mac? She never would have believed Robert would've taken his anger that far, but weren't most murders done in the heat of anger?

Robert also knew about the arctic tern her dad had carved for her.

He knew about the gold.

Then again, he couldn't get his hands on it unless they were married.

He hadn't taken her rejection of his proposal well either, and the whole time she'd been dating Gage, Robert had found excuses to 'pop' into her shop. He'd used Chloe the most, which was inexcusable. Especially because it worked, the manipulative bastard. Robert had also returned unharmed from finding the geocache full of Almond Joys. He was talented with a knife, and could have easily stolen Nadia's sleeping pills and planted them in the coffee. He'd been alone in their cabin that first night when she'd returned from her walk by the lake.

Could Robert have taken the pills?

She shook as the possibilities added up. Had she misjudged him so much?

Nadia brushed her shoulder. "Hey, you okay?"

Oh God, Robert was right behind Nadia.

Would he target her next? Tern flicked a glance at Robert, who held hers without any problem. She was the first to turn away. It hurt looking at him. She'd made love with this man. Had contemplated making a life with him, having his children. Where had she gone so wrong in her estimation of people? She used to be a good judge of character. But then she'd also fallen in love with a man who was afraid loving her would ruin him.

She gave Nadia a jerky nod and continued forward as though she was fine.

What did she do?

She had to get Nadia away from Robert, but if she let on that she knew Robert was behind this then what reasons would he have to continue the game? As long as they were 'playing' they were still alive. If she were him and he figured out she was onto him, Gage would be the next to go.

Gage was the biggest threat physically. It made sense that he would be the next target, and then Nadia, leaving Tern for last. For some reason Robert wanted her to suffer. But how did he figure to get out of this without the authorities coming after him?

Easy. Alaska.

How many people had lost their lives in the back country of Alaska? Too many to count. Most were never found, thanks to the huge population of predators. All Robert had to do was leave their bodies out for the unfriendlies to dispose of.

What a brilliant plan. He had the skills and the strength to survive out here on his own for a long time. Yeah, he was bitching about being hungry, but he was a hunter. He could pick up dinner in the same amount of time it would take him to have a pizza delivered in town if he wanted.

She needed to get Nadia away from him and warn Gage.

How did she do that when Robert—rifle in hand—hiked behind them all?

"Seriously, Gage," Nadia whined. "I need a bathroom."

Gage stopped. "Fine." He turned to face the little group and was immediately arrested by the fear in Tern's gaze. She stared at him as though trying to convey a message.

"We'll break here," he said, moving closer to Tern and glancing around the area. They were still in the woods though the trees had thinned. It was as good a place to rest for a minute as any, he figured. "Anyone else need to go?"

Tern shook her head.

"Hell, I might as well," Robert said.

Gage glanced at his watch. "You have five minutes."

"Might take me longer than five minutes to take a shit." Robert chuckled at his joke as he traipsed off into the trees.

Nadia went in the opposite direction and Tern's shoulders slumped.

"You figured something out," Gage said.

Tern waited until Nadia and Robert were out of earshot, and then stepped closer to him until their chests were almost touching. He couldn't help from reaching out and putting his hands on the sides of her hips. It was an immediate reaction, and he hated that it seemed so natural.

"I think I know who the killer is," she whispered. The words had him letting go of her and tightening his hold on his gun.

"Who?" He surveyed the surrounding trees.

"I think it's Robert." She bit her lip.

He narrowed his eyes. "Why?"

"He had opportunity and motive."

"Explain." She had his full attention now.

"He's the jealous sort. He hated Lucky and didn't warm to Mac. He also knew about the arctic tern my dad carved for me and where I kept it."

"What does he have against you?"

"Since I wouldn't marry him, I think he's out to make me suffer. He's always had a temper. He was alone in my cabin the first night when I returned. He could have found Nadia's sleeping pills. He could have easily drugged himself after he killed Mac…" She had to pause and swallow over Mac's name.

Gage knew every time Tern said his name she saw his dead body and it hurt her all over again.

"The guy was really wigged out about sleeping next to a dead man," Gage added, playing devil's advocate. "It was like he had some kind of phobia of dead people."

"It could have been an act," she suggested.

He nodded. It sure as hell could have been.

Whistling announced Robert's return. Gage studied him as he ambled out of the shadows of black spruce.

"What?" Robert stopped and checked his fly.

"Where's Nadia?" Tern asked, stepping in the direction Nadia had taken. "She should be back by now too."

"You know girls," Robert said. "They take forever."

A gunshot spilt the air, followed by Nadia's piercing scream.

CHAPTER TWENTY-FOUR

They rushed in the direction of Nadia's scream.

"If she can scream, she's alive," Gage hollered as they hurried.

Unless she was bleeding out from a gunshot wound and dying this very minute. Tern tried to dispel the image before panic overtook her.

Robert's heavy footsteps echoed like death drums behind her. A bullet ricocheted off the tree she passed.

"Get down!" Gage yelled.

Robert tackled her from behind. The breath in her body whooshed out as she hit the ground with Robert's heavy weight on top of her.

"Tern!" Gage swiveled mid-step, dropping to the ground. "Tern?"

"F-fine," she choked out.

Another gunshot penetrated the earth too close to them, dirt spraying them in the face.

"Son of a fucking bitch." Robert continued to swear a blue streak on top of her.

Gage scuttled backward on his stomach to her and Robert, his .30-06 at his shoulder pointed in the direction of the bullets. "Nadia!" he hollered.

There was no answer.

"No, no, no," Tern cried, struggling to buck Robert off her back. "Let me up!"

"Shh!" Robert settled more heavily until she could only drag in air by short, choppy breaths.

Gage scooted until he lay beside them, his finger on the trigger of his rifle, ready to shoot anything that flinched.

Then she heard it, a shuffling of brush, breaking of twigs. Thin birch branches bent, their leaves rustling against each other like sandpaper.

Nadia scurried from the forest, skidding to a stop in surprise at Gage's rifle aimed at her. Her eyes widened, becoming huge disks.

"Oh, thank God," Tern breathed out, dropping her head onto the damp earth.

"Someone's shooting at us," Nadia said, her chest heaving. "Are you shooting? Why are you shooting? You could have hit me!"

Gage reached up and pulled Nadia to the ground. "I haven't fired a damn shot."

"Who then?" Nadia asked, her voice trembling.

Gage didn't bother to answer. He looked at Tern, Robert still covering her body with his. "You hit?"

"No," Tern said.

"Yes," Robert said, rolling off Tern and grunting in pain. "I've been hit."

"What?" Tern crawled over Robert where he lay next to her. His eyes were closed, his face pale, and his shoulder and sleeve were covered in blood. "Oh, no."

"How bad?" Gage asked.

"Hurts like a son of a bitch." Robert gasped.

"How bad?" Gage repeated.

"I don't fucking know," Robert gritted out.

"Well, if you can bitch, you can't be hurt that bad. Put pressure on it. We've got to get out of here. Come on." Gage inched back in the brush, staying close to the trees, keeping his head down.

The rest of them followed suit. When they reached a large outcropping of boulders, Gage took cover, propping his rifle on the rock, and peered over.

Tern helped Robert lean against the stone shield, biting back her worry at the blood staining his left sleeve.

Nadia sidled up between her and Gage, taking in Robert. "Is it bad?"

"Of course it's bad. I took a fucking bullet!"

Tern flicked open her pocketknife and cut into the wet, sticky flannel of Robert's sleeve, then used her hands to tear the material up to the shoulder seam, revealing torn, bloody flesh. She sagged with relief, falling back on her haunches. "It's only a flesh wound."

"Sure as hell doesn't feel like a flesh wound." Robert grimaced as Tern probed around the area. "Son of a bitch. Shit."

"Everyone, quiet," Gage whispered, peaking over the boulder again. They hushed, and Tern strained until she swore she heard her own pulse thunder. After a nerve-wracking few minutes, Gage relaxed his hold on the trigger of his rifle and stared at Nadia. "We were being shot at from the direction that you relieved yourself."

"Yeah, so?"

"What do you think?"

"You can't be serious," Nadia scoffed.

"Gage, Nadia wouldn't—"

"Tern, stay out of this." His eyes didn't stray from Nadia. Silenced ticked by until Nadia yanked her pistol free of her waistband.

Tern gasped. Robert swore, and Gage pinned Nadia with his rifle. "Drop it."

"Damn it, I was just going to hand it to you, you freaking idiot. Look at it. Tell me if my gun's been fired." Nadia shoved her pistol at Gage with her thumb and forefinger.

He took her gun but didn't drop his from where it pointed at her chest. He checked her weapon before lowering his rifle. "Her gun hasn't been fired." But he didn't sound convinced. "Got an explanation for the bullets ceasing once you showed up?"

"No." She shook her head. "Don't have a clue."

"That's enough," Tern said, expelling the breath she didn't realize she'd held.

"Right." Robert swallowed. "I'm bleeding to death here."

Tern focused on what she could do something about. "Does anyone have any bandages? Disinfectant?"

"Check my backpack, I've got a t-shirt that I haven't worn," Gage said. "It's about as good as I think we can do right now." He handed Nadia her pistol back.

"I've got some water left," Nadia said, taking her gun and sliding it back in the waistband of her jeans and grabbing her water bottle.

"We'll need to sterilize it," Tern said.

"Not here." Gage glanced around the enclosed area. "It'll have to wait. This is a good place to ambush us."

"The wound needs to be wrapped, Gage," Tern said.

"Yeah," Robert added. "Plus, I don't feel like hiking another hundred miles,"

"You'd rather be dead?"

"Let's calm down," Tern said.

"Tern, wrap his arm with the sleeve you cut off his shirt." Gage surveyed the area. "Let's get moving. We'll stop as soon as we find a place where we aren't so trapped."

"Shit," Robert grumbled. Tern did as Gage said, slicing his sleeve into smaller strips and using it to tie around the wound. "Fuck, this hurts."

"Be a man," Tern said, though she wanted to swear with him. Just minutes before she was thinking he was the threat. Now she didn't know what to think.

The man had taken a bullet for her.

If Robert hadn't thrown her to the ground, she'd be the one with a bullet hole right now. She'd be dead.

Tern finished doctoring up Robert with shaky hands and glanced up at Gage, seeing fear, rage, and worry in his eyes. Their situation had been bad before, but now with one of them wounded, the stakes had gotten higher.

It was survival of the fittest, and Robert was no longer fit.

Gage reached down and pulled Tern close to him. She gladly went to him.

"Come on," Gage said. "Let's get a move on. Robert, you gotta stop that whimpering or you'll give our position away."

"Hey, I don't whimper," Robert grumbled, but he squared his shoulders and didn't make a sound as Gage and Tern help him to his feet. He sagged against Tern for a moment before straightening. She expected him to cop a feel, and was disappointed when he didn't. It meant he was hurt worse than she'd thought. Her stress level shot through the canopy of the trees closing them in.

They traipsed back to the trail of sorts they'd been hiking and continued on their trek. The goal was to get as far as they could today, putting distance between them and their supposed killer.

Everything she'd been thinking seemed all wrong now. Robert couldn't be the killer. The action, the need to protect, was so quick, so immediate. If he truly wanted her dead, why had he covered her with his body, ready to take a bullet for her?

Her head hurt with all the 'what ifs' and 'what fors.'

They hiked for what seemed like hours before Gage called a stop. Tern's feet were numb. She hoped they were stopping for the night because she didn't know how she would put one foot in front of the other if he demanded more from her.

"Thank you, God," Nadia muttered behind her, slumping against a knoll. The terrain had changed again with the altitude they'd been steadily dropping. They were at the edge of a wide expanse—thin, toothpick trees at their back, an open space dotted with cliffs and boulders in front of them. It was a glacier bed of years past that would take probably a millennium or so for the vegetation to grow back.

"Let's make camp here," Gage said, slowly taking off the two backpacks he'd been carrying, his and Robert's both. He winced—the weight must have been a strain for him over the hours they'd hiked.

The men had taken on extra weight at the beginning so that her and Nadia's packs were lighter, and now Gage had been shouldering it all.

Robert groaned as she helped him to the ground. She placed her backpack behind him so he had something to rest his head against.

Tern glanced around the open area, grateful to see a stream running a few hundred yards from them.

Gage caught where her attention had been going. "Think there's any fish in that creek?"

She doubted she had the strength to throw a knife. "Doubt it. Not deep enough."

"We gotta find something to eat," Robert started up again. "I've been shot. I need to keep my strength up."

How much food did it take to feed this man? When she was hurt, the last thing she wanted was food. Sleep, on the other hand, begged for her indulgence.

"I'm too tired to eat," Nadia said, echoing Tern's thoughts. "I say we sleep and worry about food in the morning. Though I wouldn't say no to another Almond Joy before bedtime."

Tern opened her pack, dug out the candy bars, and handed them around. Eating the chocolate shut up Robert for a few minutes, but not for long.

"This isn't going to tie me over until breakfast."

"Rob, can it." Gage said. "Let's get shelter and then we'll go hunting."

"Fine," Robert conceded.

A flare of warning had Tern sitting up. She couldn't let Gage and Robert go hunting. The four of them had to stay together.

"Can we build a fire?" Tern asked. "I need to heat water to clean Robert's wound." Maybe she could find a minute to talk to Gage if they were gathering firewood.

Gage shook his head. "I don't think it's a good idea. It would pinpoint our position."

"I can build a smokeless fire," Robert said. "And it would help keep any unwanted predators at bay."

"I'm more worried about the two-legged animals than four," Gage said. He took a moment and then nodded. "Build the fire. Nadia, gather wood."

Nadia nodded.

"Don't wander far," Gage said. "Tern, could you put your handy knowledge to work and maybe find us something to eat that we don't have to kill?"

"Sure." She motioned her head for him to follow her. He caught on without any prodding, doing so without it looking suspicious.

"I'll give you a hand." His palm settled on the small of her back. It took everything she had not to lean into him and rest her worries on his broad, strong shoulders as they walked down the slope toward the stream.

They walked in silence, still in view of the others, but with the breeze blowing behind them so their words wouldn't travel.

Gage regarded her from under hooded eyes. "Why haven't you asked if I was the one who took your dad's arctic tern?"

"I trust you."

He held her eyes and was the first to look away. "You shouldn't."

"What's that supposed to mean?"

"There are things you don't know about me either, Tern. Don't be so quick to trust me."

"I can't help it. That isn't what I wanted to talk about." She took a deep breath and blurted it out. "I was almost positive the killer was Robert until he took a bullet that could've been meant for me."

"Yeah," he said. "I was traveling along those same lines. Now I owe the son of a bitch for saving your life. Either Robert is very disciplined, which I don't see, or he isn't the killer."

"Robert reacts, he doesn't plan. I think you nailed it that the killer is very disciplined."

Gage shook his head. "I just don't see him as the one behind this." He glanced up to where Nadia was gathering sticks.

Tern followed his gaze. "Not Nadia again."

"She hadn't fired her gun, but what if she's working with a partner?"

CHAPTER TWENTY-FIVE

"A partner?" Tern sighed and rubbed a hand over her brow. "Gage, that just doesn't make sense. She's my best friend. Hell, she doesn't have the physical strength to kill Lucky or Mac, let alone the desire. What would she gain from their deaths?"

"Take a minute and entertain the possibility."

"You're barking up the wrong dog sled. Tell me how she would have been able to cut off Lucky's head?"

"Partner, remember? Even if she didn't have someone kill them, she could have surprised Lucky. Granted, cutting off his head is a stretch, but she could have done it."

"You don't sound very convinced."

"I'm not, all right." He dragged a hand through his hair. "I just know that when we go against what she wants, someone ends up dead. What if she set up this whole fiasco? She'd have to have help. Don't you think it's interesting that whoever was shooting backed off once Nadia was with us? He could have picked us off one by one, and there haven't been any attempts since then."

"I don't have an answer for that. I know Nadia better than Robert. Better than you. She doesn't have it in her to kill someone."

"Believe me, we all have it in us to kill." He glanced away from her toward the jagged, icy shroud of the Brooks Range looming in the distance.

"Gage." She put her hand on his arm. "Why didn't you call me?" He didn't pretend not to know what she was referring to.

"I couldn't." He swallowed. "I knew you would've caught a plane to New Mexico, and I couldn't let you see me like that."

"I would have understood. I do understand."

"Drop it, Tern. I don't want to talk about it." Ghosts reflected in his eyes before he blinked them away.

A stab of hurt twisted in her heart, and she turned away toward the stream.

"You say you understand, but I don't want you to. I hated that I took his life, okay, and I hate that, if given the choice, I would do it again. What kind of man does that make me?" Before she could respond he answered the question himself. "It makes me a murderer."

"You did what you needed to in order to protect those you love. That makes you a hero."

"Right," he scoffed. "My sister sure as hell doesn't see it that way."

"Give her time. Hopefully she'll get into therapy."

"I doubt it. She blames me for her shitty life, not the asshole she married."

"You're easy to blame." When his brows rose in surprise she continued, "What I meant is that it's easier to blame you than take responsibility for her part in what happened. She married the asshole, remember."

He studied her for a moment. His eyes softened. "You're very wise, do you know that?"

She quirked a smile. "I've been told."

He raised his hand to smooth back a section of her hair that had pulled loose of her braid, but stopped before he actually touched her. "I can't fall for you again."

"So you've said." She tried to deflect the hurt his words caused, to no avail.

"Don't do that."

"Do what?"

"Look hurt."

"Believe me, I'm doing my best to hide it."

She turned away and he spun her around. Swearing, he jerked her into his arms, squeezing her to his chest.

"You're killing me here, Tern," he said in a voice so low she wouldn't have caught the tortured words if he hadn't muttered them in her hair.

"Ditto," she murmured into the heavy cotton fabric of his shirt, trying to resist the urge to nuzzle.

He swore again, and tipped her chin up. She read his intent, part of her furious he would think of holding her, kissing her, when he said he wouldn't love her. But when his lips trapped hers, pressing hard in a kiss of desperation that spoke to her own, she couldn't push him away. His tongue breached her lips and tangled with hers. She groaned, her hands tangling in his shirt, her traitorous body rubbing up against him, trying with every cell to fuse to his.

He wrenched his mouth from hers and buried his lips in the crook of her neck. "What the hell am I going to do about you?"

She didn't know if he was asking some form of higher being or her. God knew she had no answers.

She freed herself of his arms, even though the action was like ripping off duct tape from a festered sore. "When you figure that out, let me know."

One last searching look and she moved away from the tempting heat of his touch. She staggered toward the stream, trying to keep one foot in front of the other, rather than fall into a helpless heap and beg him to take her. Part of her was willing to take whatever he could give her. The other wanted everything. If Gage couldn't give her that, he wasn't the man for her, but while her head knew this, her body ached.

She bent to gather water in the collapsible bladder she'd brought with her, and caught her reflection in the clear waters of the mountain run off. She was a mess. Her hair was everywhere. Sections were torn free of her braid from tree branches grabbing at her on the long hike. She didn't have an ounce of makeup to hide behind, and her eyes were deep pools of exhaustion and pain. She needed to distance herself from Gage, protect herself from further heartache, until they could get down this blasted mountain.

She needed to quit thinking of herself and think of Robert, up the hill bleeding and in pain. There was so much more to occupy her thoughts and feelings than Gage Fallon.

Gage stood silently next to Tern and mentally berated himself. He needed to start thinking with his head and not with what stretched out his fucking pants. It wasn't fair to keep playing with her affections.

Gage knew Tern cared for him. He saw it, felt it with each long look she sent his way.

He didn't say anything to Tern as he took the filled bladder and hiked beside her up the hill toward Nadia and Robert.

Robert still lay in the position they'd left him. He couldn't be hurting that bad. The jerk just didn't want to help make camp. He was milking it.

Nadia had been busy gathering dry wood scattered across the hillside. An avalanche must have wiped out this area years ago, littering the ground with lots of broken bits of trees.

Gage built a fire, doing his best to make it smokeless. He stood, stretched, and noticed a rock cropping a hundred yards or so above of them. There was a ledge that made a natural shelf. He'd bet there was a cave under the ledge. It would keep them out of the elements for the night and give them cover in case they were being followed by an outside force.

"I'm going to hike up there and check that out," he said, pointing to the rock cropping.

"What about bears?" Nadia asked. "Couldn't that be a den?"

"Yeah." He was more worried about their killer lying in wait than bears.

Tern handed him his rifle without making eye contact. "Toss in some rocks before you stick your head in there, in case it's occupied."

Guess she wasn't worried about him, but then he figured even if she did love him, she'd still hand him his rifle and tell him to be smart when poking his fool head into caves. The woman was as tenacious and resistant as any bear he might encounter. She expected a mate to be a man, to go out and hunt, protect, and provide. She would never sit back and let a man beat on her, or wait for whatever nibblets of affection he was willing to divvy out.

No, she expected everything from him, but then she'd give everything of herself in return.

The realization staggered him.

Everything Tern had to give would be a thing to experience and treasure. Could he handle that without losing who he was?

The thoughts pounded around in his head like a hail storm as he climbed to the outcropping. It looked deserted, but he'd bet it was the winter home to some large animal. He threw in some rocks as Tern suggested and waited. For good measure, he repeated the action. Silence greeted him. He crab-walked inside and gave his eyes time to adjust to the darkness. The space was roughly eight feet by ten. Big enough to shelter the four of them. Their body heat would keep them warm without a fire, unless it snowed again. There were small animal bones attesting to the spot being a favorite. But they were dry and dusty so he figured the owners wouldn't begrudge them squatting for the night.

He returned to the others and found Robert in fresh dressing, hot water on the fire with Nadia feeding the flames more wood.

But no Tern.

A shiver of warning slithered up his spine. "Where's Tern?"

CHAPTER TWENTY-SIX

"Chill, man," Robert said from his reclined position. "She's only been gone a few minutes. She probably had to answer the call of nature."

Gage wanted to strangle the man. Then Tern appeared, safe and sound, her stride confident and sure. He shook with the need to scoop her up in his arms and then shake the living daylights out of her for scaring the shit out of him.

"Where the hell have you been? How many times do we need to go over this? You don't take off alone, and if you need to be alone, you tell someone where the hell you're headed. Shit, woman, you want to be next with a knife in your chest or your head cut off and displayed on a stump!"

"Whoa, dial it back, Gage," Robert said as Tern paled. "She's obviously fine."

"I was just over that knoll, within shouting distance," Tern explained. "I noticed some arctic hares, figured they'd make a nice dinner."

He spotted the dead rabbits hanging from her grasp by the ears. His heart had a harder time slowing back to its normal rhythm. "Don't do that again."

She stared at him and then nodded. "I won't."

He heaved out a breath. "Good. You need any help with those?" He pointed to the fresh kill she'd supplied.

"No, I got it."

"Fine. The cave will make a good shelter for the night."

"Good."

They nodded at each other until he swore and had to turn away. He went over to Robert and knelt down next to him. "Listen up," he kept his voice low, "that wound of yours is nothing but a scratch. I expect you to do your share. You should have made sure Tern was protected while I was gone. Don't make me suspect you being behind this, because I won't hesitate to leave you here as food for the wild animals that roam this mountain.

"What the hell?" Robert blustered, cradling his arm.

"You know what I'm talking about. You want Tern to fawn over you, I get it. But she isn't the type of woman to find that attractive. So man up or be left behind."

"You really are a son of a bitch."

"Damn right." Gage returned to the fire to find Tern once again gone. "Where—"

Nadia pointed.

Tern was just above them picking some greens. He'd have to put a leash on her in order to settle down his blood pressure. At this rate, she was going to give him a heart attack.

He kept her in his peripheral vision as he scanned the rest of the desolated area. They seemed all alone on this deserted mountainside. Down in the valley, a migrating herd of caribou grazed peacefully. His stomach rumbled. What he wouldn't give for a caribou steak. But they wouldn't be able to consume a whole caribou before it started to spoil. Rabbit wasn't his favorite. They were usually gamey and greasy to boot, while not having a lot of meat on their bones. Plus he'd owned a rabbit as a child, and it made him feel a little sick every time he partook of one.

Tern rejoined them, ignoring him while she skinned the hares, rinsed, and stuffed them with the plants she'd picked. He tried not to show his wince as she skewered them with a stick. She set up a type of spit for the rabbits to be turned, handed one over to Nadia while she manned the other.

She was a handy woman. He'd expected to take care of her. Not the other way around.

It was peaceful while they waited for dinner to cook. The acrid smell of the fire soothed while his stomach grumbled with each sizzle of fat the meat dripped into the flames. The lush freshness of the wilderness, peppered with hidden dangers, made each sensation sharper, sweeter. The sky with its puffy clouds seemed close enough to touch if he jumped. They were near the top of the world here. If they weren't in a fight for their lives, he'd be resting back with his hands behind his head and reveling in God's backyard. Instead, apprehension pumped hot in his blood, waiting for the devil to slink out the shadows.

Robert fought his way to his feet, and ambled over to the campfire. "Sure smells good, Tern."

"Thanks."

She didn't spare him much of a glance, making Gage chuckle inside. She wouldn't go for a man who wasn't her equal, and Robert had proven he wasn't in her realm. Except he had taken a bullet for her.

Clearly, Tern didn't want to encourage him.

"How are you feeling, Robert?" Nadia asked.

"Better," he muttered his eyes never leaving Tern.

Tern removed a hare from the fire and cut into the thigh joint with her knife. It must have passed her inspection, for she handed it off to Robert. He, grabbed it with his fingers, swore as he tossed it back and forth, swore again as he pulled the wound on his shoulder, before finally grabbing the thigh with the corner of his shirt.

"Sorry," Tern said, biting back a smile. "It's hot."

"Obviously," Robert muttered, moving back to where he'd been reclining.

Nadia laughed and tried to cover it with a cough. She pulled her rabbit from the fire and offered it to Gage to cut off a piece. He did so because he was hungry and at this point it didn't matter what he ate, as long as it silenced his gnawing stomach. One bite and his saliva glands flooded his mouth. "Damn, this is good." And it was. "How'd you get rabbit to taste this good?"

"It's only because you're hungry," Tern said.

He failed to correct her because he was already tearing another bite from the thigh bone, not feeling one bit of guilt for his former childhood pet. They ate until there was nothing on the small bones of the hares.

"Tern, you should open a restaurant," Robert said, licking his fingers.

"I've already got a business I'd like to get back to," she said.

"We should bunk down and get some sleep," Gage said. "The cave above will provide us shelter and cover for the night." Not to mention give them some temporary darkness. The arctic sun blazed as bright as if it was noon rather than close to midnight.

Gage stamped out the fire, smothering it with sand before trekking up the hill after the rest of them.

"It'll be a mite cozy in here," Robert said, peering inside the cave.

"Yeah, and no offense," Gage said, "but I don't want to cozy up to you during the night. So boy, girl, girl, boy."

"Fine by me." Robert grinned.

Nadia and Tern eyed each other, did that silent communication thing women did, and seemed like they were about to object to the sleeping arrangements. While the temperature was currently pleasant, this was Alaska. Mother Nature changed her mind on the weather like a diva.

"It snowed yesterday," Gage reminded them. "We don't need anyone getting sick because they're being stupid." It went without saying that the only one of this group he was sleeping next to was Tern.

They crawled into the cave—Robert first, Nadia next, then Tern. Gage took the opening so he could keep watch. They had each packed their sleeping bags, tying them to their backpacks, and now unzipped them, laying them out on the floor of the stone cave, pulling the sleeping bags over the top of them.

They settled in to sleep, and Gage figured he'd drop right off. No such luck.

In the tight quarters, he could smell her. Fireweed and rosehips. She lay on her side, her back up against his. The heat from her body had him sweating with the need to turn over and spoon her from behind. Instead he pulled back the sleeping bag and let the arctic air cool him.

Not that it did a lot of good.

The view in front of him was priceless, but he'd pay anything to be back in Fairbanks with Tern tucked into her own bed safe and sound.

An eagle flew with deadly stealth over the valley below, hunting for prey. He heard a scattering of animals in the woods as they also hunted for prey.

And wished to God he knew who hunted them.

CHAPTER TWENTY-SEVEN

Tern awoke, blinking in the shady darkness. The inky cave roof above her twinkled with quartz as though some mythical creature had tossed stardust and it had embedded within the rough stone. She smelled damp earth and sharp grasses. At some point during the night, she'd kicked free of her sleeping bag. Heat buffeted her from one side along with the musky smell of man.

Gage. She cuddled into him, her body curling around him, and sighed with pleasure.

Her gaze connected with Gage's magnetic evergreen eyes and need shivered through her. A smothered groan and answering moan came from behind her.

Were Nadia and Robert having sex?

Gage nodded as though reading her mind.

Are you freaking kidding me? Now? The rustle of their sleeping bags became rhythmic, and so did their sighs and muffled grunts.

First Lucky and now Robert.

Wait. Nadia had already gotten it on with Robert right after Lucky was killed. She'd sure loosened her inhibitions.

Tern didn't want to move, but she couldn't stay here facing Gage. Not with him watching her. He'd see too much.

She shifted to dislodge her leg from where she had wrapped it around his hip, but his hand grabbed the back of her thigh and pulled her in tight against him. He rocked his thick, hard erection against her sex, and it was her turn to swallow a moan. His eyes glowed in the dimness, much like a wolf scenting his mate.

She couldn't do this, couldn't react sexually when two people were having sex next to her.

She was going to kill Nadia. And Robert. So much for Robert being in love with her.

Gage's eyes never left hers as he slipped his hand under her t-shirt, and his fingers danced over her ribcage to her breast. He palmed her breast, daring her to object.

She would not participate in an orgy. But then was it an orgy when you didn't change partners? Or were orgies just about group sex? She wasn't up to date on sexual fetishes.

Nadia and Robert were getting serious and didn't seem to care if they were discovered, by the sounds of it. They were past keeping quiet. Gasps and moans echoed off the walls of the cave.

Gage caught her nipple with his finger, sucking in his breath finding it as hard as the pebbles they'd swept away to the far corners of the cave before they'd laid out their sleeping bags. He rolled her nipple between his thumb and finger, flicking the tip with his thumbnail. She closed her eyes from the pleasure of the small prick of pain. Biting her lip, she tried to keep in the illicit sounds demanding a voice.

She was trapped, and the knowledge suddenly excited rather than diminished her desire. She couldn't move, sandwiched as she was between the two bodies already joined and the hard body of Gage in front of her. He was tormenting her and he knew it. His eyes glinted, their fire burning in her, heating her insides until she melted.

Two could play this game.

She reached for him and her questing fingers found his erection. She wrapped her hand around the throbbing thickness.

His eyes rolled back in his head.

There, that was more like it.

Then his hand slipped down her stomach, under the waistband of her pants and past the laughable barrier of her underwear. He found her heat. His lips descended and caught hers when she would have whimpered her surrender.

Oh God, this couldn't be happening. She wasn't the type to have sex with other people in the room. Even if the others were occupied with each other, and couldn't care less about her and Gage.

His tongue swiftly breached her lips and engaged hers in a contest of wills. Her hand tightened around his shaft while her other clutched the back of his neck. The kiss turned rougher. His fingers thrust into her, and she arched into his demanding hand. He worked her, giving no quarter, demanding all, while sealing his mouth over hers, swallowing any sound she expressed. She shuddered as her soul soared past the rock walls of the cave to burst within the rays of the midnight sun.

He held her tight against him, cushioning her fall back to earth against his heaving chest. Her hand grasped harder around him, stroking him from tip to base, determined to bring him the level of pleasure he'd given her. His mouth ground on hers as he surged against her hand.

"Ahh, Tern!" Robert's guttural shout slapped them back into the reality of the cold dark cave. Silence suddenly smothered the cramped space.

Had Robert called out her name?

"Get off me, you son of a bitch." Nadia's screech and the following smack ricocheted off the stone walls.

Gage jerked and pulled away from Tern, rolling to his feet outside the cave in one quick motion.

Accusations and apologies ensued behind her, but Tern couldn't make any sense of it. Didn't want to. She quickly chased after Gage, righting her clothes as she stumbled after him.

She didn't want any part of what just happened between Robert and Nadia. But she'd had it with Gage. No more, she was nailing him down.

Enough was enough.

She found him about a hundred yards away, leaning against a boulder, bent forward as though he were in pain.

"What the hell was that?" she asked.

His head snapped up. His nostrils flared, and his eyes glittered with temper. For a moment, she wondered if she shouldn't back up a few steps, but then she was too upset to heed the self-preservation prompting.

"Why did you do that to me?" she demanded.

"Do what?" His voice sounded as if a rope was tied around his vocal cords.

"Why do you tell me that you can't love me and then you love me like that?"

"Please let it go, Tern."

"The hell I will. You say you don't want to be with me, and then you hold me and touch me like that."

"Tern." His tone warned, and his face tightened. "I can't do this now."

Her heart was ripping from her chest, and he couldn't do this now? "I love you, you son of a bitch." She stepped nearer, wanting his touch, his heat, needing the man who'd loved her in the cave, not this cold one who stared and repressed what he felt for her. "I've been in love with you since you walked into my shop. This isn't fair."

"You need to get the hell away from me. Now."

"I don't give a damn about what you want. What about what I want?"

Okay, maybe she shouldn't engage the animal in front of her. Gage was stripped down to his Neanderthal ancestors, and that really shouldn't excite her.

"I just heard your name bellowed by another man as he climaxed," he snapped. "You need to get away from me. I'm afraid of what I'm going to do."

He advanced a step, looming over her, and the rational part of her brain nudged her to flee.

He clasped her upper arms, and drew her up on her toes. "Do you have any fucking idea how this feels?" he asked through gritted teeth.

She slowly shook her head and something that was a mix of fear and excitement skittered along her spine.

"I'm so hard I hurt. It's taking everything I've got not to strip you bare, turn you over that boulder, and pound into you until you can't remember another man's touch. I fucking *hate* knowing Robert has touched you. That he's been inside you. I want my hands around his neck until he's unable to utter your name." His fingers tightened around her arms as though he relished crushing Robert's throat. She knew she'd have imprints in her skin tomorrow.

She hung in his hands, holding her breath, almost wishing he would do the things he'd just threatened, and then hated herself for being titillated by the idea.

He could do what he wanted with Robert. But nobody branded her.

"You hypocrite," she hissed. "How dare you throw my past lovers in my face? You didn't come to me as a virgin."

His eyes bored into hers. A war waged there, as clearly as though she had ring-side seats to a clash of warriors tearing each other apart. He slowly set her back on her feet, and one by one his fingers released her. She caught sight of his trembling hands as he secured them in the front pocket of his jeans.

His expression hardened with resolve, the wildness barely contained. "You're right, I am a hypocrite. I can't be around you and leave you alone. You've turned me into a man who manipulated by his baser urges. I want to kill Robert, at the very least, beat the shit out him. You have consumed my life. I can't touch another woman without thinking of you."

Apparently neither could Robert.

"I'm losing control," he continued, "and I refuse to let that happen."

She stepped back with a shuddering breath, wishing more than ever that she'd listened to that prompting voice that told her to leave him alone.

They regarded each other, she barely breathing and him struggling to calm his. What was it about her that brought out the obsession in Robert and the resentment in Gage?

The reality of the resentment Gage felt for her tasted bitter as she swallowed the truth.

She just stood there and blinked. She could see it in each line of his rigid body, the fire in his eyes, and the throbbing vein in his temple. Her heart seemed to slow until each beat pounded in her ears and she shook from the heavy force of it.

Who did he resent more? Her or himself? The one man she wanted to spend the rest of her life with resented her.

Maybe even hated her.

How far did his hate go? Far enough to rid himself of her?

"So coming here was like the final test of your twelve-step program," she said. Hurt overshadowed the anger and she relished the burn. "You had to see if you could resist taking a taste?"

He took a step toward her, but then seemed to tighten the leash on his resolve and stopped. "It isn't that simple."

Yeah, it was.

It should have been as simple as boy meets girl. They fall in love, make a family, and live happily ever after.

"I thought you were a different kind of man, Gage. One I could make a life with, have children with, but I won't be with a man who hates that he loves me. I won't let you break me."

CHAPTER TWENTY-EIGHT

Gage watched her walk away, her shoulders straight, her stride sure, belying any hint that he could break her.

Could anything really break that woman?

He didn't think so. Everything inside begged him to follow, yank her back into his arms and beg forgiveness. He wanted all of her. Wanted it so bad that it scared the shit out of him.

The love he'd known was destructive, soul-sucking, and he couldn't give into what he felt regardless of how much his heart and soul begged him to.

But watching her walk away felt like part of him was being ripped out. With each step she took, more and more of his soul followed behind her.

He covered his eyes with his fists, surprised to find moisture there. He shuddered with the pain coursing through him. His life would be finished if he gave in and partook of what she offered.

Build a life together, have children together.

She loved him.

They were like drugs to each other. He wanted a life with her, but history had taught him his life wouldn't be his own if he gave in.

Anger and the need to throttle Robert still burned under his skin, but he was thinking more rationally. It wasn't fair for him to attack Tern because of his shortcoming. He wanted to defend his woman. But she wasn't his, and he refused to claim her. What kind of coward did that make him?

She was right. He was a hypocrite. He'd had women, more than he should, and he had no business throwing her past mistakes that she'd made with Robert in her face.

Shit, he'd have to apologize. Or did he just leave things as they stood? Tern hated him now. Wouldn't that help create the distance that he needed?

He turned and gauged the sky. There was no way to tell what time it was with the sun burning at the top of the world. Since they were up, they might as well break camp and get a move on. The sooner they were back in civilization, the better for all of them.

The ways things were going, they'd kill each other before someone else got the chance.

Tern crawled into the cave and started packing up her things. Robert lay spent on his sleeping bag and looked away when she glared at him.

Nadia struggled into her clothes, muttering obscenities under her breath. She paused when Tern entered.

"Hey," she said.

"What is with you?" Tern demanded, using her heartache over Gage to sling accusations at them. "How do the two of you have sex in a room—a freaking cave—with other people just inches away from you?"

Nadia shrugged and finished buttoning her shirt. "It just happened."

Robert, at least, had the graciousness to seem embarrassed. "Sorry, Tern. It was one of those moment things. You understand?"

"No, I don't understand." All the hurt and frustration of their situation boiled inside her. "Nadia, just a few days ago you were sleeping with Lucky. How do you jump from his bed to Robert's?"

Nadia narrowed her eyes, her fingers twisting the sleeping bag she was in the process of rolling.

Robert came to Nadia's defense. "I imagine the same way you went from my bed to Lucky's. In less time, too, if I remember correctly."

His barb connected with his target. She wadded up her sleeping bag and grabbed her backpack, taking all her items out of the cave to pack. The sooner she was away from them the better.

Funny, how you never really knew someone until you spent time in forced seclusion.

Gage stood outside the cave when she crawled out. He nodded at seeing her hands full of supplies. "Good, it's time to head out."

"Whatever."

His brows furrowed. "Something wrong?"

"You mean, what else is wrong, don't you?"

"Okay." He seemed to come to a conclusion and wisely dropped the subject. He bent and hollered into the cave. "Pack up. I want to be out of here in fifteen."

There was grumbling from inside, but Tern didn't stick around. She found a clear spot, tightly rolled up her sleeping bag, and secured it to her backpack. Then, with her gun checked and loaded and on her hip, she headed for the woods for a moment of privacy.

Once in the cover of the trees, she breathed a sigh of relief. She took care of the call of nature and hiked back, taking a different route that ended with her coming out of the woods closer to the stream. Glancing up the hill, there was no sign of Gage, but Nadia and Robert were arguing for all to see. Tern gritted her teeth. She couldn't tell what they were saying, but by the hand gestures she could imagine.

Nadia suddenly dropped her gear and kneed Robert in the groin. Ouch. Robert hit the ground with a cry, his hands cupping his injured pride.

Go, Nadia.

Tern rotated back toward the stream.

Why did the two of them hooking up bother her so much? She didn't want Robert, and with him being occupied with Nadia he'd leave her alone. That was if Nadia let him close again after his unfortunate faux pas.

At this point, Tern wouldn't be surprised if Nadia made a play for Gage.

She really shouldn't be so quick to judge. She and Gage had gotten it on too. He'd brought her to climax in the same cave. He'd sent her to heights of desire and she hadn't given a damn who was around. If Gage would have pushed it, she would have taken him inside her body and relished him coming inside her, regardless who was around to witness.

And yes, Robert had been right. She'd skipped on him that night in the bar when Lucky had appeared. But she hadn't slept with Lucky. They'd caught each other up on where their lives were over drinks, then over coffee and breakfast. She'd returned in the early morning to find Robert waiting for her inside her house. She'd never figured how'd he'd gotten in, and he'd never admitted how he had either.

At the time, it had seemed easier to let Robert think she'd cheated on him with Lucky, hoping that would finally sever their relationship. It had. Even though he'd continued to pop in whenever she least expected it.

Her sister, Raven, had suggested getting a restraining order, but then Gage had entered her life, and Robert had stayed away. It'd seemed as though her life was perfect, until Gage had disappeared, and then everything had come crashing down.

There'd been that one stupid night where she'd let Robert hold her while she'd cried her broken heart out. He'd started showing up with food and flowers, being smart enough to have his daughter in tow.

She'd done a lot of things wrong. Nobody was perfect. But had her actions brought a killer after those she loved? Was his ultimate goal to kill her after she'd suffered the deaths of the others?

Tern shook off the thoughts to dissect later, and dropped her backpack, unzipping and taking out a cloth to wash with. Filling her hands with the clear icy water from the stream, she drank deep. Next, she splashed her face, gasping when the icy water hit her skin and trickled down her neck. It helped to clear her head somewhat. She needed a baptism in this water to completely think straight.

Wetting the washcloth, she caught a flash of movement out of the corner of her eye. Blinding colors of pain exploded before her as something solid smacked her alongside the head.

Her last conscious thought, as she tumbled face-first into the glacial stream, was that she really didn't want words carved into her forehead.

CHAPTER TWENTY-NINE

Like frost on windowpanes, ice crystallized over her consciousness, cold and callous and fractured.

It wasn't half bad. Numb. Quiet in a kind of blissful way. It had been forever since she hadn't felt emotions poke at her with pinpricks. The icy darkness beckoned with a seduction that was painful to resist.

A raven cawed overhead, causing a fissure to crack the surface.

"Tern!" Gage hollered, his voice high and shaky. His arms lifted her and held her tight against his chest. "Come on, Tern. Come back to me."

God, her head hurt. She wanted to be left alone, wanted some peace. The raven caw-cawed again, sounding impatient. She moaned.

"That's it, honey. Open your eyes."

She peered through an eyelid. Bad idea. Sunlight cracked through her muddled brain matter, splintering more of the ice. She tried to raise her hand to investigate the source of the slicing pain, but it was too much trouble. Her hand fell back to the ground. She just wanted to rest, to sleep the next century away, but someone who smelled and felt a lot like Gage kept shaking and shouting at her.

Inconsiderate bastard.

"Tern, don't do this to me. Wake up!" Another hard shake. This one rattled her teeth. She tried to push him away, get him to stop, but her limbs just flopped against his stone-hard chest. It was like she was a bowl of noodles.

Overhead the raven cawed again, the sound piercing her ears. The pounding in her head increased its tempo, and she became more aware of the wet clothes clinging to her cold skin. What she wouldn't give for another dip in the hot springs. Darkness lured her back into its embrace.

"Damn it, Tern, open those beautiful brown eyes for me."

No, don't do it.

It's going to hurt. She needed to stay here, where everything was vague and words didn't have the power to slice. Objects wouldn't fly at her head from out of nowhere from unknown assailants.

The raven cawed sharp enough to break up the rest of the ice netting around her consciousness.

"I'm going to shoot that damn bird," Robert said.

Robert? Aw, man, did he have to be here?

"Shh, Raven," Tern whispered. "'S okay."

"Who the hell she talking to?" Robert asked. "The bird?"

"I don't care as long as she's talking." Gage caressed the side of her face with fingers that shook. She winced when they brushed the source of the throbbing at her temple. "You've got one hell of a goose egg here, Tern."

"No shit," she said, the words sounding like they were coming from somebody else far away.

"What the hell happened?" Gage asked.

"Somebody hit me."

"No shit," Robert repeated her words.

"Why am I wet?"

"The son of a bitch left you to drown in the stream," Gage said.

"Where's Nadia?"

"She's…fine." There was something in Gage's voice that said he wasn't telling her the whole truth.

"Help me sit up." The world spun.

Gage held her steady with an arm behind her back.

"Whoa." She wanted to close her eyes and give into that seductive darkness, but gritted her teeth and fought back the blackness. Her gaze landed on Nadia, propped up against the trunk of a birch tree holding blood-soaked fabric to her head.

"I thought you said Nadia was fine?"

"I lied," Gage said, carefully running his hands along the back of her head and neck. "Anything else hurt?"

"What happened?" Tern grabbed her head, trying to stop the spinning.

"Looks like both of you got beamed in the head," Robert said, his shotgun still pointed in the direction of the treetops. "Seems yours is harder than Nadia's, since hers spilt open." A raven croaked above him and he swung around. "Where the hell did that raven go?"

"Forget about the damn bird," Gage said. "Check on Nadia."

"I'm not turning my back on that black devil. You didn't see the way it looked at me with its beady eye. It marked me for death."

"Wrong tribal legend," Tern muttered. "Raven is the bringer of the sun."

"I thought it was a trickster?" Gage said.

"Sometimes."

"And storyteller?"

"That too."

"See, then it can also bring death," Robert muttered.

"Guess you're next then." She was in no mood to argue with him.

"Not funny," Robert said.

"Do you mind?" Nadia said. "Bleeding over here."

"Robert!" Gage hollered, making Tern wince.

"Going," Robert grumbled, but took another quick look at the treetops, waving his shotgun around, before giving it up. He knelt before Nadia, and lifted the bloodied rag. "It's stopped bleeding. You'll be fine."

"Thanks for all the concern." Nadia grabbed the rag from Robert and gingerly placed it back over her forehead.

"Want to tell me why the hell you took off?" Gage asked Tern, and then looked at Nadia. "There's a nut out there and both of you are alone."

Nadia adjusted the cloth. Her left eyebrow was cut and swollen, dried blood smeared her face and stained her shirt. She gestured to Robert. "This nitwit stalked off and left me alone without a backward glance. Where the hell were you?"

"I needed a moment," Gage said. The reason why hung heavy in the early morning air.

"You weren't the only one who needed space." Tern shivered in her damp clothes.

"You're lucky you aren't dead." Gage turned on her, fear and anger flaring in his eyes. "Both of you."

"We aren't, and I need a change of clothes, so yell at me later." She was tired and hurt and cold. She wasn't going to be interrogated until she was dry and had downed a few Tylenol. Oh, that's right. They didn't fucking have any. "Where's my backpack?"

Gage stood and grabbed it, knelt in front of her and unzipped the middle pocket. "Tell me what happened." He pulled out a sweatshirt and her only other pair of pants.

"Can it wait until I change?" she asked, giving him a pointed look to give her some privacy.

"Forget it. You're not leaving my sight." His dark look settled on Robert until he gave them his back while muttering under his breath. Gage turned back to her. His touch was gentle as he lifted her t-shirt up and over her pounding head, though his face was hard and his jaw tight with anger. "Now, tell me what happened."

"I was washing my face. Out of the corner of my eye, I saw something, and then, bam, lights out."

"Did you see who hit you?" He whipped off her bra like it was nothing, and then stuffed her into the sweatshirt.

She shrugged then wished she hadn't, as that simple movement sent jabs of pain icing over her. "It's all a blur."

Gage turned to Nadia. "What about you?"

"Sorry. I heard the splash, came around the corner, and this log came flying at me. I screamed, which brought you guys, but to save my life, I couldn't give you a description. It all happened so fast."

Gage knelt at Tern's ankles and started pulling at the laces of her hiking boots. Frustration radiated off of him.

"This is so fucked up," Robert said. "I don't want to be running from a goddamn killer. I have things to live for. My life is waiting for me. I need to get home."

"We all do, asshole," Nadia said, curling her lips in disgust. "You aren't the only one who has a life."

"Really? Who's waiting for you at home, huh? I have a little girl depending on me."

"Then why the hell did you leave her at home to begin with? Did you really think you had a chance getting back with Tern?" Nadia scoffed.

"Bitch," Robert spat.

"Guys." Tern grabbed her head as their voices escalated.

"So help me, if you two don't stop your bitching, I'll shut you up myself," Gage threatened. "You won't need to worry about some unseen killer. I'll be right in front of your fucking face. Got it?"

Both gave him jerky nods.

He was quite impressive reverting to caveman, Tern thought. That shouldn't send her heart thudding harder in her chest. Especially with how they'd ended things earlier. Maybe the bash on her head had scrambled more of her brains than she'd figured.

"Now," Gage continued. "Robert, clean Nadia up and check her over. We need to get out of here. You want to get home, put some effort into it or I'll leave you behind." He rotated toward Tern, and the combination of dread and rage blistering off him had Tern wanting to scoot back.

He knelt at her feet and took off her other boot. "Think you can stand?" His eyes bored into hers. Hidden behind the rage was fear, and it had her catching her breath.

She went to nod, and then thought better of it and gave him her hands. He slowly pulled her to her feet and the world tipped. He held her against his chest until things settled back to their rightful place.

"You okay?" he asked.

"Don't have much choice, do I?" she softly answered.

He shook his head. The only way to safety was to suck it up.

Very efficiently, Gage stripped her of her wet pants and underwear. Her body started to shake. Whether from the cold, being attacked and knocked unconscious, or from Gage impersonally stripping her of her clothes, she didn't have a clue.

"Hold onto my shoulders," Gage instructed. His tone sounded strained as he knelt and held underwear for her to step into. He smoothed them up and over her hips.

Were his hands trembling?

She didn't have time to focus on that as he now held out dry pants for her to step into, and then socks and boots. Luckily, she hadn't been submerged in the water, so her boots had remained on shore and therefore were still dry. Hiking in wet boots was never a good idea. People died of infection from raw blisters. She needed to be grateful for the killer's oversight of not tossing all of her into the swollen stream. Her boots must have acted as a type of anchor. A splitting headache and slightly blurred vision would be easier to deal with since her feet would be dry. At least, she hoped so.

Gage stood, zipped and buttoned her pants, his eyes hot and searing into hers.

"I could've done that," she whispered.

He held her gaze for a minute longer, before letting go of her completely. "You going to be okay?" he asked.

"I'll have to be."

His lips quirked into a half smile. "You are one hell of a woman." He hitched her backpack over his shoulders to rest next to his.

"I can—"

"So can I." Gage took her elbow. "It's going to be hard enough for you to keep up. I don't want to hear it." He picked up her pistol where it had been sitting on the boulder next to them, checked it to make sure it was loaded and stuck it in the waistband of his cargo pants. "Stay close to me."

The warning was clear. He didn't want her trusting anyone but him. He held her gaze until she gave a slight nod. His expression softened for just a moment but then he turned toward Robert and Nadia and his face turned to stone. "Ready?"

"Yeah," Robert answered. They were on their feet. Nadia's face was clean of blood, but her brow was swollen around the cut, the surrounding flesh already turning black and blue. Nadia would have a black eye before lunch. Hell, so would she, Tern thought. Possibly two. Weren't they a beautiful pair?

Gage led the way, but kept her beside him. She hurt too much to do anything but put one foot in front of the other. Each step felt like a hammer blow. Pretty soon it began its own kind of rhythm, with the drum solo taking center stage.

They kept to the cover of the trees, avoiding any open areas as they plodded downward. They didn't talk. Robert didn't even complain about not having breakfast. Tern was too nauseated to eat.

What did food matter anyway when they might not survive the remainder of the day?

CHAPTER THIRTY

"Can we talk?" Nadia asked.

Did they have to? They'd been walking at a brisk pace, or at least brisk for her, for what seemed hours. Just when she thought her body would betray her and give out, Gage called a halt and sat her down on a fallen log. He threatened her if she moved, and demanded that she drink some water. He'd placed an Almond Joy in her hand and said she'd better eat whether she wanted to or not. Her stomach bubbled at the thought of eating the little bit of chocolate.

"Listen," Nadia continued. "I'm sorry about...you know." She sighed and gingerly touched the cut on her eyebrow. "Hooking up with Robert was wrong. It was definitely wrong to do it with you and Gage sleeping next to us. But in my defense, I'm scared shitless out here. The last few days have been the scariest I've ever experienced. I guess having sex let me escape it for a while."

"Yeah." It was her turn to sigh. If anything this morning and the last few days had taught her was that life was too short to hold grudges. Besides, she'd never been the grudge-holding kind of woman. "Sorry I accused you like it did. I have no reasons to throw stones."

Nadia put an arm around her. "We just need to get home, then everything will be all right."

Tern didn't think her life would ever be right again.

Nadia continued to babble about inconsequential things. Tern just wanted her to shut up. Didn't her head hurt too? How did she form sentences? All Tern wanted to do was lay down and close her eyes. She wanted it so badly that she was afraid if she did, she'd never wake up. Instead, she focused on Gage. He and Robert stood a few feet away from them 'discussing' the direction they were going. Robert's side of the discussion was getting louder while Gage's voice was so low and threatening that Tern couldn't pick up the words anymore.

Finally, Robert threw his hands up in the air, swore at Gage, questioned his parentage, and stomped off.

"Well, guess we know who won that argument," Nadia commented.

Gage walked over and stopped in front them. His eyes narrowed as he studied Nadia. "How are you both feeling?" He shifted to inspect Tern, and then went back to scrutinizing Nadia.

"What?" Nadia asked, wiping her face. "Do I have dirt on my face?"

"No. Just checking on you. Your eyes seem to be dilating fine." He knelt down in front of Tern. His fingers lightly caressed the skin around her goose egg. "You, on the other hand, have me worried." He took the forgotten Almond Joy from her fingers, tore open the wrapper and held the chocolate to her lips. She gave in and opened her mouth and he placed the mini candy bar inside. She didn't have any choice but to chew and swallow. He still didn't seem satisfied as he watched her. Next he was holding the water bottle to her lips forcing her to drink. She drank. His eyes searched hers for a moment longer, and then he straightened. "All right, break's over. Let's make some distance."

"Guys!" Robert crashed through the brush. "We're being followed."

The black shadow of a raven flew overhead.

Gage held up his hand for silence, cocked his head and listened. Tern could only make out the sound of Robert's gasping breath. Then she heard it, a sight rustling in the bush alongside them. Not behind. Right alongside.

Tern vaguely remembered Robert and Gage keeping a visual as they trekked through the wilderness to make sure whoever had hit her and Nadia wasn't sneaking up behind them. There had been no sign. But obviously they were being tracked and hunted from a distance.

Gage, grabbed her hand, pulled her to her feet, and pushed her behind him. Nadia scrambled and stood next to Robert. Freeing her pistol from his waistband, Gage handed it to her and slowly positioned his rifle in the crock of his shoulder. Robert did the same. They waited, while the mosquitoes buzzed around them taking cheap bites of their exposed skin. When they been moving the mosquitoes hadn't been too bad, but now, stuck stationary in the deep forest with no breeze to reach them, the bloodsuckers feasted. Nadia slapped her arm, cursed, and then quieted from a look from Gage.

Again there was a rustling. Tern followed the sound with her eyes hoping to catch sight of the son of bitch. All she caught was a glimmer of black eyes. She blinked and they were gone. Had she imagined them? Behind her there was another rustling. She slowly turned and caught the hint of a toothy grin.

"Wolves," she whispered. "We're being hunted by a pack of wolves."

Gage nodded. "I think they're the same ones that entered camp a few days ago."

Had it only been a couple of days since wolves had scented Lucky's blood and investigated?

"How long do you think they've been trailing us?" she asked, her head no longer pounding as bad but her throat had gone dry.

"Probably since I got shot," Robert muttered. "If it's not one fucking thing, it's another."

"Why are we staying here?" Nadia asked. Panic in her voice, she made to move.

Robert grabbed her arm. "Don't move. We need to stay in a pack ourselves. A show of force. We keep moving, and they'll take us one by one."

"Robert's right," Gage said. "Move into a circle, backs to each other." They quickly did, just as the first wolf showed himself.

Tern caught her breath.

He was gorgeous. Intelligent, cunning eyes met hers, and a zing of awareness permeated her soul. His black coat tipped with white was stunning. He was easily over a hundred and fifty pounds and exuded alpha in waves. Another wolf appeared from out of nowhere ten feet from him, then another, and another, until there was a pack of eight surrounding them.

They were outnumbered two to one.

"Shoot 'em," Robert said, raising his gun.

"No!" Tern hollered, slapping Robert's rifle down until it pointed at the ground. "They aren't hungry. Look at them." The pack had thick glossy fur coats covering ropey muscles that were solid from a winter of full meals.

"What the hell do they want, then?" Robert said, his voice rising with alarm.

"I don't know."

"You want us to stand here all day until you figure it out?"

"Shut up, Robert," Gage said. "She's right. They aren't starving. Maybe they're curious."

"Have you ever heard of wolves curious about anything? They're predators. They attack."

"I know of a wolf that was curious," Tern said. "He even saved my nephew's life. So shut the hell up."

The wolves looked at them as though waiting for someone to make the first move.

"We're obviously on their territory. Could they be escorting us out of it?" Gage asked.

"Sounds like the best explanation that I can think of," Tern agreed.

"Can we quit talking about it and get out of here?" Nadia piped up. "This is really creeping me out."

The alpha male cocked a brow and shared a look with the wolf to his right as though conversing. The right-handed wolf took a few backward steps and blended into the brush. Tern knew he was there, but there was no sign of him. It was like he disappeared. One by one the other wolves did the same. Out of sight but right there ready to pounce. The alpha stayed where he was. Watching. Tern itched to feel the thickness of his fur, her hand even reached out on its own violation before she pulled her fingers away and into a fist.

What was she thinking?

"Let's follow their example," Gage said. "Tern, I want you to lead, I'll bring up the rear."

Tern knew he was afraid that Robert would be trigger-happy and doom them all.

"I should lead," Robert said. "Keep the women between us."

"No. Tern has a way. Let her lead us out of this."

"Not that native crap again."

"Shut up, Robert," Tern warned. "Or I'll shoot you and feed you to the wolves myself."

Nadia snickered. "Sorry," she admitted. "Scared silly. Can we get out of here before I pee my pants?"

"All right, slowly everyone," Gage said. "No sudden movements. Just because you can't see them doesn't mean they aren't there. In fact, I'd put money down that we have more wolves watching us than the ones who showed themselves."

Nadia whimpered, while Robert cursed. They broke formation, and Tern slowly began leading them out. The alpha flanked her a few steps ahead and perhaps ten feet to her left. It was unnerving, yet at the same time thrilling. Every now and then they would make eye contact, and she swore he was trying to communicate with his black stare. Were the wolves bored and using them as entertainment? God she hoped that was all it was. She didn't want this magnificent animal to die from one of Robert's twitchy bullets.

Suddenly the leader stopped, stood as still as marble. Tern froze too. Gage and the rest followed suit. Out of the corner of her eye she saw Robert raise his rifle. Then the wolf vaulted into the trees and disappeared.

"What the hell was that?" Robert asked.

"Something spooked him," Tern said, the hair on her arms rose.

"Who spooks a pack of wolves?" Nadia asked, her voice shaky.

Gage kept an eye on Tern as he pushed the group to make some distance between them and whatever—or whoever—startled the wolves.

She didn't look good. Her eyes were dazed and swollen, turning black, her honey-tinted skin pale. She plodded along, not making a sound, and that worried him even more.

Nadia concerned him too. It was quite the coincidence that the cut she'd sustained was in the same place as Tern's childhood scar, slashing through the left eyebrow. Seeing them both side by side, as they sat on that log earlier, with the same hair color and now the same scar, was eerie.

Could Nadia have hit herself, causing a cut the same as Tern's? Or had she been hit at all? If she'd wanted the same distinguishing mark, she'd have to literally cut herself with a knife. Why would she do that? He hadn't noticed any sign of someone else. There were no footprints in the ground around where Tern had taken the hit, other than Nadia's small boot prints.

But someone or something had scared off the wolves.

He didn't know what to think anymore. He'd already brought up the possibility that Nadia could be the one behind this, but Tern had adamantly refused to entertain the idea.

He had a hard time himself wrapping his brain around the idea. Whoever set this geocache hunt in motion had to be strong, knowledgeable, conniving, and have no remorse. How else would the person kill Lucky, chop off his head, and carve words into his forehead? Gage figured it had to take some serious strength to sever through the bones of the spinal cord, not to mention, the muscles, tendons, and arteries that held the head onto the body. The murder was so grisly that it was hard to visualize a woman doing it. Mac was a little more plausible. But then again, words had been carved into his forehead too.

Those crimes didn't fit with Tern getting hit. The others seemed more calculating, while Tern's had more passion behind it. Could Nadia have hit Tern because she was mad at Robert calling out her name? Seemed to Gage, Robert would be the one to have his head bashed in. Not Tern. But then maybe Nadia was just as mad at Tern for being the one Robert would have preferred to be with?

Could they have more than one threat?

Hell. Wolves, weather, deranged killer, and now a jealous woman. Yeah, they were doomed if he didn't hurry and figure a way to get them to safety.

They cleared the trees and came out over a rise that opened to the valley below them. The Yukon River coiled like a forgotten rope in the distance. Sweat dripped down his forehead and under his arms. The skin around the straps of his and Tern's backpacks was being rubbed raw.

Finally seeing the river was like balm to his aches and pains. Soon, maybe tomorrow, they'd reach it. There had to be traffic floating downstream. It was summer. There was tourism, supplies being shipped to small native villages in the arctic, and subsistence fishing. All of it equaled help.

Once they entered the trees again, the Yukon would be lost from sight. For the moment, he just dragged in deep breaths of the sharp clean air and scanned the best route down.

"What's that?" Robert asked, pointing to a large area of broken trees a few miles from them.

It looked as though a swath of trees had been mowed down like they were nothing more than toothpicks.

"Wind couldn't have taken out a section of trees like that," Gage said, a shiver of dread replacing the sweat coating his body. He caught a glint of metal. "There's something reflective down there. We'd better check it out. I'm getting tired of new surprises around every tree and bush."

"It's on the way," Robert said.

Nadia started up again. "I wished we'd stayed at the cabins," She'd been blissfully quiet since the wolf incident.

Tern didn't say anything, which worried Gage even more. The woman needed medical attention. She had a concussion and he didn't know how the hell she was staying on her feet, let alone hiking through the forest. Whatever strength she was drawing on, he was grateful for and even a little in awe of.

Gage cut a trail back into the tree canopy. It wasn't as dense as the last one, and thankfully the mosquitoes weren't as bloodthirsty. What he wouldn't give for some DEET.

An hour or so later they broke through the line of shorn trees. Up ahead were the remnants of a downed airplane. Pieces of red and yellow metal littered the forest floor, causing the reflections they'd seen up on the hill.

Foreboding skittered along his forearms. He'd flown in that plane. They all had.

"Gage?" Tern asked.

"Yeah, I think so," he answered.

"What?" Robert asked. "What are you two talking about? I hate it when people do that."

"Do what?" Nadia asked, huffing as she caught up to them.

"Understand each other without talking. Bugs the crap out of me."

"Robert, look around you," Gage said. "Recognize anything?"

He glanced around and threw his hands up in the air. "What the hell am I going to recognize? Someone's left a lot of junk around."

"Think about it," Gage said.

"Oh no," Nadia whispered. "It's the—" Words seemed to fail her and she turned away from them, covering her mouth with her hand.

"It's what? What the hell are you guys seeing that I'm not?" Robert slapped a half-broken branch out of his way.

"The plane," Gage said, talking slow and even. "The one that flew us here. It never made it back to Fairbanks."

Color drained from Robert's face and he shook his head. He swiveled around, his arms flying out from his sides, his mouth opening and closing. "Can't be. It can't be," he repeated and started hiking through the bigger pieces of debris. He grabbed a large section that had three numbers of the plane's call sign on it. He stared at it for a long time before throwing it away. "Where's the cockpit?"

"There, I'd imagine." Gage gestured to the long path the plane cut through the trees in its attempt to land. "Come on, guys. Nadia?"

Nadia nodded and brought up the rear as they traipsed through the wreckage. There wasn't much of the plane left, but no sign of fire. So maybe the pilot was able to walk away. Gage had heard of miraculous stories about bush pilots crash landing in the worst places and yet still able to walk away. Or at least radio for help. Sometimes even duct tape the plane back together and fly it home.

Radio.

"Gage, the radio," Tern said, echoing his thoughts. "We can call for help."

He nodded, tapping down the hope that had bloomed at the thought. They reached another knoll of sorts, and twenty feet or so below them was the cockpit, resting on the pilot's side, its nose dug into the earth. The wings were completely sheared from what was left of the body of the DeHavilland.

Gage put out his hand and stopped Tern from moving ahead. "Stay here." He caught the stench of decay on the breeze and shrugged out of the backpacks. "Come on, Robert. Let's take a look."

"Man, I can't take looking at another dead body." Robert covered his nose and shook his head, his pale skin developing a hint of green. "Seriously. Can't do it."

Gage gave him a look that spoke volumes. He took a deep breath and headed toward the plane. Tern came with him.

"Tern, I want you to stay here."

"I'll be fine. I have to know."

He tightened his lips but nodded. She followed him toward the cockpit. The passenger door was missing, as was all the sheet metal shirting the plane. Stuffing from the seat cushions littered the ground and the fabric blew in the slight breeze like curtains in an open window. Gage looked inside the cockpit, and dropped his head.

"Is he?"

"Yes. Don't come any closer." The smell triggered Gage's gag reflexes, and it was all he could do not to vomit. He stepped away from the plane. "He's been dead a while. Small animals have been feeding on him and there's insect activity." He turned back to the plane, reached into the cockpit, and fiddled with the radio. Shit. "The radio didn't make it either."

His heart sank. No radio meant no help any time soon. The hope they might be able to call for help died a quick death.

Breathing through his mouth, Gage rummaged through what was left of the cockpit, finding an unopened package of jerky and can of peanuts.

He rejoined Tern and held up the rations.

"Fitting for a pilot to have peanuts on board," she said. A giggle escaped her and she looked horrified. "God, I'm sorry. I don't know why I said that."

"Shock. It's been a hell of a few shocking days. Come on, let's return and report."

They rejoined Robert and Nadia. Robert sat against the trunk of a tree, knees up, hands falling between them. Nadia was against another tree but had her feet stretched out and crossed at the ankles.

"Well?" Nadia asked, sitting up straighter. "Is it Hugh?"

"Yes," Gage said.

"Is he…?"

"Yes."

"Shit," Robert said, throwing a rock into the trees, it crashed through branches as it fell to the earth. "When do you think?"

"By the condition of the body, I think he crashed not long after dropping us off."

"Shit," Robert said again, looking off into the horizon.

"How?" Nadia asked.

"I don't know," Gage said. "The radio is busted."

"Wait a minute," Tern said, rubbing her forehead. "When Hugh didn't report to Chena Marina and close out his flight plan, wouldn't the authorities have sent out a search party?"

"I don't know. Until we make it back to town, we won't know the answers to those questions."

"Well, we know the answer to one question," Tern said. "There wasn't going to be a plane coming back for us on Friday."

CHAPTER THIRTY-ONE

Gage returned to the plane, having partaken of his share of the jerky and nuts. It was a damn sight too coincidental that the pilot who had flown them in to this godforsaken area was dead too. Someone had thought everything out carefully and seemed damned determined not to leave any witnesses. Gage just needed to figure out if it was one of them or someone else.

He wrenched open the hood of the plane. He'd had to use a branch to pry it open like a can opener. He tossed the branch aside and gazed at the engine. Nothing jumped out at him, but then it was a torn-up mess. Crashing a plane through a forest did a number on the engine.

How would someone have sabotaged an airplane without anyone noticing, especially the pilot?

Since it wasn't something he'd ever thought about, he was having a hard time figuring out how someone would go about it. Why take out the pilot? He was their only way off the mountain other than hiking out, which was a crapshoot. The wolves they'd run into earlier in the day were proof of that. If he'd been the one to set this up, he'd first have figured out how to get home. So, he'd either make sure nothing happened to the pilot, carry a radio to call for help, or have another pilot coming in after him. But wouldn't that raise a few brows, when not only had all the people you traveled with ended up dead, but you had a separate pilot pick you up? Talk about wearing a sign for the authorities that screamed 'killer'.

He scrounged around inside the cockpit for anything that he might be able to use, doing his best to ignore the stench of Hugh's decomposing body. When that proved useless, he returned to the engine, hoping it would speak to him.

Poor bastard.

"Hey," Tern said from behind him.

He bumped his head on the hood with surprise. Rubbing his head, he scowled at her. "Shit. Make some noise when you come up behind someone, okay?"

"Sorry."

"I'm a bit on edge." He studied her. "Are you feeling better?"

She hid her hands in the pockets of her hoodie. "A bit. What are you doing?"

"Trying to figure out how someone brought down a plane."

She nodded. "You think the person who killed Mac and Lucky was taking care of loose ends."

She was a smart cookie, he'd give her that. And a sexy cookie too. How did she look so damn attractive out here? Even sporting a couple of black eyes? Nadia wasn't fairing nearly as well. But Tern seemed to have a glow about her. The sun had burnished her honey skin, and auburn highlights were more pronounced in the thick dark hair she'd braided and left to fall down her back. She didn't have on an ounce of makeup and didn't need any other than to help hide the bruising around her dark eyes. Nadia, on the other hand, was sporting blemishes. Her face was sunburned, her fine hair falling lanky on her shoulders. She'd have a tough time getting a brush through the wind-whipped mess.

"What?" Tern brushed her face.

"You look great." He cleared his throat and returned his attention to the mess of engine parts.

"Do you know anything about engines?" she asked.

"Other than the basics, not much. Any idea how someone would have sabotaged an airplane while it was being unloaded?"

She bit her lips, thinking. "They wouldn't have been able to get to the engine. We were all there, including the pilot."

"Right. So something from inside the cockpit." He didn't want to crawl in there again and see Hugh, smell him. Days of decomp had been at work. He doubted he could have stood this close to the plane if the wind hadn't been blowing some of the stench the other direction. They shouldn't stay here long. Bigger predators were going to be attracted to the smell, like the wolves that had given them a pass earlier.

"If someone did mess with the plane, it points to one of us being behind this for sure."

"I know."

"Planes crash all the time. There are more planes per capita in Alaska than any other state."

"I know."

"But you're thinking it was a nice day. The sun had been out, no weather, so why did he go down?"

"Right."

She leaned over to look at the engine. "There's no way to tell if it was mechanical with the engine busted up like this."

"Not until the authorities go through it. We might never know what happened."

"If the killer is one of us, why would they sabotage their only way out of here?"

"I've been asking that myself. It doesn't make sense." He stepped away from the plane and dusted off his hands. "I don't think going over the crash site is doing us any good. I've marked the plane's position with my GPS. There isn't any more we can do." This mission had been doomed from the beginning.

Tern fell into step beside him. "Do you think he was trying to make it to the river to land?"

"Most likely, since he had floats on the plane. He obviously didn't have the altitude to make it to the water. If he had, he might have lived." What had been going through Hugh's mind in those last moments, knowing he was going to die?

Would he go through that before this was over?

They joined Nadia, who was curled up on her side asleep. How did she sleep through this? Robert sat in the same spot they'd left him, looking shell-shocked, an uneaten piece of jerky clutched between his fingers. He glanced up at them as they returned.

"We were never going to get picked up, were we?"

Gage shook his head.

"I've got to get home. Chloe has already lost her mother." He dropped his head to his knees. "What was I thinking, coming on this geocache? I should be at home taking her to her soccer games."

Since Gage agreed with him, there was no point in reassuring him. Robert should've thought about Chloe, rather than looking at the geocache as another way of getting back into Tern's life.

"The only thing we can do is hike on. The sooner we make it to the river, the better our chances."

"Unless the killer is already there waiting for us," Robert said, but he struggled to his feet, noticed the piece of jerky still clutched in his hand and ate it.

"Tern?" Gage brushed his fingers down her arm to get her attention, since she was staring off into space. He wondered what she saw. Did her Athabascan blood speak of their demise or their salvation? She focused on him, her almond-shaped eyes heavy with sadness but also full of resolve. "Wake Nadia. I want to be on the trail in five. I don't like the look of those clouds."

Tern knelt next to Nadia and shook her shoulder, none too gently. Nadia woke with a start and jerked into a sitting position.

She raised her head and looked into Tern's eyes, her voice just loud enough to carry. "Help was never going to come. We're all going to die."

"We're not," Tern said firmly.

"I would have stayed," Nadia continued. "If you guys hadn't forced me to leave, I would have stayed at camp...and died." She dropped her face into her hands. "I don't want to die."

"None of us do. Now snap out of it, Nadia." Tern grabbed Nadia by the arm and helped haul her to her feet. "We need to move and think positive."

Nadia dropped her hands and seemed to give herself a mental shake, but continued to look exhausted and beaten. "Okay. Okay, I'll be fine. Let's go."

Gage didn't know what to think of Nadia. It seemed unlikely that she could be the mastermind behind this, but he wasn't above suspecting everyone until he knew the truth. The only one he trusted was Tern. The woman had never given him a reason not to trust her, while Nadia had.

CHAPTER THIRTY-TWO

Her legs were going to drop off.

Tern trudged along behind Gage trying not to think of how much she hurt. The ache in her skull had bloomed and spread throughout her whole body. The shock of finding the dead pilot and the harsh reality of their situation had set in like an egg timer. Their days were numbered if they didn't find help. If the killer didn't get them first, the Alaskan wilderness would finish them.

They needed to reach the river. All survival guides tell you to head for water. Rivers, and streams, flow downhill toward civilization. But the Yukon River was anything but civilized. It journeyed just shy of two thousand miles, beginning in British Columbia and meandering through the Yukon Territory and Alaska to pour into the Bering Sea through the Yukon-Kuskokwim Delta, the richest fishing grounds in the world. The Yukon River was one of the major means of transportation during the Klondike Gold Rush. Back then many paddle-wheeled boats would have traversed the river. But today fisherman, tourists, and Alaskans used the river for food, entertainment, and transportation. Most would be concentrated around towns and villages.

What were the chances that they would be able to get help clear up here, just south of the Arctic?

What would her family do without her? She didn't want to think these thoughts, but couldn't force them back. Her family had already lost so much with her dad's death. Raven would be okay. She had Aidan and Fox now. Her brother Lynx had his wife Eva and their new little girl. Her mom had just married their Uncle Pike after years of denying her feelings for the big bear of a man. So they had each other. It was her little sister Chickadee that Tern worried about the most. She was almost seventeen and the teenage years were rough. Tern had been about Chickadee's age when their dad was murdered. Their mother would do her best to be there for Chickadee, and so would Raven. Lynx was clueless when it came to the women of the family. When things got all touchy-feely, he went hunting.

Chickadee was so much like Tern. They had a special connection that had been getting stronger and richer since Chickadee had been working with her at the shop on the weekends and holidays, spending the night in Fairbanks with her, too, for that special one-on-one girl time.

Chickadee would be lost.

For that matter, so would Chloe.

It broke Tern's heart not knowing what would happen to the two girls if she and Robert didn't make it back.

She'd never thought about her life in those terms, as she was sure Robert hadn't until now either. Wasn't that how life worked? You thought you were invincible until it became apparent that you weren't. Hell, she didn't even have a last will and testament drawn up. Why should she, when she was only twenty-eight?

Raven would know how she'd want her stuff divided. The shop could go to Chickadee if she wanted it. But then Tern wanted Chickadee to attend college and have that experience. Not be saddled with the heavy responsibility of a business. Raven would think of that, wouldn't she?

Tern didn't have a lot of personal items. Car, clothes, a few pieces of nice jewelry, some art she couldn't bear to sell in the shop and had kept. She had a few lucrative investments. Surely the file would be found and her assets given to those who needed them most? Raven would divide everything between the families. Her most precious possession was the arctic tern her dad carved and she had that on her, thanks to the killer. If she was meant to die, it seemed fitting that the little bird flew with her into the spirit world.

Gage stopped in front of her and she almost ran into the back of him since she was so lost in thought.

"Let's make camp here for the night."

"Thank you, God," Nadia said, dropping her backpack and following it to sprawl on the ground.

Robert groaned as he unclipped the waistband of his large backpack and let it slide down his arms.

Tern wanted to collapse, too, but if she lay down, she wouldn't be getting up again and there was still work to do.

"I'm starving," Robert said.

Case in point, they needed to find food, gather firewood, and erect some sort of shelter. The swollen clouds looked like they were going to dump their contents at any moment.

She was so tired.

"Hey, you okay?" Gage asked.

She nodded. It was too much effort to voice anything, plus she figured if she was able to talk she'd probably cry.

Gage had picked a good spot to stop. It wasn't the Captain Cook Hotel, but there was a small brook for water, soft forest floor to sleep on instead of the rock they'd laid on the previous night. She didn't want to remember what had happened between her and Gage in that cave. Or Nadia and Robert for that matter.

"First on the list is shelter before the rain arrives." Gage gazed up at the darkening sky. "Tern, can you and Nadia see if you can find anything for dinner?"

She nodded again, really glad that she'd remained standing.

"Stay within sight," Gage warned, his eyes traveling over her with worry.

Nadia groaned as she struggled to her feet. Tern wanted to join in the groan, but sound seemed beyond her.

She opened her backpack and grabbed the plastic bladder for water, an extra t-shirt to use as a bag, and headed toward the small brook looking for anything edible.

Nadia trooped behind her. "What I wouldn't give for a cheeseburger. No offense, Tern, but I'm tired of eating like an herbivore."

She grunted her agreement. A cheeseburger with an order of onion rings sounded heavenly. Her stomach growled. She'd never take fast food for granted again.

Scanning the forest floor, there wasn't anything that looked appetizing. Not after the cheeseburger reference.

Tern glanced at the blackening sky for deliverance. The rest of them were counting on her to fill their bellies with something that would silence the biting hunger. She was just so tired, which meant more than ever that she needed to eat. Food was the only thing that would keep up her strength.

Nadia glanced along the banks of the gurgling brook. "So what goodies are you going to pull out of that?" There wasn't a lot of optimism in her tone.

Tern studied the surrounding plants, hoping her headache didn't mess with the knowledge rattling around inside her brain. What if she selected the wrong plant? She picked up a wet stone. "Stone soup?"

Nadia chuckled and then sobered. "I really hope you're not serious?"

Tern shrugged and tossed the stone back into the brook. "Not a lot here." At least, not a lot they could eat that wouldn't cause hallucinations, paralysis, or death. The area was moist and full of moss. She picked a few coltsfoot and handed them to Nadia. While good for menstrual cramps, coltsfoot could also be steamed or sautéed and the roots roasted. Though it wasn't one of her favorites because of its felt-like texture. She found some nagoonberry blossoms and popped a few into her mouth, revealing in the tart raspberry taste. She tied the top of the t-shirt she'd brought into a knot and used it as a container, picking the bush clean of flowers. If it were later in the season, there would be berries similar to raspberries, only bigger and juicer. Like the cheeseburger, there was something to be said for buying produce at the corner store rather than foraging in the forest.

"Unless we go hunting, this is the best I can do." They hadn't seen any animals since they had left the airplane and the dead pilot. They probably carried the stench of death on them and anything with a brain, no matter how small, was giving them a wide berth.

"Seriously?" Nadia asked. "That all you're going to gather? Flowers and stalks?"

"There isn't anything else edible, Nadia."

"What about this? It smells nice." She pointed to a bunch of water hemlock.

"You'll feel like your lungs are drowning as it shuts down your respiratory system."

"Seriously?" she said again, turning back with renewed interest to the plant with orange stalks and fragrant little bunches of white flowers. "Wow. What about this one here?"

"It'll take two to three weeks to kill you, but it will get the job done."

"Wow. I never knew." She gave the greenery around her a look of appreciation.

"Some of the prettiest flowers and plants are the deadliest." Tern took out her knife and cut some bark off a willow tree. She needed to get rid of her plaguing headache. "Come on. Let's fill up the water. I need to get off my feet."

They returned to Robert and Gage and found that the men had built a shelter by cutting and weaving pine branches together. One of the Mylar thermal blankets was pitched like a tent under the pine boughs and would hopefully help with the rain they were going to get. There was maybe three feet of height inside and it spanned just enough distance for the four of them to sleep side by side. Cramped quarters, to say the least, but Tern didn't care. All she wanted to do was crawl in there and sleep.

"No fire?" Nadia asked.

"Plan on getting to it," Robert said, "if the weather holds."

A raindrop hit Tern on the cheek. One drop turned into many, and before they could crawl into the opening the four of them were soaked.

"Well," Robert said with a huff. "At least it isn't snowing."

"Yet," Nadia added under her breath.

Since it could very well be snow they were dealing with rather than rain, like they had a few days ago, Tern found the comment funny. Either that or she was just so tired she was punchy. Whatever the reason, she started to laugh. Instead of humor, the sound held a kind of crazy despair. Gage looked at her with worry but she couldn't seem to stop. It wasn't long before moisture filled her eyes.

Her shoulders shook, her head pounded, and everything went gray and cold. Gage's arm wrapped around her and she didn't care that he'd broken her heart again that morning. She curled into the safety and warmth of his arms and cried.

"Shit, how long is she going to do that?" Robert said.

"As long as she needs to," Gage answered. "Go outside if it bothers you."

"Right, and get wetter than we already are?"

"Take your pick."

"Shit," he said again, scratching the growth of his four-day beard.

Tern didn't care. All she wanted was to be home in her house or at the lodge in Chatanika with her family. The thought of never seeing them again made her sobs come harder. Gage rubbed her back and held her tighter, letting her cry.

"I can't listen to this," Robert said. "Enough already."

"Tern, honey, you're killing me here," Gage whispered in her ear.

"Seriously, Tern, you're going to have us all in tears," Nadia added.

"Look, things aren't that bad," Robert said.

That had her lifting her head and staring at him in shock. "Are you kidding me?" Tern asked. "Tell me how they aren't that bad?"

"Well…we're still alive," Robert pointed out.

"You gotta do better than that." But Tern wiped her eyes and straightened away from Gage. He dropped his arms from around her and she immediately missed his heat.

"We have shelter."

"In a manner of speaking," Nadia grumbled.

"Hey, this is a very cool shelter," Robert said. "One of the best I've ever built."

"Really?" Nadia scoffed.

"With the time constraints and materials I had to work with, and the help." He indicated Gage. "It's not so bad."

"So what now?" Tern asked.

"We wait for the rain to stop," Gage said. "Did you find anything we can eat?"

"Not a lot." She wiped at the moisture on her face. "And I need a fire for half of it."

"Any candy bars left?" Nadia asked.

"A few." Tern grabbed her backpack and unzipped the pocket that held the candy. There were three. "Two of us have to share."

Silence followed her words.

"I'll share," Gage said.

"No, you need it more than I do. Nadia and I should share."

Nadia scowled. "Hey, I don't want to share. I know that sounds bitchy, but I'm hungry and I've been hiking as long and hard as the men."

"So what, you're willing to take it all and leave nothing for someone else?" Tern said.

"Give me all of them." Gage took the three candy bars, opened them and used his pocketknife to cut each of them until they all had equal parts. "We all share."

He handed out the bits of chocolate and it was quiet again while they slowly chewed, savoring the small bites, except for the rain splashing on the survival blanket over the pine branches. The air was crisp and clean smelling of freshly cut pine boughs, making her long for Christmas. Would she see another Christmas?

"I'm still hungry," Nadia said. Her voice had an angry whine to it. "What about that stuff you picked?"

"I wanted to make a soup of sorts out of it. Some of it will be bitter, like collard greens. Heating them will improve their taste. But we can eat the nagoonberry blossoms." She uncovered the blooms from the t-shirt bag she'd used to gather them and placed the fuchsia colored flowers where everyone could reach them.

"Flowers?" Nadia said. "I'm not a goat. I hate eating all this crap."

"Beats eating nothing at all," Gage said, helping himself to a handful of blossoms.

"Why are you being so bitchy?" Robert asked Nadia, taking a few flowers and testing their taste on a petal before popping the rest into his mouth.

"Why do you think, genius? I hate it here. I'm hungry, wet, dirty, cold, and scared. Those are pretty damn good reasons to be bitchy."

"Fine, but don't direct it at Tern. It's not her fault."

"Actually, it is. None of us would be here if it wasn't for her."

Tern tried to ignore the barb Nadia flung her way. She was just scared and angry and hungry. Nothing Nadia said was what she really meant. Just like the tears that had swamped Tern, Nadia's anger was her way of coping with their dire situation.

"It's nobody's fault except whoever is behind it all," Gage said. He gave Robert a pointed look.

"What are you looking at me for?"

"If I'm not mistaken, you have a pilot's license," Gage said. "You would know how to sabotage Hugh's airplane when we were occupied unpacking."

"Hey, I didn't touch the man's plane. I had nothing to do with all of this, and I'm sick of you fingering me for it."

"He's got a point," Nadia said. "And I think I remember that the police investigated you over your wife's death. Any truth to you killing her?"

The rain suddenly seemed like sharp pings of ice hitting the survival blanket in the following silence to where before it had been soothing. Now it sliced like Nadia's words.

"What's she talking about, Robert?" Tern asked.

His face turned red, and so did his eyes. He squeezed them shut as he dragged in deep breaths. "You really are a bitch, Nadia. I can't believe I—shit." He pinched the bridge of his nose as though to keep his emotions at bay.

"What happened, Robert?" Gage said, quiet and reassuring, the voice of a confidant.

"I killed my wife." When he raised his head, tears flooded his red-rimmed eyes. "She was everything to me. When she got breast cancer, she was positive she'd beat it. She was so damn optimistic that she had me believing it too. Even when they carved her up, butchered her breasts from her body, we still had hope. But then the cancer went to her bones. She was only twenty-nine. Chloe was three. How does cancer kill you at twenty-nine?" He dropped his head again and swore, angrily wiping away tears. "She was in so much pain. They'd given her weeks, maybe a month to live. She begged me to end her suffering." He raised his head and looked at Tern.

She gasped, seeing all the love and grief he still felt shining in his eyes.

"How could I say no?" he asked. "What kind of coward was I if I couldn't grant her dying wish? There was nothing else I could do to ease her suffering, except help her end it."

Holy cow, Tern had no idea. Robert was a hell of a lot deeper than she ever figured. He'd never let on that he could feel like this. That he could love like this.

"Shit. I can't—" Robert crawled out into the rain and was gone. He blended right into the forest as he disappeared.

Tern made to go after him but Gage grabbed her arm. "Let him go."

"But he could be in danger."

"Give him some time. He'll be okay."

"Why did you do that?" Tern asked Nadia.

Nadia dropped her head in her hands. "I don't know." She fisted her hands in her hair. "I'm just so damn scared and frustrated."

"We all are, but that doesn't give you the right to attack him like that."

Nadia's eyes narrowed before she dropped her gaze. "You're right. I'll apologize when he returns."

The rain continued to pour with no sign of stopping. The ground they sat on was being overcome with the runoff needing some place to go. Water seeped in and soaked their clothes where they sat. It was going to be a miserable night.

Then they heard Robert shout.

Chapter Thirty-Three

"Get out here, guys!" Robert hollered.

Tern's heart, which had jumped at Robert's first shout, bumped back into a normal rhythm, though she still felt light-headed.

"This had better be good or I'm going to kill him," Gage said. He crawled out of the shelter and held a hand out for Tern and Nadia.

"Bring all the gear," Robert yelled. His voice came from the south, but they couldn't see him.

"What the hell?" Gage said, gathering up his backpack and Robert's, and then wrestled Tern for hers. She didn't have the strength and didn't put up much of a fight. Her headache had subsided to a constant throb, one that she thankfully could handle. There were other things that she couldn't. Rain slashed her face and dripped down her neck. She hated being wet and cold. Being wet on a sandy beach in the tropics was a hell of lot better than the wilds of Alaska. She tried to visualize herself in a sunny spot with the rays of the sun shooting through a steamy tropical downpour, but she couldn't pull it off.

"Wish I had someone to carry for me," Nadia grumbled, hitching her pack onto her shoulders and ripping down the Mylar blanket. "She isn't the only one who got bashed in the head today."

"But she's the only who was really hurt," Gage said.

"Hey, I was bleeding."

"Not long enough to be of real concern." Gage turned his back on Nadia and hollered to Robert, "Where the hell are you?"

"Head south, across the brook. You'll see me."

"I hope this isn't a trap." Gage handed his rifle to Tern. "Be ready for anything."

"You don't think someone has Robert, and is using him to get us out into the open?" Tern asked.

"With the way this crazy trip keeps twisting, I wouldn't be surprised if aliens landed and asked me to take them to my leader. Just be on your guard, okay?"

"I want to go home," Nadia said.

They ignored her and crossed the brook, following the trail Robert had left. He hadn't been covert in his wanderings. They trudged through the thick trees, ending in a small oasis of a meadow. A pond, with a pair of nesting swans that would make a fine dinner, was at one end, being fed by the brook. Wildflowers bloomed like confetti. The wet smell of earth and rich plants thickened the air. It was a truly enchanting spot.

"Over here," Robert shouted. They still couldn't see him, but Tern noticed the sharp line of a roof in the mountain side, nearly taken over by the vegetation.

"Is that…"

"I sure as hell hope so," Gage said. They trudged through the tall wet grasses toward the structure. As they ventured closer, an old sod cabin materialized. It blended into the trees, the logs having been overgrown with moss and the sod roof blooming with flowers making it a part of the landscape.

Nadia screamed and fell.

"Careful, there's a fence of sorts!" Robert yelled.

"Would have been nice to know that ahead of time," Nadia complained, pulling herself up from the ground.

"You okay?" Tern asked. By the look on Nadia's face, she was ready to hurt someone.

"Yeah, just tripped." She rubbed at a muddy spot on her shin.

Robert appeared from inside the open door of the cabin. "I tripped in the same spot, that's how I noticed this." He held his arms out as though he was presenting them with the keys to the town hall. "Isn't it great?" A smile stretched across his face, a welcome relief from his earlier grief.

"It's perfect, Robert," Tern said, giving him a genuine smile.

"Way to go," Gage added.

"It's a dump," Nadia said.

"You're more than welcome to use the crappy shelter we built." Robert smirked as Nadia shut her mouth. He gestured wide with his hand. "Come in. Let me give you a tour. It's fascinating." Robert disappeared into the dark shadows of the cabin.

Gage entered first, and by the tension in his shoulders, he was ready for anything. Tern was next, followed by Nadia. It took a minute for her eyes to adjust to the darkened interior but when she did, it was like traveling back in time.

"Wow," she said, venturing farther into the one room cabin. There was an old potbelly stove in the corner, a stack of chopped wood waiting to be used. A hand pump sat on the counter with a tin bowl for a sink. In the opposite corner rested a double bed, all made up with a quilt that had faded to cream. Dust covered everything. There were fine shafts of light coming in through the rough degraded chinking of the logs, but they left the door open in order to bring in more.

"Look." Robert produced a can without the label. "What do you think is in this?"

"Nothing I want to eat," Nadia said, with a curl of her lips. "What about botulism? You don't even know how old it is."

"It isn't bulging." Robert studied the mystery can. "It's steel instead of aluminum so maybe thirty years give or take. I say we open it and take a look. It would have been frozen nine months of every year it was out here, so it can't be that bad."

"Don't let your hunger make you stupid," Gage said, but then shrugged. "What the hell, open it. We'll take a look. I'm not above walking on the wild side in order to quiet my stomach."

"I don't care if it isn't inedible. I'm just so happy to be out of the rain," Tern said. "Thanks, Robert, for wandering off." She put a hand on the back of his shoulder, offering a bit of comfort for his wife's death.

"Anytime," he said quietly, understanding.

"Let's see if we can warm this place up." Gage set his bundle down and knelt by the potbelly stove. "Whoever left this place was planning to return. I wonder how many decades ago that was?" He opened the stove and barked out a laugh. "There's a fire already set. See any matches?"

"You're not going to burn down the place if you light up that thing, are you?" Nadia asked. A scowl seemed to have permanently taken up residence on her face.

Gage looked at the rough log ceiling and back to the stove. "No, I don't think so. Whoever built all the way out here had planned to stay for a while. This was no slapstick shack."

"I think the meadow outside was cleared to build this cabin," Robert said. "Whoever homesteaded this area might have tried raising animals. It would explain the remains of the fence out there."

"Who would live all the way out here?" Nadia asked.

"A lot of people settled all over Alaska looking to escape for some reason or another," Tern said. "The town of Ruby isn't far from here, if I have my bearings right. Maybe a hundred miles or so. You have to remember that Ruby was a huge gold strike. This place was crawling with gold prospectors back in the early nineteen hundreds. Ruby rivaled Fairbanks for the center of civilization in Alaska." She looked around. "I'd say whoever built this cabin wasn't mining for gold. Miners were a tent-city kind of people. This guy wanted to put down roots. Plus, by the looks of what's left here, I'd say it's roughly fifty to seventy years old. And he had a woman with him."

"What makes you say that?" Robert asked.

"The quilt, the neatness." She picked up a porcelain teacup covered in dust and trailing a few cobwebs. "The knickknacks."

"Wonder what happened to them?" Nadia asked.

"Probably sickness, or the harshness of winter was more than they counted on." Tern shrugged. "Who knows?"

"They'd planned on coming back," Gage said, taking the lighter Robert offered him to start the fire. "The place is laid out in welcome." The flame caught on the bits of dried moss and licked the kindling until the flames greedily ate at the bigger logs. Gage looked above him to the stove pipe. "Now we just hope there isn't anything stuck in the pipe, like a buildup of creosote."

They all waited with baited breath, but the smoke continued up the pipe and out.

"I think we're good," Gage said, closing the door to the stove and adjusting the damper.

"Now, if we had some caribou steaks to cook," Robert said, rubbing his hands and holding them out for the heat. "Illegal or not, I'd settle for those swans swimming on the pond out front."

Tern looked around the neatly organized cabin. Other than dust, she doubted anyone had been in this place since the people who'd lived here had left. Even animals had left it alone. Tern studied the cabin joists. The man had been a decent carpenter. She'd seen cabins made like this. They were partially dug out of the earth, and the earth was laid back on top of the roof to add in insulation for the brutal winters and cooling for the summers.

There were people in Fairbanks who still lived in cabins constructed like this one. Her eyes followed the joists to where they met the walls. They were hand notched, snug and tight much the way the Chatanika lodge was that her father had built with the help of his father.

"This place gives me the creeps," Nadia said, rubbing her hands up and down her arms.

"I love it," Tern said.

"It's a damn sight better that than shelter Gage and I threw together," Robert said, grinning from ear to ear. He unzipped his jacket. "And downright cozy. I'm already warming up."

Gage unzipped his jacket too. "Great job, Robert. Finding this place."

"It's more like it found me." His smile turned goofy. "Weirdest thing. I felt kinda pulled here, and then when I was calling myself every kind of fool and started back, I tripped and saw it. It was like someone was leading me here. You don't think it could have been the spirit of my wife, do you?" He blushed as he spoke the words.

Tern walked up to him and laid her hand on his arm. "Maybe. This place is charmed."

"Charmed?" Nadia scoffed. "Like as in spells and witchcraft?"

"In a way. See here—" she pointed out the things she'd noticed "—in the old ways we used to protect our homes with herbs that deterred insects and such. A lot of tribal people practice what you would call pagan rituals as a means of protection. Today we know that the reason the dried plants protected against animals is because the plants produce a strong repellant that human noses can't detect. Whoever built this cabin had knowledge of such things."

"I don't believe in any of that stuff," Nadia said.

Tern studied her. Nadia was obviously agitated. Something here was bothering her, while the three of them seemed almost at peace. "Are you allergic to anything, Nadia?"

"Why?"

"It would explain why you're apprehensive about this place and the rest of us aren't. Something's got under your skin."

All eyes turned on Nadia, and she took a step back. "If I am, I don't know what it is. But this place makes my skin crawl."

"Well, you have a choice to stay here out of the rain and cold, or camp outside in the elements," Gage said. He actually seemed okay with her leaving. Even Robert seemed as though he liked the prospect.

"No one is going anywhere," Tern said. "Come on, Nadia, let's see if there's anything we can salvage from the cupboard. I don't want to eat whatever is in that can either."

"What?" Robert shrugged. "If we cook it, that should kill whatever might have taken up residence."

"You're gross," Nadia said.

"I'm game," Gage said.

"Must be a guy thing." Tern shook her head and smiled for the first time that day. Amazing what a roof and some heat could do to lighten a mood.

"Let's make a clothes line," Gage said to Robert. "More of our clothes are wet than dry."

"Smashing idea."

Nadia joined Tern in the little area cornered off for the kitchen. Other than the water pump, tin bowl for a sink, it was made up of a long split log for a counter and rough cut timbers for cabinets. Someone had used fabric, sewed in a casing, and strung string through it to make a curtain for cupboard doors. Tern very carefully moved the fragile fabric aside. It was thin and had a faded pattern of might have been sailboats.

There were more cans on the shelves, but also coffee canisters. A sniff identified one full of cocoa.

Nadia gasped. "Hot chocolate?"

"Looks like it."

She also found powdered milk, sugar, and flour, all sealed tight from bugs. She could work with this. There were also bowls, utensils, pots and pans, all meticulously put away. A woman had definitely worked in this kitchen. Tern glanced around the cabin. Had there been children?

"Here." She handed the bowl to Nadia. "I need this washed out and filled with water. Robert, would you go with her to get some water?"

"You betcha," Robert grabbed for his jacket.

"Someone's done a three-sixty," Nadia mumbled.

"You seem upset about that. What's your deal?"

"I don't know. I just don't like any of this."

"None of us like it. We're coping because we have to."

Nadia sighed. Tern watched her leave with Robert. She needed to find some alone time to talk with Nadia even though that was the last thing she wanted to do. The woman was driving her nuts. She caught Gage's eyes on her. On the other hand, Gage was also driving her crazy. Only in another way completely.

"Need anything?" he asked.

"Plenty," she said before the filter closed between her brain and mouth. His eyes heated and she knew hers had done the same. She turned back to the kitchen and resumed her rummaging.

"What can I help with?"

She cleared her throat. "Dust. Let's see if we can't dust this place out."

"Okay." Gage headed straight for the bed and carefully folded the corners of the quilt on top of itself before picking it up and taking it outside to flip it out under the roof-covered front of the cabin. He returned much sooner than she'd hoped. But he concentrated on what she'd asked him to, and when Robert and Nadia returned they had the kitchen wiped down. The place was looking downright homey.

As a summer place, it would be the perfect getaway.

There were simple carvings of fish, bear, wolves, and other animals harder to identify as the carver hadn't been that talented. She wished there were some writings or a journal to give a history of the people who'd lived here.

"No journal, I bet," Gage said. She jerked at his words. "What?" he asked.

"I was just thinking journal and then you said it." She hated that she was so in tuned with him or him with her, and pointed to the carvings sitting on the shelf, hoping to change the subject. "One of the occupants was probably Native Alaskan. Yupik or Athabascan. They told stories from generation to generation using carvings like that. Not much was written down. We'll probably never know."

"There might be record of this place. Someone had tried to homestead the area, maybe there are records in the borough. When we get back, I'll look into it."

He turned and tested the wooden chair by the stove. It held his weight, but a heavier weight settled on her heart. He was the perfect man for her. Other than his unwillingness to love her, that was.

Boy, could she pick them.

There was a sharp crack of a rifle repeating. Gage jumped to his feet and grabbed his gun. Tern's heart did a back flip. Not now. Not when they were warm and out of the elements.

They waited breathlessly for another shot and another, having decided when they'd left camp to keep to Mac's warning shot patterns.

They didn't move for a few minutes, and then Gage struggled into his jacket.

"You're not going out there."

"I have to. I know the other shots weren't fired, but I need to know that they are okay."

"I'll go with you."

"No, stay. It's warm and dry in here. The only way in is through the front door. You can take out any threat before they cross the threshold." He stared at her for a long minute before opening the door and walking through it, closing it behind him.

But how did she know which one of them was the enemy?

She palmed her pistol. She shouldn't have let Gage go out there alone. There was no one to protect his back. Did the woman who'd lived here have the same thoughts about her man that Tern was having? Had he left, leaving her behind, and then never returned? Had she died of a broken heart? As surely as Tern knew the sun wasn't setting tonight, she knew that if something happened to Gage, part of her would die too.

There weren't any windows to peek out of. Just the door. As protection it worked both for and against. No one would get past her, but then she could be trapped with no way out.

Tern heard Nadia's cry and her heart missed a beat. What the hell had happened now? She inched the door open. Gage and Robert flanked Nadia. Robert had a skinned animal by the feet. Nadia held her hands out in front of her, porcupine quills piercing her palms.

"Oh my," Tern said, biting back her smile of relief at seeing them. "What happened?"

Robert was the first to answer, as Gage was having trouble speaking past his obvious need to laugh. "Nadia scared off the swans, but tripped on this little guy. She now has a higher respect for our needled friend here."

While porcupine wasn't Tern's favorite animal, it would make a decent stew with the plants she'd already picked. She took the gutted and skinned carcass from Robert. She'd gladly handle the animal. Robert could take care of Nadia.

They entered the cabin, shaking the water from their hair and taking off their jackets, hanging them up to dry. Gage took out his Leatherman from his pocket and handed it to Robert.

"Thanks," Robert said, the sarcasm coming out clearly in his tone.

"Don't mention it," Gage said, joining Tern in the corner of the kitchen. "Tell me you have more chores for me?" he asked under his breath.

Nadia screamed, making them all wince.

"Please," Gage said, his eyes pleading.

"Water? Doesn't look like Nadia washed my bowl or got me any water."

"How the hell was I going to do that when the porcupine attacked me?" Nadia screeched.

Guess they could be heard no matter how low they kept their tones.

"Attacked you, huh?" Robert said. "That's not how I saw it go down."

"Well, that's how this story is going to be retold. Got it?"

"Whatever you say, babe."

"Don't 'babe' me. That's such a sexist thing. And an easy cover when you can't remember who you're screwing."

Robert lowered his head toward her. "I said I was sorry for that. It was a slip. That's all."

"Right, I'd buy that if you called out your dead wife's name, but not Tern's."

Did they have to revisit this subject?

"Uh…I'll be back in a few," Gage said, grabbing another bowl.

"Coward," Tern muttered, wishing she could go with him. The cabin was way too small with all the baggage suddenly packed into it.

"Genius. Not coward," Gage said.

She looked with envy at his retreating back.

"I really am sorry," Robert said, blowing on the skin punctured by the quill he'd just pulled out.

"Yeah, whatever." Nadia straightened her shoulders and looked away from what Robert was doing.

Tern took out her knife and began butchering the porcupine into small stew bites. She rolled them in flour and salt and pepper—salt and pepper! How'd she missed that the last few days. There wasn't any oil, but she figured they'd have to do with the fat from the porcupine. She put a pan on the stove and let it heat. When it was hot, she added the porcupine, caramelizing the bits of meat. The sizzle had her stomach waking up. It had kind of shut down over the last few days of not eating much.

"You really need to wash your hands and disinfect them if we can," Robert said.

"You see any disinfectant?" Nadia flicked a glance around the cabin. "Tell you what, why don't you run down to the store and pick us up some."

"You know, Nadia, I've apologized. I didn't mean to hurt you, but being a bitch isn't endeared you to any of us."

Robert stood, the legs of the wooden chair strapping on the plank floor. "I'll be outside."

Robert shut the door behind him.

"Do you think I'm out of line?" Nadia asked Tern

"I don't know. If a man did that to me, I'd probably react the same." She couldn't imagine how devastated she'd feel if

Gage called out another woman's name when she was with him. If Robert had, she knew she wouldn't take it as hard, but she'd still be royally pissed.

"Sometimes it's easy to hate you," Nadia said.

"What?" Tern faced her.

"You seem to have everything together. Men, career, family."

"I don't have it all together, Nadia. Don't be jealous of me." Her heart hurt from the statement. "Tell me you don't really feel that way?"

"It's just that gathering men seems so easy for you. Look at the great men you've had in your life. Well, Robert might have missed the mark there, but Lucky was fun and cool. And Mac. Gage—" she sighed "—being with him, well…yes, I guess sometimes I am jealous."

"I've lost all those men too," Tern pointed out. There was a hole in her heart for each one of them, though Robert's hole was more for his daughter than him. "There's nothing about my relationships to be jealous of." Especially, Gage's. Now, if she'd been able to keep him, maybe.

"Sorry, Tern. I've just been so angry since Robert called out your name."

"It doesn't do you any good to focus on it. You seem to be losing it, Nadia. Somehow you got to keep it together a little longer. We'll be home soon."

"Right." She didn't sound convinced.

CHAPTER THIRTY-FOUR

Gage gathered water and set it inside the cabin, then grabbed his bathing supplies from his backpack and headed right back outside.

"Think the coast is clear?" Robert said.

"You're an ass, Robert."

"I know."

"How do you fuck the best friend of the woman you claim to love—right next to her? And then you mess up her name. Yeah, you're an ass." Gage shook his head, returning to the pond and stripping his clothes off. He was already wet and cold.

Robert saw what he was doing and did the same.

So much for some alone time.

The pond was clear and about the same temperature as the rain—which was more of a mist than a downpour—but it didn't have him languishing over his bath. Besides, bathing with another guy gave him the willies.

A good scrubbing had him feeling more civilized and less mountain man. He tossed his soap to Robert, rinsed, and climbed out of the pond.

And found Tern.

At some point during his wash, she must have opened the cabin door. She stood watching him, and the heat of her gaze had any 'shrinkage' problem from the cold pond water disappearing in a hurry. She didn't turn her gaze away, her eyes roaming down every inch of his skin.

Damn, he loved that about her. She wasn't embarrassed over his nudity, and she'd never been embarrassed over hers when she was with him. He suddenly remembered the morning she'd cooked omelets for breakfast wearing nothing but a dishtowel.

How the hell was he going to live without her as a part of his life?

"Move it, man," Robert said. "I'm near frozen."

Gage was anything but cold now. Robert caught Tern watching them and immediately covered himself. "Damn, woman, give a guy some notice."

Tern ignored him, her attention centered on Gage. For a moment, he wished that this was his cabin and Tern his woman, and Robert and Nadia were anywhere but here.

Tern left the covered roof of the cabin and slowly sauntered toward him, her eyes never leaving his. Robert took one look at her and scowled. "You gotta be shittin' me."

"Get," Gage ground out.

Robert was smart enough to grab his clothes and run for the cabin. Gage heard the door shut behind Robert, and wished he had the strength to turn away from her. Tern had him snared. Some magical power that swam in her rich Athabascan blood had him unable to glance away. She reached a fallen log and deposited a bundle of clothes and toiletries he hadn't realized she carried.

The rain had finally stopped, but the air had turned foggy, leading a more enchanted flare to the glistening forests.

Tern toed off her shoes, bent and pulled off her socks.

He needed to move. Grab his clothes and follow Robert's sorry ass into the cabin. But for some reason he no longer wanted to save himself from Tern. Part of him knew he'd been a goner this morning when he'd barely stopped himself from taking her in the cave, right next to Nadia and Robert. No matter how turned on he'd been, he wasn't participating in an orgy with those two dingbats.

Tern straightened and his heart stuttered as she purposely strode toward him. There was a promise in her eyes that told him he'd better run now or he was hers forever.

A shiver danced over his skin.

Her fingers grabbed the hem of her sweatshirt, slowly pulling it off, leaving her bare from the waist up. He'd removed her bra earlier that morning when helping her dress and he'd tried all damn day to forget that she was bare under her top. Her honeyed breasts tightened with the cold but she didn't seem to mind. Her nipples hardened to rosy buds, and his mouth watered. She flicked the button open to her cargo pants and dragged down the zipper. In one move, she stripped off her pants along with her underwear.

She was enchanting. She paused to free her hair from her braid, her hair flowing loose around her shoulders, and falling down her back.

He couldn't move. All he could do was stare.

A few more steps and she reached him. In one fluid movement, she wrapped her arms around his neck and pulled his mouth down to hers.

Christ.

On a tortured sound, he clamped his arms around her, yanking her flush against him. Her breasts seared where they pressed against his chest. Her nipples stabbed. His heart pounded with fear and excitement. He needed to push her away, untangle her from around his body and his soul.

He never should have let her touch him.

How did he keep himself from being enslaved by her if he gave in and had her again? He'd be lost, forever hers.

As if knowing the direction of his thoughts, her hand snaked down between them and wrapped around his throbbing shaft. He groaned, thrusting into her tight grip.

Who the hell was he kidding? He was already hers. Had been from the moment he'd first seen her.

He'd done nothing but think of her, dream of her, miss her, wish for her. You name it. His world had consisted of Tern from the moment they'd met. There was nothing worth living without her.

He needed to tell her that.

After this morning, he'd known how deeply he'd hurt her, had hoped it would push her away. But here she was bringing him to climax with just the touch of her hand.

"Tern—"

"Shh." Her mouth took his again as her hand increased the friction on his shaft until his eyes rolled back in his head.

He grabbed her hand, bringing the blissful motion to an end, and took a moment to drag air into his lungs, but then she squeezed her fist around him.

"God, Tern. Not like this." He pried open her grip, and then buried his fingers in the heat between her legs. She whimpered, and her knees buckled. He grabbed her close to him again, keeping her from falling. "I need to come inside you. Later, if you want, you can have at me."

Her startled eyes met his. She licked her lips. "Okay."

Decision made, he gave in. He loved her, and he was too tired of fighting her, fighting himself, and fighting this.

Slowly he leaned down and gently kissed her, gliding over the softness of her full mouth. Her lips parted and yet he continued to innocently kiss her.

She bit his bottom lip.

Damn, he loved a woman who demanded what she wanted. He anchored his hands in her hair, and dived into the depths of her mouth, tangling with her tongue. She gasped and curved against him. They stood pressed against each other, naked in the damp air, surrounded by the lush Alaskan wilderness. An extreme paradise. They could be Adam and Eve, and he wished for one fleeting moment that they could stay here. Just the two of them. Forever.

He grabbed her ass in his palms and hiked her up, impaling her on his aching shaft. A cry of pleasure escaped Tern, and her head arched back. He refused to move, holding her suspended in his arms. He wanted time to adjust to her heat, her tightness, and give her time to adjust to him as well. As it was, he didn't know how he remained standing with her wet heat holding him locked and sheltered within her body. He couldn't resist nuzzling her throat, then traveling down her collarbone, to the sweet fullness of her breasts.

A raven cawed overhead. A slight rustling in the bushes signaled a small animal and reminded him that they weren't totally alone. He strolled with her, lashed tight against him with his arms, enjoying the movement of each step as it raised and lowered her in a slow friction on his shaft. Soft, mewing sounds came from her throat, and she sank her head into the crook of his shoulder, her nails digging into his back. He wanted to grab her hips and thrust deep inside her. So deep that he left his own mark. Branded her as his woman.

Could he enslave her as she so easily seemed to enslave him?

He sank with her into the middle of the pond, her gasp echoing his. The heat of their bodies could have raised steam off the surface of the placid water. The water afforded them some privacy, not that it mattered, but more importantly it offered buoyancy. And since there wasn't a bed nearby to fall into, he needed the extra help in order to take her the way his body demanded.

He wanted to hammer into her until his brain exploded, wanted to touch and mark every inch of her gold-dusted skin. She grabbed his hair and pulled his head back, using the lift of the water to piston herself over him. Her legs were a vice around his hips, holding him tight within her, as she took his mouth, her tongue spearing deep, while her body took his.

His hands caressed her breasts, squeezed. He captured a nipple between his fingers and tweaked hard, harder when she cried out and tightened her hands in his hair. Her hips moved faster on him, and he forgot about her beautiful breasts as the focus of his world centered on bringing her climax. He grasped her hips, taking control, bracing his feet farther apart and plunging inside her.

A cry broke free of her lips, and her head fell back, her throat exposed, her dark, raven hair, shot with fire, floating on the agitated surface of the water.

Feelings churned inside him. Tern's breathing skipped and a long drawn out moan echoed in the stillness as she came, her inner muscles wringing out his own shout of pleasure as he held her tight against him and pulsed deep inside her.

Her head fell forward onto his shoulder and her arms wrapped around his neck. "Now that is the only way I want to bathe from now on." She purred in his arms and he tightened them around her.

He chuckled. "I'll see what I can do." He nuzzled her neck, loving how she arched giving him more access. He hadn't spent a lot of time on the niceties of lovemaking the last few times they'd come together.

Movement out of the corner of his eye caught his attention. He looked up from running kisses down Tern's neck and saw Nadia watching them from the doorway of the cabin. A tremor of unease snaked through him.

He needed to come clean about her too.

CHAPTER THIRTY-FIVE

"We have company," Gage muttered.

Tern nestled deeper in his arms, wanting their time to last a little longer. She felt pleasantly buzzed. Gage's skin was hot and slick along the length of hers, a nice contrast to the cool water brushing where his skin wasn't touching hers. His hands continued to leisurely travel up and down her back, pausing to squeeze the cheeks of her ass with another small thrust as though he couldn't help himself. He still lay heavy and hard inside her, causing her inner muscles to contract around him. Her hand dipped to his backside and his shaft pulsed inside her.

"Tern." He growled, his mouth nibbled on her shoulder, and his hand cupped the underside of her breast. "Nadia's right over there."

Slivers of irritation intruded on the moment. While she hadn't given a thought to Robert and Nadia catching her and Gage devouring each other, now that the haze of passion had cleared somewhat—give them a few minutes and that fog was bound to return—knowing Nadia was purposely watching had anger heating her blood. "Let her watch." She reached up and kissed him.

Gage groaned and tore his mouth free. "Tern, there's something I need to tell you about Nadia."

"I don't want to talk about her. I don't want to talk about us. Hell, I don't want to talk at all." She pulled his mouth down again. This time he sank into her kiss, his hands getting back with the program of stroking her up and down like a cat. She liked it. Wanted more, wanted so much more loving from him that she couldn't walk afterward.

"Tern." Gage pulled away from her, his eyes seemed feverish with intent. "We have to talk."

Ah hell. Just when things were going the way she wanted them. Sounded like she needed to be dressed for this. She untangled herself from the warmth of Gage's muscled body, and swaggered out of the pond, letting her hips sway left to right. A smile quirked her lips when she heard him groan behind her. That ought to teach him.

Nadia still stood on the path from the cabin to the pond. "Have a good time?" she asked.

"Why don't you tell me?" Tern answered, picking up her clothes, struggling commando into her slightly damp cargo pants and sweatshirt.

"You made enough noise to pinpoint our location to whoever is after us," Nadia snapped. There was a nastiness in her eyes that had Tern slowing her movements and cocking her head for a better look.

"What? It's okay for you to get it on with an audience, but not me?"

"I'm just saying, now might have not been the best time for you to fuck him."

"That's enough, Nadia," Gage said, coming up behind Tern, buttoning his pants, a forgotten t-shirt hanging in his hand. "Why were you spying on us?"

"Sounded like someone was dying. Besides, it's not like there's a TV to switch on." She sauntered closer to Gage, licked her lips, and trailed her fingers down his bare chest. "Ever thought of trying a threesome?"

Tern growled, pushing between Nadia and Gage, forcing Nadia back. "What is with you?"

"It's not like I haven't been touched by him before," Nadia smirked. "Though never quite like that."

Gage stiffened behind her, and Tern suddenly felt the cold of the evening chill settle into her bones. "Excuse me?"

Nadia arched her newly cut brow. The action and resulting expression was so like one of Tern's that she shivered.

"You never told her about us?" Nadia asked Gage with a pout in her tone.

"Told me what?" Tern had a chilling feeling she knew what Nadia was implying.

"Tern, we need to talk," Gage said, laying his hand on her shoulder.

She shrugged it off and spun toward him. "You slept with her?"

"Now, why say it like that?" Nadia said. "Like it's something to be ashamed of. I have very fond memories of our night together."

"Tern, it was nothing." Gage's words came fast, tumbling over themselves. "A few dates and the one night when we'd had too many drinks at a University function. It was over a year and half ago. Way before I met you."

"It wasn't nothing to me," Nadia said, her tone trying to sound hurt, but coming out more biting instead.

Tern swiveled and pinpointed Nadia with a stare. "Why didn't you tell me? You're supposed to be my friend. Friends don't keep things like sleeping with my boyfriend a secret."

"Boyfriend? Is that what he is to you? He left you without a word, besides you weren't together that long. There was no point in telling you."

"Hey," Robert said, at some point having joined them. Not that any of them noticed until he spoke. "What's all the drama?"

"Shut up," Tern and Nadia said together.

His eyes widened, and his mouth flopped open once and then closed. He might be smarter than Tern had given him credit for.

"Tern," Gage said, taking her elbow. "I wanted to tell you, but the time never seemed right."

She wrenched her arm free and took a few steps back. "You couldn't have mentioned it before?" Did she have everything wrong? She'd thought they had been together, a couple, exclusive. For her there hadn't been any time for someone else. If she'd slept with his best friend previous to their relationship, she'd have told him. "We've been together nonstop the last four fucking days and you never had a moment to tell me that you'd slept with Nadia? Don't give me that bullshit."

"Whoa," Robert said with a gasp. "Gage and Nadia?" He turned toward Nadia. "Is there anyone on this trip that you haven't spread your legs for?"

Nadia let her hand swing. It connected with a loud smack across Robert's cheek. "You're a bastard," she spat.

Robert cupped his cheek and flexed his jaw. "Holy hell, did you sleep with Mac too?" His eyes widened with dread. "Is anyone using any freaking condoms? Shit, do I need to get tested?"

Silence spilt the open meadow, even the birds had the sense to hush as the repercussions ping-ponged between the four of them.

In a nauseating way, they had all slept together.

Tern's head pounded with the disturbing information. She'd been with only four men in her whole life. Nadia had admitted to being with the same men. No that wasn't right. It couldn't be right. She hadn't slept with Mac, had she? Tern suddenly felt the need to throw up.

Nadia turned toward Robert, her fingers in the shape of claws. A deep scary sound came from her throat. Tern grabbed her by the waist in case she went for Robert. They were all going to kill each other if someone didn't start thinking rationally.

"Shake it off, Nadia," Tern gritted out. "Robert, apologize."

"You are one crazy bitch." Robert slowly backed up not taking his eyes from Nadia. He continued his careful retreat until he was at the door of the cabin.

Nadia shuttered. Tern felt the tension in her body and didn't blame her for wanting to go after Robert. Tern wouldn't mind having a go at Gage, who continued to stand stoic next to her. Betrayal beat at her from both sides, and Tern didn't know which to examine first. The betrayal of her best friend or the betrayal of the man she loved? Instead, she let go of Nadia and followed in Robert's steps.

Let them have each other.

"Tern," Gage said.

"I can't," she said, meeting his eyes and letting him see the pain and turmoil swimming in hers. How much heartbreak could she take at his hands? "Leave me alone."

Gage dragged in a deep breath and hardened his jaw. "I won't do that."

"You don't have a choice, Gage. Besides, it's what you wanted." She cocked a sardonic smile. She shut the door on the two people she loved, who apparently had loved each other, lied to her, and betrayed her.

Was anything what it seemed?

"You are a bitch." Gage turned on Nadia. "What in the hell possessed you to hurt her like that?" His hands fisted. He'd never hit a woman. Never thought he could. But then maybe there was more of his father in him than he thought, because he wanted to beat the shit out of this one. It took everything he had not to give in to the temptation.

Nadia dropped her face into her hands and moaned. "I don't know what overcame me."

"You're jealous."

Her head snapped up.

"We were over." He advanced a step, his muscles tensing as he got within arm's reach. It would take nothing to snap her neck. The last time he'd felt like this he'd killed his brother-in-law. Sweat broke out over his body at the realization, and he anchored his feet. "You pushed me in her direction," he gritted out through locked teeth.

"I was helping you out because you said you needed a gift for your mother. I didn't mean for you to fall at her feet."

"Did you set all this up as a way of getting back at her? At me?" He waved his hands in the air to encompass the hell they'd been going through.

"Of course not. Why would I do that?"

"For the same reason you blurted out that we'd slept together. You want to hurt her. Why?"

"She's my best friend. The last thing I want is to see Tern hurt. I was saving her."

"From me? If that was truly your motivation you would have told her about us back in December."

"Back in December, I thought you might be good for her. Why should I have ruined what was developing between you? You did that without my help when you took off. Maybe I was trying to keep that from happening again. Now she knows how deceiving you can be."

"You mean how deceiving both of us can be, don't you?"

Chapter Thirty-Six

Tern slammed the pot of water on top of the wood stove. Water sloshed up and out, sizzling on the heat of the cast-iron, sounding like the blood scorching through her veins. She was burning up inside, but relished the anger over the hurt that crept like a disease. Grabbing a wooden spoon, she stirred the porcupine stew she'd set to simmer before she'd been stupid enough to go outside. Before she'd caught Gage naked, and decided to take him.

"Hey, you okay?" Robert asked.

She jumped, forgetting she wasn't alone. What she wouldn't give to be alone. It seemed like forever since she'd had a minute to herself.

"Right, you're not fine. Sorry. That was a stupid thing for me to ask. Here let me do that." Robert took the spoon out of her hand. "Why don't you take a minute to fix your hair, change into dry clothes, and for God's sake, wipe the tears off your face."

She reached up and found moisture on her cheeks. "Shit."

Robert gave her his back as he mindlessly stirred the pot of porcupine stew. "Want me to take care of them both? I'll do it. No one would know but us."

She choked on a laugh and made sure there were no remaining tears on her face. If she wasn't careful, she'd end in hysterics. "Don't tempt me." She snatched dry clothes and changed into them, grateful for Robert giving her a minute to compose herself. "How's the graze on your arm?" she asked, wanting the attention off her situation. Besides, she should have asked how he was doing before now.

His chest swelled and he looked pleased that she'd asked.

"It looks good. Already scabbing over with no sign of infection."

"I'm so relieved. That could have been bad all the way out here."

She was running a brush through her damp, tangled hair when Nadia entered the cabin. Tern met her eyes, but couldn't look at her long without tears welling up again. She turned away and took a fair amount of time to locate a hair-tie from inside the front pocket of her backpack and began braiding her hair.

"Tern," Nadia said. "Can we talk?"

"Nope. Not yet."

"If I were you," Robert said, "I'd find a corner to sit in and stay out of everyone's way."

"Don't tell me what to do," she spat.

Tern straightened and faced Nadia. "Either do what he says, or leave, because I sure as hell don't want to see you right now."

"It's raining again," she whined.

If she didn't stop her damn whining, Tern was going to do it for her. "I don't care." Tern tried not to think of Gage out there getting soaked in the rain, maybe even stalked by a killer. If there was a killer out there, he probably had more sense than Gage and was hold up somewhere nice and cozy, waiting out the weather. Or the killer was right now in the room with her. Even with all that Gage had done, she didn't think he could have killed Lucky or Mac. What would be his reasoning?

Unless he was the psycho jealous type and was one-by-one killing all the men she'd slept with.

Could she believe that? It would mean that he was obsessively in love with her. And insane. Two things he hadn't demonstrated, but he had killed someone. Maybe she shouldn't discount it so fast.

Her rambling thoughts were driving her insane. She finished with her hair and took over the cooking from Robert, needing something to keep her busy.

"Whatever you're cooking," Nadia said from her corner. "It sure smells good."

"Nadia, I don't want to hear you either," Tern said.

The door flew open and Gage entered.

She couldn't help the shiver as her eyes met his from across the small space. He was wet, his hair almost black and wild around his unshaven face. If anything the rain seemed to have darkened his features, giving him shadows and hallows that were damned attractive. He exuded alpha male and her blood quickened in response.

Damn it, she wanted to look away, but her heart strangled in her throat, and it was all she could do not to fall at his feet in a pool of want and misery.

In two quick strides, Gage was in front of her and had her arm in the vise-like hold that didn't hurt, but said in no uncertain terms that she wasn't getting away from him without a fight. That traitorous part of her twittered to life.

"You're coming with me," he said, the gruffness of his voice raising the little hairs on her arms and the back of her neck.

She took a few steps with him before her mind cleared enough to ask what the hell she was doing. She dug in her feet. How many times was she going to let him break her?

She wrenched her arm free. "I'm not going anywhere with you."

"The hell you aren't." He swung her up into his arms. Iron bands locked her in place against his rock-solid chest. He held her so tight she felt his heart pound in quick heavy thumps. That sick woman inside her thrilled at being swept off her feet and spirited away. She was suddenly Scarlett and he was one sexy Rhett Butler.

Robert barred the door, his shotgun clenched in his hands.

"Get out of the way," Gage said.

"She doesn't want to go with you, and I don't want to be stuck with her." He indicated Nadia who had risen to her feet when Gage came crashing into the small one room cabin. Robert raised the shotgun across his chest. "No one is leaving. I don't trust anyone here. We all stay together until we get fucking home and let the authorities figure out this goddamn mess. Until then, no one is alone unless they need to take a shit in the woods."

Gage had a staring contest with Robert. After a period of time, he rolled his shoulders, coming to a decision, and dropped his hold on Tern's legs. She gained her feet and pushed out of his grasp. Her insides trembled but thankfully her backbone snapped in place and she stood tall, faking some self-control she'd secured from somewhere. She turned back to the porcupine stew. It wasn't going to taste any better with more stirring, so she grabbed some bowls that she'd cleaned earlier and filled them.

They ate in silence. The porcupine was tough and chewy and had a strong gamey taste, but it was better than going hungry.

"We'd better get some sleep." Robert stood and set his bowl on the counter. "Tomorrow's going to be a long day."

"Every day here has been freaking long," Nadia muttered. The three of them stared at her. "What? It's the truth."

"One you don't have to constantly point out," Robert said. He faced Tern. "Thanks for dinner. It was...filling."

"You're welcome." Not a bad compliment considering how the stew sat like a stone in her stomach. Tern took the empty bowls and washed them in the heated water and set them out to dry.

"I say we stay here," Nadia said. "It's comfortable, out of the weather. We can hunt for food, there's water. Besides, in another couple of days, when we don't return to Fairbanks, they'll send a rescue party looking for us."

"No one knows where the hell we are," Robert said. "If they did, they would have sent out Search and Rescue when the pilot never returned to Fairbanks. Obviously, he hadn't filed a flight plan."

"He had to have gotten off a mayday or something. We should stay here."

"You are fucking crazy," Robert said. "We're a day away from the river."

"Don't call me crazy!" She half rose to her feet, the look in her eyes downright freaky.

308

"Oh my hell," Tern said, hoping to inject some sense. "We need some rest. I'll take first watch." She didn't think she could sleep anyway, not with Gage staring at her as though trying to convey some secret message. Didn't matter how much he tried, she didn't understand him. Didn't even want to right now.

"She's right," Gage finally spoke up. "Nadia and Tern take the bed. Robert, you and I will bunk down on the floor."

"Don't have to tell me twice. I'm dead on my feet." Robert was already unrolling his sleeping bag. "Can't remember when I've been this dog-tired," he muttered.

"Tern, get some sleep," Gage said, standing. "You cooked dinner and cleaned up. I'll take first watch."

She wasn't going to fight him for it. While her mind refused to quit its racing, her bones seemed to liquefy. Any minute now and her body would collapse.

Gage stopped in front of her and took her chin in his hand. "How's the head?" His fingers trailed over the goose egg near her temple.

"It's fine." The concern in his stare and the gentleness in his fingers had tears threatening.

"Are you okay to sleep?"

Like she was going to sleep. She was too tired and worked up to sleep.

"I'll be fine," she repeated. He let go of her and stepped back. It was all she could do not to reach out for him. She fisted her hands to keep from doing just that.

"No one's asked me how my head feels," Nadia muttered.

"We all know how you feel, since you keep telling us," Robert returned.

That took Tern's mind off Gage. She grabbed her sleeping bag, laid it next to Nadia's, and carefully eased herself onto the old bed. It took her weight with a few groans.

Gage took the chair and positioned it in front of the cabin door and laid his shotgun across his knees. Robert extinguished the candle and plunged them all into darkness. A few cracks of midnight sun eased through the chinking of the logs.

Robert rotated in his sleeping bag, left and right, trying to get comfortable. The bed squeaked as Nadia rustled around and the wooden chair creaked under Gage's weight. She heard the brush of tree branches against the cabin walls. A cry of a bird, howl of a wolf, the slap of the wind as it pelted rain at the cabin. All the noise seemed to escalate into a racket she couldn't escape. Tern twisted onto her side and sank farther into her sleeping bag, laying her upper arm over her ears. The noise turned to a drone of static. Who said sleeping in the wilderness was relaxing? She used to think it was. Now she just wanted to get home and away from these people. Nadia made the bed squeak again as she adjusted her position.

How could Nadia have lied to her like this? She'd thought they'd been friends, good friends, best friends. But all this time Nadia had slept with Gage and never told her? What did that say about the type of person she was? What other deep dark secrets did Nadia have?

Tern inched away from her to the edge of the bed. What if right now she was sleeping beside a killer? Nadia could have taken Lucky down if she'd gotten the jump on him, surprised him. They were having sex, could she have killed him then, when his guard was down?

Oh, God. How could she even suspect Nadia of such a thing? But then she'd suspected Robert of the same until he'd been grazed by a bullet. A bullet that Nadia could've shot at him. No, her. Robert had saved Tern from being shot. He'd tackled her to the ground and had been winged for his trouble.

She was going round and round until the thoughts were knocking at the roof of her skull, making her head pound. She'd had enough head pounding today. She needed to examine the possibility that Gage was behind this. She didn't want to, but then if she didn't at least consider him it could be the death of her.

Obviously Gage wasn't the man she thought him to be. First he'd left her without a word, kept secrets from her. Could he be willing to kill her too? Whoever had set this up wanted her dead.

Wanted all of them dead.

A hand fell on her shoulder and she jumped.

"Hey, it's okay," Nadia whispered. "It's just me."

And that was supposed to reassure her?

By the direction of light flittering into the cabin, she'd been playing round robin with her thoughts for some time. She heard Robert's soft snoring on the opposite side of the room. But nothing from the chair where Gage kept watch. Was he still awake? Was he even still there? The shadows were deeper where he'd taken up his position. She would have heard him leave. Right?

"Listen," Nadia continued to whisper. "I'm really sorry you had to find out about Gage and me that way. I didn't mean to hurt you or blurt it out like that. It's just that this whole situation is so messed up that I'm saying and doing things I wouldn't normally do."

"I don't want to talk about it, Nadia." She wanted peace. She wanted sleep. Escape. Above all, she wanted this burning in her heart to stop.

"I don't like you being mad at me." The whine was back in Nadia's voice, and it had Tern grinding her teeth.

"You should have told me about you and Gage way before now." And why had she told her when she'd caught them together. That spoke of jealously. Which had Tern rethinking how Nadia could be behind all this.

"Can't we work it out? You have to forgive me."

Not going to happen tonight or anytime soon. "Nadia, right now you need to stay the hell away from me. I'll let you know when and if I'm ready to talk."

"Okay, but you might want to consider something I've been bothered about. Robert's been shot, you've been knocked out, me too, but nothing has happened to Gage. I think there's something fishy about that." Nadia turned and lay on her back. "Just know that I love you Tern."

Sure, twist the knife in her heart.

How did Nadia love her and then betray her like this? For that matter how did Gage? And damn it, Nadia had a good point.

Why hadn't Gage been attacked, when the rest of them had?

Gage sat in the dark, listening to Nadia beg Tern to forgive her. If Tern was smart, Nadia had lost her position as friend. It didn't miss his attention that he sat where he could see the bed, see Tern, and that his shotgun was more trained on Nadia than the front door.

Telling Tern that they'd slept together one night when they'd both drank too much had been vicious and possibly cunning. There was more to Nadia than she'd let on.

She'd come on to him strong when they'd first met at UAF. They worked in different departments, she a professor of mathematics, he a scientist for the Geophysical Institute specializing in the study of the aurora borealis. Most of his time was spent outside Fairbanks in Poker Flats, Normally, they wouldn't have met even professionally, but the University was small and Fairbanks, while the second largest city in Alaska, was by no means a major metropolis. Yet, they'd kept 'running' into each other. He wouldn't put it past Nadia to have hunted him out.

Could she have stalked him? Or was he completely losing it?

She'd been sweet. Too sweet. Too accommodating. In a moment of weakness, he'd ignored his big brain for his smaller one and taken her up on her blatant invitation. He'd regretted it immediately. As kindly as he could, he explained that a relationship was not for him. Had he been the trigger?

Didn't they say with every psychopath, there was a trigger that started them on a killing spree?

What if him hooking up with Tern had flipped something inside Nadia? But then he'd left Tern. He was ashamed to admit it now, but he'd run from Tern like a scared hare from a hungry wolf. Yes, the situation with his sister, and his incarceration, were valid reasons to have left and stayed gone, but he should have called and explained things to her.

It didn't make sense for Nadia to have flipped over that. What kind of proof did he have that she was a psychopath other than she was a bitch and bothered the shit out of him?

It wasn't like Tern hadn't slept with anyone before him. Hell, he faced them all on this trip. What was the big deal that she found out about Nadia?

Oh, this was so not the way to go.

Lucky must have been her experimental stage. God knew that man had more thrill genes than brains. Robert must have been a rebound. He represented family and Gage knew how important family was to Tern and how much she wanted children of her own. Mac was easy. He was the father figure. Gage couldn't find anything negative to say about Mac. He'd respected the man, had looked forward to getting to know him better.

The bed squeaked as Tern adjusted her position. How he wanted to lie next to her. It had been too long since they had actually shared a bed, and he wanted time. Time to be with her, explore her, and make amends that were long overdue. He was such an idiot not to see what he had. She was his match. His soulmate. It was so sappy, but that was how he felt. He was complete with her, fulfilled, and not just in a sexual way. Though the sex rocked.

He'd done nothing but fuck up his chances with her from the beginning. Not telling her the full truth about his acquaintance with Nadia. Because of that, he might have lost her completely. She loved him, but did she love him enough to forgive his sorry ass?

His hands tightened around the shotgun. He had to keep them all alive, prove to Tern that he was worthy of her love, her respect. Then maybe she'd give him a chance to grovel at her feet.

CHAPTER THIRTY-SEVEN

Tern looked around the quiet cabin once more before shutting the door. Was it weird of her to GPS this location for future reference? She wanted to know who had lived here and what happened to them. Hopefully she'd be given the chance to find out if they made it out of here alive. She'd like to return to this spot, even though her memories of it were bittersweet.

She glanced at the pond with longing as they traipsed by on their way into the forest. If only Nadia had kept her mouth shut. But then she'd rather know the truth than be deceived, right? Of course she wanted the truth.

She watched the movements of Gage's broad shoulders in front of her. He still insisted on carrying her pack. She'd told him she was fine, but he'd taken it from her anyway. She kind of felt bad because no one offered to help Nadia's with hers. Thankfully, Nadia had stopped bitching about it, but insisted she take the rear and Robert at least break the trail for her.

The weather had cleared. Bringing heat that filtered through the birch leaves and helped keep the buzzing mosquitoes down to a slower slapping level. They didn't seem to bother her as much as the men and Nadia.

Everything bothered Nadia.

She even complained about the sun. It had to be by far the most beautiful day since they'd left Fairbanks. Tern tried to shut her out, as the men were doing. Men could ignore women as though it was an art form. Nadia was only doing this because Tern hadn't forgiven her yet. Like this behavior would endear her into forgetting that she'd lied to Tern all this time. Gage had been smart enough to leave Tern alone, other than checking out the bump on her head. She sported a nice pair of shiners today, and the never-ending headache continued to beat on, but she was fine.

The terrain was steep as they hiked down to the river. The trail narrowed on the rocky cliff with the rushing river below. The cold humidity of the water was a welcome relief as they struggled over the rough landscape. Rapids rushed by some fifty to sixty feet below them as they carefully navigated the loose shale. It was a deadly drop to the gunmetal, silt-filled waters below. It was a relief to know they'd soon be at the riverbank. They just needed to find a safe way down the razor-sharp edge without falling to their deaths.

"Watch your footing," Gage hollered. "Hold onto something. Trail looks easier up ahead."

Good. She was getting vertigo from climbing so high over the rushing water. They made the bit Gage called 'easier', but they still needed to stay alert and watch every step. At least here there were struggling birch trees to hold onto.

A gunshot rang out, followed by Nadia's horrifying scream, and then a splash echoed from far below. Tern swiveled as Gage knocked her to the uneven ground.

"Nadia!" Tern screamed.

Robert had hit the dirt, too, but there was no sign of Nadia. Another shot rang out close to them. Shattered shale flew into the air like shards of glass. Robert swore, rivaling the cursing coming from Gage as he attempted to flatten her into the ground with the heavy blanket of his body.

"*Nadia!*" Tern screamed again. A sob lodged in her throat. "Where the hell is she?" No one answered her and Tern was afraid she knew why.

"Move back, take cover!" Gage yelled, the words ringing in her ears as he dragged her into the safety of the trees away from the cliff face and raining bullets.

"Shit, shit, shit!" Robert muttered a litany of swear words like a prayer as he belly-crawled after them.

Gage picked Tern up, half-carrying her to a thick stand of birch where he deposited her behind the trunk of the largest tree. He knelt in front of her, his eyes wild and filled with fury and dread.

"You all right?" His hands roved over her body checking to see if she was hit.

"Nadia," she pleaded, grabbing his shoulders. "You've got to help Nadia."

"She's beyond help now."

"No, we have to go after her."

"You heard the splash. If she wasn't shot, the fall killed her."

"She's a good swimmer," Tern argued. "What if she's hanging onto the side of the cliff right now?"

"I saw her go over," Robert said, joining them. "I'm sorry, Tern."

"No!" Tern scrambled to stand and rush passed the men. Gage caught her around the waist and swung her off her feet. "There's got to be a way to save her."

"Even if she survived the fall, the water's too cold, moving too fast, and has already drowned her with silt."

"We have to do something," she begged on a sob, struggling in his rigid hold.

Gage twisted Tern in his arms and shook her. "There's nothing to do. She's gone. And unless you want to die, too, you'll have to grieve later. Robert?"

"Ready."

"Ready for what?" Tern asked. The men ignored her as they went into some type of combat mode.

Robert was on his knees, the muzzle of his rifle cocked between branches, the butt of the gun snug against his shoulder, one eye closed and the other looking through the scope.

"We'll head southeast, away from the river into deeper brush," Gage said, his hold on her tightening in readiness. "You got enough bullets?"

"Yes. Now go!" Robert started shooting, the repeat of the rifle deafening.

They ran as Robert laid down cover for them. Tern did her best to keep up with Gage. She knew he'd staggered his stride to make it easier for her, but he still had to drag her along behind him, helping her when she stumbled. They ran until she gasped for air and her legs turned to jelly. Yet they still ran, dogging branches and tearing through brush.

Would they ever stop? Would this nightmare ever end?

Were they all going to die?

She could no longer hear the gunfire. Did that mean Robert had taken care of the killer, or was he now dead himself?

Just like Nadia.

CHAPTER THIRTY-EIGHT

"We'll stop here," Gage said, his breathing heavy, his chest heaving. He struggled out of the backpacks he'd been shouldering and bent at the waist trying to catch his breath.

Everything that she'd been running from crashed into her. "This can't be happening. Why?" She gasped as the pain of Nadia's loss cut through her. "Why her? She never hurt anybody."

Gage pulled her into his arms. "I'm sorry, Tern." He kissed her forehead. Then he was helping her to sit on the ground as her body crumbled in on itself with grief.

Just last night she'd lain next to Nadia while Nadia begged for forgiveness.

She'd gone to her death thinking Tern hated her. Another series of sobs racked her body. What were the last words she'd spoke to her? They came crashing back with sharp clarity.

Right now you need to stay the hell away from me.

If they'd stayed at the cabin, like Nadia had wanted to, she'd still be with them.

Robert crashed through the bushes. "I scared off the motherfucker. Guy tucked tail and scurried back into the trees like the coward he was. I gave chase for a few but couldn't catch up to the murdering asshole."

Tern lurched to her feet and threw herself into Robert's arms. She'd been so terrified he'd been killed too. Robert staggered back under her weight but wrapped his arms tightly around her. "Now this I like." He nuzzled his lips into the crook of her neck, and his hand cupped her butt. She pushed out of his grasp.

"What? No kiss?"

A tear escaped her and she angrily whipped it away. She knew he was attempting humor to dispel the tragedy they'd just experienced, but it didn't do any good. Tears streamed down her cheeks again, and the sobs came harder.

"Hey, you don't have to kiss me. Just stop that. Please." His voice cracked.

Gage wrapped an arm around her and brought her carefully, like she was glass, into the safety of his broad shoulders. "We have to keep moving, Tern."

She nodded, but the tears wouldn't stop.

"Oh, shit. Shut her up, man." Robert turned and suspiciously wiped at his own eyes.

"Are you sure?" Tern choked out. "Absolutely positive?"

Robert didn't pretend he didn't know what she was asking. "Yeah. Everything happened so fast, but I saw that bright pink backpack of hers hit the river. I'm so sorry, Tern."

Tern nodded, but her lips wouldn't stop trembling.

"Come on," Gage said.

"No. We need to recover Nadia's body. Make sure she's…"

"There's nothing we can do for Nadia," Gage said, his tone hardening.

"I don't have a body to bury for Lucky—"

"Don't forget his head's bagged and on ice with Mac."
Robert backed up a few steps from the look she shot his way.
"Sorry. But I'm not going after Nadia's body. Not when
someone's been shooting at us."

"He's right," Gage said. "He's a jerk, but he's right."

"Hey!"

"Shut up, Robert."

"We need to go after the son of a bitch." Tern fists
tightened, wanting them around the throat of the murderer
who'd brought her so much heartache.

"Think it through, Tern," Gage said. "You're riding on
emotions. We don't know where he is, why he's doing this.
We're running out of ammo. We don't have any food, and no
way to contact help. Our best chance to stay alive is to make it
to the river."

"I'm not running any more. If I sit here long enough, the
murdering coward will find me, and I'll get him."

"The hell you will. I'm not going to let you get yourself
killed."

"What? Like Lucky and Mac and Nadia got themselves
killed?"

"You're smarter than this. You know we need to get to
safety." Gage stared at her, willing her to understand.

She swallowed the biting remark dying to fly from her
mouth and wrangled in her emotions. He was right. She was
reacting. Not thinking.

She nodded.

"Good," Robert said. "Glad that's settled. I need a minute
to give nature my best, and then we'll get out of this fucking
forest." He headed into the trees, one hand unbuckling his belt,
the other still tightened around his rifle.

"I gotta hand it to Robert," Gage said with a small smile. "While he's useless most of the time, he's good in a gunfight. I'm grateful he had our backs today."

"I should have told him that."

Gage cracked a smile. "You did when you plaster yourself to him."

"Yeah, well. Jerk copped a feel while I was showing him my 'gratitude'."

"Can't say I blame him." Gage swallowed. "Listen, Tern, about what happened yesterday with Nadia—"

"I don't want to talk about it." Tern grabbed her pack and struggled into the straps, hitching it onto her shoulders.

"We need to before—"

"Before what? Another one of us dies, and it's too late?"

The look in his eyes answered for him.

"You'll just have to keep us alive then, won't you?"

"Loving you isn't going to be easy, is it?"

"Nothing worth having ever is."

Robert's terrified scream echoed through the forest.

CHAPTER THIRTY-NINE

They found Robert on his back, pants around his knees, blood covering his head and torso. "Damn bitch caught me with my pants down, taking a shit!" At least he was conscious and still breathing.

Tern rushed over to him. Gage was a little slower as he surveyed the area, his gun ready.

"What happened?" Tern dropped to her knees, reaching out to touch him but not knowing where to help first. There was so much blood, and had he finished his nature call? "How bad are you hurt? Where are you hurt?"

"She hit me on the head. About cracked open my skull. Dazed me something awful. She probably thought it was enough to make it easy to knife me. Bitch. Shit, this hurts." He moaned.

"Who are you talking about? Who did this to you?"

"Nadia! She's the one behind all this."

"She's alive?" Tern quickly glanced around, hope blooming in her heart.

"And deadly as a snake. Knew there was something off about her. Son of a bitch!"

"Nadia did this?"

"Yes, that bitch did this to me! Haven't you been listening? Your best friend is our fucking psycho killer!"

"Robert," Gage said, bending on one knee, keeping an eye on the surrounding forest. "Tell us what happened. Where are you hurt?"

"Shit. I hurt everywhere. First the blow to the head, when I came to enough, bitch was straddling me, knife ready to plunge into my heart. Do you think that's the way she killed Lucky? She seems to prefer being on top." His uninjured hand shook as it covered his throat. "She was going to knife me in the heart, and then cut off my head, wasn't she?" He grabbed Gage, his hand twisting in his shirt. "You gotta kill her for me, man. I gotta be avenged. Oh, shit, shit, shit." A sob escaped him, tears filled his eyes, and his lips trembled. "Chloe. My poor little girl." He looked at Tern, his eyes wild and swimming with pain. "Promise me you'll take care of her. Love her like she's your own."

"Stop talking like that," Tern said. "You're going to be fine." Tern clamped her hands over the wound in his arm that was bubbling blood the worst. The others on his chest seemed superficial, but the one in his arm might have cut an artery. "You'll be there for Chloe."

Robert let go of Gage and grabbed Tern's wrist with surprising force. "Promise me, goddamn it! I need to know my baby's going to be cared for."

Tern met his scared, fierce stare and nodded. "I promise, Robert. I've always loved Chloe. Anything happens to you, she'll be mine as though I gave birth to her myself."

His head fell back and he shut his eyes. "Thank you."

"Come on, let's patch you up and get out of here," Gage said. "Any chance you might have hurt Nadia?"

"A black eye, some bruised ribs as I was trying to shake her off me. She's taunting us, man. She's going to kill us all."

"Enough," Gage said. "You're not that hurt. It's just a lot of blood."

Tern stared at Gage. Was he serious? Gage looked at her, his mouth tight, eyes bleak, and the truth of Robert's condition sank in. He needed medical help and he needed it now, or the only doctor that would do him any good was a coroner.

"I've got to give it to Nadia," Robert said. "The bitch is sure handy with a knife."

Gage reached for the waistband of Robert's pants.

"Dude?" Robert tried to cover his privates.

"Relax, I need your belt." Gage yanked the belt free of Robert's belt loops. "This might pinch." Gage wrapped the belt around Robert's upper arm, above the gushing wound, and wrenched it tight.

"Shit, damn, fuck!"

"Suck it up, cupcake. You're whining like a girl. Tern, grab me one of my shirts out of my pack." Gage secured the belt around Robert's arm as Tern gathered clothes from Gage's backpack.

Gage took the t-shirt she handed him and tore it into strips. He handed a few to Tern. "Let's make this fast." He looked around them. "We need to get out of here."

She felt it then. Someone was watching them.

CHAPTER FORTY

A raven cawed overhead, settling on a birch branch above them, its beady eyes taking in everything.

"Oh shit, it's that raven again," Robert said with a whimper. "Tell me he isn't here for my soul. I don't want to die."

"Shut up, Robert," Gage said, tying off ends of the makeshift bandage. "Thinking that way isn't helping anyone."

"Right. Right. Think positive. Law of attraction and shit. Got it." He closed his eyes. "Okay, visualizing no fucking ravens."

"Robert, you're too stupid to die," Gage said with a shake of his head.

"Thanks, that means a lot right now." He sniffed.

Tern stuffed the remains of Gage's clothes back into his pack. The hair on the back of her neck was standing up, and she was chilled with fear. She didn't think it was just the raven watching them. Either a bigger animal or a human. Most likely Nadia. Why didn't she just end it rather than playing this cat and mouse game? Why was she doing this to begin with?

"You're going to have to walk, Rob." Gage helped Robert into a sitting position. He swooned. They'd strapped his arm to his body by wrapping strips of fabric around his chest. The belt worked to clamp off the hemorrhaging, keeping him alive but killing his limb as long as he was without medical care. They'd bandaged his head, since it wouldn't stop bleeding either. His skin color was pasty. His lips had a bluish tint.

Maybe the raven had come for him.

"He won't make it to the river," Gage said.

"The cabin?" Tern asked.

"But—"

"Nadia."

"She'll figure that's our plan."

"Crap, stop doing that," Robert said, his eyes rolling. "Damn it, Tern. Why'd you have to love this asshole?"

She ignored him, knowing it was the pain and fear talking.

"I don't see another choice," Gage said. "We backtracked when we were running. We're actually closer to the cabin than the river. There's shelter, water, a place for him to lie down. Have your gun ready and use your spidey sense."

"Got it." She made sure the safety was off the rifle.

Could she even shoot Nadia?

Robert groaned as Gage helped him to his feet. "Come on, man. Now's the time to show Tern what you're made of. Let's impress the hell out of her."

Tern opened up every sense she had. Ears, eyes, and that little extra that her dad always said she possessed. All her siblings believed there was something more in their Athabascan blood. She'd never tried to use it like this. She'd always had a feeling about things. Though, obviously, not about choosing her friends.

The trek back to the cabin felt the longest by far. though Gage was moving at a steady clip and Robert as fast as he could.

Gage stopped when they approached the clearing and lowered Robert to the ground. "I'm going to go and check it out. Tern, keep an eye on him. Robert, keep your mouth shut."

Gage slinked off, as quiet as a wolf.

The minutes ticked by. Every glance she gave Robert scared her further.

He was slowly dying.

Gage showed up. "Okay, I didn't see her. Doesn't mean she isn't there." He helped a too-quiet Robert to his feet.

A little bitching from him would make Tern feel a lot better about his situation.

She rushed to open the cabin door for Gage, and then shut it tight behind them with relief. Gage steered Robert toward the bed, and Tern helped him lay Robert down. A groan of pain escaped him and then a heavy sigh.

Gage untied a sleeping bag from his backpack and unzipped it, laying it over Robert.

They'd left a fire laid in the stove, just like they'd found one waiting for them. Tern quickly lit it and had flames licking the dried wood. She heated water they'd also left in a bucket for whoever might need the cabin in the future. Who would have guessed it would be them and within hours after leaving it?

She brought some warm water and had him drink. They needed to ward off shock. If the blood loss didn't kill him, shock would. He sipped. Gage was busy reloading their rifles. He placed Robert's next to him on the bed, along with a box of bullets.

"You guys need to leave me here," Robert said.

"Robert—"

"Don't. Just listen." Robert took a labored breath. "Tern, Nadia wants you and everyone you've cared about dead. She thinks I'm dying. She's probably not far from the mark on that one." He tried to smile but it fell flat. "The only way we're going to live through this is for you and Gage to get to the river and find help."

"We can't leave you," she protested, taking his good hand. "I won't leave you." Not to die alone.

"You have to. I'm dead if you stay. Nadia wants you. The best way to keep me alive is to stay the hell away from me."

The words were brutal and sliced at her, but he was right. "I don't want to leave you here."

He freed his hand from hers and cupped her cheek. "I know, but you must. There's more than just us at stake here. Chloe. Your family. If she isn't stopped, she'll go after them. Hell, they might already be dead."

"No, they're fine. I'd feel it if something bad happened to them."

"How?" He rolled his eyes. "Let me guess, the native crap again."

"'That native crap' has saved your ass a few times."

This time his smile was less forced. "I sure wished you'd fallen for me like you did for this asshole."

The asshole in question stayed off to the side and let them continue their conversation.

She leaned over and kissed him, letting her lips linger on his.

His eyes fluttered open when she sat back on the edge of the bed. "Thanks for that. There's something else I need you to do…in case…well, you know. Tell Chloe I love her, and the combination to my private safe is taped behind the refrigerator. There's enough money and investments in there to provide Chloe with higher education and a comfortable life."

"Stop talking like that," Tern said.

"Chances are I won't make it out of here alive. No, don't interrupt. Let me have some peace of mind."

"Okay. Don't worry, Robert. I'll take of everything."

CHAPTER FORTY-ONE

They lightened their load, just taking what they absolutely needed so they could move faster. Nadia was out there somewhere. Tern had her pistol tucked into her waistband. If they didn't get help today, Robert would be dead. They had too far to travel in terrain not meant for speed, and they were being hunted.

Tern's nerves were at a fever pitch, twanging with every little sound, expecting attack from every angle. She felt the same tension in Gage.

Suddenly an icy tingling in her blood gave warning.

"Get down!" she yelled, but she wasn't fast enough to save Gage.

Gage grunted, gasped, and hit his knees, going down right in front of her. A knife protruded from his chest. He fell to his back and reached to yank out the knife.

"No! Don't!" Tern skidded on her knees and grabbed his hand where it had tightened on the hilt of the hunting knife. "You could bleed to death."

"Hurts," he wheezed. His eyes widened. "Behind you."

Tern swiveled. Nadia strolled out of the forest her rifle trained on them, looking pretty damn good for someone who'd supposedly fallen to her death.

Tern's fingers itched for her weapon.

"Don't do it." Nadia shook her head. There was a demonic gleam of pleasure in her eyes. "Toss the guns toward me." She motioned with the barrel of her rifle. "Pistols too."

"Nadia—"

"Make it fast, or I'm going to shoot him."

There was no hesitation in Nadia's stance or her tone. To buy time, until she could think of something, Tern did what Nadia had ordered and lugged the guns toward her. She made sure she threw them like a girl. A ten-year-old girl.

Nadia shot Gage in the gut. Gage's body jerked and a guttural moan escaped him.

Tern screamed, her hands pressing the wound low on Gage's abdomen. "Why'd you do that? I did everything you said."

"Oops." Nadia shrugged. "Trigger happy, I guess."

"You bitch!"

"Careful. You don't want to provoke me."

Tern yanked off her hoodie and used it to try and stop the bleeding.

Nadia poked her with the shotgun. "Stand up."

Gage muttered an objection, his hands grabbing her. She took his hands and placed them over her sweatshirt, trying to convene with her eyes how much she loved him.

Nadia nudged her harder with the barrel of the shotgun

Madder than hell, and more scared than she'd ever been in her life, Tern stood and faced Nadia, putting herself between Gage and the murdering bitch. "Why are you doing this?"

Nadia laughed. The sound sent chills cascading like rapids down Tern's spine. Nadia pointed the gun toward Gage again. "You took him from me. But that won't matter because soon I will be you."

"What?"

"Like my outfit?" She cocked her hip.

They were going to talk fucking fashion? Tern cleared the rage and fear from her mind long enough to look at Nadia.

"Those are my clothes," Tern said, frowning. Nadia actually looked like her. At least superficially. The recently dyed hair, the cut through her eyebrow, Tern's porcupine quill earrings, especially made for her by her grandmother. Tern wanted to rip them from Nadia's ears. Where the hell had she gotten those? When she'd stolen the little arctic tern from her bedroom?

"Yep. And soon everything you have will be mine. Heck, I've already had all the men you've had. Lucky was a treasure. What the man could do with his tongue." Her eyelids went half-mast in remembered pleasure. "I sliced his throat while riding him to climax. I never knew how stimulating something like that could be." Nadia poked her with the barrel of the gun again, hard enough to leave a bruise. "You stopped me from killing Robert in the same way, not once, but twice." She tilted her head in order to regard Gage. "Hmm. Think he's too far gone for a ride to heaven?"

Behind her, Gage made a gagging sound, his breathing raspy as he struggled to breathe with the knife in his chest.

Tern moved to block Nadia's view. "Did you have sex with Mac too?" The conversation made her sick, but she had to get Nadia's attention off Gage, somehow distract her so Tern could take her down.

"Mac." Nadia rolled her eyes. "He had to take command. Talked everyone into leaving the game I'd taken so much time to set up. There were so many great surprises in store. He ruined everything with his big mouth." She suddenly giggled. "Using my sleeping pills was a stroke of genius, don't you think?" She didn't wait for Tern to answer. "I really wanted to kill him like I did Lucky, but the pills took that out of the equation. You know there is something so intimate about a knife. So killing Mac like I did was very much like having sex with him."

Tern tried to look meek and scared, not really a stretch in the situation, hoping Nadia would keep talking until she could think of some way out of this.

"Killing Mac had been so simple. Anticlimactic, actually." She laughed at her own joke. "He didn't even move, just sighed as his last breath left his body. And Robert, what a laugh. Caught the man with his pants down and his weapon out of reach. Some outdoorsman he is."

Tears started to fall from Tern's eyes, delighting Nadia.

"I do believe you would have married Mac if he had asked. Tell me, does it hurt that he didn't? After all, isn't he the only one of your many suitors who didn't ask you to marry him? Oh, but Gage never asked you to marry him, did he? He actually left you. Almost destroyed you." She smirked.

"What's your point?"

"Really don't have one. Just wanted to torture you a little bit more."

"What about Hugh?" Tern asked. "Was he in cahoots with you?"

"Who? Oh, the pilot." She shook her head. "He was a lapdog. He helped me set up the competition, but he was clueless."

"But you killed him, didn't you? How?"

"He was a witness. He had to go. It was easy enough to plant a small explosive in the tail of the plane, which I activated when I helped unload the bags."

She'd killed so many people. How had Tern been so naïve about her? They were friends. "Why do you hate me so much?"

"Oh, I don't hate you, Tern. I love you. You know it's the highest form of compliment to emulate someone. I've looked at this competition as my metamorphosis. I am becoming you. And now with all of you dead, I will be welcomed into the bosom of your family. I'll take over your business, nurturing Chickadee in the process. Such a lovely girl, your baby sister. Raven and I will become the best of friends." Nadia shrugged. "I'm thinking your brother Lynx might make a nice replacement for Gage, since he won't live through this. Your sister-in-law would have to go, but I can take care of that easy enough."

She didn't know Eva very well.

"You weren't the right woman for Gage anyway. What kind of spell do you have over men?" Nadia gave another sadistic sound. "Doesn't matter anymore since you'll be dead. Doubt you'll attract anything other than bugs from now on."

"But why kill Gage? Why not just kill me?"

Gage made a hiss of protest.

"I hadn't planned on killing him, but you guys figured it out. I'd planned on consoling him after you died a horrible and tragic death. We would have had a wonderful life together."

Nadia advanced closer. "He was supposed to love me. Killing him will be so disappointing."

Tern felt the sudden need to vomit.

A raven cawed and landed on a branch overhead, flapping its blue-black wings, startling Nadia.

Tern jumped her, knocking the gun out of her hands. She grabbed her hair and pulled, clawed at her face. "You won't look like me now, bitch."

Nadia screamed, blood dripped from her cheek in three nice deep scratches. She punched Tern, knocking her to the ground. Tern swept her foot under Nadia's, knocking her off her feet. She scrambled on top of her and they rolled toward the cliff. Nadia slammed a rock into Tern's head and stars exploded behind her eyelids and her body went limp with pain.

Nadia struggled to her feet and picked up the rifle. She stood over Tern, breathing hard.

"Die, bitch." With an unholy gleam in her eye and a malicious smile twisting her lips, Nadia pulled the trigger.

CHAPTER FORTY-TWO

Gage yanked the knife out of his chest and threw it at Nadia's heart. The blade sunk deep. Nadia's shot went wild and the rifle fell from her hands.

"You die, bitch," Gage said.

Nadia stumbled back and teetered on the edge of the cliff, her arms flailing wild. A breath of wind, and she tumbled over the same precipice she'd pretended to fall off earlier.

Gage gasped for breath as blood gurgled into his lung. It felt like he'd been mowed down by a herd of caribou and one of them was sitting on his chest.

"Gage?" Tern crawled over to him. "What did you do?" Her hands pressed on his wounds, attempting to staunch the blood now seeping from his chest as well as his gut. Pain flared at her touch and he groaned.

"I love you," he wheezed. "Sorry. Should...have...told you...so many things."

"Damn words don't mean anything if you die on me!" Tears ran unchecked down her cheeks.

He wiped at the blood flowing down the side of her head. "You're hurt."

"I'll be fine." Pain thundered in her head the likes of which she'd never felt. Made getting hit by the log and being left to drown feel like a prank. Nadia had done that to her too. Had she winged Robert the day before that? Gage had checked her gun. Had she'd been carrying another one they hadn't known about? Obviously, there was a lot she hadn't known about Nadia.

She checked Gage's injures, all the while praying to the gods of her ancestors and to Gage's God. To anyone who would listen and answer, she prayed. Either there was a lot more blood around her, or there was blood pooling behind her eyes. Everything suddenly had a bloody tint. Tern struggled not to lie down alongside Gage to rest for just a moment.

"Tern, your…eyes," Gage struggled to say.

"Just shut up! I swear if you die on me I'll hunt you down in the afterlife and hurt you." Her voice caught on a sob. "I love you, Gage. Please, please stay with me."

Already the hoodie she'd used to staunch the gunshot in his stomach was soaked with blood. There was too much blood and the gurgling in his chest was louder. It sounded like he was drowning.

Tern's vision started to dim, the edges blurring. For a moment she thought her sister flew out of the trees. "Raven?" Then darkness swooped down like death.

CHAPTER FORTY-THREE

"'Bout time you opened your eyes," Mac said, leaning over Tern, a gentle sun backlighting him in a halo. "I have to say, you've looked better."

"Mac?" Tern asked. Either he was alive or she was...

"Did you miss me, babe?" Lucky asked, walking into her line of vision.

Now she knew she was dead. A person couldn't live without their head attached. Lucky looked healthy with all his body parts intact like the last time she'd seen him before—

"Oh, no." She closed her eyes on a moan. How had she let that bitch kill her?

"We've been asking that ourselves," Mac said.

She hadn't voiced that, had she?

"Nope," Lucky said. "In the hereafter, seems as though we can read each other's minds." Lucky gestured with his thumb toward Mac. "Sure is freaky to hear what this guy is thinking."

"While this dingbat doesn't have an original thought in his head," Mac said, his eyes bright and full of life. She'd never thought to see them like that again. "So, why are you here,

Tern? You aren't going to let that little bump on the head do you in, are you?"

Her attention was caught by the meadow of wildflowers in which they were currently convalescing. Bright and sharp in their beauty, they rivaled any she'd ever seen. Amethyst, snow-frosted mountains soared into an azure sky. "Wow." She sat up with an ease that borrowed on weightlessness, as though she was the bird she was named for. If she put her arms out, she wondered if she could fly.

"Now don't get any ideas," Mac warned. "This place is something, don't get me wrong, but it isn't your time to experience it."

"Ahh, come on, Mac. Let her stay," Lucky said, sitting next to her on the sweet-smelling grass. "I've missed you, babe."

"I've missed you guys too." Tern wanted to wrap her arms around them.

"No hugging, we don't have time for that," Mac said. "The longer you stay here, the harder it will be to go back. Listen, I've got my Shannon waiting for me and Lucky, well, he's got every damn mountain he could ever imagine climbing. We're content."

Lucky nodded. "It's pretty rad."

"I'm so sorry, guys. This is all my fault. I should have known Nadia was crazy."

"Stop that. It's nobody's fault but the one who killed us."

"Nadia was like a black widow or something," Lucky said.

"You had to be married to her in order for her to be a black widow," Mac scoffed. "She was a psycho. You were too busy getting into her pants to find out anything about her."

"Yeah, well, paid for that in spades." Lucky rubbed his neck.

Mac ignored him and knelt in front of Tern, his piercing eyes arrowed right into hers. "Tern, you have a full life ahead of you. Many things to do. Go, forgive that man, make him yours, settle down with a few kids and get fat."

"No, not fat," Lucky said, shaking his head. "You can do all that other stuff if you want, but don't get fat. You're too hot the way you are. Mac's right, though, go 'climb every mountain.' Yeah, I saw the movie," he replied sarcastically at the look Mac gave him. "Geez."

"Good thing I'm not stuck in eternity with you. That would be some kind of hell." Mac regarded Tern again. "Gage is a good man. He was cuckolded by Nadia like all of us were. You included. He kind of reminds me of myself a few years ago."

"More like decades," Lucky muttered under his breath.

"Do you think my dad's here?" She didn't want to revisit the heartache Gage was attached to.

"Near as I can tell, this is a holding place. A type of limbo. Neither Lucky nor I were willing to move on until we knew you were out of danger. You have a family and a man who loves you waiting for you."

"Why isn't Gage here with me?" Tern asked. He'd pulled the knife out of his chest. Sacrificed his life for hers. "There's no way he could have lived." She didn't want life, or death, without him.

"Help came just in time. He's sitting next to your hospital bed, crying like a baby," Lucky said. "Really touching if you ask me."

"He would have died if not for Raven and Aidan showing up when they did, along with Search and Rescue. They'd been just a step behind you for days. Pretty cool magical connection you two have. It saved all of your lives."

"Robert?"

"They found him first. He'll live."

"How did Raven and Aidan know where we were? I never told them where I was headed. None of us knew until we landed."

"Raven knew as soon as you'd flown out of Chena Marina that something was wrong. She questioned everyone until someone told her where Hugh had been flying the last month, helping this woman set up some competition."

"So if we had stayed in camp, like Nadia had wanted, none of this would have happened?"

"If you had stayed in camp, Nadia would have been able to play out her game the way she'd planned rather than on the fly," Mac said. "Doesn't do any good to second-guess everything."

"How had Nadia planned to be rescued?"

"She had a satellite phone on her the whole time. Once her plan was complete, she'd call in a mayday, act devastated over the tragedy that had befallen all of you, and gain your family's sympathy."

"Girl knew how to spin a yarn," Lucky said. "I fell for it."

"Any more questions?" Mac asked. "You need to head back before it's too late and you're stuck here."

"Doesn't seem like such a bad place," Tern said, gazing at the pink-tinged clouds floating in the blue-purple sky.

"Gage won't survive without you," Mac said.

CHAPTER FORTY-FOUR

Gage sat in a wheelchair, praying over Tern. She lay like death swallowed up by the hospital bed. He'd wasted so much time pushing her away. Now she was so far away, he couldn't reach her. She hadn't woken since she'd lost consciousness in the wilderness.

They were currently patients of Fairbanks Memorial Hospital thanks to Tern's sister and brother-in-law, who'd been on their trail from about the time they'd been stalked by the raven and the wolves. He needed to know more out this 'link' Tern's family had. Whatever it was, he was eternally grateful.

They'd been life-flighted right to Fairbanks, after being triaged in Ruby's medical clinic, as their injures were too severe for the little village clinic to handle.

Robert had been the worst. They'd rushed him right into surgery. He'd live, but the doctors had to amputate his arm. Gage also had surgery the minute they'd landed, resulting in two blood transfusions and a slight reduction of his intestines. Nadia's knife had punctured his lung and it had been touch and go there for a bit. In a few months he'd be roughly as good as new.

But Tern…

That last bash on the head, combined with the hit she'd taken the day before, had done something. Problem was, the doctors had run every test they could think of and couldn't figure out why she wouldn't wake up. She was currently in ICU and there was nothing more they could do but wait and pray.

It had been five days.

The same length of time they'd fought for their lives in the arctic wilderness.

It was after midnight and he'd refused to be taken back to his room. The nurse had given up and let him be with Tern. He wasn't leaving her side. Her family had been visiting in shifts, but the nights were his. Tern lay prone on the bed, multiple tubes and IVs stuck in her, machines monitoring her vitals. Even with her honey-golden Athabascan skin, she was as white as the sheets she lay on.

Why wouldn't she wake up? What kept her from him now?

He'd been talking to her since they let him enter her room. She had to wake up. He couldn't think that she wouldn't. Life would be no life without Tern in it. Why hadn't he realized that before he almost lost her? Hell, he could still lose her.

"You die on me, and I'll haunt you in the afterlife. Isn't that what you threatened me? I'll not only haunt you, I'll haunt your ancestors." He lightly applied chapstick to her dry lips and smoothed back her hair. "Just wake up and swear at me. Tell me I'm an idiot. Tell me to shut up. Something. Just come back to me, Tern."

Tears choked him, and he pressed the heels of his hands over his eyes. Pain in his chest burned, but it wasn't coming from his injuries. Unless there was some way they could treat a broken heart. Exhausted, he laid his head down on the bed, next to her side.

He must have dozed, for the next thing he was aware of were fingers softy sifting through his hair. He slowly lifted his head, afraid to let hope flare in his soul. He gazed into Tern's beautiful eyes.

"Hey," he said, softly. They'd warned him that if she woke up, she might not be the same person. Head wounds and comas were tricky.

"Hey, yourself," she returned, her eyes clear with recognition. "Water?"

He reached for the container with the straw sticking out the top and helped her drink. "Just a little bit." He let her take a few small sips, and then set the water on the rolling table next to the bed. "How do you feel?"

"Jet-lagged," she murmured, closing her eyes. He had a moment of panic when it took her longer than a normal blink for them open again. She focused on him. "You look like shit."

He croaked out a laugh. "So do you."

She grimaced. "Did I hear you threaten to haunt me?"

His mouth went dry and a tingling of awareness shot through him. "What else did you hear?"

She gave him a slight smile, but her eyes shown with love. "Your undying devotion and willingness to be my love slave."

"Yeah, that about covers it." He swallowed passed the emotion thickening his throat. "So, what do you say?"

"What drugs do they have you on?"

Did she still think with everything they'd been through that he'd leave her again? Had he really hurt her that badly?

"I love you, Tern Maiski, with everything that's in me. This is me finally talking from my heart. I should have listened to it before, instead of some cracked-up idea that was rooted in fear. I'm no longer afraid of loving you. I never want to be without you in my life again." His voice cracked as emotion overwhelmed him. "Marry me, Tern. Please." His 'please' came out sounding like a pitiful whine. He didn't care anymore. "You're the reason I fought to live. There's nothing without you in this lifetime or the next. I love you so much my heart can't contain it all."

He took her hand and carefully cradled it in both of his. Tears slowly seeped from his eyes, but he refused to turn away from her and wipe them off his face, letting her see as deep as she needed into his soul.

Tern opened her mouth to speak and only a croaking sound came out, then a whispered, "Water?"

He let go of her hand and let her sip some more, his hand shaking as he replaced the cup.

"Thanks." Tern swallowed and did one of those long blinks again. Just when he thought the suspense was going to do him in, she smiled the sweetest smile. "Yes, I'll marry you, Gage."

His heart swelled, making his chest hurt—the best kind of hurt of all—and then he froze as she held up a finger.

"On one condition."

"Anything." He'd give her whatever was in his power to give.

"We never go geocaching again."

A PREVIEW OF

DREAMWEAVER

the sequel to DEATH CACHE

Tiffinie Helmer

CHAPTER ONE

Gemma's lips trembled apart on a moan of pleasure so intense her body shivered with it. Synapses fired behind eyes she dared not open for fear he'd leave her wanting again.

Last time, he'd taken her right to the brink of release before disappearing, leaving her writhing with hunger. Not this time. This time he'd better take her all the way, damn it.

Her body came alive under the tutelage of his skillful hands. The way he knew just how to caress her, tease, and torment, until she wept, threatened, and begged for more.

Her hips arched off the bed, seeking, wishing for more, but once again he strung her out until she was mindless with need.

Oh, please, please. Quit dinking around and take me, already.

He chuckled as though able to read her thoughts, while his hands breezed over her breasts, the heat of his mouth hovered over her nipple, until she sunk her teeth into her lower lip to keep in the whimper. Sensations flooded her, tightening her muscles, and her hands clenched the sheets beneath her as little cries escaped her bitten lips, betraying her.

A growl of satisfaction vibrated from him, pouring into her body, pushing her closer to that delirious edge.

The alarm blared in her ear, jerking her awake.

"Nooo," Gemma groaned. Her sound of distress battered around the empty bedroom. "Not again." Would her dream man ever truly make love to her?

She opened her eyes and found herself alone. Of course she was alone. He was just a dream, part of her imagination. Her very creative imagination.

But he *felt* like more than that.

For weeks now he'd been visiting, always in the deepest of night. That magical time where the world slept and passions awoke.

She threw back the covers, the chill hitting her nakedness.

What the—?

She *never* slept naked.

A quick glance around the room showed her flannel pajamas tossed to the floor, along with her pink polka dotted cotton underwear.

Huh? She knew she'd crawled into bed last night fully clothed, including her hand-knitted woolen socks currently hanging off the top of the dresser. Her copy of *The Three Musketeers* lay face down, where she'd placed it before turning off the light. She'd given up on her love of romance books once the erotic dreams had started, not needing the added stimuli. She'd hoped reading the classics would settle down whatever the heck was going on with her subconscious mind while she slept.

She grabbed a robe hanging over the back of a chair and slipped into the warm terrycloth. It was springtime in Alaska and just like Johnny Horton was famous for singing, it was currently forty below.

No one in their right mind slept naked.

And she was very worried that she was no longer in her right mind.

He'd almost had her.

Lucky Leroy Morgan fell back onto the sweet smelling grass, his hands fisted, his jaw clenched, and aching with sexual frustration down to the cellular level. No, that was no longer true.

Not since he was dead and trapped in this fucking paradise.

He roared up at the perfectly blue skies, his back arching, and his lungs emptying of pent up emotions, praying the sound reached farther up into the Heavens from where he was currently trapped.

If he didn't know better, he'd think this was hell.

She'd been so close. He'd literally brushed her soft skin this time. Smelled her, and she'd smelled like high mountain Himalayan Impatiens with hints of rich, dark coffee.

What he wouldn't give for a cup of coffee.

He sat up, his hands tearing at the lush grass beneath him, and came to face to face with Hansen.

"Failed again?"

Nothing like stating the obvious. "Fuck, yes."

Hansen glanced around and lowered his voice, "Reverence, man."

"I don't give a shit. I shouldn't be here."

"You aren't going anywhere with that attitude."

"Fuck you too."

"She got to you this time, didn't she?" Hansen gave him that knowing smile. "You're starting to care, to fall in love." Nothing seemed to ruffle the calmness the man radiated. That used to impress him.

Lucky Leroy Morgan came by the nickname "Lucky" naturally. He loved women. Not just one. Many. And caring this much about one woman freaked him out.

"You're running out of time," Hansen said. "If you can't get her to accept you before these strong solar storms are over, you're stuck here, my friend."

"Like I don't know that." Lucky clawed his fingers through his shaggy, sun-bleached hair. Here wasn't that bad, for a spirit detention hub so to speak. A lush valley full of sharp-painted wildflowers intermixed with the sweet smelling grass all framed by purple snowcapped mountains jutting into an azure sky. Puffy, porcelain clouds floated by without a care in the Universe. When he'd first arrived, it had been one more adventure. More mountains to climb, a different world to conquer, but the thrill had quickly lost its appeal when he'd realized there was no risk.

He was already dead. What more could happen to him? The worst had already happened. What he needed was to get back to the land of the living.

And Gemma Star was his ticket.

CHAPTER TWO

Gemma flipped the sign to open and unlocked the doors to Chinook Books. Of course, her mother Siri and her Aunt Rosie were the first ones to breeze in.

"Did you see the Aurora last night?" Siri asked after Gemma shut the door behind them.

Siri was garbed in her traditional winter woolen dress pieced together from a variety of rainbow recycled sweaters surged in a haphazard design. Added to the outfit were clashing arm warmers with just her fingers uncovered. Silver rings fitted every finger, and her painted nails shimmered with a glittery crimson today. White bunny boots and a royal purple coat, that was more of a cloak, completed the ensemble. Rosie helped Siri out of her cloak, while Siri stared at Gemma.

Oh Lord, she hoped her mother wasn't off her meds.

"Mom?" Gemma prompted. "You okay?"

Siri blinked her dark blue eyes rimmed with thick black lashes. Her shocking red hair was long and curly and had yet to fade with age.

Gemma glanced at Rosie who shrugged. Aunt Rosie was the complete opposite of Siri. Her brunette hair had been left to gray naturally, and cut in a no-nonsense bob. She wore jeans, a man's flannel shirt and a sensible parka that she shrugged off, along with removing her gloves and knit hat. She resembled Gemma's father who had died when she was eight that it sometimes hurt to look upon her. Gemma took their coats and hung them up behind the counter.

She turned back to find Siri's eyes burrowing into her, as though trying to see into Gemma's soul.

"Gemini Star, what have you been up to?"

She hated it when her mother looked at her like that. "What do you mean?" She'd better clarify. She'd learned early not to volunteer information.

"You've been touched by a Dreamweaver." Siri continued her slow sweep, traveling up and down Gemma's simple brown slacks and cream cable knit sweater. "Tell me you haven't given yourself to him."

"What? No. What are you talking about?" A premonition prickled up Gemma's spine, and she tried to suppress the sudden need to shudder.

"You mustn't do it. Do not invite him in. Your soul will be compromised."

"Huh? What? Mom, you're talking nonsense." But it didn't feel like nonsense. Sometimes the things her mother said were downright freaky. Her dream lover was just that, a dream. No more. Unfortunately she knew enough having been raised by her New Age mother not to completely discount the supernatural. There was too much out there left unexplained. But a Dreamweaver? What the hell was that?

"Siri, let's get you a cup of tea." Rosie shared a here-we-go-again glance with Gemma.

"Yes, tea. Must have tea, and then we'll consult the cards," Siri said.

"Mom—"

"I'm reading your cards today, Gemini. You can't stop me. I'll find out what's going on."

Oh great.

"Siri, you have a full day of customers scheduled today," Rosie said. "Let's concentrate on them first. What do you say?"

"Fine. You're right of course. But if there's time...."

Gemma mouthed "thank you" as Rosie turned Siri toward the café. Amie, the barista who had been with Gemma for years, already carried a tray with a brewing teapot, along with matching cups and saucers to Siri's favorite bistro table right in the middle of the room. No disposable coffee cups for her mother. Tea was a ritual and needed to be respected as such with purified water and a specialized Silver Tip White Tea imported from Sri Lanka.

"This looks charming, Amie, thank you." Siri adjusted her skirts as she sat. "So, Amie, when are you due?"

Amie looked at Gemma, her eyes wide with panic and then back to Siri. "No, ma'am, I'm not pregnant." She smoothed down the fabric of her apron as though to show off the flatness of her stomach.

"Hmm, interesting. I see a new baby in your immediate future." Siri shrugged and helped herself to one of the shortbread cookies also on the tray.

"Amie, I'm going to need a brownie this morning," Rosie said, attempting to get Amie's attention off her nonexistent bump.

"Coming right up." Amie undid the ties to her apron and wrapped them around her front, tying them tighter around her middle as she walked back behind the counter to get Rosie's brownie.

Gemma hurried across the café and whispered over the dessert case, "You know not to take anything she says to heart, right?"

"Yes, I know that," Amie said. The mass of bracelets on her thin wrist jangled as she slammed open the bakery case. "But I'm *late*. Gemma, I can't be pregnant, I just can't. Drew hasn't even asked me to marry him. And I don't know if I *want* to marry him. A baby? What am I going to do with a baby? I'm not ready to be a mother."

"Stop. It's nothing. *Nothing*."

"But you heard her," Amie's voice rose in worry.

"Yes, and last Tuesday she told Mrs. Halverson that she'd find cockroaches. This is Fairbanks, Alaska. Have you ever seen a cockroach?"

Amie took a deep breath, closed her eyes and let it out. "Right. Okay, but you know I'll need to leave early so that I can buy a pregnancy test to put my mind at ease." Amie put Rosie's brownie on a plate and took it to her.

Gemma studied Amie's trim figure. It was just as fit and petite as it was when Gemma had hired her right out of high school. No way could she be over a hundred and ten pounds. She just topped five feet. With her dyed black hair, multiple ear piercings, coupled with her kohl rimmed eyes and dark purple lipstick, Amie fit more into Chinook Books than Gemma did.

The eclectic bookstore used to be hippie central when Siri ran it. Incense had burned at the counter. Brownies could be ordered "organic" instead of the dark chocolate, nut-filled ones Gemma stocked. And customers hung out all day gazing up at the celestial ceiling her father had commissioned for Siri's birthday. There was still a New Age vibe, and the ceiling still received a lot of oohs and ahhs, but the more years that went by, the more Gemma had lessened the influence. Though she hadn't been able to get rid of Tarot Tuesday, or what she secretly referred to as Trial Tuesday.

When Gemma's perky part-timer, Callista, reported to work at noon, Gemma grabbed a book on dreams and hid herself in the back office. She let Callista run the book floor while Amie continued to fret about her possible pregnancy in the café. Siri was too occupied with her Tarot readings to pay attention to what Gemma was up to.

She wished she could just ask her mother what she meant about the Dreamweaver comment, but she'd learned a long time ago not to show too much interest in her mother's "second sight." At least medicated, Siri didn't talk to people who weren't there and predict the future or the sex of unborn children. Well, as much.

She hoped Amie wasn't pregnant. Maybe she'd run out and pick up a pregnancy test to put both their minds at ease. Until she could get away, she had some investigating to do. She opened the book she'd swiped on dreams and found the table of contents.

The chapter on "Astral Sex" leapt off the page.

CHAPTER THREE

"Well, you look awful," Tern Maiski said, entering Gemma's little back office.

There wasn't much room for more than a desk in the closet-like space. Gemma had tried to lighten it up from the multi-colored rainbow arching across the walls her mother had painted to a much more soothing sage green. Though the rainbow still bled through in the right light as if refusing to be covered up.

Gemma planted her elbows on the old walnut desk that had been her father's, and rested her chin in her hands. "I'm having astral sex."

Tern sank into the chair opposite. "You're having *what?*"

"Astral sex."

"Before I draw any wrong conclusions, explain exactly what astral sex is." Tern shrugged off her stylish black wool coat that reached to her calves and unwound a hand-painted red silk scarf from around her neck. Tern owned the Arctic Tern Art Gallery just down the street, and they had a standing date to eat lunch together on Trial Tuesdays.

"Here, read this." Gemma held up the book for Tern, her head still spinning with the otherworldly implications.

Tern took the book and read the passage Gemma indicated. She glanced up. "You're having sex dreams? What a relief. I thought—never mind what I thought."

"Geesh, Tern. I'm not even seeing anyone special and you thought I'd—holy balls, just keep reading."

Tern followed the passage with her finger. "Astral sex—damn but that's funny to say—is the theosophical belief, belonging to the ethereal region that is believed to exist at a higher level than the material world. Personal auras are said to have non-corporeal sex with astral playmates." Tern leaned forward, the book cradled to her chest. "So you have a spiritual playmate."

"Be serious for a minute."

"I am being serious." Tern's Athabascan skin glowed under the harsh fluorescent lights, picking up the auburn strains highlighted in her thick ebony hair. But it was her dark almond eyes looking grave that had Gemma swallowing.

"Don't tell me you buy into this?"

"Of course I do."

"Come on, I was counting on you to bring me back to earth." At Tern's lift of an eyebrow, Gemma added, "Ground me at least. I need to talk to someone and I can't tell anyone out *there*." Gemma gestured wide with her hand to include all the occupants currently in Chinook Books who believed what the pretty painted cards told them.

"Your mother probably has more information on the subject than this book." Tern held up the Dreamology Dictionary.

"I've been trying my whole life to get away from this kind of stuff. Don't tell me you believe in it?"

"There is a lot I believe in." Tern's tone more than the words had Gemma feeling ashamed as she remembered Tern's close call with death last summer. "There's so much we don't understand," Tern continued. "It's arrogant to discount the unexplained."

Wow, nice way to put her in her place. "Help explain this to me then. I'm so confused."

"Tell me what's happening."

"I'm having the most intense, sexual dreams. It's like he's there. I can feel him, smell him, hear him until I open my eyes. Then he's gone and usually before I ...well, you know."

Tern's lips twisted into a smile. "No, I don't know."

"Don't make me say it."

"Yeah, you're going to need to say it."

"*Come* on, Tern."

"Well, I guess that's close enough."

Gemma felt the blush heat her face.

"How long has he been 'visiting'?" Tern asked.

"Three weeks as of last night."

"Every night?" Those brows of hers arrowed in thought. One brow was split at the apex by a scar giving her a somewhat rakish look for a woman. Very becoming on her and said more than words that she held her own.

"Except two days ago," Gemma admitted, though leaving out how despondent she'd felt when her dream man hadn't put in an appearance.

"So you have been having astral sex—damn, I love that phrase—for three weeks and you haven't orgasmed?"

Gemma's blush flamed, and she couldn't respond.

"You might have to help yourself out for your own peace of mind."

"Forget all that. How do I get rid of him?"

"Your astral partner?"

"Will you quit saying that word?"

"Nope." Tern shook her head and laughed. This time it was full-bodied, and Gemma couldn't help being pulled into the magic of the melodious sound.

"Oh my hell, what am I going to do?"

"Figure out why he's sought you out and vice versa."

"Me? I haven't sought him out. How would I even go about doing something like that?"

"Your subconscious has. Maybe you need to have a talk with yourself and figure out what is missing in your life that you're seeking in the astral plane."

"Well, the obvious. I must be sexually frustrated."

"Are you?"

"I didn't think I was until *he* started visiting me every night."

"Wait, you said he didn't visit two days ago. That was Sunday. So why not Sunday? What was happening that was different that night?"

"Nothing really. The bookstore was closed, so I took care of errands and cleaned the house. I did meet up with Cub and had dinner."

"Oooh, how did that go?"

"Eh. He's good looking, that's for sure." Jacob "Cub" Iverson resembled a Norse god. Cool blond looks with ice blue eyes and muscles that bore witness to his ancestors throwing tree trunks. She should be climbing all over him from the moment he'd moved to town six months ago. "But there wasn't any spark."

"No, spark with Cub Iverson? My goldfish lights up when he's in the room. The man was made for worshiping."

"Don't let Gage hear you talk like that."

"Just because I'm married doesn't mean I can't appreciate art when I see it. So why no spark? Did he kiss you?"

"Yeah." Gemma sighed. "It was nice but not as nice as my Dreamweaver's."

Tern's smile fell, and she became very still. "What did you just call him?"

"Dreamweaver." A shiver skittered across her skin. "Why?"

"Pull up the weather report for the last three weeks." Tern pointed to Gemma's laptop. "Come on. Do it."

Gemma did as Tern instructed while Tern came around the desk to see the results. They quickly scanned through the past weather reports for the last month. Fairbanks had actually fared well for March. Other than the snow storm Sunday night, they'd had cold but clear weather and amazing Aurora Borealis displays due to the record solar flares.

"I don't want you to freak out with what I'm about to say," Tern said, slowly retaking her seat.

"You're already freaking me out."

"Well, hold onto something then. Your Dreamweaver is using the Northern Lights as a conduit to travel between the astral planes. If you aren't careful, he'll snatch your spirit and take you back with him. You need protection."

"Really? You'd think having astral sex would be the ultimate solution for having unprotected sex. You can't get pregnant or catch anything."

"Don't joke about this. There is so much you can lose." Tern tightened her lips. "What's the forecast for the Aurora tonight?"

Gemma glanced back to her computer screen. "Intense."

"Don't go to sleep. Promise me." Tern waited until Gemma promised. "Okay, you wire yourself with caffeine. I'll talk to Gage."

"Gage? Tern, no." Gemma rose out of her chair as Tern stood and hurriedly slid her coat back on. "I don't want anyone else knowing about this."

"We're going to need his help. He works for the Geophysical Institute, remember. He's an Aurora genius. We need to know what we're up against if this 'thing' is using the Northern Lights as a stream into our world."

"This sounds like *Star Trek*," Gemma muttered rushing to catch up with Tern as she exited the office onto the book floor.

"Until I get back with you, it wouldn't hurt to find out what Siri knows. She might have some other ways of protecting you."

"I can't talk to my mother about this." She'd wished now she hadn't talked to Tern.

Tern stopped and faced her. "Your soul is at risk. Talk to her. And no sleep." She held up her finger when Gemma went to interrupt. "No naps either."

"You've got to be kidding?"

"The Aurora is out there even during the day. We humans can only see them at night." Tern took Gemma by the arm and steered her toward the café. A few tables were taken by regulars who liked to hear Siri's readings. Siri was currently deep in the middle of another reading for Mrs. Halverson who never missed a week.

"Amie, large coffee with a double shot of espresso for Gemma," Tern ordered. "I want you to make sure she drinks enough of those to make her twitchy."

Amie, paler than when Gemma had left her, pointed at Mrs. Halverson. "Did you see Mrs. Halverson's cockroach?"

Gemma followed Amie's shaky finger. There on Mrs. Halverson's pink lapel jacket was pinned a huge emerald cockroach.

Siri stood, holding the moon card in her hand for Gemma to see. "Dreamweaver," she whispered.

About the Author

Photo by: Kelli Ann Morgan

Tiffinie Helmer is an award-winning author who is always up for a gripping adventure. Raised in Alaska, she was dragged 'Outside' by her husband, but escapes the lower forty-eight to spend her summers commercial fishing on the Bering Sea.

A wife and mother of four, Tiffinie divides her time between enjoying her family, throwing her acclaimed pottery, and writing of flawed characters in unique and severe situations.

To learn more about Tiffinie and her books, please visit www. tiffiniehelmer.com

ALSO BY TIFFINIE HELMER

NOVELLAS

Bearing All (sequel to Edge)
Impact (prequel to Hooked)
Moosed Up (prequel to Shiver)
Dreamweaver (sequel to Death Cache)
Bait (sequel to Hooked)
Reel Trouble (sequel to Hooked)
Bushwhacked (sequel to Edge)
Fireweed (sequel to Bait)
Icebreaker
Mooseletoe

BUNDLE

Wild Men of Alaska
Wild Women of Alaska

ROMANCE ON THE EDGE NOVELS

Edge
Hooked
Shiver
Death Cache

THE WITCHES OF PORT TOWNSEND SERIES

Which Witch is Which?
Which Witch is Wicked?
Which Witch is Wild?